"I can say of David Gemmell that he's the only writer of hist ... ose I actuall ... w he produc ...

—S ...

a ... ar

"I am truly amazed at David Gemmell's ability to focus his writer's eye. His images are crisp and complete, a history lesson woven within the detailed tapestry of the highest adventure. Gemmell's characters are no less complete, real men and women with qualities good and bad, placed in trying times and rising to heroism or falling victim to their own we ...

"I ... at
Ge ... e,
cle ... ve
all ... es
sup ... gs
are ...

"G ... d
an ...

"G ... a
cro ...

By David Gemmell
(*published by Ballantine Books*)

LION OF MACEDON
DARK PRINCE
ECHOES OF THE GREAT SONG
KNIGHTS OF DARK RENOWN
MORNINGSTAR
DARK MOON
IRONHAND'S DAUGHTER
THE HAWK ETERNAL

THE DRENAI SAGA
LEGEND
THE KING BEYOND THE GATE
QUEST FOR LOST HEROES
WAYLANDER
IN THE REALM OF THE WOLF
THE FIRST CHRONICLES OF DRUSS THE LEGEND
THE LEGEND OF DEATHWALKER
HERO IN THE SHADOWS
WINTER WARRIORS
WHITE WOLF
THE SWORDS OF NIGHT AND DAY

THE STONES OF POWER CYCLE
GHOST KING
LAST SWORD OF POWER
WOLF IN SHADOW
THE LAST GUARDIAN
BLOODSTONE

THE RIGANTE
SWORD IN THE STORM
MIDNIGHT FALCON
RAVENHEART
STORMRIDER

TROY
LORD OF THE SILVER BOW (October 2005)

THE
HAWK
ETERNAL

A NOVEL OF THE HAWK QUEEN

DAVID
GEMMELL

BALLANTINE BOOKS · NEW YORK

The Hawk Eternal is a work of fiction. Names, places, and incidents either are products of the author's imagination or are used fictitiously.

2005 Del Rey Mass Market Edition

Copyright © 1995 by David A. Gemmell
Excerpt from *Lord of the Silver Bow* by David Gemmell copyright © 2005 by David A. Gemmell

All rights reserved.

Published in the United States by Del Rey Books, an imprint of The Random House Publishing Group, a division of Random House, Inc., New York.

DEL REY is a registered trademark and the Del Rey colophon is a trademark of Random House, Inc.

Originally published in Great Britain by Legend Books, a division of Random House UK Limited, London, in 1995.

This book contains an excerpt from the forthcoming edition of *Lord of the Silver Bow* by David Gemmell. This excerpt has been set for this edition only and may not reflect the final content of the forthcoming edition.

ISBN 0-345-45839-7

Printed in the United States of America

www.delreybooks.com

OPM 9 8 7 6 5 4 3 2 1

The Hawk Eternal is dedicated to the memory of Matthew Newman, a young writer from Birmingham who never had the chance to see his name in print. He should have. He was talented, dedicated, and gifted with great determination. But he was also one of the many hemophiliacs whose lives were further blighted by HIV-contaminated blood products. In the short time I knew him I gained a great insight into his courage and his amazing lack of outward bitterness.

He desperately wanted to finish his book and see it in print before he died. He didn't make it.

But the effort was truly heroic.

Prologue

The young priest was sitting in the sunshine, studying an ancient manuscript. Slowly he ran his index finger over the symbols upon it, mouthing each one. It was cold up here by these ancient stones, but Garvis had wrapped himself in a hooded sheepskin cloak, and had found a niche in the rocks away from the wind. He loved the solitude of these high, lonely peaks, and the distant roar of the mighty falls of Attafoss was a faraway whisper upon the wind. *"All the works of Man are as dust upon a flat rock,"* he read. *"When the winds of time blow across them they are lost to history. Nothing built of stone will endure."* Garvis sat back. Surely this was nonsense? These mountains had existed since the dawn of time and they would be here long after he was dead. He glanced up at the old stone circle. The symbols upon each standing stone had weathered almost to nothing. Yet still they stood, exactly where the ancients had placed them a thousand years ago. The sun was high now, but there was little warmth in the rays. Gaunt shadows stretched out from the stones. Garvis pulled his cloak more tightly about him.

According to Lord Taliesen, this was once one of the Great Gates. From here a man could travel across time and space. Garvis rubbed a slender hand over his pockmarked face. Time and Space: the legends fascinated him. He had asked Lord Taliesen about the Ancient Gates and had been rewarded with extra study. The Lesser Gates still allowed a man to move through space. He himself had traveled with Lord Taliesen from the mountains to the outskirts of Ateris—

that was more than sixty miles of space, but the journey had taken less than a heartbeat. According to Metas, the Lesser Gates could carry a man all over the land. So why were the Great Gates special?

Garvis's attention was distracted momentarily, as his fingers found a ripe spot upon his chin. Idly he squeezed it. It was not ready to burst, and pain flared across his face. Garvis gave a low curse and rubbed at the wounded skin. A hawk landed on the tallest of the standing stones, then flew away. Garvis watched it until it rose high on the thermals and was lost to him. "I would like to have been a hawk," he said aloud.

Lightning flashed across the stones, a blaze of brightness that caused Garvis to fall backward from the rock on which he sat. Rolling to his knees, he blinked and tried to focus. The stones seemed darker now. Violet light blazed out, and pale blue lightning forked up from the tallest stone. More lights flared, gossamer threads of light forming a glittering web around the stones. It seemed to Garvis as if tiny stars were caught in a pale blue net, gleaming like diamonds. It was the most beautiful sight. At the center of the light storm one diamond grew larger and brighter than all the others, swelling until it was the size of a boulder. Then it flattened, spreading out like a sheet upon a wash line, moving from circle to square, its four corners fastening to the top and bottom of two standing stones. The wind increased, howling over the crags, and for less than a heartbeat two suns hung in the sky.

All was silent as Garvis knelt, mouth open, shocked beyond words. Standing between the central stones was a tall warrior in bloodstained armor. He was supporting a woman, also attired for war; blood was flowing from a wound in her side. Garvis had never seen armor quite like that worn by this fearsome pair. The man's helm was full-faced, and boasted a white horsehair plume. His bronze breastplate had been fashioned in the shape of a human chest, complete with pectorals and a rippling solar plexus. He wore a leather kilt reinforced with bronze, and high, thigh-length riding boots. With a start Garvis realized that the warrior was looking at him. "You!" he called. "Help me."

Garvis scrambled to his feet and ran forward as the man lowered the warrior woman to the ground. Her face was grey, and blood had stained her silver hair. Garvis gazed down upon her. Old she was, but once she had been beautiful.

"Where is Taliesen?" asked the warrior.

"Back at the falls, sir."

"We must take her to shelter. You understand, boy?"

"Shelter. Yes."

The woman stirred. Reaching up, she gripped the warrior's arm. "You must go back. It is not over. Leave me with the boy. I will . . . be fine."

"I shall not leave you, my lady. I have served you these thirty years. I cannot go now." Reaching up, he made to remove his helm.

"Leave it," she said, her voice ringing with authority. "Listen to me, my dear friend. You must go back, or all may be lost. You are my heir; you are the son I never had; you are the light in my life. Go back. Set a lantern for me in the window."

"We should have killed the bitch all those years ago," he said bitterly. "She was warped beyond evil."

"No regrets, my general. Not ever. We win, we lose. The mountains do not care. Go now, for I can feel the air of the Enchanted Realm healing my wounds even as we speak. Go!"

Taking her hand, he kissed it. Rising, he gazed around at the mountains. With a sigh he drew his sword and ran back to the stones. Lightning flickered once more. Then he was gone.

Garvis ran into Taliesen's chambers, his face flushed, eyes wide with excitement. "A warrior woman has appeared by the Ancient Gate," he said. "She is wounded, and nigh to death."

The old man rose and gathered up his cloak of feathers. "The Ancient Gate, you say?"

"Yes, Lord Taliesen."

"Where have you taken her?"

"I helped her to the supply cave on High Druin. It was the closest shelter I could find. Metas was there and he has stitched her wounds, but I fear there is internal bleeding."

Taliesen took a deep breath. "Has she spoken of herself?"

"Not a word, lord. Metas is still with her."

"That is as it should be. Go now and rest. Make sure that not one word is spoken of this—not even to a brother druid. You understand me?"

"Of course, lord."

"Be sure that you do, for if I hear any whisper of it I shall turn your bones to stone, your blood to dust."

Taliesen swung the cloak of feathers about his skinny shoulders and strode from his rooms.

Two hours later, having activated one of the Lesser Gates, he was climbing the eastern face of High Druin and feeling the bitter wind biting through his cloak. The cave was deep, and stacked with supplies to help wandering clansmen through the worst of the winter—sacks of dried oats and dried fruit, salt and sugar, salted meat and even a barrel of smoked fish. It was a haven for crofters and other travelers who needed to tackle the high passes in the winter months. There was a man-made hearth in the far corner, and two pallet beds; also a bench table, rudely fashioned from a split log, and two log rounds that served as seats.

The druid Metas was seated upon one of the rounds, which he had placed beside a pallet bed. Upon it lay an old woman, bandages encasing her chest and shoulder. As Taliesen approached the bed, Metas rose and bowed. Taliesen praised him for his skill in administering to the woman, then repeated the warning he had given to the young druid when in his chambers.

"All will be as you order, lord," said Metas, bowing once

more. Taliesen sent him back to Vallon and seated himself beside the sleeping woman.

Even now, so close to death, her face radiated strength of purpose. "You were a queen without peer, Sigarni," whispered Taliesen, taking hold of her hand and squeezing the fingers. "But are you the one who will save my people?"

Her eyes opened. They were the grey of a winter sky, and the look she gave him was piercing. "Again we meet," she whispered with a smile. The smile changed her face, returning to it the memory of youth and beauty he recalled so well. "I fought the last battle, Taliesen . . ." He held up his hand.

"Tell me nothing," he said. "Already the strands of time are so interwoven that I find it hard to know when—or where—I am. I would dearly love to know how the Ancient Gate was opened, but I dare not ask. I will only assume that I did it. For now you must rest, and regain your strength. Then we will talk."

"I am so tired," she said. "Forty years of war and loss, victory and pain. So tired. And yet it is good to be back in the Enchanted Realm."

"Say nothing more," he urged her. "We stand at a delicate place on the crossroads of time. Let me say only this. Two days ago you urged me to hunt down Caracis, and return to you the sword, Skallivar. You remember asking me this?"

She closed her eyes. "I remember. It was almost thirty years ago. And you did."

"Yes," he said, his gaze drawn to the fabled sword that stood now against the far wall beside the fire.

"You sent the goddess walking on the water of the pool below the falls. All my generals saw the miracle, and when word spread of it men came flocking to my banner. I owe you much for that, Taliesen." Her words faded away, and she fell into a deep sleep.

Taliesen stood and walked to the sword; his thin fingers stroking the ruby pommel. He sighed and moved back into the sunlight. "The goddess upon the water," he repeated. What did she mean? Taliesen had spent the last two days desperately trying to think of a way to achieve what the Queen told him he already had!

And he remembered the words of his master, Astole, many centuries before. *"Treat the Gates with respect, Taliesen, lest you lose your mind. They are not merely doorways through time. You must understand that!"*

Oh, how he understood! He glanced back at the sleeping Queen. How many times had he seen her die? Thirty? Fifty? Again the words of Astole drifted back to haunt him.

"Hold always to a Line, my boy. A single thread. Never move between the threads, for that way lies madness and despair. For every moment that the past can conjure gives birth to an infinity of futures. Cross them at your peril."

The sun was hot upon Taliesen's face, though the wind remained cool. "I crossed them, Astole," he said, "and now I am trapped in a future I cannot unravel. Why is she here? How was the Gate opened? How was it that I returned her sword? Help me, Astole, for I am lost, and my people face annihilation."

No answer came, and with a heavy heart Taliesen returned to the cave.

Chapter One

Caswallon watched the murderous assault on Ateris, a strange sense of unreality gripping him. The clansman sat down on a boulder and gazed from the mountainside at the gleaming city below, white and glorious, like a child's castle set on a carpet of green.

The enemy had surprised the city dwellers some three hours before, and black smoke billowed now from the turrets and homes. The distant sound of screaming floated to his ears, disembodied, like the echo of a nightmare upon awakening.

The clansman's sea-green eyes narrowed as he watched the enemy hacking and slaying. He shook his head, sadness and anger competing within him. He had no love for these doomed Lowlanders and their duplicitous ways. But, equally, this wanton slaughter filled him with sorrow.

The enemy warriors were new to Caswallon. Never had he seen the horned helms of the Aenir, the double-headed axes, nor the oval shields painted with hideous faces of crimson and black. He had heard of them, of course, butchering and killing far to the south, but of their war against the Lowlanders he knew little until now.

But then, why should he? He was a clansman of the Farlain, and they had little time for Lowland politics. His was a mountain race, tough and hardy and more than solitary. The mountains were forbidden ground for any Lowlander and the clans mixed not at all with other races.

Save for trade. Clan beef and woven cloth for Lowland sugar, fruits, and iron.

In the distance Caswallon saw a young girl speared and lifted into the air, thrashing and screaming. This is war no longer, he thought, this is merely blood sport.

Tearing his gaze from the murderous scene he glanced back at the mountains rearing like spear points toward the sky, snowcapped and proud, jagged and powerful. At their center the cloud-wreathed magnificence of High Druin towered above the land. Caswallon shivered, drawing his brown leather cloak about his shoulders. It was said that the clans were vicious and hostile to outsiders, and so they were. Any Lowlander found hunting clan lands was sent home minus the fingers of his right hand. But such punishments were intended to deter poachers. The scenes of carnage on the plain below had nothing to do with such practices; this was lust of the most vile kind.

The clansman looked back at the city. Old men in white robes were being nailed to the black gates. Even at this distance Caswallon recognized Bacheron, the chief elder, a man of little honesty. Even so, he did not deserve such a death.

By all the Gods, no one deserved such a death!

On the plain three horsemen rode into sight, the leader pulling a young boy who was tied to a rope behind his mount. Caswallon recognized the boy as Gaelen, a thief and an orphan who lived on scraps and stolen fruit. The clansman's fingers curled around the hilt of his hunting dagger as he watched the boy straining at the rope.

The lead rider, a man in shining breastplate and raven-winged helm, cut the rope and the boy began to run toward the mountains. The riders set off after him, lances leveled.

Caswallon took a deep breath, releasing it slowly. The flame-haired boy ducked and weaved, stopping to pick up a stone and hurl it at the nearest horse. The beast shied, pitching its rider.

"Good for you, Gaelen," whispered Caswallon.

A rider in a white cloak wheeled his mount, cutting across

the boy's path. The youngster turned to sprint away and the lance took him deep in the back, lifting him from his feet and hurling him to the ground. He struggled to rise and a second rider ended his torment, slashing a sword blade to his face. The riders cantered back to the city.

Caswallon found his hands shaking uncontrollably, and his heart pounded, reflecting his anger and shame.

How could men do such a thing to a youth?

Caswallon recalled his last visit to Ateris three weeks before, when he had driven in twenty long-horned Highland cattle to the market stalls in the west of the city. He had stolen the beasts from the pastures of the Pallides two days before. At the market he had seen a crowd chasing the red-haired youngster as he sprinted through the streets, his skinny legs pounding the marble walkway, his arms pumping furiously.

Gaelen had shinned up a trellis by the side of the inn and leaped across the rooftops, stopping only to make an obscene gesture to his pursuers. Spotting Caswallon watching, he drew back his shoulders and swaggered across the rooftops. Caswallon had grinned then. He liked the boy; he had style.

The fat butcher Leon had chuckled beside him. "He's a character, is Gaelen. Every city needs one."

"Parents?" asked Caswallon.

"Dead. He's been alone five years—since he was nine or ten."

"How does he survive?"

"He steals. I let him get away with a chicken now and then. He sneaks up on me and I chase him for a while, shouting curses."

"You like him, Leon?"

"Yes. As I like you, Caswallon, you rascal. But then he reminds me of you. You are both thieves and you are both good at what you do—and there is no evil in either of you."

"Nice of you to say so," said Caswallon, grinning. "Now, how much for the Pallides cattle?"

"Why do you do it?"

"What?" asked Caswallon innocently.

"Steal cattle. By all accounts you are one of the richest clansmen in the Farlain. It doesn't make any sense."

"Tradition," answered Caswallon. "I'm a great believer in it."

Leon shook his head. "One of these days you'll be caught and hanged—or worse, knowing the Pallides. You baffle me."

"No, I don't. I make you rich. Yours is the cheapest beef in Ateris."

"True. How is the lovely Maeg?"

"She's well."

"And Donal?"

"Lungs like bellows."

"Keeping you awake at nights, is he?"

"When I'm not out hunting," said Caswallon with a wink.

Leon chuckled. "I'm going to be sorry when they catch you, clansman. Truly."

For an hour they haggled over the prices until Leon parted with a small pouch of gold, which Caswallon handed to his man Arcis, a taciturn clan crofter who accompanied him on his raids.

Now Caswallon stood on the mountainside soaking in the horror of Aenir warfare. Arcis moved alongside him. Both men had heard tales of war in the south and the awful atrocities committed by the Aenir. Foremost among these was the blood-eagle: Aenir victims were nailed to trees, their ribs splayed like tiny wings, their innards held in place with wooden strips.

Caswallon had only half believed these tales. Now the evidence hung on the blood-drenched gates of Ateris.

"Go back to the valley, my friend," Caswallon told Arcis.

"What about the cattle?"

"Drive them back into the mountains. There are no buyers today."

"Gods, Caswallon! Why do they go on killing? There's no one fighting them."

"I don't know. Tell Cambil what we have seen today."

"What about you?"

"I'll stay for a while."

Arcis nodded and set off across the slopes, running smoothly.

After a while the Aenir warriors drifted into the city. The plain before the gates was littered with corpses. Caswallon moved closer, stopping when he neared the tree line. Now he could see the full scale of the horror and his anger settled, cold and malignant. The cattle dealer, Leon, lay in a pool of blood, his throat torn open. Near him was the boy thief Gaelen.

Caswallon swung away and moved back toward the trees.

I am dying. There was no doubt in Gaelen's mind. The pain from his lower back was close to unbearable, his head ached, the blood was seeping from his left eye. For a long while he lay still, not knowing if the enemy was close by; whether indeed an Aenir warrior was at this moment poised above him with a spear or a sharp-edged sword.

Fear cut through his pain but he quelled it savagely. He could feel the soft, dusty clay against his face and smell the smoke from the burning city. He tried to open his eyes, but blood had congealed on the lashes. I have been unconscious for some time, he thought.

An hour? Less? Carefully, he moved his right arm, bringing his hand to his face, rubbing his right eye with his knuckle to free the lashes. The pain from his left eye intensified and he left it alone, sealed shut. He was facing the shuttered gates and the ghastly ornaments they now carried. Around him the crows were already settling, their sharp beaks ripping at moist flesh. Two of them had landed on the chest of Leon. Gaelen looked away. There were no Aenir in sight. Gingerly he probed the wound above his left hip, remembering the lance that had cut through him as he ran. The wound still bled on both sides, and the flesh was angry and raw to the touch.

Turning his head toward the mountains, and the tall pine trees on the nearest slope, he tried to estimate the time it would take him to reach the safety of the woods. He made an effort to stand, but a roaring began in his ears, like an angry sea. Dizziness swamped him and he lost consciousness.

When he awoke it was close to dusk. His side was still bleeding, though it had slowed to a trickle, and once again he had to clear his eye of blood. When he had done so he saw that he had crawled twenty paces. He couldn't remember doing it, but the trail of blood and scored dust could not lie.

Behind him the city burned. It would not be long before the Aenir returned to the plain. If he was found he would be hauled back and blood-eagled like the elders.

The boy began to crawl, not daring to look up lest the distance demoralize him, forcing him to give in.

Twice he passed out for short periods. After the last he cursed himself for a fool and rolled to his back, ripping two strips of cloth from his ragged tunic. These he pressed into the wounds on his hip, grunting as the pain tore into him. They should slow the bleeding, he thought. He crawled on. The journey, begun in pain and weakness, became a torment. Delirious, Gaelen lived again the horror of the attack. He had stolen a chicken from Leon and was racing through the market when the sound of screaming women and pounding hooves made him forget the burly butcher. Hundreds of horsemen came in sight, slashing at the crowd with long swords and plunging lances.

All was chaos and the boy had been petrified. He had hidden in a barn for several hours, but then had been discovered by three Aenir soldiers. Gaelen had run through the alleys, outpacing them, but had emerged into the city square where a rider looped a rope over his shoulders, dragging him out through the broken gates. All around him were fierce-eyed warriors with horned helms, screaming and chanting, their faces bestial.

The rider with the rope hailed two others at the city gates.

"Sport, Father!" yelled the man, his voice muffled by his helm.

"From that wretch?" answered the other contemptuously, leaning across the neck of his horse. The helm he wore carried curved horns, and a face mask in bronze fashioned into a leering demon. Through the upper slits Gaelen could see a glint of ice-blue eyes, and fear turned to terror within him.

The rider who had roped Gaelen laughed. "I saw this boy on my last scouting visit. He was running from a crowd. He's fast. I'll wager I land him before you."

"You couldn't land a fish from a bowl," said the third rider, a tall wide-shouldered warrior with an open helm. His face was broad and flat, the eyes small and glittering like blue beads. His beard was yellow and grimy, his teeth crooked and broken. "But I'll get him, by Vatan!"

"Always the first to boast and the last to do, Tostig," sneered the first rider.

"Be silent, Ongist," ordered the older man in the horned helm. "All right, I'll wager ten gold pieces I gut him."

"Done!" The rider leaned over toward the boy, slicing the dagger through the rope. "Go on, boy, run."

Gaelen heard the horse start after him, and throwing himself to the ground, he grabbed a rock and hurled it. The yellow-bearded warrior—Tostig?—pitched from his rearing mount.

Then the lance struck him. He tried to rise, only to see a sword blade flash down.

"Well ridden, Father!" were the last words he heard before the darkness engulfed him.

Now as he crawled all sense of time and place deserted him. He was a turtle on a beach of hot coals, slowly burning; a spider within an enamel bowl of pain, circling; a lobster within a pan as the heat rose.

But still he crawled.

Behind him walked the yellow-bearded warrior he had pitched to the ground. In his hand was a sword and upon his lips a smile.

Tostig was growing bored now. At first he had been intrigued by the wounded boy, wondering how far he could crawl, and imagining the horror and despair when he discovered the effort was for nothing. But now the boy was obviously delirious, and there was little point in wasting time. He raised the sword, pointing downward above the boy's back.

"Kill him, my bonny, and you will follow him."

Tostig leaped back a pace, his sword flashing up to point toward the shadow-haunted trees as a figure stepped out into the fading light. He was tall, wearing a leather cloak and carrying an iron-tipped quarterstaff. Two daggers hung from a black leather baldrick across his chest, and a long hunting knife dangled by his hip. He was green-eyed, and a dark trident beard gave him a sardonic appearance.

Tostig looked beyond the man, straining to pierce the gathering darkness of the undergrowth. The warrior seemed to be alone.

The clansman stepped forward and stopped just out of reach of the Aenir's sword. Then he leaned on his staff and smiled. "You're on Farlain land," he said.

"The Aenir walk where they will," Tostig replied.

"Not here, my bonny. Not ever. Now, what's it to be? Do you leave or die?"

Tostig pondered a moment. His father, Asbidag, had warned the army not to alienate the clans. Not yet. One mouthful at a time, that was Asbidag's way.

And yet this clansman had robbed Tostig of his prey.

"Who are you?" Tostig countered.

"Your heart has about five beats of life left in it, barbarian," said Caswallon.

Tostig stared deeply into the sea-green eyes. Had he been sure the man was alone, he would have risked battle. But he was not sure. The man was too confident, too relaxed. No clansman alive would face an armed Aenir in such a way. Unless he had an edge. Tostig glanced once more at the trees. Archers no doubt had him in range at this moment.

"We will meet again," he said, backing away down the slope.

Caswallon ignored him, and knelt by the bleeding youngster.

Gently he turned him to his back, checking his wounds. Satisfied they were plugged, he lifted the boy to his shoulder, gathered up his staff, entered the shadows, and was gone from the sight of the Aenir.

Gaelen turned in his bed and groaned as the stitches front and back pulled at tender, bruised flesh. He opened his eyes and found himself staring at a grey cave wall. The smell of burning beechwood was in his nostrils. Carefully he moved onto his good side. He was lying on a broad bed, crafted from pine and expertly joined; over his body were two woolen blankets and a bearskin cloak. The cave was large, maybe twenty paces wide and thirty deep, and at the far end it curved into a corridor. Looking back, the boy saw that the entrance was covered with a hide curtain. Gingerly he sat up. Somebody had bandaged his side and his injured eye. Gently he probed both areas. The pain was still there, but more of a throbbing reminder of the acute agony he remembered from his long crawl.

Across from the bed, beyond a table and some chairs rough-cut from logs, was a man-made hearth skillfully chipped away at the base of a natural chimney in the cave wall. A fire was burning brightly. Beside it were chunks of beechwood, a long iron rod, and a copper shovel.

Bright sunlight shafted past the edges of the curtain and the boy's gaze was drawn to the cave entrance. Groaning as he rose, he limped across the cave, lifting the flap and looking out over the mountains beyond. He found himself gazing down into a green and gold valley dotted with stone buildings and wooden barns, sectioned fields and ribbon streams. Away to his left was a herd of shaggy long-horned cattle, and elsewhere he could see sheep and goats, and even a few horses in a paddock by a small wood. His legs began to tremble and he dropped the curtain.

Slowly he made his way to the table and sat down. Upon it was an oatmeal loaf and a jug of spring water. His stomach tightened, hunger surging within him as he tore a chunk from the loaf and poured a little water into a clay goblet.

Gaelen was confused. He had never been this far into the Highlands. No Lowlander had. This was forbidden territory. The clansmen were not a friendly people, and though they occasionally came into Ateris to trade, it was well known to be folly for any city-dweller to attempt a return visit.

He tried to remember how he had come here. He seemed to recall voices as he struggled to reach the trees, but the memory was elusive and there had been so many dreams.

At the back of the cave the man called Oracle watched the boy eating and smiled. The lad was strong and wolf-tough. For the five days he had been here he had battled grimly against his wounds, never crying—even when, in his delirium, he had relived fear-filled moments of his young life. He had regained consciousness only twice in that time, accepting silently the warm broth that Oracle held to his lips.

"I see you are feeling better," said the old man, stepping from the shadows.

The boy jumped and winced as the stitches pulled. Looking around, he saw a tall, frail, white-bearded man dressed in grey robes, belted at the waist with a goat-hair rope.

"Yes. Thank you."

"What is your name?"

"Gaelen. And you?"

"I no longer use my name, but it pleases the Farlain to call me Oracle. If you are hungry I shall warm some broth; it is made from the liver of pigs and will give you strength."

Oracle moved to the fire, stooping to lift a covered pot to the flames. "It will be ready soon. How are your wounds?"

"Better."

The old man nodded. "The eye caused me the most trouble. But I think it will serve you. You will not be blind, I think. The wound in your side is not serious, the lance piercing just above the flesh of the hip. No vital organ was cut."

"Did you bring me here?"

"No." Using the iron rod, Oracle lifted the lid from the pot. Taking a long-handled wooden spoon from a shelf, he stirred the contents. Gaelen watched him in silence. In his youth he must have been a mighty man, thought the boy. Oracle's arms were bony now, but the wrists were thick and his frame broad. The old man's eyes were light blue under thick brows, and they glittered like water on ice. Seeing the boy staring at him, he chuckled. "I was the Farlain Hunt Lord," he said, grinning. "And I was strong. I carried the Whorl boulder for forty-two paces. No man has bettered that in thirty years."

"Were my thoughts so obvious?" Gaelen asked.

"Yes," answered Oracle. "The broth is ready."

They ate in silence, spooning the thick soup from wooden bowls and dipping chunks of oatmeal loaf into the steaming liquid.

Gaelen could not finish the broth. He apologized, but the old man shrugged.

"You've hardly eaten at all in five days, and though you are ravenous your stomach has shrunk. Give it a few moments, then try a little more."

"Thank you."

"You ask few questions, young Gaelen. Is it that you lack curiosity?"

The boy smiled for the first time. "No, I just don't want any answers yet."

Oracle nodded. "You are safe here. No one will send you back to the Aenir. You are welcome, free to do as you wish. You are not a prisoner. Now, do you have any questions?"

"How did I get here?"

"Caswallon brought you. He is a clansman, a Hunt Master."

"Why did he save me?"

"Why does Caswallon do the things he does? I don't know. Caswallon doesn't know. He is a man of impulse. A good friend, a terrible enemy, and a fine clansman—but still a man of impulse. When he was a youth he went tracking deer. He was following a doe when he came upon it caught in a Pallides snare. Now, the Farlain have no love for the Pallides, so Caswallon cut the deer loose—only to find it had an injured leg. He brought the little beast home upon his back and nursed it to health; then he released it. There's no accounting for Caswallon. Had the beast been fit he would have slain it for meat and hide."

"And I am like that injured doe," said Gaelen. "Had I run into the trees unharmed, Caswallon might have killed me."

"Yes, you are sharp, Gaelen. I like quick wits in a boy. How old are you?"

The boy shrugged. "I don't know. Fourteen, fifteen . . ."

"I'd say nearer fourteen, but it doesn't matter. A man is judged here by how he lives and not by the weight of his years."

"Will I be allowed to stay, then? I thought only clansmen could live in the Druin mountains?"

"Indeed you can, for indeed you are," said Oracle.

"I don't understand."

"You are a clansman, Gaelen. Of the Farlain. You see, Caswallon invoked the *Cormaach*. He has made you his son."

"Why?"

"Because he had no choice. As you said yourself, only a clansman can live here and Caswallon—like all other clansmen—cannot bring strangers into the Farlain. Therefore in the very act of rescuing you he became your guardian, responsible in law for everything you do."

"I don't want a father," said Gaelen. "I get by on my own."

"Then you will leave," agreed Oracle, amiably. "And Caswallon will give you a cloak, a dagger, and two gold coins for the road."

"And if I stay?"

"Then you will move into Caswallon's house."

Needing time to think, Gaelen broke off a piece of bread and dipped it into the now lukewarm broth.

Become a clansman? A wild warrior of the mountains? And what would it be like to have a father? Caswallon, who-ever he was, wouldn't care for him. Why should he? He was just a wounded doe brought home on a whim. "When must I decide?"

"When your wounds are fully healed."

"How long will that be?"

"When you say they are," said the old man.

"I don't know if I want to be a clansman."

"Reserve your judgment, Gaelen, until you know what it entails."

That night Gaelen awoke in a cold sweat, screaming.

The old man ran from the back of the cave, where he slept on a narrow pallet bed, and sat down beside the boy. "What is it?" he asked, stroking Gaelen's brow, pushing back the sweat-drenched hair from the boy's eyes.

"The Aenir! I dreamed they had come for me and I couldn't get away."

"Do not fear, Gaelen. They have conquered the Lowlands, but they will not come here. Not yet. Believe me. You are safe."

"They took the city," said Gaelen, "and the militia were overrun. They didn't even hold for a day."

"You have much to learn, boy. About war. About warriors. Aye, the city fell, and before it other cities. But we don't have cities here, and we need no walls. The mountains are like a fortress, with walls that pierce the clouds. And the clansmen don't wear bright breastplates and parade at festivals, they don't march in unison. Stand a clansman against a Lowlan-der and you will see two men, but you will not be seeing clearly. The one is like a dog, well trained and well fed. It looks good and it barks loud. The other is like a wolf, lean and deadly. It barks not at all. It kills. The Aenir will not come here yet. Trust me."

*   *   *

When he woke Gaelen found a fresh-baked honey malt loaf, a jug of goat's milk, and a bowl containing oats, dried apple, and ground hazelnuts awaiting him at the table. There was no sign of Oracle.

Gaelen's side was sore and fresh blood had seeped through the linen bandages around his waist, but he pushed the pain from his mind and ate. The oats were bland and unappealing, but he found that if he crushed the honey cake and sprinkled it over the mixture the effect was more appetizing.

His stomach full, he made his way outside the cave and knelt by a slender stream that trickled over white rocks on its journey to the valley below. Scooping water to his face, he washed, careful to avoid dampening the bandage over his injured eye. He had thought to take a short walk, but even the stroll to the stream had tired him and he sat back against a smooth rock and gazed down into the valley.

It was so calm here. Set against the tranquillity of these mountain valleys the events at Ateris seemed even more horrifying. Gaelen saw again the crows settling on fat Leon, squabbling and fighting over a strip of red flesh.

The boy was not surprised by the Aenir savagery. It seemed a culmination of all that life had taught him about people. In the main, they were cruel, callous, and uncaring, filled with greed and petty malice. The boy knew all about suffering. It was life. It was being frozen in winter, parched in summer, cold-soaked and trembling when it rained. It was being thrashed for the sin of hunger, abused for the curse of loneliness, tormented for being a bastard, and despised for being an orphan.

Life was not a gift to be enjoyed, it was an enemy to be battled, grimly, unremittingly.

The old man had been kind to him, but he has his reasons, thought Gaelen sourly. This Caswallon is probably paying him for his time.

Gaelen sighed. When he was strong enough he would run away to the north and find a city the Aenir had not sacked, and he would pick up his life again—stealing food and scraping a living until he was big enough, or strong enough, to take life by the throat and force it to do his bidding.

Still dreaming of the future, he fell asleep in the sunshine. Oracle found him there at noon and gently carried him inside, laying him upon the broad bed and covering him with the bearskin cloak. The fur was still thick and luxuriant, yet it was thirty years since Oracle had killed the bear. An epic battle fought on a spring day such as this . . . The old man chuckled at the memory. In those days he had been Caracis, Hunt Lord of the Farlain, and a force to be considered. He had killed the bear with a short sword and dagger, suffering terrible wounds from the beast's claws. He never knew why it had attacked him; the large bears of the mountains usually avoided man, but perhaps he had strayed too close to its den, or maybe it was sick and hurting.

Whatever the cause it had reared up from the bushes, towering above him. In one flowing motion he had hurled his hunting knife into its breast, drawn sword and dagger, and leaped forward, plunging both blades through the matted fur and into the flesh beyond. The battle had been brief and bloody. The beast's great arms encircled him, its claws ripping into his back. He had released the sword and twisted at the dagger with both hands, seeking the mighty heart within the rib cage.

And he had found it.

Now the bear, the lord of the high lonely forest, was a child's blanket, and the greatest of the Farlain warriors was a dry-boned ancient, known only as Oracle.

"Time makes fools of us all," he whispered.

He looked down at the boy's face. He was a handsome lad, with good bones and a strong chin, and his flame-red hair contained a glint of gold, matching the tawny flecks in his dark eyes.

"You will break hearts in years to come, Gaelen, my lad."

"Hearts . . . ?" said Gaelen, yawning and sitting up. "I'm sorry. Were you talking to me?"

"No. Old men talk to themselves. How are you feeling?"

"Good."

"Sleep is the remedy for many of life's ills. Especially loss of blood."

"It's peaceful here," said Gaelen. "I don't normally sleep so much, even when I've been hurt. Is there anything I can do to help you? I don't want to be a burden."

"Young man, you are not a burden. You are a guest. Do you know what that means?"

"No."

"It means you are a friend who has come to stay for a while," the old man told him, laying his hand on the boy's arm. "It means you owe me nothing."

"Caswallon pays you to look after me," said Gaelen, pulling his arm away from Oracle's touch.

"No, he does not. Nor will he. Though he may bring a joint of venison, or a sack of vegetables the next time he comes." Oracle left the bedside to add several chunks of wood to the fire. "It's so wasteful," he called back, "keeping a fire here in spring. But the cave gets cold and my blood is running thin."

"It's nice," said Gaelen. "I like to see a fire burning."

"Chopping wood keeps my body from seizing up," said the old man, returning to the bedside. "Now, what would you like to know?"

Gaelen shrugged. "About what?"

"About anything."

"You could tell me about the clans. Where did they come from?"

"A wise choice," said Oracle, sitting at the bedside. "There are more than thirty clans, but originally there was one: the Farlain. Under their leader, Farla the First, they journeyed to Druin more than six hundred years ago, escaping some war in their homeland. The Farlain settled in the valley below here, and two neighboring valleys to the east. They prospered and multiplied. But, as the years passed, there was discord and several families broke from the clan. There was a little trouble and some fighting, but the new clan formed their own settlements and began calling themselves Pallides, which in the old tongue meant Seekers of New Trails. In the decades that followed other splits developed, giving birth to the Haesten, the Loda, the Dunilds, and many more. There have been several wars between the clans. In the last, more than one hundred years ago, six thousand men lost their lives. Then the mighty king Ironhand put an end to it. He gave us wisdom—and the Games."

"What are the Games?" asked Gaelen.

"Tests of skill in a score of disciplines. Archery, swordsmanship, racing, jumping, wrestling . . . many, many events. All the clans take part. It lasts two weeks from Midsummer's Night, and concludes with the Whorl Feast. You will see it this year—and you will never forget it."

"What are the prizes?"

"Pride is the prize—and always has been." The old man's blue eyes twinkled. "Well, pride and a small sack of gold. Caswallon took gold in the archery last year. A better bowman has never been seen in these mountains."

"Tell me of him."

The old man chuckled and shook his head. "Caswallon. Always the children seek stories of Caswallon. If Caswallon were a swallow he would stay north for the winter, just to see how cold it gets. What can any man tell you of Caswallon?"

"Is he a warrior?"

"He is certainly that, but then most clansmen are. He is good with sword and knife, though others are better. He is an expert hunter and a good provider."

"You like him?" asked Gaelen.

"Like him? He infuriates me. But I love him. I don't know how his wife puts up with him. But then Maeg's a spirited lass." Oracle rose from the bedside and moved to the table, filling two clay goblets with water. Passing one to Gaelen, he sat down once more. "Aye, that's the story to give you a taste of young Caswallon.

"Three years ago at the Games, he saw and fell in love

with a maid of the Pallides, the daughter of their Hunt Lord
Maggrig. Now, Maggrig is a formidable warrior and a man
of hasty and uncertain temper. Above all things on this earth
he hates and despises the Farlain. Mention the clan name and
his blood boils and his face darkens.

"So imagine his fury when Caswallon approaches him and
asks for his daughter's hand. Men close by swore his veins
almost burst at the temples. And Maeg herself took one look
at him and dismissed him for an arrogant fool. Caswallon
took the insults they heaped on him, bowed, and departed to
the archery tourney, which he won an hour later. Most of us
thought that would be the last of the affair." Oracle rose and
stretched his back, then moved to the fire and added two
thick logs. He sighed and refilled his goblet.

"Well, what happened?" urged Gaelen.

"Happened? Oh, yes. I'm sorry, my boy, but the mind wan-
ders sometimes. Where was I? Caswallon's courting of Maeg."
Returning to the bedside, he sat down again. "Many of the
Farlain enjoyed the jest for such it had to be. Maeg was almost twenty and unmarried and it was considered she was a
frosty maiden with little interest in men.

"Two months later, in dead of night, Caswallon slipped
into the Pallides lands, past their scouts and into the heart of
Maggrig's own village. He scaled the stone wall of the old
man's house and entered Maeg's room unseen. Just before
dawn he awoke Maeg, stifled her scream with a kiss, climbed
from the window, and was gone into the timberline. Oh, they
chased him all right. Fifty of the fleetest Pallides runners, but
Caswallon was the racer to beat them all, and he made it
home without a scratch.

"Now, back at Maggrig's house there was rare fury, for the
young Farlain hunter had left a pair of torn breeches, a worn
shirt, and the hide cut out in the shape of a new pair of shoes.
Soon the entire Highlands chuckled at the tale and Maggrig
was beside himself with fury. You have to understand the
symbolism, Gaelen. The trousers, shirt, and hide were what
you'd leave a wife to mend and make. And the fact that he'd

spent the night alone in her bedroom made sure no other man would marry her.

"Maggrig swore he'd have his head. Pallides hunters spent their days hoping Caswallon of the Farlain would darken their territory with his shadow. Finally, some three months later, as winter took its hold making the mountains impassable, the Pallides withdrew to their homes. On this night in the long hall, where the clan chiefs were celebrating the Longest Night, the doors opened and there, covered in snow and with ice in his beard, stood Caswallon.

"He walked slowly down the center of the hall, between the tables, until he stood before Maggrig and his daughter. Then he smiled and said, 'Have you finished my breeches and shirt, woman?'

" 'I have,' she told him. 'And where have you been these last months?'

" 'Where else should I be?' he answered her. 'I've been building our house.'

"I tell you, Gaelen, I would have given much to see Maggrig's face that night. The wedding took place the following morning and the two of them stayed most of the winter with the Pallides. Caswallon would not hear of taking Maeg back the way he had come, for he had scaled the east flank of High Druin—no easy task in summer, but in winter fraught with peril.

"Now, does that help you understand Caswallon of the Farlain?"

"No," answered Gaelen.

The old man laughed aloud. "No more should it, I suppose. But keep it in your mind and the passing years may explain it to you. Now strip off that shirt and let me check that wound."

Oracle carefully cut away the bandages and knelt before the bed, his long fingers prizing away the linen from the blood-encrusted stitches. Gaelen gritted his teeth, making no sound. As the last piece of linen pulled clear Gaelen looked down. A huge blue and yellow bruise had spread from his hip to his ribs and around to the small of his back. The wound itself had closed well, but was seeping at the edges with yellow pus.

"Don't worry about that, boy," said Oracle. "That's just the body expelling the rubbish. The wound's clean and healing well. By midsummer you'll be running with the other lads at the Games."

"The wound seems wider than I remember," said Gaelen. "I thought it was just a round hole."

"Aye it was—on both sides," Oracle told him. "But round wounds take an age to heal, Gaelen. They close up in a circle until there is just a bright tender spot at the center which never seems to close. I cut a wider gash across it. Trust me; I know wounds, boy. I have seen enough of them, and suffered enough of them. You are healing well."

"What about my eye?" asked Gaelen, tenderly fingering the bandage.

"We'll know soon, lad."

Maeg placed the babe in his crib and covered him with a white woolen blanket. She ran her fingers over the soft, dark down on his head and whispered a blessing to protect him as he slept. He was a beautiful child, with his father's sea-green eyes and his mother's dimpled chin. Tomorrow his grandfather would arrive, and Maeg was secretly delighted that the child had Maggrig's wide cheekbones and round head. She knew it would please the fiery Hunt Lord of the Pallides. For all that he was a warrior and a man to be respected, Maeg knew that within the crusty shell was a soft-hearted man who had always doted on children.

Men walked warily around the old bull, but children clambered over him, shrieking with mock terror at his blood-curdling threats and tugging at his rust-red beard. He was a man who had always wanted sons, and yet had never made his daughter feel guilty, nor blamed his wife for becoming barren thereafter.

And Maeg loved him.

The sound of the axe thudding into logs drew her to the thin north-facing window. In the yard beyond, stripped to the waist, Caswallon was preparing the winter fuel. An hour a day through spring and summer and the logs would be stacked against the side of the house three paces deep, thirty paces long, and the height of a tall man. In this way the wood performed a double service, keeping the fire fed and the north wind away from the wall, insulating their home against the ferocity of the winter.

Caswallon's long hair was swept back from his face and tied at the nape of the neck in a short ponytail. The muscles of his arms and shoulders stretched and swelled with each smooth stroke of the axe. Maeg grinned as she watched him, and rested her elbows on the sill. Caswallon was a natural showman, imbuing even such a simple task as chopping wood with a sense of living poetry. His movements were smooth and yet, every now and then, as he swung the axe, he twisted the handle flashing the blade in a complete turn before allowing it to hammer home in the log set on an oak round. It was almost theatrical and well worth the watching. It was the same with everything he did, Maeg knew; it wasn't that he needed to impress an audience, he was merely creative and easily bored, and amused himself by adding intricacy and often beauty to the most mundane of chores.

"You will win no prizes at the Games with such pretty strokes," she called as the last log split.

He grinned at her. "So this is why my breakfast's late, is it? You're too busy gawking and admiring my fine style? It was a sad day, woman, when you bewitched me away from the fine Farlain ladies."

"The truth of it is, Caswallon, my lad, that only a foreign woman would take you—one who hadn't heard the terrible tales of your youth."

"You've a sharp tongue in your head, but then I could expect no more from Maggrig's daughter. Do you think he'll find the house?"

"And why shouldn't he?"

"It's a well-known fact the Pallides need a map to get from bed to table."

"You tell that to Maggrig when he gets here and he'll pin both your ears to the bedposts," she said.

"Maybe I will, at that," he told her, stooping to lift his doeskin shirt from the fence.

"You will not!" she shouted. "You promised you'd not aggravate the man. Did you not?"

"Hush, woman. I always keep my promises."

"That's nonsense. You promised you'd seal the draft from this very window."

"You've a tongue like a willow switch and the memory of an injured hound. I'll do it after breakfast—that is, if the food ever sees the inside of a platter."

"Do the two of you never stop arguing?" asked Oracle, leaning on his quarterstaff at the corner of the house. "It's just as well you built your house so far from the rest."

"Why is it," asked Maeg, smiling, "that you always arrive as the food is ready?"

"The natural timing of an old hunter," he told her.

Maeg dished up hot oats in wooden platters, cut half a dozen slices of thick black bread, and broke some salt onto a small side dish, placing it before the two men. From the larder she took a dish of fresh-made butter and a jar of thick berry preserve. Then she sat in her own chair by the fire, taking up the tiny tunic she was knitting for the babe.

The men ate in silence until at last Caswallon pushed away his plate and asked, "How is the boy?"

Maeg stopped her knitting and looked up, her grey eyes fixed on the old man's face. The story of Caswallon's rescue of the lad had spread among the Farlain. It hadn't surprised them, they knew Caswallon. Similarly it hadn't surprised Maeg, but it worried her. Donal was Caswallon's son and he was barely four months old. Now the impulsive clansman had acquired another son, many years older, and this disturbed her.

"He is a strong boy, and he improves daily," said Oracle. "But life has not been good to him and he is suspicious."

"Of what?" Caswallon asked.

"Of everything. He was a thief in Ateris, an orphan, un-loved and unwanted. A hard thing for a child, Caswallon."

"A hard thing for anyone," said the clansman. "You know he crawled for almost two hours with those wounds. He's tough. He deserves a second chance at life."

"He is still frightened of the Aenir," said Oracle.

"So should he be," answered Caswallon gravely. "I am frightened of them. They are a bloodthirsty people and once they have conquered the Lowlands they will look to the clans."

"I know," said the old man, meeting Caswallon's eye. "They will outnumber us greatly. And they're fighters. Killers all."

"Mountain war is a different thing altogether," said Caswallon. "The Aenir are fine warriors but they are still Lowlanders. Their horses will be useless in the bracken, or on the scree slopes. Their long swords and axes will hamper them."

"True, but what of the valleys where our homes are?"

"We must do our best to keep them out of the valleys," answered Caswallon with a shrug.

"Are you so sure they'll attack?" asked Maeg. "What could they possibly want here?"

"Like all conquerors," Oracle answered her, "they fear all men think as they do. They will see the clans as a threat, never knowing when we will pour out of the mountains onto their towns, and so they will seek to destroy us. But we have time yet. There are still Lowland armies and cities to be taken, and then they must bring their families over from the south land and build their own farms and towns. We have three years, maybe a little less."

"Were you always so gloomy, old man?" asked Maeg, growing angry as her good humor evaporated.

"Not always, young Maeg. Once I was as strong as a bull and feared nothing. Now my bones are like dry sticks, my muscles wet parchment. Now I worry. There was a time when the Farlain could gather an army to terrify the world, when no one would dare invade the Highlands. But the world moves on . . ."

"Let tomorrow look after itself, my friend," said Caswallon, resting a hand on the old man's shoulder. "We'll not make a jot of difference by worrying about it. As Maeg says, we are growing gloomy. Come, we'll walk away and talk. It will help the food to settle, and I know Maeg will not want us under her feet."

Both men rose and Oracle walked around the table to stand over Maeg. Then he bowed and kissed her cheek. "I am sorry," he said. "I promise I'll not bring gloom to this house—for a while, at least."

"Away with you," she said, rising and throwing her arms around his neck. "You're always welcome here—just bear in mind I've a young babe, and I don't want to hear such melancholy fear for his future."

Maeg watched them leave on the short walk through the pasture toward the mountain woods beyond. Then she gathered up the dishes and scrubbed them clean in the water bucket by the hearth. Completing her chores the clanswoman checked on the babe, once more stroking his brow and rearranging his blanket. At her touch he awoke, stretching one pudgy arm with fist clenched, screwing up his face and yawning. Sitting beside him, Maeg opened her tunic and held him to her breast. As he fed she began to sing a soft, lilting lullaby. The babe suckled for several minutes, then when he had finished, she lifted him to her shoulder. His head sagged against her face. Gently she rubbed his back; he gave a loud burp that brought a peal of laughter from his mother. Kissing his cheek, she told him, "We'll need to improve your table manners before long, little one." Carefully she laid him back in his cot and Donal fell asleep almost instantly.

Returning to the kitchen, Maeg found Kareen had arrived with the morning milk and was busy transferring it to the stone jug by the wall. Kareen was a child of the mountains, orphaned during the last winter. Only fifteen, it would be a year before she could be lawfully wed and she had been sent by the Hunt Lord, Cambil, to serve Maeg in the difficult early months following the birth of Donal. In the strictest sense Kareen was a servant under indenture, but in the Highlands she was a "child of the house," a short-term daughter to be loved and cared for after the fashion of the clans. Kareen was a bright, lively girl, not attractive but strong and willing. Her face was long and her jaw square, but she had a pretty smile and wore it often. Maeg liked her.

"Beth's yield is down again," said Kareen. "I think it's that damned hound of Bolan's. It nipped her leg, you know. Caswallon should chide him about it."

"I'm sure that he will," said Maeg. "Would you mind seeing to Donal if he wakes? I've a mind to collect some herbs for the pot."

"Would I mind? I'd be delighted. Has he been fed?"

"He has, but I don't doubt he'll enjoy the warmed oats you'll be tempting him with," said Maeg, winking.

Kareen grinned. "He's a healthy eater, to be sure. How is the Lowland boy?"

"Healing," Maeg told her. "I'll be back soon." Lifting her shawl cloak from the hook by the door, Maeg swung it about her shoulders and stepped out into the yard.

Kareen placed the last of the stone jugs by the wall, hefted the empty bucket, and walked out to the well to wash it clean.

She watched Maeg strolling toward the pasture woods, admiring the proud, almost regal movements and rare animal grace that could not be disguised by the heavy woolen skirt and shawl. Maeg was beautiful. From her night-dark hair to her slender ankles she was everything Kareen would never be. And yet she was unconscious of her beauty and that, more than anything, led Kareen to love her.

Maeg enjoyed walking alone in the woods, listening to the birdsong and reveling in the solitude. It was here that she found tranquillity. Caswallon, despite being the love of her life, was also the cause of great turmoil. His turbulent spirit would never be content with the simple life of a farmer and cattle breeder. He needed the excitement and the danger that came from raiding the herds of neighboring clans, stealing into their lands, ghosting past their sentries. One day they would catch and hang him.

You'll not change him, Maeg, she thought.

Caswallon had been a child of the mountains, born out of wedlock to a flighty maid named Mira who had died soon after childbirth—supposedly of internal bleeding, though clan legend had it that her father poisoned her. She had never divulged the name of her lover. Caswallon had been raised in the house of the Hunt Lord, Padris, as foster brother to Cambil. The two boys had never become friends.

At seventeen Caswallon left the home of Padris with a dagger, a cloak, and two gold pieces. Everyone had assumed he would become a crofter, eking out a slender existence to the north. Instead he had gone alone to Pallides land and stolen a bull and four cows. From the Haesten he stole six cows, selling three in Ateris. Within a year every out-clan huntsman watched for Caswallon of the Farlain.

Maggrig, the Pallides Hunt Lord, offered two prize bulls to the man who could kill him. Caswallon stole the bulls.

At first his fellow clansmen had been amused by his exploits. But as his wealth grew, so too did the jealousy. The women, Maeg knew, adored Caswallon. The men, quite naturally, detested him. Three years ago, following the death of Padris, Cambil was elected as Hunt Lord and Caswallon's stock among the men plunged to fresh depths. For Cambil despised him, and many were those seeking favor with the new lord.

This year, Caswallon had even declined to take part in the Games, though as defending champion he could have earned points for the clan. What was worse, he had given as his reason that he wished to stay home with his lady, who had a showing of blood in her pregnancy. He had put her to bed and undertaken the household chores himself—an unmanly action.

Yet, as his stock had fallen with the men, so it climbed in direct proportion with the women.

Now there was the business of the Lowland boy, and the almost perverse use of clan law to accommodate the act. How could he invoke *Cormaach* for such a one? The old law—crafted to allow for the children of a fallen warrior to be adopted by relatives of the hero—had never been invoked to bring a Lowlander into the clans.

Cambil had refused to speak publicly against Caswallon, but privately he had voiced his disgust in the Council. Yet Caswallon, as always, was impervious to criticism.

It was the same when he caught two Haesten hunters on Farlain lands. He had thrashed them with his quarterstaff, but he had not cut off their fingers. That and his marriage to Maeg had left the Council furious: a slight, they called it, on every Farlain maiden.

Against their fury Caswallon adopted indifference. And in some quarters this fanned the fury to hatred.

All of this Maeg knew, for there were few secrets among the Farlain, and yet Caswallon never spoke of it. Always he was courteous, even to his enemies, and rarely had anyone in the three valleys seen him lose his temper. This was read by many as a sign of weakness, but among the women, who often display greater insights in these matters, there was no doubt as to Caswallon's manhood.

If he didn't maim the hunters, there was a reason that had naught to do with cowardice. And Caswallon's reasons, whatever they were, were good enough for his friends. Since no answer would justify his actions to those who hated him, Caswallon offered them exactly that—no answer.

It was a matter of sadness for Maeg that the result of the hatred would be the letting of blood and a death feud between Farlain houses. But that was a worry for tomorrow, and there were always more pressing problems of today to concern the women of the mountains.

Chapter Two

Unaware of the controversy, of which he was now a part, the boy Gaelen sat in the cave slowly unwinding the bandage around his head, gently easing it from the line of stitches on his brow and cheek.

With infinite care he rubbed away the clotted blood sealing the eyelid and gently prized the eye open. At first his vision was blurred, but slowly it cleared and perspective returned, though a pink haze disturbed him. By the hearth was a silver mirror. Gaelen picked it up and gazed at his reflection. No expression crossed his face as he looked upon his scars, but something cold settled on his heart as he saw the eye.

It was totally red, suffused with blood, giving him a demonic appearance. The top of his head had been shaved to allow the stitches to be inserted, though now the hair was growing again. But it was growing white around the scar.

A change came over him then, for he felt the fear of the Aenir drift away like morning mist, making way for something far stronger than fear.

Hatred filled him, instilling in his soul a terrible desire for vengeance.

For three weeks Gaelen stayed in or around the cave, watching the rain and the sunshine that followed it turn the mountain gorse to gold. He saw the snow recede from the mountain peaks and the young deer emerge from the woods to the fast-flowing streams. In the distance he saw a great brown bear stretching to claw his territorial mark on the trunk of a wiry elm, and the rabbits hopping in the long grass of the meadow in the pink light of dawn.

At night he talked to Oracle, the two of them sitting on a rug before the fire. He heard the history of the clans, and began to learn the names of the legendary heroes—Cubril, the man known as Blacklatch, who first carried the Whorl stone; Grigor, the Flame-dancer who fought the enemy even as his house burned around him; Ironhand and Dunbar. Strong men. Clansmen.

Not all of them were from the Farlain, that was the strange thing to Gaelen. The clansmen hated each other, yet would glory in tales of heroes from other clans. "It's no use trying to understand it yet, Gaelen," the old man told him. "It's hard enough for us to understand ourselves."

On the last evening of the month Oracle removed the boy's stitches and pronounced him fit to rejoin the world of the living.

"Tomorrow Caswallon will come, and you'll meet with him and make your decision. Either you'll stay or you'll go. Either way, you and I will part friends," said Oracle gravely.

Gaelen's stomach tightened. "Couldn't I just stay here with you for a while?"

Oracle cupped the boy's chin in his hand. "No, lad. Much as I've enjoyed your company it cannot be. Be ready at dawn, for Caswallon will come early."

For much of the night Gaelen was unable to sleep, and when he did he dreamed of the morning, saw himself looking foolish before this great clansman whose face he couldn't quite see. The man told him to run, but his legs were sunk in mud; the man lost his temper and stabbed him with a spear. He awoke exhausted and sweat-drenched and rose instantly, making his way to the stream to bathe.

"Good morning to you."

Gaelen swung to see a tall man sitting on a granite boulder. He wore a cloak of leaf-green and a brown leather tunic. Slung across his chest was a baldric bearing two slim daggers in leather sheaths, and by his side a hunting knife. Upon his long legs were leggings of green wool, laced with leather thongs crisscrossed to the knee. His hair was long and dark, his eyes sea-green. He seemed to be about thirty years of age, though he could have been older.

"Are you Caswallon?"

"I am indeed," said the man, standing. He stretched out his hand. Gaelen shook it and released it swiftly. "Walk with me and we'll talk about things to interest you."

Without waiting for a reply Caswallon turned and walked slowly through the trees. Gaelen stood for a moment, then grabbed his shirt from beside the stream and followed him. Caswallon halted beside a fallen oak and lifted a pack he had stowed there. Opening it he pulled clear some clothing; then he sat upon the vine-covered trunk, waiting for the boy to catch up.

Caswallon watched him closely as he approached. The boy was tall for his age, showing the promise of the man he would become. His hair was the red of a dying fire, though the slanted sunlight highlighted traces of gold, and there was a streak of silver above the wound on his brow. The scar on his cheek still looked angry and swollen, and the eye itself was a nightmare. But Caswallon liked the look of the lad, the set of his jaw, the straight-backed walk, and the fact that the boy looked him in the eye at all times.

"I have some clothes for you."

"My own are fine, thank you."

"Indeed they are, Gaelen, but a grey, threadbare tunic will not suit you, and bare legs will be cut by the brambles and gorse, as naked feet will be slashed by sharp or jagged stones. And you've no belt to carry a knife. Without a blade you'll be hard-pressed to survive."

"Thank you then. But I will pay you for them when I can."

"As you will. Try them." Caswallon threw him a green woolen shirt edged with brown leather and reinforced at the elbows and shoulders with hide. Gaelen slipped off his own dirty grey tunic and pulled on the garment. It fitted snugly, and his heart swelled; it was, in truth, the finest thing he had ever worn. The green woolen leggings were baggy but he tied them at the waist and joined Caswallon at the tree to learn how to lace them. Lastly a pair of moccasins were produced from Caswallon's sack, along with a wide black belt bearing a bone-handled knife in a long sheath. The moccasins were a little too tight, but Caswallon promised him they would stretch into comfort. Gaelen drew the knife from its scabbard; it was double-edged, one side ending in a half-moon.

"The first side is for cutting wood, shaving, or cleaning skins; the second edge is for skinning. It is a useful weapon also. Keep it sharp at all times. Every night before you sleep, apply yourself to maintaining it."

Reluctantly the boy returned the blade to its sheath and strapped the belt to his waist.

"Why are you doing this for me?"

"A good question, Gaelen, and I'm glad you asked it early. But I've no answer to give you. I watched you crawl and I admired you for the way you overcame your pain and your weakness. Also you made it to the timberline, and became a child of the mountains. As I interpreted clan law, that made you clan responsibility. I took it one stage further, that is all, and invited you into my home."

"I don't want a father. I never did."

"And I already have a son of my blood. But that is neither here nor there. In clan law I am called your father, because you are my responsibility. In terms of Lowland law—such as the Aenir will not obliterate—I suppose I would be called your guardian. All this means is that I must teach you to live like a man. After that you are alone—should you so desire to be."

"What would you teach me?"

"I'd teach you to hunt, and to plant, to read signs; I'd teach you to read the seasons and read men; I'd teach you to fight and, more importantly, when to fight. Most vital of all, though, I'd teach you how to think."

"I know how to think," said Gaelen.

"You know how to think like an Ateris thief, like a Lowland orphan. Look around and tell me what you see."

"Mountains and trees," answered the boy without looking around.

"No. Each mountain has a name and reputation, but together they combine to be only one thing. Home."

"It's not my home," said Gaelen, feeling suddenly ill at ease in his new finery. "I'm a Lowlander. I don't know if I can learn to be a clansman. I'm not even sure I want to try."

"What *are* you sure of?"

"I hate the Aenir. I'd like to kill them all."

"Would you like to be tall and strong and to attack one of their villages, riding a black stallion?"

"Yes."

"Would you kill everyone?"

"Yes."

"Would you chase a young boy, and tell him to run so that you could plunge a lance into his back?"

"NO!" he shouted. "No, I wouldn't."

"I'm glad of that. No more would any clansman. If you stay among us, Gaelen, you will get to fight the Aenir. But by then I will have shown you how. This is your first lesson, lad, put aside your hate. It clouds the mind."

"Nothing will stop me hating the Aenir. They are vile killers. There is no good in them."

"I'll not argue with you, for you have seen their atrocities. What I will say is this: A fighter needs to think clearly, swiftly. His actions are always measured. Controlled rage is good, for it makes us stronger, but hatred swamps the emotions—it is like a runaway horse, fast but running aimlessly. But enough of this. Let's walk awhile."

As they strolled through the woods Caswallon talked of the Farlain, and of Maeg.

"Why did you go to another clan for a wife?" asked Gaelen as they halted by a rippling stream. "Oracle told me about it. He said it would show what kind of man you are. But I didn't understand why you did it."

"I'll tell you a secret," said the older man, leaning in close and whispering. "I've no idea myself. I fell in love with the woman the very first moment she stepped from her tent into the line of my sight. She pierced me like an arrow, and my legs felt weak and my heart flew like an eagle."

"She cast a spell on you?" whispered Gaelen, eyes widening.

"She did indeed."

"Is she a witch?"

"All women are witches, Gaelen, for all are capable of such a spell if the time is right."

"They'll not bewitch me," said the boy.

"Indeed, they won't," Caswallon agreed. "For you've a strong mind and a stout heart. I could tell that as soon as I saw you."

"Are you mocking me?"

"Not at all," he answered, his face serious. "This is not a joking matter."

"Good. Now that you know she bewitched you, why do you keep her with you?"

"Well, I've grown to like her. And she's a good cook, and a fine clothes-maker. She made those clothes you are wearing. A man would be a fool not to keep her. I'm no hand with the needles myself."

"That's true," said Gaelen. "I hadn't thought of that. Will she try to bewitch me, do you think?"

"No. She'll see straightaway the strength in you."

"Good. Then I'll stay with you . . . for a while."

"Very well. Place your hand upon your heart and say your name."

"Gaelen," said the boy.

"Your full name."

"That is my full name."

"No. From this moment, until you say otherwise, you are Gaelen of the Farlain, the son of Caswallon. Now say it."

The boy reddened. "Why are you doing this? You already

have a son, you said that. You don't know me. I'm . . . not good at anything. I don't know how to be a clansman."

"I'll teach you. Now say it."

"Gaelen of the Farlain, the . . . son of Caswallon."

"Now say, 'I am a clansman.' "

Gaelen licked his lips. "I am a clansman."

"Gaelen of the Farlain, I welcome you into my house."

"Thank you," Gaelen answered lamely.

"Now, I have many things to do today, so I will leave you to explore the mountains. Tomorrow I shall return and we'll take to the heather for a few days and get to know one another. Then we'll go home." Without another word Caswallon was up and walking off down the slope toward the houses below.

Gaelen watched until he was out of sight, then drew his dagger and held it up before him like a slender mirror. Joy surged in him. He replaced the blade and ran back toward the cave to show Oracle his finery. On the way he stopped at a jutting boulder ten feet high. On impulse he climbed it and looked about him, gazing with new eyes on the mountains rearing in the distance.

Lifting his arms to the sky he shouted at the top of his voice. Echoes drifted back to him, and tears coursed from his eyes. He had never heard an echo, and he felt the mountains were calling to him.

"I am going home!" he had shouted.

And they had answered him.

"HOME! HOME! HOME!"

Far down the slopes Caswallon heard the echoes and smiled. The boy had a lot of learning to do, and even more problems to overcome. If he thought it was hard to be a thief in Ateris, just wait until he tried to walk among the youths of the Farlain!

A Lowlander in Highland clothing . . .

A sheep to be sheared . . .

And being the son of Caswallon would make life no more easy.

Caswallon shrugged. That was a worry for tomorrow.

*   *   *

For three days the new father and son wandered the Far-lain mountains and woods, into the high country where the golden eagle soared, and on into the timberline where bears had clawed their territorial marks deep into the trunks of young trees.

"Why do they do that?" asked Gaelen, staring up at the deeply scored gashes.

"It's very practical," Caswallon answered him, loosening his leather pack and easing it to the ground. "They rear up to their full height and make their mark. Any other bear in the vicinity will, upon finding the mark, rise to reach it. If he can't he leaves the woods—for the other bear is obviously bigger, and therefore stronger, than he is. Mind you, the bear that lives here is a canny beast. And he can't reach his own mark; in fact, he's quite small."

"I don't understand," said Gaelen. "How then did he make the gashes?"

"Think about it for a while. Go and gather some wood for a fire and I'll skin the rabbit."

Gaelen scoured the clearing for dead wood, snapping each stick as Caswallon had taught him, discarding any that retained sap. Every now and again he glanced back at the tree. Could the bear have rolled a boulder against the trunk? He didn't know. How clever were bears? As he and Caswallon sat by the fire he told the older man his theory about the boulder. Caswallon listened seriously.

"A good theory," he said at last, "but not true. Now look around you and describe your setting."

"We are in a hollow where our fire cannot be seen, and there is protection from the wind."

"But exactly where in the hollow are we?"

Taking his bearings from the mountains, as Caswallon had taught him, the boy answered with confidence, "We are at the north end."

"And the tree, how is it placed?"

"It is growing ten paces into the hollow."

"Where does the wind come from in the winter—the freezing wind?"

"From the north," answered Gaelen.

"Picture the hollow in winter," prompted the clansman.

"It would be cold, though sheltered, and snow-covered."

"How then did the bear make his mark?"

"I see it!" yelled Gaelen. "The wind whipped the snow into the hollow, but it built up against the bole of the tree like a huge step and the bear climbed up the snow."

"Very good."

"But was that just luck? Did the bear intend to fool other bears?"

"I like to think so," said Caswallon. "You see bears tend to sleep through the winter. They don't hibernate as other animals; they just sleep a lot. Mostly a bear will only come out in winter if it's hungry, and then it wouldn't be thinking about territorial marks.

"But the lesson for you, Gaelen my lad, is not about the bear—it's about how to tackle a problem. Think it through, all the way. A question about the land involves all four seasons."

As Gaelen rolled into his blankets that night, beneath the hide roof Caswallon had made, his mind overflowed with the knowledge he had gained. A horse always kicks the grass back in the direction from which it has come, but the cow pushes it down in the direction it is facing. Deer avoid the depths of the forest, for they live on saplings and young shoots which only grow in strong sunlight, never in the darkened depths. Never kill a deer on the run, for in its terror its juices flood the muscles making it tough and hard to chew. Always build your fire against a cliff wall, or fallen tree, for the reflected heat will double its warmth. That, and the names of all the mountains, floated through his mind and his sleep was light, his dreams many.

He awoke twice in the night—once as it began to rain, and the second time when a large fox brushed against his foot. In the moonlight the beast's face seemed to glow like some hellish demon of the dark. Gaelen screamed and the fox fled.

Caswallon did not stir, though in the morning as he packed their makeshift tent he told Gaelen grimly, "In the mountains a man can pay with his life for a moment's panic. That was a good lesson for you. In future, make no noise when faced by a threat. You could have been hiding from the Aenir, and felt a snake upon your leg. One scream, one sudden movement—and you would face death from both."

"I'm sorry. It won't happen again."

Caswallon ruffled the boy's hair and grinned. "It's not a criticism, Gaelen. As I said, it's a valuable lesson."

Throughout the morning the companions followed the mountain paths and trails. Gaelen listened to the older man's stories of the clans and learned. He learned of the Farlain march to the island of Vallon and the mysterious Gates, and their entry to the mountains. He learned of the structure of the society and how no kings were permitted within the clans, but that in times of war a High King would be elected: a man like the legendary Ironhand. But most of all he learned of Caswallon of the Farlain. He noticed the smooth, confident manner in which he moved and spoke, the gentle humor in his words, the authority in his statements. He learned that Caswallon was a man of infinite patience and understanding, a man who loved the high country and its people, despite lacking the harsh cruel quality of the former and the volatile, often violent passions of the latter.

Toward the afternoon Caswallon led the way into a small pine woods nestling against the base of a towering rock face. As they entered the trees the clansman stopped and Gaelen started to speak, but Caswallon waved him to silence. They could hear the wind swishing the leaves above them, and the rustle of small animals in the dry bracken. But inlaid into the sounds was an occasional squealing cry, soft and muted by the trees, like an echo.

Caswallon led the boy to the left, pushing his way through

intertwined bushes until they reached a larger clearing at the base of the cliff.

Here, before the cave mouth, lay the evidence of a mighty struggle. A dead mountain lion was locked in a grotesque embrace with a huge dog, the like of which Gaelen had never seen. The dog's jaws were clamped together in the throat of the lion that in its death throes had disemboweled the hound with the terrible claws of its hind legs. The dead animals had already begun to putrefy, the lion's belly bloated with gases.

"What kind of hound is that?" asked Gaelen.

"The best there is," answered Caswallon. "That is Nabara, the War Hound, she who belonged at one time to Cambil, the Farlain Hunt Lord. But she was a vicious beast and she ran away to the hills the day before she was to be slain."

Gaelen walked close to the bodies. "Her jaws are huge, and her body is long. She must have been formidable," he said.

"There are few war hounds left now. I don't know why. Maybe because we don't have the old-style wars. But yes, they are formidable. Terrifying, in fact. As you see, they can even be a match for a lion."

The squealing began again from within the cave.

"Her pups are inside," said Caswallon. "That is why she fought to the death. Little good it will do them."

"Are you going to kill them?"

"Yes."

"But why?"

"She's been living in the mountains for over a year. The only animal she's likely to have mated with is a wolf. But we'll see."

The cave ceiling was low and the companions entered warily on hands and knees. Inside, the cave narrowed into a short tunnel bearing right. Beyond that was a deep cleft in which the hound had left her pups. There were five small bodies and a sixth struggling to stand on shaking legs. Caswallon reached over, lifted the black and grey pup, and passed it back to the boy. Then he checked the bodies. All were dead.

Once back in the sunlight Caswallon retrieved the pup, tucking it half into his tunic where his body heat would warm it.

"Build a fire over there, Gaelen, and we'll see if the beast is worth saving."

Gaelen built a small circle of stones, laid his tinder, and struck sparks from his dagger and a small flint block. The tinder began to smoke. He blew on it softly until the first tongue of flame rose, then he added small twigs and finally thinner sticks. Caswallon eased his pack from his shoulders, pulling out the strips of dried meat packed by Maeg.

"We need a pot to boil some thick broth," he said. "And here is another lesson for you. Cut me a long strip of bark from that tree over there."

Gaelen did as he was bid and watched amazed as Caswallon shaped the edges and then twisted the bark into the shape of a deep bowl. Half filling it with water from the canteen, he laid the pot on the small fire.

"But it will burn away," said Gaelen. "It is wood."

"It will not burn as long as water is in it and the flames stay below the waterline." Taking his dagger, Caswallon sliced the dried meat into chunks and added them to the pot.

Before long the stew began to bubble and steam, the meat expanding. Caswallon added more meat, stirring the contents with his dagger. Gaelen moved beside him, reaching to stroke the small dark head poking out from Caswallon's tunic.

As the sun sank behind crimson clouds, bathing the mountain peaks in glowing copper, Caswallon ordered the lad to remove the bowl and allow the stew to cool. As they waited, the clansman opened his tunic and lifted the pup to his lap. Then he cut a section of the dried beef and began to chew it. "Can you give some to the pup?" pleaded Gaelen. "He is starving!"

"That's what I am doing, boy. It's too tough for him. I am doing what his mother would do."

Removing the half-chewed meat from his mouth, Caswallon shredded it and offered a small amount to the pup. Its tiny tongue snaked out, nose wrinkling at the smell of the meat. The tiny beast ate a little, then its head sank against Caswallon's hand. "Still too tough for him," said the clansman. "But see the size of his paws? He will be big, this one. Here, hold him."

The pup began to whine as Caswallon passed him over, but he settled down as Gaelen stroked behind his floppy ears.

"As I thought, he is half wolf," said the clansman. "But there's enough dog in him to be trained, I think. Would you like to keep him?"

Gaelen lifted the pup to his face, staring into the tiny brown eyes. Like him, the helpless beast was an orphan, and he remembered his own long crawl to the high ground.

"He is a child of the mountains," said Gaelen. "I shall adopt him. Is it my right?"

"It is," said Caswallon gravely. "But first he must live."

After a while Caswallon tested the stew. When it had reached blood heat he passed it to Gaelen. "Dip your smallest finger into it and get the beast to lick it. He's obviously too young to take it any other way." The stew was thick and dark and Gaelen followed the instructions. The pup's nose wrinkled again at the smell, but its tongue licked out. The boy continued to feed the animal until at last it fell asleep in his arms.

"Do you think it will live?"

"I don't know. Tomorrow we will have a better idea."

"I hope it does, Caswallon."

"Hope is akin to prayer," said the clansman, "so perhaps it will." He rose to his feet. "Wait here, there's something I must check. I should not be long." With that he was gone into the undergrowth. The sun had set, but the moon was high and bright in the clear sky, and Gaelen sat with his back against a tree, staring into the flickering coals of the fire.

This was life, this was a peace he had never known. The little pup moved in its sleep and he stroked it absently. In the distance the mountains made a jagged line against the sky like a wall against the world—deeply comforting and immensely reassuring.

Caswallon returned silently and sat beside the boy.

"We have a small problem, Gaelen," he said. "I saw a couple of footprints at the edge of the woods as we entered, but I was intent on finding the pup. I have followed the track to softer ground where the prints are clearer. There is no doubt they are made with iron-studded boots. Clansmen all wear moccasins."

"Who made the footprints then?"

"The Aenir. They are in the mountains."

In the morning as Gaelen fed the pup the remains of the stew that had been warmed on the glowing coals of the fire, his mind was clear, the terror of the night condensed and controlled into a manageable apprehension.

"How many are there?" he asked the clansman.

"Somewhere in the region of twenty. I think they're just scouting, but they're headed into Farlain lands and that could prove troublesome. We will walk warily today, avoiding the skylines. Have no fear, though, Gaelen, for these are my mountains and they shall not surprise us."

Gaelen took a deep breath, and his gaze was steady as he met Caswallon's eyes. "I am not afraid today," he told the clansman. "Last night I was trembling. Today I am ready."

"Good," said Caswallon, gathering up his quarterstaff and looping the straps of the pack across his shoulders. "Then let us put the Aenir from our minds and I will show you something of rare grandeur."

"What is it?"

"Do not be impatient. I'll not spoil it with words."

The clansman set off toward the west, and Gaelen gathered up the pup and followed him.

Throughout the morning they climbed through the timberline, over rocky scree slopes, down into verdant vales, and finally up into a sandstone pass. A sound like distant thunder growled in muted majesty and Gaelen's heart hammered.

"Is it a beast?" he asked.

"No. Though legends have it otherwise. What you are about to see is the birthplace of many myths. The Rainbow bridge to the home of the Gods is but one that springs from Attafoss."

Once through the pass, Caswallon led the way along a grassy track, the thunder growing below and to the right. Finally they climbed down toward the noise, clambering over rocks and warily walk-sliding down scree slopes, until Caswallon heaved the pack from his shoulders and beckoned the boy to him. Caswallon was standing on the lip of a slab-like ledge. As Gaelen approached he saw for the first time the glory of Attafoss, and he knew deep in his heart that he would never forget the moment.

There were three huge falls, the water split by two towering boulders before plunging three hundred feet to a foaming pool beneath, and onto one great waterfall whose roar deafened the watchers. Sunlight reflected from black, basaltic rock, forming rainbows in the spray, one of which spanned the falls and disappeared high in the air above the mountains. The falls were immense, almost half a mile wide. Gaelen stood openmouthed and stared at the Rainbow bridge. Even in Ateris he had heard stories of it.

Caswallon lifted his arms to the sky and began to speak, but the words were whipped from his mouth by the roaring voice of Attafoss. The clansman turned to the boy and grinned. "Come on," he bellowed.

Slowly they worked their way above the falls to sit beside the surging water in the lea of a rock face that deadened the cacophonous noise.

Caswallon pointed to a tear-shaped island in the center of the lake. It was heavily wooded, and from here the boy could see the mouths of deep caves in the rocky hills above the tree line.

"That is Vallon," he said, "and upon it lies one of the magic Gates through which the Farlain passed hundreds of years ago. We came in winter when the water was frozen solid, and we walked upon the ice."

They stayed the night above the falls, and Gaelen fed the pup with dried meat that he had first chewed to softness; this time the hound ate with relish. The following day Caswallon led them south toward the Farlain. The boy saw that Caswallon moved more cautiously, scanning the surrounding countryside and waiting in the cover of woods, checking carefully before moving out into open country.

Twice they came upon Aenir tracks, and once the remains of a campfire. Caswallon worked his fingers into the grey ash, and down into the earth beneath.

"This morning," he said. "Be watchful."

That night they made camp in a narrow cave and lit no fire. At first light they moved on. Caswallon was uneasy.

"They are close," he said. "I can almost smell them. To be honest, Gaelen, I am worried. I may have underestimated these Aenir. For all that there are twenty of them they leave little spoor, and they avoid the skylines in their march. They are woodsmen and good scouts. And that concerns me; it could mean the Aenir are preparing to march upon us far earlier than I anticipated."

By dusk Caswallon's unease had become alarm. He didn't talk at all but checked the trail many times, occasionally climbing trees to scan the horizon.

"What is wrong?" Gaelen asked him as he pored over a near-invisible series of scuffs and marks on the track.

"They have split up into small parties. Three have gone ahead, the rest have moved into the woods. My guess is that they know we are close and they have formed a circle around us."

"What can we do?"

"We do not have many choices," said the clansman. "Let's find a place to make camp."

Caswallon chose a spot near a stream, where he built a small fire against a fallen trunk and the two of them ate the last of the food Maeg had prepared. Once again the night sky was cloudless, the moon bright. Gaelen snuggled into his blankets with the pup curled against his chest, and slept deep and dreamlessly until about two hours before dawn when Caswallon gently shook him awake. Gaelen opened his eyes. Above him knelt Caswallon, a finger held to his lips, commanding silence. Gaelen rose swiftly. Caswallon pointed to the pup and the boy picked it up, tucking it into his tunic. The clansman filled Gaelen's bed with brush and covered it with a blanket. Then he added fuel to the fire before moving into the darkness of the woods. He stopped by a low, dense bush in sight of the clearing and the flickering fire.

Putting his face close to Gaelen's ear, he whispered, "Crawl into the bush and curl up. Make no sound and move not at all. If the pup stirs—kill it!"

"I am willing to fight," whispered Gaelen.

"Willing—but not yet ready," said Caswallon. "Now do as I bid."

Dropping to his knees Gaelen crawled into the bush, pushing aside the branches and wrapping himself in the cloak Caswallon had given him. He waited with heart hammering, his breath seeming as loud as the Attafoss thunder.

Caswallon had disappeared.

For more than an hour there was no sign of hostile movement in the woods. Gaelen was cramped and stiff, and the pup did stir against him. Gently he stroked the black and grey head. The tiny hound yawned and fell asleep. Gaelen smiled—then froze.

A dark shadow had detached itself from the trees not ten paces from the bush. Moonlight glistened on an iron-rimmed helm and flashed from a sword blade in the man's hand.

The warrior crept to the edge of the clearing, lifted his sword and waved it, signaling his companions. His view partly screened by leaves and branches, Gaelen could just make out the assault on the camp. Three warriors ran across the clearing, slashing their swords into the built-up blankets.

As the boy watched the Aenir drew back, realizing they

had been fooled. No word passed between them, but they began to search the surrounding trees.

Gaelen was terrified. The bush stood alone, out in the open, plainly in sight of the three hunters. Why did Caswallon leave him in such an exposed place? He toyed with the idea of crawling clear and running, but they were too close.

One of the warriors began to search at the far side of the clearing, stepping into the screen of gorse. Gaelen's eyes opened wide as Caswallon rose from the ground behind the warrior, clamped a hand over his mouth, and sliced his dagger across the man's throat. Releasing the body, he turned and ducked back into the gorse.

Unsuspecting, the remaining hunters checked to the west and east. Finding nothing, they moved toward the bush where Gaelen sat rigid with fear.

The first warrior, a burly man in bearskin tunic and leather breeches, turned to the second, a tall, lean figure with braided black hair.

"Fetch Karis," said the first. The warrior moved back toward the clearing, while the leader walked toward Gaelen's hiding place. The boy watched in amazement. The man never once looked down; it was as if he and the bush were invisible.

The warrior was so close that Gaelen could see only his leather-clad legs and the high, laced boots he wore. He did not dare look up. Suddenly the man's body slumped beside the bush. Gaelen started violently, but stopped himself from screaming. The Aenir lay facing him, his dead eyes open, his neck leaking blood on the soft earth.

The dead man began to move like a snake, only backward. Gaelen looked up. Caswallon had the man by the feet and was pulling him into the undergrowth. Then, dropping the body, the clansman vanished once more into the trees.

The last Aenir warrior, sword in hand, stepped back into the clearing. "Asta!" he called. "Karis is dead. Come back here."

Caswallon's voice sounded, the words spoken coldly. "You're all alone, my bonny."

The warrior spun and leaped to the attack, long sword raised. Leaning back, Caswallon swiveled his quarterstaff, stabbing it forward like a spear. It hammered into the warrior's belly and with a grunt he doubled over, his head speeding down to meet the other end of the iron-capped staff. Hurled from his feet, he hit the ground hard. Groggy, he tried to rise. Strong fingers lifted him by his hair, ramming his face into the rough bark of an old oak. He sank to the ground once more, semiconscious.

Ongist could feel his hands being tied, but could find no strength to resist. He passed out then, returning to consciousness some hours later for the sun had risen. His head ached and he could taste blood in his mouth. He tried to move but he was bound to a tree trunk.

Several paces before him sat the two he had been tracking, the man and the boy. Both were obviously clan, but there was something familiar about the lad although the warrior couldn't place him.

"I see you are back with us," said the clansman. "What is your name?"

"Ongist, son of Asbidag."

"I am Caswallon of the Farlain. This is my son Gaelen."

"Why have you not killed me?"

"I like a man who makes his point swiftly," said Caswallon. "You are alive by my whim. You are here to scout Farlain lands. Your instructions were probably to remain unseen, or kill any who discovered you—in which case you have failed twice. You had us encircled, and the circle is now tightening. Therefore if I leave you here you will be found, and you can give this message to your leaders: Leave now, for I shall summon the Farlain hunters before the day is out and then not one of you will live to report to your lord."

"Strong words," muttered the Aenir.

"Indeed they are, my friend. But understand this, I am

known among the Farlain as a mild-mannered man and the least of warriors. And yet two of your men are slain and you are trussed like a water fowl. Think what would happen if I loosed two hundred war carles upon you."

"What are your two hundred?" spat the warrior. "What are your two *thousand,* compared to the might of the Aenir? You will be like dry leaves before a forest fire. The Farlain? A motley crew of semisavages with no king and no army. Let me advise you now. Send your emissaries to the Lord Asbidag in Ateris and make your peace. But bring presents, mind. The Lord Asbidag appreciates presents."

Caswallon smiled. "I shall carry the words of your wisdom to the Farlain Council. Perhaps they will agree with you. When your men find you, tell them to head south. It is the fastest way from the Farlain."

The warrior hawked and spat.

"Look at him, Gaelen. That is the Aenir, that is the race that has terrorized the world. But for all that he is merely a man who smells strong, whose hair is covered in lice, and whose empire is built on the blood of innocents. Warriors? As you saw last night they are just men, with little skill— except in the murder of women, or the lancing of children."

Ongist's eyes flashed in recognition. The boy was the lad Asbidag had speared at the gates of Ateris. He bit his lip and said nothing. His brother Tostig had told them all how the boy had crawled to the mountains and been rescued by twenty clansmen. It had worried Asbidag.

"Would you like to kill him, Gaelen?"

Ongist felt the hatred in the boy's gaze, and he stared back without fear. "I see we made our mark upon you, boy," he sneered. "Do they call you Blood-eye or Scar-face?"

The boy said nothing, but the cold gaze remained. "Did someone cut your tongue out?" hissed Ongist.

Gaelen turned to his father. "Yes, I want to kill him," he said. "But not today."

The man and the boy left the clearing without a backward glance and Ongist settled back to wait for his brother and the others. It was nearing midday when the Aenir found him; they cut him loose and hauled him to his feet. His brothers Tostig and Drada supported him, for his head was dizzy and his vision blurred as he stood.

"What happened?" asked Drada, his elder by three years.

"The clansman tricked us. He killed Karis and Asta."

"I know. We found the bodies."

"He told me to leave Farlain lands. He says he will alert their hunters."

"Good advice," said Drada.

"Asbidag will be angry," muttered Tostig. Ongist rubbed at his bruised temple and scowled. Tostig was the largest of the brothers, a towering brute of a man with braided yellow hair and broken teeth. But he was also the most cautious—some would say cowardly. Ongist despised him.

"What was he like?" asked Drada.

Ongist shrugged. "Tall. Moved well. Fought well. Confident."

"Then we'll take his advice. Did you talk to him, try to bait him?"

"Yes."

"And?"

"No reaction, he just smiled. I told him the Aenir would sweep his people away. I advised him to come to Asbidag and beg for peace. He just said he would take my words of wisdom to the Council."

"Damn," said Drada. "I don't like the sound of that. Men who don't get angry make the worst enemies."

Ongist grinned, draping his arm over Drada's shoulder. "Always the thinker, brother. By the way, the boy he claimed was his son is the same lad Father speared at the city gates."

Drada swore. "And still he didn't get angry? That does make me shiver."

"I thought you'd enjoy that," said Ongist. "By the way, Tostig, how many men did you say rescued the boy?"

"I couldn't see them all. They were hidden in the bushes."

"How many could you see?" asked Drada, his interest caught by Ongist's question.

"I could see only the leader clearly. Why? How many men did he say he had?"

"He didn't say," answered Ongist, "but I know."

"A curse on you!" shouted Tostig, storming to the other side of the clearing.

Drada took Ongist by the arm and led him to the fallen trunk where Caswallon had made their fire. The two men sat down and Drada rubbed his eyes. "What was the point of all that?" he asked.

"There were no twenty clansmen," sneered Ongist. "Just the one—the same man, I'd stake my life on it."

"You are probably right," Drada agreed. "Did he give a name?"

"Caswallon of the Farlain."

"Caswallon. Let's hope there are not too many like him among the clans."

"It won't matter if there are. Who can stand against thirty thousand Aenir warriors?"

"That is true," agreed Drada, "but they remain an unknown quantity. Who knows how many there are? Our estimate is less than seven thousand fighting men if all the clans muster. But suppose we are wrong?"

"What do you suggest?"

"I think we ought to deal with them gently. Trade first and earn a welcome among them. Then we'll see."

"You think they'll be foolish enough to allow us into the mountains?" asked Ongist.

"Why not? Every other conquered nation has given us the same facility. And there must be those among the clans who are disenchanted, overlooked, or despised. They will come to us, and they will learn."

"I thought Father wanted to attack in the summer?"

"He does, but I'll talk him out of it. There are three main Lowland areas still to fall, and they'll yield richer pickings than these mountains."

"I like the mountains. I'd like to build a home here," said Ongist.

"You will soon, my brother. I promise you."

Oracle sat alone, gazing into the fire, lost in yesterday's dreams when armies swept across the land with their lances gleaming and banners raised.

A red hawk on a field of black. The Outlanders streaming from the battlefield, broken and demoralized. Sigarni raising her sword in the sunset, the Battle Queen triumphant.

Such had been the glory of youth when Oracle crossed the Gate to the kingdom beyond. The old man drew his grey cloak about his shoulders, stretching his legs forward, soaking in the heat from the burning beech in the hearth. He stared down at the backs of his hands, wrinkled and spotted with the drab brown specks of age.

But once upon a time . . .

"Dreaming of glory?" asked Taliesen.

Oracle jerked up as if struck, twisting in his seat. He cursed softly as he recognized the ancient druid. "Pull up a chair," he said.

The druid was small, and skeletally thin, his white hair and beard sparse and wispy, clinging to his face and head like remnants of winter mist. But his eyes were strangely youthful and humorous, antelope-brown and set close together under sharp brows. From his skinny shoulders hung a cloak of birds' feathers, many-hued, the blue of the kingfisher flashing against raven-black, soft pale plover and eagle's quill.

He leaned his long staff against the cave wall and seated himself beside Oracle. "The boy came then," said the druid, his voice soft and deep.

"You know he did."

"Yes. And so it begins: the destruction of all that we love."

"So you believe."

"Do you doubt me, Oracle?"

"The future is like soft clay to be molded. I cannot believe it is already set and decided."

The druid gave a low curse. "You of all men should know that the past, present, and future exist together, woven like a cloth, interweaving. You crossed the Gate. Did you learn nothing?"

"I learned the error of pride. That was enough for me."

"You look old and tired," said the druid.

"I am both. How is it that you still live, Taliesen? You were old when I was a babe at the breast."

"I was old when your grandfather was a babe at the breast."

For a while both men sat in silence staring into the flames, then Oracle sighed and shifted in his seat. "Why have you come here?" he whispered.

"Sigarni has crossed the Gate. She is at the cave on High Druin."

Oracle licked his lips, his mouth suddenly dry. "How is the girl?"

Taliesen gave a dry laugh. "Girl? She is a woman near as old as you. As I said, you do not understand the intricacies of the Gateways."

"Well, how is she anyway, damn you?"

"Gravely wounded, but I will heal her."

"May I see her?"

The druid shook his head. "It would not be wise."

"Then why come to me at all?"

"It may be that you can help me."

"In what way?"

"What happened to the sword you stole from her?"

Oracle reddened. "It was payment for all I had done for her."

"Do not seek to justify yourself, Caracis. Your sin led to more wars. You cost Sigarni far more than you were worth; then you stole Skallivar. You told me you lost it in the fight that brought you back to us, but I no longer believe you. What happened to it?"

Oracle rose and walked to the rear of the cave. He returned carrying a long bundle wrapped in cloth. Placing it on the table, he untied the binding and opened the bundle. There lay a shining sword of silver steel. "You want it?" Oracle asked.

Taliesen sighed, and flipped the cloth back over the blade. "No. Damn you, man! You crossed the Lines of Time. You will die and never know the chaos you gave birth to. I have tried to put it right, and have only succeeded in creating fresh paradoxes."

"What are you talking about?"

"Without the sword Sigarni was crushed, defeated, and slain."

"But you said she was here!"

"As she is. I tried to help her, Caracis, but she died. I crossed the Lines finding another Sigarni, in another world. She died. Time and time again I traveled the Gates. Always she died. I gave up for a long while, then I returned to my quest and found another Sigarni who was fated to die young. She defeated her first enemy, and then the second, Earl Jastey. She did it with the help of Caracis. You remember that, do you not?" Oracle looked away. "And Caracis, once again, stole her sword. But this time she asked *me* to return it to her. That had never happened before. I did not know what to do. And now—suddenly—she is here. A victorious queen carrying *this* sword."

"I did not want to part with it," whispered the man who had been Caracis.

"You had such talents, Caracis," said Taliesen softly. "How was it that you became such a wretch?"

"I wanted to be a king, a hero. I wanted songs sung about me, and legends written. Is that so shameful? Tell me, did she rule well?"

"She won the final battle, and held the clans together for forty years. She is a true legend and will remain so."

Oracle grinned. "Forty years, you say? And she won." Hauling himself to his feet, the old man fetched a jug of honey mead and two goblets. "Will you join me?"

"I think I will."

"Forty years," said Oracle again. "I could not have done it. Forty years!"

"Tell me of the boy Gaelen."

Oracle dragged his mind back to the present. "Gaelen? He's a good lad, bright and quick. He has courage. I like him. He will be good for Caswallon."

"How does Caswallon fare?"

"As always, he walks his own path. He has been good to me . . . like a son. And he eases my shame and helps me forget . . ."

"Have you told him of your past?" inquired Taliesen, leaning forward and staring hard at Oracle.

"No, I kept my promises. I've told no one of the worlds beyond. Do you doubt me?"

"I do not. You are a willful man and proud, but no one ever accused you of oath-breaking."

"Then why ask?"

"Because men change. They grow weak. Senile."

"I am not senile yet," snapped Oracle.

"Indeed you are not."

"What will happen to the Queen?"

Taliesen shrugged. "She will die, as all die. She is old and tired; her day is gone. A sorcerer long ago sent a demon to kill her. He made a mistake and cast his spell too close to a Gateway. The beast is almost upon her."

"Can we not save her?"

"We are talking of destiny, man!" snapped Taliesen. "The beast must find her." His stern expression relaxed. "Even should the demon fail, she will die soon. Her heart is old and worn out."

"At least she achieved something with her life. She saved her people. I've destroyed mine."

"I cannot make it easier, for you speak the truth. But it is done now."

"Is there truly no hope?" Oracle pleaded.

The druid sighed and stood, gathering his long staff. "There is always hope, no matter how slender or unrealistic.

Do not think that you are the only one to feel regret. The Farlain are my people, in a way you could never comprehend. When they are destroyed my life goes with them. And all the works of my life. You! You are just a man who made a mistake. I must bear the cost. Hope? I'll tell you what hope there is. Imagine a man standing in Atta forest at the birth of autumn. Imagine all the leaves are ready to fall. That man must reach out and catch one leaf, one special leaf. But he doesn't know which tree it is on. That is the hope for the Farlain. You think the idiot Cambil will catch the leaf?"

"Caswallon might," said Oracle.

"Caswallon is not Hunt Lord," said Taliesen softly. "And if he were . . . the clans are sundered, and widely spread. They will not turn back an enemy as strong as the Aenir."

"Did you come here to punish me, druid?"

"Punish you? I sometimes wish I had killed you," said Taliesen sadly. "Damn you, mortal! Why did I ever show you the Gate?"

Oracle turned away from him then, leaning forward to add fuel to the fire. When he looked back the druid had gone.

And he had taken the sword . . .

"You are a little unfair on Caswallon," Maeg told her father as he sat in the wide leather chair, chuckling as the infant Donal tugged at his beard. Maggrig was well into middle age, but he was still powerful and his thick red beard showed no grey. Donal yawned, and the Pallides Hunt Lord brought the babe to his chest, resting him in the crook of his arm.

"Unfair to him?" he said, keeping his voice low. "He married my only daughter, and still he raids my herds."

"He does not."

"I'll grant you he's stayed out of Pallides lands recently— but only because the Aenir have cut off his market."

"It is tradition, Father," argued Maeg. "Other clans have always been fair game; and Caswallon is Farlain."

"Don't give me that, girl. That tradition died out years ago. By God, he doesn't need to raid my cattle. Or Laric's. And sooner or later someone will catch him. Do you think I want to hang my own son-in-law?"

Maeg lifted the sleeping child from Maggrig's arms, laying him in his crib and covering him.

"He needs excitement, he does it because he enjoys it." The words sounded lame, even to Maeg. For all his intelligence and quick wit, Caswallon refused to grow up.

"He used to enjoy taking other men's wives, I hear," said Maggrig.

Maeg turned on him, eyes flashing. "Enough of that!" she snapped. "He's not looked at another woman since we wed . . . well, he's looked, but that's all."

"I can't think why you married him. Did you know he's got my prize bull in the meadow behind the house? Now there's a sight to greet a visitor, his own stolen bull!"

"Take it with you when you go," said Maeg, smiling.

"And be seen by all the men of the Farlain? I'd sooner they thought it was a present." He shook his head. "I thought you'd change him, Maeg. I thought marriage would settle him."

"It has. He's a wonderful husband, he cares for me."

"I don't want to kill him," admitted Maggrig. "Damn it all, I like the boy. There must be other ways to get excitement."

"I'll talk to him again. Are you sure that's your bull?"

"Sure? Of course I'm sure. The night he took it, Intosh and seven others chased him for hours—only he and that damn crofter Arcis had split up. Caswallon led Intosh a merry run."

"He must have been furious," said Maeg, keeping the smile from her face.

"He's promised to have Caswallon's ears for a necklace."

"That wasn't because of the bull," said his daughter. "It is said that when Intosh came back to his house he found his bed had been slept in and his best sword stolen."

"The man is unreasonable," said Maggrig, unable to suppress a grin. "I gave Intosh that sword after he won the Games."

"Shall I get it for you, Father? I'm sure Intosh would like it back."

"He'd bury it in pig's droppings rather than use it now."

"Caswallon plans to wear it at the Games."

"Ye Gods, woman! Has he no shame?"

"None that I've noticed."

From the hearth room below they heard a door open and close, and the sound of whistling floated up the stairs.

"Well, I suppose I'd better see him," said Maggrig, pushing himself to his feet.

"Be nice," said Maeg, linking her arm with his.

"Be nice, she says. What should I say? 'Been on any good raids lately?' "

Maeg chuckled, looped her arm around his neck, and kissed his bearded cheek. "I love you," she told him.

He grinned at her. "I was too soft in the raising of you, child. You always had what you wanted."

The two of them walked downstairs where Caswallon was standing before the hearth, hands stretched out to the flames. He turned and smiled, green eyes twinkling. "How are you, Father?" he asked.

"Not a great deal better for seeing you, you thieving swine," snapped Maggrig. Maeg sighed and left them together.

"Is that any way to talk to the husband of your daughter?" Caswallon asked.

"It was a miserable day when you crossed my doorway," said Maggrig, walking to the far table and pouring a goblet of honey mead. It was full-flavored and rich, and he savored the taste. "This has a familiar feel to it," he said. "It is not unlike the special mead that Intosh brews."

"Really?" said Caswallon.

Maggrig closed his eyes. "That is all I need to complete my day—my own bull grazing in your meadow, while I drink mead stolen from my comrade."

"You must give him my compliments. It is the finest mead I've tasted."

"I'll do that. Where is Gaelen?"

"I've sent him out to meet the other lads."

"Was that wise?"

The smile faded from Caswallon's mouth as he moved to Maggrig's side and poured himself a goblet of mead. "It had to happen sooner or later," he said, gesturing Maggrig to a chair. Sitting opposite him, Caswallon gazed at the golden liquid, then sipped at it slowly. "He's a good boy, Maggrig, but he's been through much. I think they'll make him suffer. Agwaine will lead them."

"Then why send him?"

"Because he has to learn. That's what life is—learning how to survive. All his life he has done that. Now he must find out that life in the mountains is no different."

"You sound bitter. It is not like you."

"Well, the world is changing," said Caswallon. "I watched the Aenir sack Ateris and it was vile. They kill like foxes in a henhouse."

"I hear you had words with them in the mountains?"

Caswallon grinned. "Yes."

"You killed two."

"I did. I had no choice."

"Will they attack the clans, do you think?"

"It is inevitable."

"I agree with you. Have you spoken to Cambil?"

Caswallon laughed aloud. "The man hates me. If I said good day he would take it as an insult."

"Then talk to Leofas. Make plans."

"I think I will. He's a good man. Strong."

"More than that," said Maggrig, "he's canny."

"He sounds like you, Maggrig."

"He is."

"Then I'll see him. And you needn't worry about your herds. Those days are behind me. After watching Ateris I lost my appetite for the game."

"I'm glad to hear it."

Caswallon refilled their goblets. "Of course I might just sneak back for some more of Intosh's mead."

"I wouldn't advise it," said Maggrig.

Chapter Three

Gwalchmai listened as Agwaine planned the downfall of the Lowlander. Around the Hunt Lord's son, in a wide circle, sat fifteen other youngsters—the sons of councilmen, who would one day be councillors themselves. They listened as Agwaine spoke, and offered no objections. Gwalchmai wasn't happy with such conversation. An orphan child of the mountains, he knew what loneliness was, the pain it brought, and the inner chill. He had always been popular, but then he worked at it—jesting and joking, seeking approval from his peers. He ran errands for the older boys, always willing to help in any chore, but in his heart his fears were great. His father had died when he was seven—killed while poaching Pallides lands. His mother contracted lung fever the following year and her passing had been painful. Little Gwalchmai had been sent to live with Badraig and his son, and they had made him welcome. But Gwalchmai had loved his parents deeply, and their loss hurt him beyond his ability to cope.

He was not a big child, and though he approached fifteen, he was by far the smallest of his group. He excelled in two things: running and bowmanship. But his lack of strength held him back in both. At short distances he could outpace even Agwaine, and with a child's bow at twenty paces he could outshoot the Farlain's best archers. But he had not the strength to draw a man's bow, and failed in tourneys when the distance grew beyond thirty paces.

Agwaine was talking now about humiliating Caswallon's new son. Gwalchmai sat and stared at the Hunt Lord's son.

He was tall and graceful, with a quick and dazzling smile, and normally there was little malice in him. But not today. Agwaine's dark eyes glittered, and his handsome face was marred as he spoke of tormenting the Lowlander. Gwalchmai found it hard to understand, and he longed to find the courage to speak out. But when he looked inside himself he knew that his nerve would fail him. Nervously his eyes sought out Layne. While all others would follow Agwaine blindly, Layne would always go his own way. At the moment the son of Leofas was saying nothing, his aquiline face showing no emotion. Beside him his giant brother Lennox was also silent. Layne's grey eyes met Gwalchmai's gaze and the orphan boy willed Layne to speak out; as if in answer to prayer Layne smiled at Gwalchmai, then spoke.

"I think this Gaelen has already been harshly treated, Agwaine," said Layne. "Why make it worse for him?" Gwalchmai felt relief flow through him, but Agwaine was not to be persuaded.

"We are talking about a jest," said Agwaine smoothly. "I'm not suggesting we *kill* him. Where's the harm?"

Layne ran a hand through his long, dark hair, his eyes holding Agwaine's gaze. "Where is the good in it?" he countered. "Such an action is beneath you, cousin. It is well known that your father has no love for Caswallon, but that is a matter for the two of them."

"This is nothing to do with my father," said Agwaine angrily. He swung to Lennox. "What about you?" he asked. "Do you side with your brother?"

Lennox shrugged his huge shoulders. "Always," he said, his voice deep as distant thunder.

"Do you never think for yourself, you ugly ox?" snapped Agwaine.

"Sometimes," answered Lennox amiably.

"What about the rest of you?"

"Oh, let's have a little fun with him," said Draig, Gwalchmai's foster brother. "Where's the harm? What do you think, Gwal?"

All eyes turned to Gwalchmai and his heart sank. He spent his life avoiding argument, and now whatever he said would hurt him. Layne and Lennox were his friends. Layne was stern of nature but a loyal youth, and his brother Lennox, though strong as an ox, was a gentle companion. But Agwaine was Cambil's son and the accepted leader of the Farlain youth, and Draig was Gwalchmai's foster brother and a boy given to hot temper and malice-bearing. Of the other five, all were larger than Gwalchmai.

"Well, what do you think?" urged Draig.

"I don't mind," mumbled Gwalchmai. "Whatever you think best." He tried not to look at Layne, but his eyes were drawn to the other's gaze. Layne merely smiled at him, and he felt the pity in that smile; it hurt him more than he could bear.

"Then let's do it!" said Agwaine, grinning.

The plan was a simple one. Kareen had innocently told them that Caswallon planned to send his son to the meadow that morning to meet the other boys of the village. Agwaine had suggested they take his clothes and chase him back to his house, lashing him the while with birch sticks.

Now Layne and Lennox moved away from the group to lounge on the grass. Gwalchmai sat miserably on a fallen tree, wishing he had stayed at home.

He looked up as the conversation died. Coming toward them was a slender boy in a green woolen tunic edged with brown leather; his hair was red, with a white flash above the jagged scar that ran down the left side of his face. He wore a wide belt and from it hung a hunting knife. There was no swagger in his walk, but he seemed nervous. Layne and Lennox ignored him as he passed, and Gwalchmai saw the boy's jaw was clamped tight.

He approached the group with eyes fixed on Agwaine. Gwalchmai saw that his left eye was filled with blood and he shivered.

"I am Gaelen," said the boy, addressing Agwaine.

Agwaine nodded. "Why tell me?"

"I see from the way your friends are grouped around you
that you are the leader."

"How observant of you, Lowlander."

"Will you tell me your name?"

"To what purpose? You will never address us directly, you
are like the wolf pup you brought home—of no account to
those with pedigree."

Gaelen said nothing but his mind raced. In Ateris there
had been many thieves and many gangs, but he had always
been alone. This scene was no different from many in his
life. There would be a little more talk, then tempers would
grow and the violence would begin. The difference was that
in Ateris he always had somewhere to run; he knew every
alley and tall building, every rooftop and hiding place. As he
had approached the group he had scanned them, making
judgments, deciding which were the boys to be feared, which
to be ignored. Two were lounging on the grass away from
their comrades; one of these was slender, but athletically
built, his face strong. Beside him was a veritable giant, bigger than most clansmen Gaelen had seen. But since they
were apart from the group Gaelen ignored them. His eyes
had been drawn to a small boy sitting with the others. Slight
of build, with short-cropped ginger hair, he had seemed nervous, frightened. Gaelen put this one from his mind. The
others had gathered around the young man now facing him.
These would not act—only react. Therefore everything depended on the outcome of this confrontation with the leader.
Gaelen took stock of him. His face was strong, the eyes dark,
the gaze steady. And he was proud. In that instant Gaelen
knew that he was facing no cowardly bully who could be
browbeaten, or dominated by words. His heart sank.

Still, one thing he had learned early was that you never
allow the enemy to dictate the pace of the game. "Well, don't
just stand there," he told Agwaine, forcing a grin, "teach this
wolf pup the lesson you have planned."

"What?" said Agwaine, momentarily taken aback.

"It's obvious that you and your mongrel playmates have already decided how this game is going to be played, so let's be at it. Here, I'll make it easy for you." Casually he stepped forward and then, with a lack of speed that dulled Agwaine's reflexes, punched the other boy full in the face, toppling him backward to the grass.

Gaelen drew his knife and leaped back as the other youths surged to their feet. Agwaine shook his head and slowly rose, eyes glittering. He too drew a knife.

"I'll kill you for that, Outlander," he said. His face was set and he moved forward, perfectly in balance. The other youths drew their blades, spreading out in a half circle.

"That's enough!" said the tall young man Gaelen had seen sitting apart from the others. Walking forward, he stood by Gaelen. "In fact, it is more than enough. The joke has soured, Agwaine." Another figure moved to the other side of Gaelen; he was enormous, towering above all the other youths.

"Do not interfere," Agwaine warned them. "I mean to cut his heart out."

"Move behind me," Layne told Gaelen.

"I'm not afraid of him."

"Move behind me!" The voice was not raised, and yet had great authority. Even so, Gaelen's anger was so great now that he was ready to refuse. Then the giant laid a massive hand on his shoulder and Gaelen felt the power in the grip.

"Best do as he says," said the huge youth softly. "Layne's usually right."

Gaelen obeyed and Layne stepped forward until his stomach pressed against Agwaine's dagger.

"Do you really want to kill me, cousin?" he asked.

"You know I will not."

"Then think on it. The boy did well. He knew you planned to thrash him and he took you all on; he has courage. It would not be fitting to punish him now—would it?"

Agwaine sheathed his blade. "He is a Lowlander, and I will never accept him. Neither will my friends. He will be shunned by all who follow me."

"I'll not shun him, Agwaine. Neither will Lennox."

"Then you are my friend no longer. Let's go!" he told the others. As they trooped away Gwalchmai hung back, but Draig spotted him and called out.

"I'll see you later," Gwalchmai replied.

Draig trotted back to his side. "You can't stay here," he said. "You heard what Agwaine said."

"I stay with my friends," said Gwalchmai.

"You're a fool, Gwal. No good will come of it." Draig strode off. Gaelen slid the knife back in its sheath. The tall youth with the dark hair and grey eyes turned to him, holding out his hand.

"I am Layne, son of Leofas," he said. "This is my brother Lennox and my cousin Gwalchmai."

Gaelen shook hands with them all. "Why did you do this for me?" he asked.

"It wasn't for you, it was for Agwaine," Layne told him.

"I don't understand."

"Agwaine is a fine friend and a brave one," said Layne. "He acted in anger and would have regretted slaying you. He is not evil, not malicious. But he has the conceit of his father and he loves to lead."

"I have caused you trouble. For that I am sorry."

Layne shook his head. "You caused nothing. It was not you they were seeking to humble, but your father. Caswallon is not liked."

"Why?"

"It is not for me to prattle on with gossip. I like Caswallon but others do not, and among the clans such matters usually end in bloodshed and family feuds. We are a violent race, Gaelen, as you have discovered."

"Caswallon is not violent."

"Indeed he is not. But he has the capacity for it, as you saw in the mountains with the Aenir."

"You heard of that?"

"Who has not? My father led the hunters that escorted them from the Farlain."

The lads settled themselves on the grass, enjoying the sunshine. Lennox and the ginger-haired Gwalchmai said little.

Layne asked Gaelen about life in Ateris, and the Aenir invasion. Gaelen found the memories too painful and switched the conversation back to Caswallon. "I know you don't want to gossip," he said, "but I am a stranger here, and I need to know how my . . . father earned such dislike."

"Caswallon is the richest man in the valley. He has the largest herds and his fields carry more wheat than any save Cambil's. But he holds himself apart from other clansmen, and the Hunt Lord hates him."

"He doesn't appear rich," said Gaelen. "In Ateris rich men have . . . had . . . marble palaces and carriages of gold. And many servants. They wore rings and necklets, bracelets and brooches."

"We have no use for such finery," Layne told him. "We live free. Caswallon supports more than one hundred crofters. If he desired, he could start a new clan. That is rich—believe me."

"Then why doesn't he? I mean, if he's so disliked it would seem to be good sense. Then he would be his own Hunt Lord."

"He would have to surrender his valley land and find somewhere else to live, and that is no longer easy. To the northeast the Haesten control the land bordering the Lowlands. North of them are the Pallides. The rest of the land for a six-day march is all Farlain, and beyond that the minor clans—the Loda, the Dunilds, and the Irelas—fight over territory. Anyway, Caswallon is Farlain and always will be."

"I'm damned hungry," said Lennox suddenly.

Gaelen fished in his leather hip pouch and produced a thick slice of cold meat pie. He passed it to Lennox. Thanking him, the huge youth wolfed the pie down at speed.

"My father would also be rich," said Layne dryly, "were it not for my brother's appetite."

"He's big," said Gaelen. "I don't think I've seen anyone his age bigger." Lennox was already more than six feet tall, with a bull-like neck and an enormous frame. His face was broad, his eyes deep-set and brown. His chin and cheeks were already darkening with the promise of a beard.

"And he's as strong as he looks. Also, despite what you will hear, he's no fool. He just says little. Isn't that right, brother?"

"Whatever you say," said Lennox, grinning.

"I don't know why, but he likes to play the fool," said Layne. "He lets people think he has no brains."

"It does no harm," said Lennox mildly.

"No, but it irritates me," replied his brother, scowling. Gaelen would not have guessed them to be brothers. Layne, though tall, was of more slender build, his face fine-boned.

"I can't think why it should, Layne," said Lennox, smiling. "You are the thinker in the family."

"Nonsense." Layne swung to Gwalchmai. "Why so silent, little one?"

"I was thinking about Agwaine," answered Gwalchmai. "I don't like to make anyone angry."

"He won't be angry with you for long. And besides, I'm proud of you. What do you think, Lennox?"

"I think it took nerve to stay with us. You'll not regret it, Gwal, my lad."

"Do you think they'll attack Gaelen again?" Gwal asked.

"No," replied Layne. "When he has had time to think on it, Agwaine will realize that Gaelen acted like"—he grinned—"like a Highlander," he said. "He will respect that."

Gaelen blushed and said nothing.

"Well," said Layne, "I think it's time we told Gaelen about the Hunt."

Caswallon stood nervously outside the door biting his lip, a habit he thought he had left behind in childhood. But then standing before the door of Leofas brought back memories, none of them pleasant.

When Caswallon was a child he had stolen a dagger from the home of the Sword Champion, Leofas. His foster father, Padris, had been furious when Cambil informed him of Caswallon's misbehavior—and had sent the boy to Leofas to confess.

Caswallon had stood before the door then as now, on edge and fearful. The clansman chuckled. "You fool," he told himself. But it didn't help.

Rapping the door with his knuckles, he took a deep breath.

Leofas let him in without a word of greeting and pointed to a chair before the hearth. Removing his cloak, Caswallon sat down. The room was large, strewn with rugs of goatskin and wolf hide, and on the far wall hung a bearskin, dust-covered and patchy with age.

Caswallon stretched out his legs before the fire. "The last time I was here, you thrashed me with your belt," he remarked.

"I recall that you deserved it," said Leofas. He was a big man, not tall, but wide in the shoulder with a thick neck and heavy beard streaked with grey. But his blue eyes were keen, the stare forbidding.

"Indeed I did."

"State your business, Caswallon," snapped the older man.

Caswallon pushed himself to his feet, a knot of anger deep within him. "I don't think that I will," he said softly. "I am not the child who stole your knife, I am a man. I came here because Maggrig advised it, and it seemed sensible, but I'll not sit here swallowing your discourtesies."

Leofas raised his eyebrows, waiting as Caswallon reached for his cloak.

"Would you like a drink, boy?" he asked.

Caswallon hesitated for a moment, then dropped his cloak across the back of a chair and turned to the older man. "That would be pleasant," he said.

Leofas left the room, returning with two jugs of ale. Then he sat opposite Caswallon. "Now will you state your business?"

"Before I do, let's clear the air. When you were young you raided all over the Druin to build your herds. So why are you set against me?"

"That's easily answered, and I like a man who states his grievance swiftly. When I was a lad there was open warfare between the clans.

"No man knew what it was like to be rich. Raiding was often the difference between starvation and small comfort. But times changed and clans prospered. I applauded you when you began, I thought you were spirited and cunning. But then you grew rich, and yet the raids continued. And then I knew that the raids were not a means to an end but the end itself.

"Sometimes in life a man must risk death for the sake of his family, but you risk it merely for pleasure. Most men in the mountains value their clan, for it is like a great family and we depend on one another to survive. Children of the mountains are cared for; no one man starves while another gluts himself. But you, Caswallon, you don't care. You avoid responsibility, and your very existence eats away at what makes the clan strong. Children imitate you. They tell tales of your exploits and they want to be like you, for you are exciting, like a clansman out of time. A myth from the past.

"Cuckoo Caswallon they used to call you, because of your amorous exploits. Women yearn for you and I can understand that and don't begrudge it. But when you creep into the bed of another man's wife, and sire him a son, all you have done is destroy that man's life. He cared for his wife deeply, loved her and cherished her. She surrenders all that for a few nights of passion with you. You don't stick by her, so she despairs. And her life is ruined too.

"As for your raids . . . you encourage other clans to copy you. Last autumn I caught three Pallides poachers making off with my prize bull. I had to mutilate them, it was the law. But why did they do it? Why? Because Caswallon had stolen *their* bull. Now state your business."

Caswallon leaned back in his chair, his heart heavy for he could not refute a word of Leofas's damning indictment.

"Not yet, Leofas. First let me say this: Everything you accuse me of is correct and I cannot gainsay it. But I never intended evil. Cuckoo Caswallon? Sometimes a man gives in to selfishness, telling himself there is a nobler reason—he is bringing a little happiness into a dull life. But since I married Maeg I have been faithful, for I learned by my mistakes.

"As for the raids, they too were selfish, but I don't regret them for I enjoyed every moment. If men suffered by imitating me, then it is on their heads, for my risk was as great as theirs. But that too is now a thing of the past.

"I came to you because of the Aenir; that is my *business* with you. I seek not your friendship nor your approval. I care for neither. The Aenir are killers and they will invade the clans."

"Cambil is Hunt Lord," said Leofas guardedly. "Have you seen him?"

"You know I have not. Nor will I. If I told Cambil that sheep ate grass he would deny it and feed his flock on beef."

The older man nodded. "That is true enough. And I agree with you about the Aenir, but Cambil thinks differently. He seeks new trade agreements, and he has invited an Aenir captain to watch the Hunt."

"He didn't see the sack of Ateris," said Caswallon.

"No. But you did and it changed you."

"I won't deny that."

"How is the boy you brought home?"

"He is well. Your lads helped him, I think, though he has not spoken of it."

"Neither have they, but I heard. They're good boys. Layne would not allow Agwaine to harm him and Lennox stood by him. That made me proud, for it's hard bringing up boys without a mother. And they've turned out well."

"They are a credit to you."

"As is Gaelen to you," said Leofas, "for he took them all on."

"He is a credit to himself. Will you argue against Cambil on the Council?"

"On the question of the Aenir, I will."

"Then I'll take up no more of your time."

"Man, you haven't finished your ale. Sit and be comfortable for a while. I don't get many visitors."

For an hour or more the men sat, drinking ale and swapping stories. It came to Caswallon that the older man was lonely; his wife had died six years before and he had never taken another. On the death of Padris three years ago Leofas had refused to stand for Hunt Lord, claiming it was a young man's duty. But he remained on the Hunt Council, and his words were heeded.

"How long do you think we have—before they invade?" asked Leofas suddenly, his eyes clear despite the jugs of ale.

Caswallon fought to clear his mind. "I'd say a year, maybe two. But I could be wrong."

"I don't think so. They're still fighting in the Lowlands. Several cities are holding out."

"We need a plan of our own," said Caswallon. "The valley is indefensible."

"Seek out Taliesen," Leofas advised. "I know these druids raise the hairs on a man's neck, but he is wise, and he knows much about events outside Druin."

For two months Caswallon took Gaelen with him on every hunt, teaching him more of the land and the creatures of the land. He taught him to fight hand-to-hand, and to wrestle and to box, to roll with the punches, and to counter swiftly. The lessons were sometimes painful, and Gaelen was quick to anger. Caswallon taught him to hold his fury and use it coolly.

"Anger can strengthen a man or destroy him," he told the youth as they sat on the hillside above the house. "When you fight, you stay cool. Think with your hands. When you strike a blow it should surprise you as well as your opponent. Now pad your hands and we will see what you have understood." Warily the two circled each other. Caswallon stabbed a straight left to Gaelen's face. Gaelen blocked it, hurling a right. Caswallon leaned out of reach, the punch whistling past his chin. He countered with a swift left that glanced from the boy's jaw. Off balance, Gaelen hit the ground hard, rolled, and rose to his feet with eyes blazing. Caswallon stepped in to meet him, throwing a right cross. It never landed, for Gaelen ducked inside the punch and caught the taller man with an uppercut that sent him reeling in the grass.

"Good. That was good," said Caswallon, rubbing his jaw. "You are beginning to move well. A little too well." Reaching up, he took Gaelen's hand and the younger man pulled him to his feet. "Let's sit for a while," he said. "My head is still spinning, I think you've shaken all my teeth."

"I'm sorry."

Caswallon laughed. "Don't be. You were angry, but you kept it under control and used the power of your anger in your punch. That was excellent." The two sat together beneath the shade of an elm.

"There is something I have been meaning to ask you," said Gaelen, "about the bush you hid me in when the Aenir were close."

"It was a good hiding place."

"But it wasn't," insisted Gaelen. "It was out in the open, and had they looked down they would surely have seen me."

"That's *why* it was good. When they attacked their blood was up. They were moving fast, thinking fast, seeing fast. You understand? They didn't examine the clearing, they scanned it swiftly, making judgments at speed. The bush was small and, as you say, in plain sight. It offered little cover and was the last place, so they believed, that anyone would choose as a hiding place. Therefore they ignored it. Similarly that made it the best place to hide in."

"I see that," said Gaelen, "but what if they had stopped to examine the clearing?"

"Then you would probably have been slain," said Caswallon. "It could have happened—but the odds were vastly against it. Most men react to situations of violence—or threatened violence—by animal instinct. Understanding that instinct allows an intelligent man to win nine times out of ten."

Gaelen grinned. "I do understand," he said. "That's why when you raided the Pallides you chose to hide in the village itself. You knew they would expect you to flee their lands at speed, and so they raced from their village to catch you."

"Ah, you've been listening to the tales of my wicked youth. I hope you learn from them."

"I am learning," agreed Gaelen. "But why did you choose the house of Intosh to hide in? He is the Sword Champion of the Pallides, and everyone says he is a fearsome opponent."

"He is also a widower with no children. No one would be in the house."

"So you had it planned even before you did it. You must have scouted the village first."

"Always have a plan, Gaelen, *always*."

Later, as they sat on the hillside above Caswallon's house, awaiting the call to the midday meal, Caswallon asked the boy how he was settling in with the other lads in the small village.

"Very well," Gaelen told him guardedly.

"No problems?"

"None that I can't handle."

"Of that I have no doubt. How do they compare with the boys of Ateris?"

Gaelen smiled. "In the city I used to watch them play games: hunt-seek, spider's folly, shadowman. Here they play nothing. They are so serious. I like that . . . but I always wanted to join in back in Ateris."

Caswallon nodded. "You joined us a little late for children's games, Gaelen. Here in the mountains a boy becomes a man at sixteen, free to wed and make his own life. It is not easy. Two in five babes die before their first birthday, and few are the men who reach fifty years of age. Childhood passes more swiftly here. Have you teamed yet for the Hunt next week?"

"Yes, I travel with Gwalchmai, Lennox, and Layne."

"Fine boys," said Caswallon, "although Gwalchmai is a little timid, I think. Are you content with the teaming?"

"Yes. We are meeting today to plan the Run."

"What problems will you face?"

"Lennox is strong, but no runner. We may not beat Agwaine's team to the first tree."

"Speed is not everything," said Caswallon.

"I know."

"Which of you will lead?"

"We're deciding that this afternoon—but I think it will be Layne."

"Logical. Layne is a bright fellow."

"Not as bright as Agwaine," said Gaelen.

"No, but you are. You should enjoy yourselves."

"Did you lead when you ran in the Hunt?"

"No. Cambil led."

"Did you win?"

"Yes."

"Was Cambil a good leader?"

"In his way. He still is. And he has been a good Hunt Lord for the Farlain."

"But he doesn't like you, Caswallon. Everyone knows that."

"You shouldn't listen to idle chatter. But you are right. He doesn't like me—but then he has good cause. Three years ago I robbed him of something. I didn't mean to, but it worked out that way, and he has not forgotten."

"What did you steal?" asked Gaelen.

"I didn't actually steal anything. I just refused to stand against him for the position of Hunt Lord. I didn't want the role. So he was voted to it by the elders."

"I don't understand. How can he hold that against you?"

"That's a difficult question, Gaelen. Many people assumed I would try for Hunt Lord. In truth I would have lost, for Cambil is—and always was—worthy of the role. But had I stood and lost, he would have known he was considered the better man. Because I did not stand he will never know."

"Is that why Agwaine doesn't like me?" asked Gaelen. "Because his father doesn't like you?"

"Perhaps. I have been very selfish in my life, doing only that which I enjoyed. I should have acted differently. If I am nominated for the Council again I shall accept. But that is not likely."

From the house below they heard Kareen calling. Gaelen waved at her, but Caswallon remained where he was.

"Go and eat," he said. "I will be down soon."

He watched the boy running down the hillside and smiled, remembering his own Hunt Day fifteen years before. Every lad in the Farlain over the age of fourteen, and not yet a man, was teamed with three others and sent out into the mountains to recover a "treasure." Skillful hunters would lay trails, hide clues and signs, and the teams would track them down until at last one team returned with the prize. For Caswallon the prize they had sought was a dagger, hidden in a tree. Often it was an arrow, or a lance, or a helm, or a shield. This year it was a sword, though none of the lads knew it.

Every year Caswallon helped lay the trails and delighted in his work. But this year was special for him, for Gaelen would be taking part.

He removed from his pouch the strip of parchment Taliesen had given him and he reread the words written there.

> Seek the beast that no one finds,
> always roaring,
> never silent,
> beneath his skin,
> by silver wings,
> bring forth the
> long-lost
> dream of kings.

After the meal Caswallon would read the verse to his new son, even as, all over the Farlain, fathers would be doing likewise. There were times, Caswallon considered, when tradition was a wholesome thing.

In the wide kitchen Caswallon's young son Donal lay on a woolen blanket by the hearth. Beside him slept the pup Gaelen had brought home; it had grown apace in the last two months, showing signs of the formidable beast it would be in the years ahead. Kareen sat beside Maeg opposite Gaelen, and they were all laughing as Caswallon entered.

"And what is amusing you?" he asked.

"Rest your poor bones at the table," Maeg told him, "and tell us, gently, how Gaelen here dumped you to the earth."

"It was a wicked blow and I was unprepared," he answered, seating himself beside the boy, who was blushing furiously.

"Have you been bragging, young Gaelen?" he asked.

"He has not," said Maeg. "Kareen herself saw the deed done as she fed the chickens."

"Fed the chickens, indeed," said Caswallon. "It could not be seen from the yard. The lazy child climbed the hill and spied on us, for a certainty." Now Kareen began to blush, casting a guilty glance at Maeg. "In fact," said Caswallon, smiling broadly, "on my way back here I saw two sets of tracks. One had the dainty footprints of young Kareen, the other I could not make out except to say the feet must have been uncommonly large."

"So!" said Maeg. "It's back to gibes about my feet, is it?"

"You have beautiful feet, Maeg, my love. There isn't a woman in the Farlain who could match them for beauty—or length."

Throughout the meal they good-naturedly sniped at each other, and only when she began to list Caswallon's faults did he open his arms in surrender and beg her forgiveness.

"Woman," he said, "you're full of venom."

After the meal he gave leave to Gaelen to seek his friends, and read him the druid's parchment. "Do not be home late. We've an early start tomorrow."

Later, as Maeg and Caswallon lay arm in arm in the broad bed, she leaned over him and kissed him gently on the lips. "What troubles you, my love?" she asked him, stroking his dark hair back from his eyes.

His arm circled her back, pulling her to him. "What makes you think I am troubled?"

"No games, Caswallon," she said seriously. She rolled from him and he sat up, bunching a pillow behind him.

"The Council has voted to resume trade with Ateris, and allow an Aenir group to visit the Farlain."

"But we had to trade with them," said Maeg. "We always have dealt with Ateris, for iron, seed corn, seasoned timbers, leather."

"We didn't always, Maeg. We used to do these things ourselves. We're no longer dealing with merchant Lowlanders; this is a warrior race."

"What harm can it do to allow a few of them to visit us? We might become friends."

"You don't make friends with a wolf by inviting it to sleep with the sheep."

"But we are not sheep, Caswallon. We are the clans."

"I think the decision is shortsighted and we may live to rue it."

"I love you," she said, the words cutting through his thoughts.

"I can't think why," he said, chuckling. Then he reached for her and they lay silently enjoying the warmth of each other's bodies and the closeness of their spirits.

"I cannot begin to tell you what you mean to me," he whispered.

"You don't have to," she said.

One moment the mountainside was clear, rolling green slopes, the occasional tree, two streams meeting and foaming over white boulders. Sheep grazed quietly near a small herd of wild ponies.

Suddenly the air reeked with an acrid smell none of the animals recognized. Their heads came up. Blue light replaced the gold of the sun. Rainbows danced on the grass and a great noise, like locust wings, covered the mountainside. The ponies reared and wheeled, the sheep scattering in all directions.

For a fraction of a second two suns hung in the sky, then

they merged and the golden sunlight bathed the mountain. But all was not as it had been . . .

In the shadow of a great boulder stood a towering figure, six-inch fangs curving from a wide snout, massive shoulders covered in black fur, huge arms ending in taloned fingers. The eyes were black and round, the brows deep, and it blinked as its new surroundings came into focus.

Lifting its shaggy head, the beast sniffed the air. The sweet smell of living flesh flooded its senses. The creature leaned forward, dipping its colossal shoulders until its talons brushed the earth. Its eyes focused on a three-year-old ewe, which stood trembling on the hillside.

Dropping fully to all fours, the beast bunched the muscles of its hind legs and leaped forward, bearing down on the sheep with terrible speed. Startled, the ewe turned to run. It had made only three running jumps before the weight of the hunter smashed its spine into jagged shards.

Taloned fingers tore aside the ewe's flesh and the blood ran.

The beast ate swiftly, lifting its shaggy black head often, peering shortsightedly around the mountainside, ready for any enemy that might chance upon it. It was uncomfortable out in the open, unused to shimmering horizons and bright light. But the blood was good upon its tongue, the flesh rich and greasy. Casually it ripped out the ewe's entrails, hurling them far from the body, concentrating instead on the flesh of the loins. Slowly, methodically, the giant creature fed, snapping bones and sucking out the marrow, splitting the skull with one blow and devouring the brains.

Hunger satisfied, the beast sank back to its haunches. It blinked in the sunlight as an image fashioned itself in its mind. A bright image. Grunting, it shook its head, then gave a low growl. Dimly it remembered the circle of stones and the red-clad sorcerer whose fingers danced with fire. The fire had entered the creature's breast, settling there without pain. The beast howled as hunger returned.

It would always be hungry—until it devoured the image-woman. Angrily the beast slammed its hands against the ground.

Away to the left it saw the line of trees that merged into the forest above Vallon. Hunger returning, it began to lope toward them, stopping at a stream to drink. The trees were smaller than the ones it had known and climbed, less closely packed and strangely silent. No chittering monkeys swung from the vines, few birds sang, and there was no sign of fruit upon the boughs.

The wind shifted and a new smell filtered to the beast's flaring nostrils. The black eyes glittered with the memory of salty-sweet flesh and marrow-filled bones. The sorcerer had implanted a soul scent upon its senses—and this creature was not the victim ordained. Nor was the spell scent close by. Yet it could almost taste the sweet meat of the approaching man-beast.

Saliva dripped from its maw and its dark tongue licked out over its fangs. The smell was growing stronger. There was no need to stalk, for the simpleminded creature was moving this way.

A hundred paces to the west Erlik of the Pallides, a tall young hunter from the house of Maggrig, leaned on his staff. Beside him his war hound Askar growled deep in his throat. Erlik was puzzled. An hour ago he had seen the blue haze across the mountains, and the two suns appear in the sky. And despite this being Farlain land he had ventured here, led by the curiosity of the young. Less than a year before Erlik had gained his manhood in the Hunt, and was now a contender for the Games.

And where a more seasoned veteran would hesitate, Erlik, with all the confidence of youth, had crossed the border and ventured into the lands of the enemy. He did not fear Farlain hunters, for he knew he could outrun them, but he had to know why the air burned blue. He sensed it would be a fine tale to tell his comrades at the evening feast.

He leaned down and stroked Askar, whispering it to silence. The hound obeyed unwillingly. It didn't like the idea of moving with the direction of the breeze, and it sensed danger ahead that made the fur on its shoulders rise. With the natural cunning of the canine it began to edge left, but Erlik called it back.

The young hunter moved forward toward an area of thick bracken and gorse. Askar growled once more and this time the dog's unease filtered through to the man. Carefully he laid down his quarterstaff, then swung his bow from his shoulder, hastily notching an arrow to the string.

The gorse exploded as a vast black creature reared up from the ground at Erlik's feet. A taloned arm flashed out, half severing the hunter's left arm and hurling him to the ground. The war hound leaped for the beast's throat, but was brutally swatted aside. Erlik drew his hunting knife and struggled to rise, but the talons flashed once more and his head toppled from his shoulders.

Minutes later the war hound came to its senses, pain gnawing at its broken ribs. The great head came up slowly, ears pricking at the sounds of crunching bones.

With infinite care the hound inched its way to the west, away from the feeding beast.

In the valley of the Farlain fourteen teams of youngsters were packing shoulder sacks with provisions ready for the hunt. Families and kin thronged the Market Field.

The brothers Layne and Lennox were seated side by side on a fallen oak while Gaelen lay on his back, eyes closed, nearby. Beside him sat the slender Gwalchmai, whittling with a short dagger.

"I wish they would announce the start," said Layne. "What are they waiting for?"

Gaelen sat up. "Caswallon said the druid must give his blessing."

"I know that," snapped Layne. "I meant why the delay?" Gaelen lay back on the grass and said nothing. Layne was not normally this edgy.

"Are you looking forward to it?" asked Gwalchmai. Gaelen could see that the ginger-haired youth was worried by Layne's tension and seeking to change the mood.

"Yes, I am," said Gaelen.

"Do you understand the meaning of the riddle?"

"No. Have you deciphered it?"

Gwalchmai shrugged. "Maybe it will be clearer when we find the second clue."

In the house of Cambil, beyond the field and the waiting teams, sat the Druid Lord, Taliesen. Opposite him, pacing before the hearth, was the tall Hunt Lord Cambil, a golden-haired, handsome young man wearing a leaf-green tunic and a red cloak.

By the hearth sat a stranger clad in leather shirt and breeches, his long blond hair braided beneath a round leather helm. He too was handsome, but unlike Cambil, there was no softness in him. His eyes were the cold blue of the winter sky, and upon his mouth was a mocking half smile. That the druid disliked him was obvious and seemed to amuse the Aenir; but for Cambil the meeting was a monstrous embarrassment.

The druid was angry, though he showed nothing of it as he sipped water from a clay goblet. Cambil was uneasy and pulled at his golden beard. The stranger sat back in the leather-covered chair, his face expressionless.

"It is rare," the druid said at last, "for a stranger to be present at the Youth's Hunt—though it is not without precedent. There shall be no blessing today, for the words of power cannot be spoken in the presence of Lowlanders. In this there is no disrespect intended for your guest, Cambil, it is merely the weight of tradition which forbids it."

Cambil bit his lip and nodded.

"May I ask," continued the druid, "that we speak privately?"

Cambil turned to the man beside him. "My apologies, Lord Drada, but please feel free to join the men at the food table beyond and refresh yourself."

Drada stood and bowed to Cambil, then he turned to the

druid. "I am sorry to have caused you problems. Had I known my presence would disrupt the ceremony I would have turned down the invitation." Neither Taliesen nor Cambil missed the stress he placed on the word *invitation,* and the Hunt Lord felt himself blushing.

The Aenir warrior carefully hung his black cloak upon his broad shoulders and left the room, closing the door quietly behind him.

The ancient druid turned his dark eyes on the Hunt Lord and leaned forward across the table. "It was not wise to invite him into Farlain lands," he said.

"He is friendly enough," insisted Cambil.

"He is the Enemy to Come," snapped the druid.

"So you say, old man, but I am the Hunt Lord of the Farlain, and I alone decide whether a man is a friend or enemy. You are a druid and as such are to be respected in religious matters, but do not exceed your authority."

"Are you blind, Cambil, or merely stupid?"

Anger shone in the Hunt Lord's eyes, but his response was calm. "I am not blind, druid. And I make no great claims to be wiser than any other clansman. What I do know is that war brings no advantage to either side. If the Aenir can be convinced that we offer them no threat, and that there is no wealth to be found in the mountains, I see no reason why we cannot exist together—if not as friends, then at least as good neighbors. Keeping them out will only cause suspicion, and make war more likely."

Cambil walked to the door, wrenching it open. "Now, the boys are waiting and I shall send them off, and I don't doubt the lack of your words of power will affect them not at all."

At the edge of the field Caswallon sat with Maeg and Kareen, watching the boys line up for the first race to the trees. Once there, they would find a leather pouch hanging from the branch of the central pine. Within the pouch were four clues, written on parchment. The first team to reach the tree would be able to read all the clues, and remove one. The next team would find three clues, and remove one. And so on until the fourth team would find only one remaining.

Gaelen, who could not yet read, would be useless to his team on this first run, but they had chosen Gwalchmai to lead the sprint, and he was almost as fast as Cambil's son Agwaine.

The teams sprinted away at Cambil's command and Caswallon watched as Gwalchmai and Agwaine forged a lead over the rest, with Gaelen loping beside the lumbering Lennox at the rear.

At that moment Caswallon caught sight of the black-coated Aenir warrior standing by the grey house. Leaving Maeg and Kareen, he walked the short distance to the building. As he walked he gauged the man. The Aenir was tall and well built, but slim of hip. He looked what he was—a warrior. As Caswallon approached the man turned and the clansman knew he was undergoing the same appraisal.

"The lads move well," said the Aenir, pointing toward the youngsters who were now halfway up the hillside.

"I see your men took my advice," said Caswallon. "That was wise."

Drada smiled. "Yes, I always listen to wise counsel. But I saw no sign of the Farlain hunters you promised to send after us."

"They were there."

"I was surprised to find you are not a councillor, Caswallon."

"Why so?"

"I gained the impression that you were a man of influence but Cambil tells me this is not so. He says you are a thief and a bandit."

"What do you think of the Farlain mountains?" Caswallon countered.

"They are beautiful. Most especially this valley."

"There are many valleys in the Farlain, and a vast number more in the Druin range," said the clansman.

"I have no doubt I shall see them all eventually," Drada told him, with a wolfish smile.

"Travel alone when you do so."

"Really, why?"

"The mountains can be tranquil and a man alone can best enjoy their harmony."

"And if he is not alone?" asked Drada.

"If he travels with many, then the mountains can be hostile, even deadly. Why, even now two Aenir corpses are rotting in the mountains. And there is room for many more."

"That is no talk for new friends, Caswallon."

Caswallon laughed with genuine humor; then the smile faded. "But then I am not your friend, my bonny. Nor ever shall be."

More than fifty youngsters pounded up the slope, feet drumming on the hard-packed grass-covered clay of the hillside. Gwalchmai tucked himself in behind Agwaine, fastening his eyes on the other boy's pack and running on grimly. After forty paces he loosened the straps of his own heavy pack and let it fall to the ground behind him. Then, as Gaelen had instructed him, he once more moved up behind Agwaine.

Here the hillside was at its steepest and the young Agwaine was breathing heavily, his legs began to burn as the body's waste acids settled to the muscles of his calves. He did not look back. He could afford no wasted energy. And besides, he was the fastest runner for his years in the Farlain.

Back down the slope, Lennox scooped up Gwalchmai's pack and continued to lope alongside Gaelen, way to the rear of the other runners.

"I hope this is allowed," shouted Lennox.

Gaelen said nothing. Caswallon had told him that the rules were specific. All runners had to start the race carrying their own provisions. Well, Gwalchmai had done that.

Layne had not been easy to convince, for he was a youth who lived on traditions of honor and would sooner lose than cheat. But Gaelen had called a vote, as was his right, and had won the day. Layne seemed to harbor no grudge.

Gwalchmai and Agwaine had now increased their lead over the following pack to fifty paces, and it was obvious that they would reach the trees well ahead of their rivals.

As the timberline neared Gwalchmai sped past his astonished opponent. Agwaine was furious. Sweat-soaked and near-exhausted, he released his pack and set off after the sprinting youth. Fury pumped fresh adrenaline to his tired legs and against all the odds he began to close the gap.

Fifty paces from the trees Agwaine was running in Gwalchmai's shadow, but the canny youngster had one more ploy. As Agwaine came abreast of him Gwalchmai kicked again, releasing the energy he had held in reserve. Agwaine had nothing more to offer. In an agonizing effort to match his opponent, he stumbled against a stone and pitched to the earth.

Gwalchmai ran ahead, eyes flickering from tree to tree, seeking the pouch. It was in plain view, fastened to a low branch. He pulled it clear, removing the small pieces of paper it contained. Reading them all, he selected one and tucked it in his belt. Then he rehung the pouch and wandered back toward Agwaine.

The Hunt Lord's son ignored him, racing past to tear the pouch clear. He read the three remaining strips, took one, and replaced two. Then he turned after Gwalchmai.

"You dog!" he shouted, his breathing labored. "You . . . cheating . . . cur!"

Frightened, Gwalchmai backed away and opened his hands. "The rules did not forbid it, Agwaine."

Other runners came between them in the last frantic dash for clues, and Agwaine turned away to sit in the shade of a spreading elm.

Gwalchmai was grinning broadly as Layne reached him and he handed the parchment over. Layne read it, nodded, then walked over to where Agwaine was sitting.

"Well run, cousin," he said, squatting beside him.

"Thank you. That was a devious strategy. But, as Gwalchmai says, it was within the rules and therefore I can have no complaint." Layne offered Agwaine the parchment. "What is this? What are you doing?"

"There may be nothing in the rules against our tactic," said Layne, "but I am not happy with it. Here. Read the line, and from now we start level."

"No, cousin," said Agwaine, gripping the other's shoulder, "though I thank you for your courtesy. I must confess that were I not the fastest runner it is likely I would have used the tactic myself. I take it the Lowlander conceived it?"

"Yes."

"He has quick wits, I'll give him that."

Layne nodded. Then he stood and returned to the others, who had been watching the scene, puzzled. "Let's find a place out of earshot and discuss our next move," he said, walking past them to the trees. Gaelen bit back his anger and followed. He had seen Layne offer the clue to Agwaine and noted the other's refusal. It was confusing and deeply irritating.

In a deep hollow, away from the crowds, the four squatted in a huddled circle. Layne nodded to Gwalchmai, who began to speak in a hushed whisper. They were all aware that those teams without clues would now seek to follow and spy on the leading four.

"The clues were simple to understand," whispered Gwalchmai. "The one we have is the simplest: 'That which Earis lost.' So, it is a sword we seek. The other clues confirm it: 'A King's Sorrow,' 'The Light that brings Darkness,' and 'The Bane of Eska.' The question now is, where is it hidden?"

"It's hidden at, or near, Attafoss," whispered Gaelen.

"What?" said Layne, astonished. "How do you know?"

"The rhyme: 'Seek the beast that no one finds, always roaring, never silent . . .' When Caswallon took me to Attafoss it sounded like a great monster, but when we arrived there was no monster, merely a roaring fall of water."

"It could be," said Layne. "What do you think, Gwal?"

"I agree with Gaelen."

"Lennox?"

The youth raised his shoulders in a noncommittal shrug.

"So," said Layne, "we are agreed. Well done, Gaelen. If we look at the rest of the verse it becomes even more obvious. 'Beneath its skin, by silver wings, bring forth the long-lost dream of kings.' The blade is hidden under the water, guarded by fishes. But where? Attafoss is huge."

"There will be other clues," said Gwalchmai. "We must follow the right tracks."

"True," said Layne. "All right. We'll make camp higher up in the trees, then slip away before dawn and strike for Vallon."

Dawn found the four of them miles from the first timber and well on their way. Layne led them down rocky slopes and over difficult terrain, constantly checking on what tracks they were leaving. By midmorning he was content. Even the most skillful hunters would have difficulty finding them, and above all, the task would be time-consuming.

As they strolled through patches of yellow-gold gorse and across meadows bedecked with blooms, Gaelen rediscovered the strange sense of joy he first felt when Caswallon formally adopted him. He was home. Truly home.

Beside him Gwalchmai was whistling a merry tune and ahead Layne and Lennox were deep in conversation. Gaelen rubbed at his scarred eye, for it itched now and then, usually when he was tired.

"Is it troubling you?" asked Gwalchmai. Gaelen shook his head and Gwalchmai resumed whistling, but his thoughts remained on the youngster beside him. Gwalchmai had liked Gaelen from the first. He didn't know why, but then he rarely rationalized such things; he relied on his emotions to steer him and they rarely played him false. He remembered his shock when he first saw the boy, his red hair streaked with a white slash, his left eye filled with blood—for all the world like a ruby set in his skull.

He had been prepared to dislike the Lowlander, having listened to Agwaine speak sneeringly of Caswallon's rescue.

But there had been something about the way Gaelen carried himself—like a clansman, tall and proud. Gwalchmai stopped whistling as he noticed a track some ten paces from the trail.

"Layne!" he called. "Hold on." Gwalchmai stepped from the trail and knelt by the soft earth beside the gorse. The three companions gathered around him, staring in wonder at the footprint.

"It's as long as my forearm," said Gwalchmai. "And look, the thing has six toes." All four lads scouted back along the line of tracks, but they found nothing. The earth by the gorse was soft, but the surrounding ground was rocky and firm.

"What do you think it is?" asked Gaelen, whose knowledge of mountain animals was still sparse.

"It isn't anything I've ever seen," said Gwalchmai. "Layne?"

The leader grinned suddenly. "It's perfectly obvious, my friends. It's a hunter's joke. When they were laying the trails for our Hunt they made a jest of the rhyme 'Seek the beast . . .' the footprint points toward Vallon and the print was created to show we're on the right track."

Gwalchmai's freckled face split into a grin. "Yes, of course," he said.

An hour before nightfall Layne scouted a small hollow where they could build a fire against a towering granite stone. The tiny blaze could not be seen from any distance and the four travelers unrolled their blankets and settled down for a light meal of oatcakes and water.

As the night closed in and the stars shone bright, Lennox curled up like a dozing bear and slept, leaving the others seated by the fire talking in low voices.

"Who was Earis?" Gaelen asked as he fed the fire with dry sticks.

"The first High King," Layne told him. "Hundreds of years ago the Farlain lived in another land, beyond the Gates. There was a great war and the clans were nigh obliterated. Earis gathered the remains of the defeated army and launched one last desperate assault on the enemy, smashing their army and killing their leader, Eska. But it was only one of several armies facing him. The druids told the King of a way to save his people. But it was hazardous: They had to pass a Gate between worlds. I don't know much about that side of it, but the legends are many. Anyway, Earis brought the Farlain here and we named the mountains Druin.

"During the journey a strange thing happened. As Earis stepped through the Gate of Vallon, into the bitter cold of winter, his sword disappeared from his hand. Earis took his crown and hurled it back through the Gate. The sword, he said, was the symbol of kingship, and since it had gone so too would his position. From henceforth there would be no king for the Farlain. The Council voted him to the position of Hunt Lord and so it has remained."

"I see," said Gaelen. "So 'the Bane of Eska,' that is a clue I can understand. But why the light that brings darkness?"

"The sword was called Skallivar, meaning Starlight on the Mountain," said Gwalchmai. "But in battle whoever it touched found only the darkness of death."

"And that is what we seek? Skallivar?"

Layne laughed. "No. Just a sword. It makes the clues more poetic, that's all."

Gaelen nodded. "There is much still to learn."

"But you will learn, cousin," said Layne. Gaelen felt a surge of warmth and comradeship within him as Layne spoke, but it was shattered by a sound that ripped through the night. An eerie, inhuman howling echoed through the mountains.

Lennox awoke with a start. "What was that?" he asked, rolling to his knees.

Gaelen shuddered and said nothing.

"I've no idea," said Layne. "Perhaps it's a wolf and the sound is distorted."

"If it's a wolf," muttered Gwalchmai, "it must be as big as a horse."

For several minutes they sat in silence, straining to hear any more sounds in the blackness of the night. But there was nothing. Lennox went back to sleep. Layne exchanged glances with Gwalchmai.

"It wasn't a wolf, Layne."

"No, but it could have been a hunter trying to frighten us."

"I hope so," said Gwalchmai. "I think we should stand watches tonight, though."

Chapter Four

Gaelen awoke at Gwalchmai's touch, his eyes flaring open, his troubled dreams fragmented and instantly forgotten.

"I can't keep my eyes open any longer," whispered Gwalchmai. "I don't think there's anything out there. I saw a fox, that's all."

Gaelen sat up and yawned. "It's chilly," he whispered. Gwalchmai rolled himself swiftly into his blanket, laying his head on his pack. Within seconds he was asleep. Gaelen stretched, then crept to the fire, easing himself past Lennox. Taking a dry stick he poked around the embers of the dying fire, gently blowing it to life. Adding more sticks, he watched the flames flicker and billow. Then he looked away. Caswallon had told him never to stare into a fire, for the brightness made the pupils contract, and when you looked away into darkness you would be blind.

Gaelen wrapped his blanket around his shoulders and leaned back against the granite boulder. An owl hooted and the boy's fingers curled around the hilt of his hunting knife. You fool, he told himself. You've never been afraid of the dark. Calm down. These are your mountains, there is nothing to harm you.

Except wolves, bears, lions, and whatever made that bestial howling . . .

Gaelen shuddered, and fed more sticks to the fire. The supply was growing short and he didn't relish the prospect of entering the menacing darkness of the surrounding trees to replenish the store.

Slowly the fire died and Gaelen cursed softly. He had hoped it would last until first light, when the woods would become merely trees and not the frightening sentinels they now appeared. He stood up, loosening the dagger in its sheath, and walked carefully toward a fallen elm at the edge of the woods. Swiftly he collected dead wood and thicker branches. Back at the fire, relief washed over him. He was comforted by the sound of Lennox snoring and the sight of his other two friends sleeping soundly.

It was ridiculous. If danger was upon them they would be no use to him, sleeping as they were. And yet he felt at ease.

Layne muttered in his sleep and turned onto his back. Gaelen gazed down at his square, honest face. He looked so much younger asleep, his mouth half open and childlike.

Gaelen turned his gaze to Lennox. Where Layne was clean-cut and athletic, Lennox was all bulk, with sloping shoulders of tremendous power, barrel-chested, thick-waisted. His hands were huge and the strength in them awesome. A year before he had straightened a horseshoe at the Games, having seen it done in the Strength Test. Too young to be entered, he had shamed several of the contestants and caused great merriment among the Farlain clan.

Later that day a dozen youths of the Haesten clan, having seen their man shamed, lay in wait for Lennox as he strode home. They came at him out of the darkness bearing cudgels and thick branches. As the first blow rapped home against his thick skull Lennox had bellowed in anger and lashed out, sending one luckless youngster through a bush. Two others followed him as Lennox charged among them; the rest fled.

Gaelen had heard the story and chuckled. He believed it. He wished he had seen it.

To the east the sky was brightening and Gaelen stood and wandered through the trees, on and up, scrambling over the lip of the hollow to stare at the distant mountains. In the trees around him birds began to sing, and the eldritch menace of the night disappeared. The boy watched as the snowcapped peaks to the west began to burn like glowing coals, as the sun cleared the eastern horizon. Fields below were bathed in glorious colors as blooms opened to the golden light.

Gaelen breathed deeply, filling his lungs with the sweet mountain air. He slid back down the slope and burrowed into Lennox's large pack, more than twice the weight of his own, and produced a copper bowl. Stoking up the fire, he placed the bowl upon it, filling it with water and adding the dry oats Maeg had wrapped for him.

Layne was the first to wake. He grinned at Gaelen. "No monsters of the night, then?"

Gaelen grinned back and shook his head.

Had he remained on the rim of the hollow for a minute more he would have seen a Farlain hunter racing back toward Cambil's village, his cloak streaming behind him.

Badraig was a skillful huntsman whose task it was to set the trails for those of the boys traveling toward Vallon. He enjoyed his role. It was good to see tomorrow's generation of clansmen testing their mettle, and his son Draig and foster son Gwalchmai were among them.

But today his mind was on other matters. During the night, as he made cold camp by a narrow stream, he had heard the howling that so disturbed Gaelen and his companions. They had half dismissed it as a hunter's prank; Badraig knew it was not, for he was the only hunter in the area.

Being a cautious man, with over twenty years' experience, Badraig waited until near dawn before checking the source of the cry. With infinite patience he had worked his way through the woods, keeping the breeze in his face. As it shifted, so too did he.

And he found the butchered, broken remains of Erlik of the Pallides. In truth he didn't know it was Erlik, though he had seen the man many times at the Games. But no one could have recognized the bloody meat strewn across the track. Badraig lifted a torn section of tunic, recognizing the edging

as Pallides weave. In the bushes to the left he found part of
a foot.

At first he thought it was the work of a bear, but he scouted
for tracks and found six-toed footprints the like of which he
had never seen. There were also the tracks of foxes and other
small carrion creatures, but they had obviously arrived long
after the killing beast had departed.

The prints were enormous, as long as a short sword. Badraig measured the stride. He was not a tall man, neither was
he the shortest clansman in the Farlain, but he could not
match the stride except by leaping. He gauged the height of
the beast as half that again of a tall man. And it walked upright. The deepest impression was at the heel. He followed
the track for a little way until he reached the foot of the
slope. Here the spoor changed. The creature dropped to all
fours and scrambled up at speed, gouging great tears in the
clay. Badraig dug his fingers into the earth with all his
strength, then compared his efforts with those of the killer.
He could barely scratch the surface.

So it was big, bigger than a bear, and much faster. It could
run on all fours or walk upright like a man. Its jaws were
enormous—the fang marks in the leg he had found proved
that. He considered following the beast up the slope, but dismissed the idea.

From the remains he could see that the Pallides hunter had
been carrying his bow with the arrow notched. He had been
given no time to shoot. Badraig was confident of his own
skills, but his strength lay also in the understanding of his
weaknesses. Armed with only a hunting knife and a quarterstaff, he was no match for whatever had wreaked this carnage. His one duty was to carry the news to Cambil and clear
the mountain of youngsters.

Luckily, so he believed, no teams had passed his vantage
point, so he would be able to stop any he came across as he
returned. By midafternoon every village in the Farlain had
the message and by nightfall six hundred clansmen, in groups
of six, were scouring the mountains. By noon the next day

forty-eight puzzled and disappointed youngsters had been shepherded back to their villages.

Only two teams remained to be found, those led by Layne and Agwaine. At dusk on the second day Cambil sat with his advisers around a campfire half a day's march into the mountains.

"They've just vanished," said Leofas. "Layne's group made camp near the elm grove, and then moved northeast. After that the tracks cease."

"It was a cunning ploy," said Badraig. "They obviously thought they had a clue and didn't wish to be followed. It doesn't make it any easier for us, though—except that we know they didn't head for Vallon."

"I disagree," said Caswallon.

"A pox on you, Caswallon," snapped Badraig. "That was my area. Are you saying I'm that poor a huntsman that I could have missed eight callow boys?"

"What I am saying is that we've searched everywhere and found no sign," answered Caswallon softly.

Badraig snorted. "Then maybe it's you who've missed the trail."

"Enough of this quarreling," ordered Cambil. "What shall we do now?"

"Look in Vallon," said Caswallon. "We have two missing teams. Both are led by the brightest, most able of our young men. The rhyme was not easy, but the answer was there for those with the wits to work at it. Agwaine I am sure would have deciphered it. Do you not agree, Cambil?"

Cambil bit his lip and stared into the fire. "Yes, he misses little."

"Now, all the boys who headed west say they saw no sign of Agwaine. Or Layne. In fact, after the first night they just dropped from sight. No team headed for Vallon, because none of the others deciphered the rhyme. To my mind the conclusion is inescapable."

"So you *are* saying I'm lacking in skill!" stormed Badraig.

"Please be calm, cousin," said Caswallon. "We are talking

about two teams who traveled carefully so that no rivals would spot them. It doesn't mean you lacked skill because you missed them."

"I still say they headed west."

"Then go west and find them," said Caswallon. "I'm heading for Vallon."

Badraig swore, but Cambil cut across him. "Hold your tongue, man! In this I think Caswallon is right. Now we have men hunting the west, and we'll lose nothing by visiting Attafoss. I just wish that druid would get here. I'd like to know what Hell spawn we're facing."

"Well, 'that druid' can help you," said Taliesen, moving out of the tree shadows and seating himself among them. "The beast crossed a Gateway and it is following the youngsters toward Attafoss. Caswallon is right. Let these arguments cease."

"Are you sure, Lord Druid?" asked Badraig.

"As sure as death," answered Taliesen. "You had best move now, for there is tragedy in the air, and more blood to be spilt before you find them."

"A curse on your prophecies," said Cambil, lurching to his feet. "Is this beast more of your magic?"

"None of mine, Hunt Lord."

"Have you seen who will die?" asked Badraig. "Can you tell us that?"

"No, I cannot tell you."

"But my son is with Agwaine."

"I know. Go now, for time is short."

The men rolled their blankets and set off without a backward glance at the druid, whose dark eyes followed them seemingly without emotion. Taliesen watched them go, his heart heavy, a great sadness growing within him. The threads were beginning to come together now. In another time the sorcerer Jakuta Khan had sent a beast to kill the young Sigarni. That beast had vanished into the mists of time. Now it was here, in the Farlain, and being drawn inexorably toward the frail and wounded Queen. And between the hunter and his victim were the boys of the Farlain. Taliesen longed to intervene. He remembered the long nights sitting at the Queen's bedside, in the cave on Druin's flanks. He had told her to say nothing of events in her own world, lest the knowledge cause even more fractures in the Time Lines. But when she became delirious with fever she had spoken in her sleep, and Taliesen had felt the weight of sorrow bear down on him like a huge rock.

He longed to rescue the boys. And he could not. "It rests with you now, Gaelen," he whispered.

And with the Hawk Eternal, he thought.

The four men walked for most of the night, stopping only to snatch an hour's sleep before dawn. Then they moved on, crossing hills, running across narrow valleys, scaling tree-lined slopes. During the afternoon they were joined by six hunters cutting in from the east. A hurried conference was held. One man was sent back to the village to fetch more bowmen, and the remaining nine hoisted their packs and ran single file toward the towering peaks of the northeast.

They drove themselves hard, calling on reserves of endurance built during years of tough mountain living. Only Leofas, the oldest of them, struggled to maintain the pace; but maintain it he did, giving no sign of the pain from his swollen knee.

Just before nightfall Badraig halted the column, spotting something to the right of the track; it was a half-eaten oat-cake. Badraig picked it up, breaking it into crumbs. At the center it was still dry.

"Yesterday," he said. Then he scouted carefully around the area. Rather than destroy any faint traces of spoor, the other hunters squatted down to wait for Badraig's report. Within minutes he returned.

"Four lads," he said. "One is very large and can only be Lennox. You were right, Caswallon; they passed me."

The group pushed on into the mountains, and as the sun

sank, Caswallon found the hollow Layne had chosen for their camp. The men gathered around.

"Tomorrow should be easier going," said Cambil, stretching his long legs in front of him and resting his back against the granite boulder. "The tracks will be easy to find." His strong fingers kneaded the muscles of his thigh, and he grunted as the pain flowed.

Leofas sank to the ground, his face grey, his eyes sunken. With great effort he slipped his pack from his shoulders and unrolled his blanket. Wrapping himself against the night chill, he fell asleep instantly.

Badraig took two huntsmen and began to scour the area. The moon was bright and three-quarters full and the tracks left by the boys could be clearly seen. Badraig followed them halfway up the north slope of the hollow. Here he stopped.

Overlapping Lennox's large footprint was another print twice as long. Badraig swore, the sound hissing between clenched teeth. Swiftly he returned to the men in the hollow.

"The beast is hunting them," he told Cambil. "We must move on."

"That might not be wise," the Hunt Lord replied. We could miss vital signs in the darkness. Worse, we could stumble on the beast itself."

"I agree," said Caswallon. "How close behind them is it, Badraig?"

"Hard to say. Several hours, perhaps less."

"Damn all druids!" said Cambil, his broad face flushed and angry. "Damn them and their Gates."

Caswallon said nothing. Wrapping himself in his blanket, he leaned back, closed his eyes. He thought of Gaelen and wondered if Fate could be so cruel as to save the boy on one day, only to have him brutally slain thereafter. He knew that it could. All life was chance.

But the Gates were a mystery he had never been able to fathom.

The elders had a story of a time just before Caswallon was born, when a leather-winged flying creature had appeared in the mountains, killing sheep and even calves. That had been slain by the then Hunt Lord, a strong proud man who sought to be the first High King since Earis. But the people had voted against him. Embittered, he had taken thirty of his followers and somehow found a way to cross the churning waters of Attafoss to the island of Vallon. There he had overpowered the druids and led his men through the Forbidden Gate.

Twenty years later he returned alone, gravely wounded. Taliesen had asked for his death, but the Druid Council denied him and the man was returned to the Farlain. No longer Hunt Lord, he would tell no man of his adventures, saying only that a terrible vision had been revealed to him.

Many thought him mad. They mocked him and the once-proud lord took it all, making his home in a mountain cave where he lived like a hermit. Caswallon had befriended him, but even with Caswallon the man would not speak of the world beyond the Druid's Gate. But of the Gates themselves he spoke, and Caswallon had listened.

"The feeling as you pass through," Oracle had told him, "is unlike any other experience life can offer. For a moment only you lose all sense of self, and experience a great calm. Then there is another moment of sense-numbing speed, and the mind is full of colors, all different, moving past and through you. Then the cold strikes marrow-deep and you are human again on the other side."

"But where did you go?" Caswallon asked.

"I cannot tell you."

The wonder of it, Caswallon knew, was that Oracle had returned at all. There were many stories of people disappearing in the mountains, and even rare occasions when strange animals or birds appeared.

But Oracle was the only man he had heard of—save for Taliesen—to pass through and return. There were so many questions Oracle could have answered. So many mysteries he could lay to rest.

"Why can you not tell me?" Caswallon asked.

"I promised the druids I would not."

Caswallon asked no more. A promise was a thing of steel and ice and no clansman would expect to break such an oath.

"All will be revealed to you, Caswallon. I promise you," Oracle had told him cryptically.

Now as the young clansman sat beneath a moonlit sky his mind harked back to that conversation. He wasn't at all sure he desired such knowledge. All he wanted was to find the boys and return them safely to the valley.

Badraig prepared a fire and the men gathered around it silently, fishing in their packs for food. Only Leofas slept.

Cambil pushed back the locks of blond hair from his forehead and wiped sweat from his face. He was tired, filled with the exhaustion only fear can produce. Agwaine was his only son, and he loved him more than anything else the world could provide. The thought of the lad being hunted by a beast from beyond the Gates filled him with terror; he could not face the possibility that Agwaine might die.

"We will find them," said Caswallon softly.

"Yes," answered the Hunt Lord. "But alive?"

Caswallon saw the man's angular, honest face twist, as if a sudden pain had struck him. Beneath the wiry yellow-gold beard Cambil was biting his lip hard, seeking to prevent the collapse into tears of frustration.

"What did you think of the pack incident?" asked Caswallon suddenly.

"What?"

"Gwalchmai dropping his pack and outstripping Agwaine."

"Oh, that. Clever move. Agwaine did not give up, though. He ran him to the end."

"Bear that in mind, Cambil. The boy is a fighter. Given half an opportunity he will survive."

"The thing will probably seek to avoid Man," said Badraig. "It is the way with animals of the wild, is it not? They know Man is a killer. They walk warily around him."

"It didn't walk too warily around the Pallides scout," said a balding bearded clansman from the west.

"True, Beric—but then, from the tracks, the Pallides was stalking it, though I can't see why. Still, it is well known the Pallides are long on nerve and short on brain."

Slowly, as the night passed, the men drifted off to sleep until at last only Cambil and Caswallon remained sitting side by side before the fire.

"It's been a long time since we sat like this, cousin," said Cambil, breaking a lengthy silence.

"Yes. But we walk different paths now. You have responsibility."

"It could have been yours."

"No," said Caswallon.

"Many would have voted for you."

"They would have been wrong."

"If Agwaine is taken I shall take my daughter and leave the Farlain," said Cambil, staring into the glowing ashes of the dying blaze.

"Now is not the time to think of it," Caswallon told him. "Tomorrow we will talk as we walk the boys home."

Cambil said nothing more. He unrolled his blanket, curled it around his shoulders, and settled down against his pack.

Caswallon stood and made his way slowly up the farthest slope into the deep, cool pine woods beyond. From the tallest point he gazed to the northeast, seeking sign of a campfire, yet knowing he would see nothing. The boys were too well trained.

Sixteen miles northeast the four companions were arguing over the choicest morsels of a freshly cooked rabbit. Lennox, who had cooked the coney and served it, was protesting innocence, despite his plate bearing twice as much meat as any other.

"But I am bigger," he said seriously. "My pack carries all the cooking equipment. And it was my snare."

Gwalchmai broke from the argument for long enough to

pop a small piece of meat in his mouth and begin chewing. He dropped from the discussion instantly, tugging surreptitiously at Gaelen's cloak. Gaelen saw the expression on his face. He tried his own meat, chewed for a moment, then removed the offending gobbet. Lennox and Layne were still arguing furiously. "I think Lennox is right," said Gaelen suddenly. "He is the largest and he has the greatest burden. Here, take mine too, my friend."

"I couldn't," said Lennox, his eyes betraying his greed.

"No, truly. One small rabbit is scarce enough to build your strength." Gaelen tipped the contents of his plate on Lennox's own. In the meantime Gwalchmai had whispered to Layne.

"I'm sorry, brother," said Layne, smiling. "Gaelen has made me realize how selfish I am. Take my portion too."

"And mine," added Gwalchmai eagerly.

Lennox sat back on his haunches. "You are all true friends," he said, gazing dreamily at his plate. Discarding his knife he scooped a handful of meat into his mouth. For several seconds he chewed in silence, then his face froze. His three companions waited in nerve-tingling silence until he doggedly finished the mouthful and swallowed.

"Is it good?" asked Layne, his face set and serious.

"Yes, it is," said Lennox. "But look, I feel bad about taking it all."

"Think nothing of it," said Gwalchmai swiftly. "Your need is the greatest."

"Yes, but . . ."

"And you cooked it," put in Gaelen.

"I know, but . . ."

"Eat on, brother," said Layne. "See, it grows cold and . . . congeals."

The dam burst and all three broke into giggling laughter. Realization struck Lennox and he hurled the diseased meat into the bushes. "Swine!" he said.

A hundred paces above them, on the edge of the trees, the beast squatted on its haunches glaring down at the fire. The laughter puzzled it, for the sound was similar to the screeching of the small apes of its homeland. Its black nostrils flared, catching the aroma of scorched flesh—rancid-smelling sickly flesh.

The beast snorted, blowing the scent away. It stretched its powerful legs, moving several paces left. Here the flesh scent was different, warm-blooded, salty, and alive. The creature's eyes glittered. Hunger urged it to charge the camp and take the meat. Instinct made it fear the fire.

The beast settled down to wait.

Gaelen's dreams were troubled. Once more the Aenir killers pursued him, the pounding of their horses' hooves drumming fear into him as he ran. His legs were heavy, his movements sluggish. Suddenly a calming blue light filled his mind and the warriors faded. A face appeared, wrinkled and ancient, only the dark eyes giving a hint of life.

"The fire," said a deep melodious voice, though the lips did not move. "The fire is dying. Awake!"

Gaelen groaned and rolled over, trying to force the man from his mind.

"The fire, fool! Your life is in danger! Awake!"

The calming light disappeared, to be replaced by a red haze. Within the haze was a monster, black and menacing. Its huge jaws slavered, and its taloned hands reached for him.

Gaelen awoke with a jolt, eyes opening to the bright moonlight and the glittering stars in the velvet-dark sky. He glanced at the fire. As the dream had told him, it was failing fast, the last flickering twigs turning to ash and glowing embers.

The boy did not want to leave the warmth of his blanket, but the dream left an edge of fear in him. He sat up, running his fingers through his hair, scratching at the scar beneath the blaze of white above his left eye. Swiftly he broke twigs and small branches, feeding them to the tiny blaze and blowing life back into the fire. He felt better as the flames danced.

A rustling to his right made him turn. A large bush quivered and a low growl reverberated in the clearing. Gaelen drew his hunting knife and narrowed his eyes, trying to pierce

the darkness. He felt a fool. Had Caswallon not warned him
endlessly about staring into fires? Now he could not see
clearly. A giant shadow rose above the bush and Gaelen
screamed a warning to the others.

Layne rolled from his blanket with knife in hand, standing
in a half crouch beside Gaelen. "What is it?" Gaelen pointed
at the thing beyond the bush. It was at least eight feet high,
its head round like a man's except that the jaws were huge
and rimmed with curving fangs. Gwalchmai and Lennox had
left their beds and were staring horror-struck at the creature.

Gaelen pushed his trembling hand toward the fire, grasp-
ing the last of the branches they had stacked. It had not been
stripped of its dry leaves for they would be good tinder for
the morning blaze. Lifting the branch, Gaelen held it over the
flames. The leaves caught instantly, flaring and crackling. On
trembling legs, Gaelen advanced toward the beast, holding
the torch before him.

Layne and Lennox exchanged glances, then followed behind him. Gwalchmai swallowed hard, but he could not force
his legs to propel him forward and stood rooted to the spot,
watching his friends slowly advance on the nightmarish
beast. It was colossal, near nine feet in height, and the light
from the blazing branch glinted on its dagger-length talons.

Gaelen's legs were trembling as he approached the mon-
strosity. It reared up and tensed to leap at the youth but he
drew back his arm and flung the blazing brand straight at the
creature's face. Flames licked at the shaggy fur around its
eyes, flaring up into tongues of fire on its right cheek. A fearful howl tore the silence of the night and the beast turned and
sprang away into the night. The boys watched until it blended
into the dark woods. Layne placed his hand on Gaelen's
shoulder. "Well done, cousin," he said, his voice unsteady.
"I'm glad you woke."

"What in the seven hells was that?" asked Gwalchmai as
they returned to the comfort of the fire.

"I don't know," said Layne grimly. "But from the look of
those jaws it's not after berries and grubs."

Gwalchmai retrieved the blazing torch and examined the beast's tracks. Returning to the fire he told Layne, "It's the same track we saw in the valley. And we know no hunter made it. Congratulations, Gaelen, you saved our lives. There is no doubt of that."

"I had a dream," Gaelen told him. "An old man appeared to me, warning me."

"Did you recognize him?" asked Layne.

"I think he was the druid with Cambil on Hunt Day."

"Taliesen," whispered Gwalchmai, glancing at Layne.

"What are we going to do?" asked Lennox. "Go back?"

"I don't see that we need to," said Layne. "We turned the beast away easily enough. And most animals avoid men anyway. Also, we will be at Attafoss in the morning, so we might just as well see it through."

"I'm not sure," said Gwalchmai. "That thing was big. I wouldn't want to face it without fire."

"If it's hunting us," said Gaelen, "it can do so equally well whether we go forward or back."

"Are we all agreed, then?" Layne asked them. Gwalchmai longed to hear Lennox suggest a swift retreat back to the valley, but Lennox merely shrugged and donned his pack.

Dawn found the companions on the last leg of their journey, climbing the steep scree-covered slopes of the last mountain before Attafoss. As they crossed the skyline the distant roar of the falls could be heard some miles ahead.

"Always roaring, never silent," quoted Gwalchmai. "Whenever I hear it I feel the hairs rise on the back of my neck."

Layne hitched his pack into a more comfortable position. "No sign of the beast, anyway," he said, leading them on down the slope to cross a narrow stone bridge and on to a winding trail through gorse-covered countryside. Layne bore right down a rock-strewn slope and on, at last, to a narrow strip of black sand nestling in a cove below the falls. Here they loosened their packs and settled down for breakfast. The jutting wall of rock deadened the thunder of the falls, but the wind carried the spray high into the air before them, and the sun made rainbows dance above the camp.

"It occurs to me," said Gwalchmai as they ate, "that we have not come across a single clue. No pouches. No stones marking the trail. It is an unpleasant thought, but we might be wrong."

"I've been thinking that," said Layne, "but then the rhyme is clear. Perhaps the clues are all at the falls."

After the meal they gathered at the water's edge to indulge in the age-old sport of stone-skimming, at which Gwalchmai excelled, beating Layne by three jumps. Refilling their water canteens, the boys picked their way up the slope and into the timberline above the falls.

Lennox prepared a fire in the afternoon and Layne suggested a quick search of the woods for clues. Leaving their packs by the fire they set off to scout, traveling in pairs—Lennox and Layne moving south, Gaelen and Gwalchmai north.

From a highpoint on the hillside Gaelen gazed once more at the majesty of Attafoss, watching the churning white water thunder to the river below.

"That, my friend, is the soul of the Farlain," said Gwalchmai.

Gaelen turned to his comrade and grinned. "I can believe it."

Gwalchmai's face shone with pride and his green eyes glittered.

"Everything we are is contained there," he said. "All the poetry, the grandeur, and the strength that is Clan."

Gaelen watched him as he soaked in the sight. Gwalchmai was not built on the same powerful lines as Lennox or Layne—he was slight and bird-boned, his face almost delicate. But in his eyes shone the same strength Gaelen had come to see in all clansmen—a sense of belonging that rooted them to the land, allowing them to draw on its power.

"Come on, Gwal, let's find the clues," he said at last, and the two of them reentered the timberline.

By midafternoon they had found nothing, and then Gwalch-mai discovered a set of tracks that set him cursing loudly.

"What is it?" asked Gaelen. "Hunters?"

"No," snapped Gwalchmai. "It's Agwaine. They reached here this morning. That's why there are no clues; he's taken them. Curse it!"

"Let's follow them," said Gaelen. "We have nothing to lose."

The trail led south and was easy to follow. After less than an hour they reached a gentle slope, masked by thick bushes. Here Gwalchmai stopped.

"Oh, my soul!" he whispered. "Look!"

Overlaid upon the moccasin tracks was a huge print, six-toed, and as long as a man's forearm.

Pale-faced, Gwalchmai looked at Gaelen. "Are we going up the slope?"

"I don't want to," answered his friend. "But is there a choice?" He licked dry lips with a dry tongue.

Slowly they made their way to the top of the slope and entered a grove of pine. The sun was sinking slowly and long shadows stretched away from them.

"The beast was upon them here," hissed Gwalchmai. "Oh, Gods, I think it killed them all. Look at the tracks. See, they scattered to run, but not before one was downed. Look there! The blood. Oh, God."

Gaelen could feel his heart racing and his breathing becoming shallow: the beginning of panic. Caswallon had told him to breathe deeply and slowly at such times, and now he did so, calming himself gradually. Gwalchmai was inching his way into the bushes, where he stood and covered his face with his hands at what he saw lying there. Gaelen joined him.

His stomach turned and bile filled his throat. He swallowed hard. Inside the screen of bushes were the remains of three bodies, mutilated beyond recognition. A leg was half-buried in rotting leaves, and a split skull lay open and drained beside it.

Everywhere was drenched in blood.

Gwalchmai stumbled back from the sight, and vomited onto the grass. Gaelen forced himself to look once more, then he rejoined Gwalchmai who was shivering uncontrollably.

"Gwal, listen to me. We must know where the beast has gone. Check the tracks. Please."

There was no indication that Gwalchmai had heard him.

Gaelen took him by the shoulders and shook him gently. "Gwal, listen to me. We must find out; then we'll tell Layne. Can you hear me?"

Gwalchmai began to weep, slumping forward against Gaelen, who put his arms around him, patting his back as with a child. "It's all right," he whispered.

After a few moments Gwalchmai pulled away, breathing deeply. "I'm sorry," he said, drying his eyes on his sleeve.

"That's all right, cousin," said Gaelen. "They were your friends."

"Yes. All right. Let's see where the swine went."

For several minutes Gwalchmai circled the scene of the massacre, then he returned.

"The beast waited for them, hidden at the top of the slope. It reared up and killed the first as he cleared the top. The second, it was Ectas I think, turned to run and he too was slain. The other two ran west. The beast overtook one of them, but the fourth—Agwaine—got clear. The beast has followed him now. But first it . . . it ate."

"So," said Gaelen, "the creature is in the west. Now let's find Layne."

Gwalchmai nodded and set off in a loping run, his green eyes fixed to the trail. Gaelen ran just behind him, eyes flickering to the undergrowth around them. Fate was with them and they found the brothers within the hour. They were sitting by a stream. Swiftly Gaelen explained about the slaughter.

"How long ago did this happen?" Layne asked Gwalchmai.

"This morning, while we sat on the beach. I think the beast was following us, but when we cut away down to the waterside it picked up Agwaine's trail."

"Do you think Agwaine survived?"

"He certainly survived the first attack, for the beast returned to the bodies. But then it set out after him once more. What kind of creature is it, anyway? I mean, it's fed. Why hunt Agwaine?"

"I don't know, but we must help our cousin."

"We will not help him by dying, brother," observed Lennox. "Gwal says the beast has gone west. If we follow the wind will be behind us, carrying our scent forward. And we will be walking straight toward it."

"I know that's true," said Layne. "Yet we cannot leave Agwaine."

"Would you mind a suggestion from a Lowlander?" Gaelen asked.

Layne turned to him. "You're not a Lowlander, cousin. Speak on."

"Thank you. But I am not as wise in these things as the rest of you, so my plan may be flawed. But I think we should find a hiding place where we can watch the . . . food store. Once the beast has returned, unless the wind changes we should then be able to travel west without it picking up the scent. What do you think?"

"I think you are more clan than you realize," said Layne.

They left the stream at a brisk run and headed for the line of hills less than half a mile distant—Layne leading, Gaelen and Gwalchmai just behind, and Lennox at the rear.

Once on the hillside they settled down on their bellies to watch the trail. From their vantage point they could see clearly all the way to the lake above the falls and beyond, while to the northwest a range of rocky hills cut the skyline. Above them the sky was red as blood as the sun sank to the level of the western mountain peaks.

"I hope it comes back before nightfall," said Layne.

Luck was with them for, in the last rays of the dying sun, Gwalchmai spotted the beast ambling on all fours along the trail. It moved carefully, hugging the shadows before disappearing into the bushes where the corpses lay.

The companions wormed their way back down the slope, cutting a wide circle around the beast's lair before picking up its trail and beginning the long process of backtracking it to the west. They ran through the timberline and on toward the rocky hills. The moon had risen before they arrived, but the night sky was clear and Gwalchmai pointed up to the boulder-covered hillside.

"I think Agwaine sought refuge in the caves," he said, and they climbed the slope, seeking a sign.

"We must bear in mind," said Layne, "that the beast will come back tonight after it has fed."

It was Gaelen who found the boy, wedged deep in a narrow cleft in the rocks halfway up the slope. "Agwaine, are you all right?" he called.

"Sweet Gods, I thought it was the beast come back," said Agwaine. Tears rolled down his cheeks and he gritted his teeth to strangle the sobs he knew were close to the surface. Gaelen reached down as Agwaine climbed closer and he pulled him clear as the others gathered around. Agwaine was unhurt, but his face showed the strain he had endured. His eyes seemed sunken and blue rings stained the sockets.

"It came at us from nowhere," he said. "It beheaded Cael. Ectas was next; as he turned to run, the beast opened his back with one sweep of its talons. There was nothing to do but run. I was at the back and I turned and sprinted away. Draig was right behind me. I heard his screaming, but it was cut short and I knew I was the only one left. I could hear it chasing me and I ran as never before. It found me here, but it couldn't reach me."

"We must get away, cousin," put in Layne.

"Yes. No! First I must get something. I threw it away as we ran."

"We can't go back in those woods," hissed Gwalchmai.

"We must. It's not far; I threw it as I saw the slope."

"What can be that important?" asked Layne. "Even now the beast may be coming."

"You set off then and I'll catch up," said Agwaine.

"Damn you, cousin, you know we cannot do that."

"Let's find the cursed thing," said Gaelen. "I don't want to spend all night discussing this."

Agwaine led them back to the woods. Gaelen was furious, but he held himself in check. He knew what Agwaine was seeking. The sword. Agwaine had found the sword.

The woods loomed dark and threatening and the boys drew their knives. Little good would they be, thought Gaelen. He glanced at Gwalchmai. His friend's face was pinched and ashen in the moonlight. Only Lennox seemed unconcerned.

Agwaine held up his arm and then stopped. The Hunt Lord's son disappeared into the bushes, returning quickly with a long closely tied package.

"Let's go," he said, and led them away down toward the falls. The shifting wind made them take wide detours to avoid their scent being carried to the beast, and dawn found them below Attafoss with the river to the left, a section of woods before them. They were tired, but the fear of the beast was upon them and they hesitated before entering the woods.

Daggers held firm, they walked warily, but as they moved under the overhanging branches a voice jolted them. Gwalchmai dropped his dagger in fright, then scooped it up swiftly.

"Good morning, boys."

To their right, in a circular clearing, a woman was sitting on a fallen oak. At her feet was a blanket on which was laid a breakfast of black bread and cold meat.

She was dressed in a manner they had never seen before. Upon her shoulders was a mail scarf of closely linked silver rings. Beneath this she wore a fitted breastplate of silver, embossed with a copper hawk, its wings spread wide, disappearing beneath the mail scarf. About her waist was a leather kilt, studded with copper and split into sections for ease of movement. She wore dark leggings and silver greaves over riding boots. Her arms were bare save for a thick bracelet of silver on her right wrist; on her left was a wrist guard of black leather.

And she was old. Thick silver hair swept back from a face lined with wisdom and sorrow. But her eyes were bright, ice-blue, and her bearing straight and unbending.

Gaelen watched her closely, noting the way she looked at them all.

She must have been beautiful when young, he thought. But there was something in her expression he could not pinpoint; it seemed a mixture of wonder and regret.

"Will you join me for breakfast?" she invited.

"Who are you?" asked Agwaine.

The woman smiled. "I am Sigarni—the Queen," she said.

"We have no queens in the Farlain," said Layne.

"I am the Queen Beyond," she said, with a slow smile.

"You are on Farlain land," Agwaine told her sternly. "No stranger is allowed here. Are you from the Aenir?"

"No, Agwaine. I am a guest of the Lord Taliesen."

"Can you prove this?"

"I don't feel the need to. You boys are here on the Hunt. Taliesen asked if he could borrow my sword for it. If you open the package you will find it—a beautiful weapon of metal which one of you will have seen. The hilt is of ebony, and shaped for a warrior to hold with both hands, while the guard is of iron decorated with gold and silver thread. The scabbard is embossed with a hawk, even as on my breastplate. Now open the package and return what is mine."

"Open it," said Layne. "If it is true, then the sword must be returned to its rightful owner."

"No, it is mine," said Agwaine, flushing. "I won the Hunt and this is my proof."

"You don't need proof," said Gaelen. "We know you won, the sword is only a symbol. Open the package."

Agwaine drew his dagger and sliced the leather thongs binding the oilskins. As the woman had predicted, the sword was indeed a wondrous weapon. Reluctantly Agwaine handed it over. The woman swiftly buckled the scabbard to her waist. Had there been any doubt as to the ownership, it was laid to rest as she placed it at her side. It was like watching a picture completed, thought Gaelen.

The sword in place, she returned to her seat on the tree. She gestured at the food. "Come. Eat your fill," she said. "I was expecting eight of you. Where are the others?"

The boys exchanged glances.

"They are dead," said Gaelen.

"Dead?" asked the Queen, rising to her feet gracefully. "How so?"

Gaelen told of the beast and their flight from the mountains.

"Damn!" she said. "Taliesen came to me in a dream yestereve. He told me you were lost upon the mountain and that I should seek you here. He said nothing of a beast."

"He came to me also," said Gaelen. "And he said nothing of a queen."

She smiled without humor. "So be it, then. The ways of wizards are a mystery to me and I pray they'll stay that way. Now, describe this creature."

All of them started to speak at once, but she waved them to silence and pointed to Agwaine. "You saw it closely. You speak."

Agwaine did as he was bid, recalling vividly the power of the brute and its awesome size, its speed, and its semihuman appearance.

"You are right to consider running," said the woman when he had finished. "I have seen the like of the beast before in my own kingdom. More than once. They are terrible—and hard to slay. Although it kills to eat, once it has fixed on a prey it will pursue it damn near forever. This beast has—in a way—been hunting me for forty years."

"Why you?" whispered Gaelen.

"It was sent a long time ago by a sorcerer named Jakuta Khan. But that is a story for another day, Gaelen."

"What can we do?" asked Layne.

"You can eat breakfast and put some strength in your limbs. Then we will plan for battle."

The companions seated themselves at her feet and dug into the loaves and meat. The bread tasted fresh-baked and the beef was tender and pink. They ate without gusto, except for Lennox who tore great chunks of bread and crammed them into his mouth.

The Queen watched him, eyebrows raised. "You were perhaps expecting a famine?"

"Either that or he's going to cause one," observed Gwalchmai.

Agwaine said nothing. The appearance of this strange woman had angered him, and he was loath to hand over the great sword—their only real defense against the beast—to a woman.

"How will we fight this beast?" asked Layne.

"How indeed?" she replied, her pale eyes showing sorrow.

"We could make spears," suggested Gaelen, "by fastening our daggers to poles."

"Come to that, I could make a bow," said Gwal. "It wouldn't be a great weapon, or very accurate. But it might serve at close range."

"Then do it swiftly," said the Queen, "and we will talk again."

The boys rose and spread out nervously into the woods, searching for saplings or stout straight branches. Gaelen and Agwaine selected an infant elm and began to hack at it with their daggers.

"What do you think of her, Lowlander?" Agwaine asked as the sapling snapped.

"I think she is what she says she is," snapped Gaelen. "And if you call me Lowlander again, you'll answer for it."

Agwaine grinned. "I don't like you, Gaelen, but you are right. Whatever your pedigree, you are now a clansman. But I'll never call you cousin."

"I don't care about that," Gaelen told him. "You are nothing to me."

"So be it."

They stripped the sapling of twigs and leaves and short-

ened it to a manageable five feet. Then Gaelen unwound the
thongs of his right legging and bound his knife to the wood.
He hefted it for balance and hurled it at a nearby tree. The
spear hammered home with a dull thud. Gaelen tugged it
loose and examined the binding; it remained firm.

It seemed a formidable weapon, but he summoned the
image of the beast to mind and then the spear seemed puny
indeed.

"Were you surprised I found the sword?" Agwaine asked
him.

"No, disappointed."

"That was a good trick with the pack."

"I'm glad you enjoyed it."

"I didn't, but it was good anyway." Gaelen nodded. He
waited while Agwaine fashioned his spear, then wandered
away; he didn't enjoy Agwaine's company and he knew the
feeling was reciprocated.

He made his way back to the clearing where the old woman
sat. She was deep in thought and Gaelen watched her for
some time from the edge of the woods. It was easy to believe
she was a queen, for her bearing was proud and confident
and she was clearly used to being obeyed. But there was
more to her than that: a kind of innate nobility, an inner
strength, which shone through.

"Are you going to stand there all day, Gaelen?" she asked
without moving her head.

Gaelen stepped forward. "How did you know I was here?
And how do you know my name?"

"Let's leave it at the first question. I heard you. Come and
join me for a while, and eat something. To work efficiently
the body must be fed."

"Are you no longer a queen?" asked Gaelen, seating himself cross-legged before her.

The woman chuckled and shook her head. "A queen is
always a queen. Only death can change that. But I am, at present, without a realm. Yet I hope to return soon. I promised my
people I would—just as my father did before me."

"Why did you leave your land?" Gaelen asked.

"I was wounded, and likely to die. And so the prophecy was fulfilled and . . . my captain . . . sought the Gate and passed me through. Taliesen healed me."

"How were you wounded?"

"In a battle." She looked away, her eyes distant.

"Did you win?"

"I always win, Gaelen," she said sadly. "My friends die and yet I win. Winning is a hard habit to break; we can come to feed on it to the exclusion of all else."

"Is that a bad thing?"

"Not when you're young," she said, smiling again.

"Why have you stayed up here and not in the village?"

"As I told you, I am a guest of the Lord Taliesen. He felt it would be wiser to remain near Vallon. Now, enough of questions. Look around you. Is this a good place to face the beast?"

"Is there a good place?" countered Gaelen.

"There are places you should avoid, like open ground."

"Is here a good place?"

"Not bad. You have the trees to shield you, and yet there is no dense undergrowth so it cannot creep up on you unnoticed."

"Except at night," said Gaelen.

"Indeed. But it will be over, for good or ill, long before then."

"What about you? You have no spear."

The Queen smiled. "I have my sword; it has been with me these forty years. I thought it had been left behind when I passed through the Gateway, but Taliesen brought it to me. It is a fine weapon."

Lennox came into view carrying an enormous club of oak. "I found this," he said. "It will do for me."

The Queen laughed loud. "There is nothing subtle about you, Lennox, my lad. Nor ever will be. Indeed it is a fine weapon."

Gwalchmai had fashioned a short bow and had found six pieces of wood straight enough to slice into shafts for it. "It's a clumsy thing," he said, "and the range will be no greater than twenty paces." Squatting down, he began to shape pieces of bark into flights for his arrows.

By noon they had completed their preparations and they sat waiting for the woman's instructions. But she said nothing, merely sitting among them slowly chewing the last of the bread. Gaelen caught the Queen's eye and she smiled, raising an eyebrow questioningly. He turned to Gwalchmai. "You are the lightest of us, Gwal. Why don't you climb that tree and keep a watch for the creature?"

Gwalchmai nodded. "Wouldn't the oak be better? It's more sturdy."

"The beast might be able to climb," said Gaelen. "The elm would never support its weight."

"How will you tackle it when it comes?" asked the Queen, staring at Gaelen.

"We must confuse it," he said, his mind racing. He had no idea how five boys and an old woman should tackle a creature of such speed and strength, but the Queen asked him a question and seemed to expect a rational reply. "If we spread out, the beast must attack us one at a time. Each time it does, one or all the others must stab at it, turning the creature all ways. Gwal, you will stay in the tree," he called to the climbing boy. "Shoot when you have a clear target."

"That is all good thinking," said the Queen, "but, even so, to confuse the beast you must surprise it. Once it is sighted, and we know which direction it is coming from, you must hide yourselves, forming a rough circle. But one of you must act as bait and stay in plain sight. With luck the beast will charge; I've seen that before. Ideally we must make it charge onto a spear. That way its weight will carry the point home far more powerfully than any thrust of yours."

"I will be the bait," said Gaelen, surprising himself.

"Why you?" asked Agwaine. "I am the fastest here, and I've outrun it before."

"Speed is not usually required of bait," Gaelen told him.

Agwaine chuckled and shook his head. "All right. I will

stay on your right, Lennox and Layne can take the left. And may God give us luck."

"Do not ask for luck, ask for courage," said the Queen.

"How will you fight?" Agwaine asked her.

"With my sword," she replied softly. "As I always have, against man and beast. Don't worry about me, boy."

"Why should you fight for us at all?"

"That is a mystery you will one day understand, but it is not for me to explain to you."

"It's coming!" called Gwalchmai from high in the elm. They could all see where he was pointing; the beast was moving from the northwest.

"Take up positions," said the woman. Lennox and Layne ran to the left, crouching behind a large bush. Agwaine moved to the right, spear held before him, and squatted behind the bole of an oak. High in the elm Gwalchmai strung his bow, hooked his leg around a thick branch, and wedged himself in position, notching an arrow to the string.

The Queen drew her sword and held the blade to her lips. Then she smiled at Gaelen. "This should be something to tell your five children," she said.

Gaelen did not reply. Some fifty paces ahead the beast had come into view. This close it seemed even more colossal. Seeing Gaelen, the creature reared up to its full height and bellowed a bloodcurdling howl. Then it dropped to all fours and charged.

The boy glanced to his left, seeking assurance from the warrior. But the Queen had gone.

The ground beneath Gaelen's feet shook as the beast thundered toward him. He gripped his spear and waited, all fear vanishing like mist in a breeze. In that moment a strange euphoria gripped him. All his life he had been alone, afraid, and unhappy. Now he was part of something; he belonged. Even if his life had to end in the next moments nothing could take away the joy he had known in these last few precious months.

He was no longer alone.

He was Clan.

The beast slowed, rearing to its full height with arms spread, fangs gleaming in the morning sun. Gaelen gripped his spear firmly, muscles tensed for the thrust. The beast came on, drawing abreast of the hidden Agwaine. Fear swept over the Hunt Lord's son, shrouding him in a tidal wave of panic. He wanted to run. To hide.

But he too was Clan.

Rising up from his hiding place as the creature's shadow fell across him, Agwaine rammed the spear into the beast's side. A blood-chilling scream filled the clearing. Agwaine vainly tried to pull his weapon clear. A taloned arm swept backhanded, punching the boy from his feet; he hit the ground on his face and rolled to his back. The beast stepped over him, jaws slavering and talons reaching out. Agwaine screamed.

At that moment Layne raced from the left, hurling his spear with all his strength. The weapon flashed through the air to bury itself in the beast's broad back. It came upright, swinging to meet the new attack. Behind it Agwaine tried to stand, but his legs gave way and he pitched to the earth, nausea filling his throat. Layne, weaponless, stood transfixed as the beast bore down on him. Lennox grabbed him by the shirt and hauled him aside, then stood waiting for the creature, his club raised, his eyes defiant.

Gaelen ran in to attack, screaming at the top of his voice. The beast's black eyes flickered toward the charging boy and in that moment Lennox struck, stepping forward to thunder the oak club against the creature's head. It staggered, but blocked Lennox's next blow with a raised arm. Gaelen's spear sliced into the flesh above its hip, then broke, pitching the boy to the ground at the monster's feet.

Now only Lennox remained in the fight. The young giant hit once more, but this time the beast was ready—it parried the blow with its paw and a taloned hand gripped the youth's upper arm, smashing the bone and ripping the flesh from the shoulder. Lennox staggered back but did not fall. Transferring the club to his right hand, he waited for the beast's next attack.

An arrow cut deep into the monster's thigh, causing it to bellow in pain and rage. A second glanced from its thick skull. Lennox crashed his club into the creature's mouth, but a backhanded blow hurled him from his feet.

Injured though the beast was, none of the wounds were mortal, and the battle had turned. From his precarious position in the tree, Gwalchmai fired a third shaft that buried itself in the ground by the beast's right foot. Leaning out for the fourth shot, the young archer toppled from the branch, landing on his back.

Running behind the beast, Gaelen grabbed Layne's spear and plucked it from the creature's back. As it turned he stabbed at its face, the point slashing a jagged line up and into the sensitive nostrils. To Gaelen's right Layne gathered up Lennox's club and tried to help, but the monster turned on him, slashing the boy's chest. The talons snaked out again. Gaelen leaped backward, tumbling to the earth.

The beast's jaws opened and another terrifying howl pierced the air.

The boys were finished.

"Ho, Hell spawn!" shouted the Queen. The beast swung ponderously, glittering black eyes picking out the tall, armored figure at the center of the clearing. "Now face me!"

She stood with feet apart, her silver sword before her.

The beast reared to its full height—eight feet of black, merciless destruction. Before its power the woman seemed to Gaelen a frail, tiny figure. The monster moved forward slowly—then charged, dropping to all fours. The Queen sidestepped, her silver sword swung arcing down to rebound from the creature's skull, slicing its scalp and sending a blood spray into the air. The beast twisted, launching itself in a mighty spring, but the woman leaped to the right, the sword cutting across the creature's chest to open a shallow wound.

Agwaine crawled to where Gaelen crouched.

"She cannot win," whispered the Hunt Lord's son.

"Run, boys!" yelled the Queen.

But they did not. Gaelen scooped up the broken spear, while Layne helped Lennox to his feet and gathered once more the club of oak.

The old woman was breathing hard now. Taliesen had stitched her wounds, but her strength was not what it was. Under the breastplate stitches had parted and blood oozed down her belly. Sweat bathed her face and her mouth was set in a grim line.

Once more the beast reared above her. Once more she hammered the sword in its face. The creature shook its head, blood spraying into the air.

The woman knew she could last but a little longer, while the creature was only maddened by the cuts it had received. A plan formed in her mind and weighed down her heart. It had been her hope to return to her realm and lead it out of the darkness of war. Now there would be no going home. No future. No golden days of peace watching the nation prosper.

In that final moment, as the creature prepared to attack once more, it was as if time slowed. Sigarni could smell the forest, the musky brown earth, the freshness of the breeze. Images leaped to her mind and she saw again the handsome forester, Fell, the first great love of her life. He had died in the battle against the Baron, cut down by the last arrow loosed in that fateful battle. Faces from the past glittered in her memory: Ballistar the dwarf, who had sought a new life in a new world; Asmidir, the black battle captain; Obrin, the renegade Outlander; and Redhawk—above them all, Redhawk.

I will never see you again, she thought, though you promised to be with me at the end. You gave me your word, my love. You promised!

Talons lashed toward her. Ducking beneath them she leaped back, lifting her sword toward the beast. It sprang forward, but this time the Queen did not sidestep. With a savage battle cry she launched herself into its path, driving the blade deep into the creature's huge chest. The silver steel slid between its ribs, plunging through its lungs and cleaving the heart.

As it screamed in its death throes its great arms encircled the woman. The breastplate buckled under the immense pressure and the Queen's ribs snapped, jagged bone ripping into her. Then the beast released her and toppled to the earth. The woman staggered back, then fell. She struggled to rise, but agony lanced her.

The boys ran to her side, Gaelen kneeling by her and raising her head to lay it on his lap. Gently he stroked the silver hair from her eyes.

"Give the word to Taliesen," whispered the Queen, blood staining her lips. She coughed weakly and swallowed. "We did it, lads," she said. "You did well, as I knew you would."

Agwaine knelt on her right, taking her hand.

"You saved us; you killed it," said Gaelen.

"Listen to me, for I am dying now, but remember my words. I shall return to the Farlain. You will be older then. Men. Warriors. You will have suffered much and I will aid you again."

Agwaine glanced at Gaelen. "What does she mean?"

Gaelen shrugged. The sound of running feet echoed in the clearing as Caswallon, Cambil, and the clansmen raced into view. Caswallon knelt by Gaelen. "Are you all right?"

"Yes. She saved us. She slew the beast."

"Who is she?" asked Caswallon.

The Queen's eyes opened. "Ah, it is you," she whispered, smiling. "Now the circle is complete, for you told me you would be with me at my death. How well you look. How young. How handsome! No . . . silver in your beard."

Caswallon gazed down into the bright blue eyes and saw that the woman was fading fast. Her hand lifted toward him and he took it, holding it firm.

"Did I do well, Caswallon? Tell me truly?"

"You did well," answered Caswallon. "You saved the boys."

"But my kingdom? Was I . . . truly the Queen you desired me to be?"

"Yes," answered Caswallon, nonplussed.

She smiled once more, then a tear formed and slowly fell to her pale cheek. "Poor Caswallon," she whispered. "You do not know whose hand you hold, but you will." Tears filled her eyes.

Lifting her hand to his lips, he kissed the fingers. "I know you are brave beyond words," he said, "and I do not doubt you were a queen beyond compare."

Her eyes closed and a long broken sigh hissed from her throat. Caswallon sat for a moment, still holding on to the hand. Then he laid it gently across the Queen's chest.

Cambil knelt beside him. "Who was she?" asked the Hunt Lord.

Caswallon stared down at the dead warrior woman. "Whoever she was, I mourn her passing."

"She was the Queen Beyond," said Gaelen, "and she always won."

Then he began to weep.

Chapter Five

Lennox sat with his back against a tree as they stitched his shoulder and strapped his broken arm. His face was grey with pain, but he uttered no groan, merely squeezed his eyes shut and gritted his teeth.

His father, Leofas, said nothing, but pride shone in his eyes. Layne lay beside his brother, enduring the stitches in his chest in the same stoic fashion. Away from the others sat Badraig, tears flowing and head in hands. His son Draig had been killed the day before.

Even through his own immense relief Cambil felt the other man's sorrow, and leaving his son Agwaine, he walked over to sit beside the hunter. He put his hand on Badraig's shoulder.

"I am sorry, my friend. Truly."

The man nodded, but neither lifted his head nor answered.

Caswallon stood with the other clansmen looking down on the beast. Even in death it was a terrifying sight, its great jaws drawn back in a last snarl, its fangs, as long as a man's fingers, bared and bloody.

"I have never seen the like," muttered Caswallon, "and I pray I never shall again."

They buried the Queen deep, marking the grave with flat white stones. Cambil promised to have a headstone carved. Then the men split into two groups, Badraig leading the five hunters back to the falls and burying what was left of the bodies; Cambil, Leofas, and Caswallon staying with the boys. It was decided they would rest in the clearing until morning and then attempt the long walk back to the village.

The main worry was Lennox, who had lost a great deal of blood. Gwalchmai, though stunned by his fall, was back on his feet and unhurt. He alone of the boys had missed the Queen's last battle.

That night around the campfire the boys were unnaturally silent. Lennox, in great pain, sought refuge in sleep, but the others sat together staring at the flames. Agwaine had lost friends and suffered the terror of being hunted; Layne had seen the leadership of the group taken quietly from him by the former Lowlander; and Gaelen had discovered in his heart a strength he had not known existed. Only Gwalchmai was untouched by the drama, but he remained silent, for he sensed his friends' needs.

Caswallon prepared a strong broth for them all. His own thoughts were many. Through his sorrow at the death of the three lads he felt a surging pride at the way the others had tackled the beast, and a sense of joy at the manner in which Gaelen had conducted himself. Thinking back, he did not know if he could have duplicated the feat at Gaelen's age. But overriding these thoughts he could not help but remember the words of the Queen. At first he had thought the woman delirious, but her eyes had been clear.

Caswallon had always enjoyed an ability to read character truly, and he knew instinctively that the dying warrior was a great woman, a woman of courage, nobility of spirit, and great inner strength. That she was a queen was no surprise.

But queen of where? And how did she know him?

Beyond the Gate. What was beyond the Gate?

Only Oracle knew. And Taliesen.

The night wore on and Caswallon strolled away from the fire, seeking solitude and a place to think. But Cambil joined him and they sat together on a high hillside under the clear sky.

"Badraig is a broken man," said Cambil softly, gathering his green cloak about his broad shoulders.

"Yes. What can one say?"

"I feel a burden of guilt for it," said Cambil. "Last night I prayed that Agwaine would survive. I would willingly have exchanged any life for his. When I saw he was alive I didn't care anything for Badraig's loss; it only struck me later."

"That is understandable."

"Don't patronize me, Caswallon!" snapped the Hunt Lord, eyes blazing.

"I was not trying to. How do you think I felt when I saw Gaelen?"

"It's not the same thing, is it? You may be fond of the boy, but he's not of your blood. You didn't watch him take his first faltering steps, hear his first words, take him on his first hunt."

"No, that is true," admitted Caswallon, realizing the futility of the argument.

"Still Gaelen did well," said Cambil. "He proved his right to be a clansman."

"Yes."

"But he can never be Hunt Lord."

Caswallon turned then, catching Cambil's eye, but the Hunt Lord looked away, staring into the woods. At once Caswallon understood the man's meaning. Gaelen had planned the battle with the beast, had taken over leadership from Layne. Agwaine had done his bidding. On such talents were future Hunt Lords built. Cambil's dream was that Agwaine would succeed him, but now he was unsure.

"Be content that your son is alive," said Caswallon. "The future will look to itself."

"But you agree it would not be fitting for a Lowlander to lead the clan?"

"The Council can decide on the day you step down."

"So, it is your plan to supplant Agwaine with this boy?" accused Cambil, face reddening.

Caswallon sighed. "Nothing could have been further from my mind."

"It was Agwaine who found the sword."

"Indeed it was."

A long silence enveloped them, until at last Cambil stood to leave. We will never be friends, Caswallon," he said sadly.

"You see ogres where there are none," Caswallon told him. "I have no ambition, cousin—not for myself, nor my sons. They will be what they desire to be, and what they are able to be. I want to see them happy, married well, and content. All else is dross, for we all die and there is no evidence we take anything with us when we go."

Cambil nodded. "I wish I could believe you, but I see a different Caswallon. I see a man who could have been Hunt Lord. Children imitate your walk, tales are told about you around the campfires. And yet what have you done? You steal other men's cattle. What is it about you, Caswallon?"

"I have no idea. I never listen to the stories."

Caswallon watched as Cambil walked slowly down the slope toward the fire. Gathering his own cloak about him, he stared at the stars, mind wandering.

After about an hour he felt a cold wind blow against his neck, but the leaves about him did not stir. He turned. Behind him stood Taliesen, wrapped in his cloak of shimmering feathers and holding a staff of oak entwined with mistletoe.

"Three boys are dead," he told the druid, gesturing to a place beside him on the flat boulder. The druid sat, leaning forward on his staff.

"I know. The Queen also."

"Who was she?"

"Sigarni the Hawk Queen. Did she say anything before she died?"

"She said she would come again, so the boys tell me. And she thought I was someone she once knew."

"The old man you know as Oracle brought this upon us," said Taliesen. "I only hope I can make it right."

"What are you talking about?"

"Seek Oracle and tell him you have spoken to me. Tell him that it pleases me for you to know his story. But when you have heard it, promise me you will repeat it to no one. Do you agree to this?"

"I do."

Maeg ran from the house, Kareen beside her, as the men appeared on the far hill. Other women streamed from crofts and homes. Men working in the fields dropped their tools and joined the rush.

Within minutes the hunters and the boys were surrounded. Cambil answered all questions and Caswallon led Gaelen through the throng to where Maeg waited. She moved forward, cupping Gaelen's face with her hands.

"Are you well, my bonny lad?"

"Yes."

She read the sorrow in his eyes and linked her arm in his for the long walk to the house. He had suffered so much in his life and now it was obvious that he had endured more pain. Her heart ached for him.

At the house the crofter Durk was waiting for Kareen. He asked after Gaelen and then left, taking the girl with him to walk up the hillside.

Gaelen was exhausted and stumbled to his bed while Caswallon and Maeg sat together by the hearth. The clansman told her of the ordeal in the mountains and how well the boys had handled themselves.

"He is a lad to be proud of, Caswallon," she said.

He grinned sheepishly. "I know. I was close to tears as he told me the tale."

"He'll be a fine man."

"Sooner than you think," said Caswallon.

"And how did you fare with Cambil for so many days?"

He shrugged. "The man fears me, Maeg. He thinks I plan to supplant Agwaine with Gaelen. Is it not madness? His doubts must sit on his shoulders like a mountain."

"He is a sad, lonely man. I'm glad you harbor no ill will."

"How can I hate him? I grew up with him. He was always the same; he believed his father liked me more than him. Always he strived to beat me, and he never did. Had I been wiser, I would have lost at least once."

"It's not in you to lose," she said. "You are a clansman. And a proud man—too proud, I think."

"Can a man be too proud? It harms no one. I have never insulted another man, nor abused my strength by destroying a weaker opponent. I do not parade my talents, but I am aware of them."

"Nonsense. You're as vain as a flamingo. I've seen you trimming your beard by the silver mirror and using my brush to comb it flat."

"Spying on me now, is it?"

"Yes, it is. And why shouldn't I? Am I not your wife?"

He pulled her to his lap and kissed her. "Indeed, you are the best thing I ever stole from the Pallides. Except for that bull of your father's."

"When I think that Intosh proposed to me," said Maeg, tugging his beard, "and instead I ended up with you, I wonder if the Gods hold a grudge against my family."

"Intosh? He was my rival? You'd have hated it, Maeg. The man has ticks in his bed. I was scratching for days after I stole his sword."

"You dog! So that's where they came from."

"Now, now, Maeg my love," he said as she pulled from his grasp, eyes blazing. "Let's not have a row. The boy needs his sleep, he's been through much."

"You've not heard the last of this, my fine Farlain," she said softly.

"And now, while you're quiet for a moment," he said, pulling her to him once more, "perhaps you'll welcome me home. It's been a tiring journey."

"Then you'll be wanting to sleep?"

"Indeed I do. Will you join me?"

"You can bathe first. I'll have no more of your ticks."

"Is there any heated water?"

"There is not."

"You'd not expect me to bathe in the yard in the cold?"

"Of course not. You can sleep down here and bathe tomorrow in the warm water."

"Sleep here?" Their eyes met and there was no give in her.

"It's the yard then," he said.

Later, as Caswallon slept, Maeg heard Gaelen moaning in his sleep in the next room. She rose quickly, wrapping a blanket around her naked body, and made her way to his bedside. It was a familiar nightmare and she knew he was once more running from the Aenir, his legs leaden, his wounds bleeding.

She sat beside him stroking his hair. "It's all right, Gaelen," she whispered. "You're here with Maeg. You're safe. Safe."

He groaned and rolled to his back. "Maeg?"

"I'm here."

"Dreaming," he whispered and his eyes closed once more.

She remembered the first time Caswallon had brought him home. He had been nervous then, and his eyes had flickered from wall to wall as if the house were a prison. And he had avoided her. When she showed him his room, his delight had stunned her.

"This is my room?"

"Yes."

"My very own? To share with no one?"

"Your very own."

"It's wonderful. Thank you."

"You are very welcome."

"You cannot bewitch me," he said suddenly.

"I see," she said, smiling. "Caswallon has told you about my spells?"

"Yes."

"But he didn't tell you my powers faded soon after we were wed?"

"No."

"It happens to women once they've snared their men."

"I see," he said.

"So let us be friends. How does that sit with you?"

"I'd like to be friends," he said, grinning. "I've never had friends."

"It'll be nice to have someone to talk to," she told him.

"I don't talk very much," he said. "I never had anyone to practice with. I'm not terribly clever at it."

"It's not clever that counts, Gaelen. Clever comes from the mind, truth from the heart. Now I will begin our friendship by telling you the truth. When Caswallon first rescued you I was worried, for we have a son. But I have thought long about it, and now I am glad. For I like you, and I know you will be happy with us. For our part, we will teach you to be a clansman."

"I may not be very good at that either," admitted the boy.

"It's not a matter of being good at it. Merely *being* is enough. It will not be easy for you, for Caswallon is not a popular man, and some will make it hard—perhaps even unpleasant—for you."

"Why is he not popular?"

"That is a complex question. He is independent, and it has made him all that he has. He holds to the old ways of raiding and stealing from other clans. But there are other reasons that I think it best you find out for yourself."

"He is a thief?"

She chuckled. "Yes. Just like you."

"Well, I like him. I don't care about the others."

She laid a hand on his shoulder. "Here is a first lesson for you, Gaelen: Care. That is what the clan is. We care. For one another. Even if we dispute matters, we still care. I tell you this. If Caswallon's house burned to the ground, even those who disliked him would gather around and help rebuild. If Caswallon died, I would be cared for should I need it. If Caswallon and I both died, little Donal would be taken in by another family—perhaps one that disliked us both—and raised with love."

He had been hard to convince, especially after the early trouble with Agwaine. But at least he had found friends.

Maeg sat by the bedside for a while, then moved to the window.

The moon was high, the mountains silver, the valley at peace. Behind her, Gaelen stirred and opened his eyes, seeing her silhouetted against the sky. "Maeg," he whispered.

She returned to the bedside. "Yes?"

"Thank you."

"For what?"

"For caring."

Leaning down, she kissed his brow. "Sleep well, young warrior," she said.

Caswallon strolled up toward the cave, aware that the old man was watching him. Oracle's sunken blue eyes looked hard at the clansman. "You look tired, man," said Oracle as Caswallon sat beside him in the cave mouth.

"Aye, I am tired. And hurt by the suffering of those poor boys."

"A bad day," agreed the older man. For a time they sat in silence, then Oracle spoke again. "It is always good to see you, my boy. But I sense there is something on your mind, so spit it out."

Caswallon chuckled. "As always, you miss little. Taliesen told me to speak to you; he said it would please him for you to tell the story of what happened beyond the Gate."

"Aye, please him and shame me." Oracle stood and wandered back into the cave, sitting beside the glowing fire. Caswallon joined him. Oracle filled two clay cups with watered wine, passing one to the younger man. "I have told no one else this tale in twenty-five years. I trust you not to repeat it while I live."

"You have my word on it," Caswallon assured him.

"I wanted to be High King," said Oracle. "I felt it was my right after the battles I had led—and won. But the people rejected me. This much you know already. I took my followers and we overpowered the druids guarding the Vallon Gate. We passed through. At first it seemed that nothing had changed;

the mountains remained the same, High Druin still stood
sentinel over the lands of the clans. But it was different, Caswallon. In a land beset by war, a woman had become High
Queen. Her name was Sigarni. For reasons which I cannot
explain now—but which you will understand later—I shall
say no more about her, save that my men and I helped her in
her battles with the Outland army. We stayed for two years. I
still wanted to be a king, to found my own dynasty. I returned, with the survivors of my men, to the Vallon Gate, and
passed through once more. It was the biggest mistake of my
life."

The old man drained his wine and refilled the cup, this
time adding no water. Looking at Caswallon, he smiled grimly.
"Cursed is the man who achieves his dreams. In this new
land—after ten blood-drenched years—I did become king. I
led my armies to victory after victory. Great victories, Caswallon. Great victories . . ." He fell silent.

"What happened?" asked the clansman.

"Failure and flight," responded Oracle, with a sad smile. "I
was betrayed—but then I deserved to be. Just because a man
desires to be a king, it does not necessarily follow that he
will make a good one." He sighed. "But this is not what Taliesen wanted me to tell you. While I was fighting for my
kingdom I made an alliance with a butchering killer named
Agrist. I told him the secrets of the Gateways. After he had
betrayed me, and plundered his way across my kingdom, he
led his army through another Gate." Oracle licked his lips.
"They arrived here forty years ago; they are the Aenir,
Caswallon. I brought the Aenir to destroy us all."

"They haven't destroyed us yet," Caswallon pointed out.

"They are demons, Caswallon, unsurpassed in violence
and terror. I have seen them fight. I told Gaelen the clans
were strong, like wolves. It's true. But the Aenir will outnumber us by twenty to one. They live to conquer and kill."
Oracle looked up. "Did Sigarni speak to you before she
died? Did she mention me?"

"No, but she knew me, Oracle. Can you tell me how?"

Oracle shook his head. "I could—but I won't. Trust me, Caswallon. All will be revealed to you. I can say no more."

During the months that followed the horror in the mountains the five survivors found their lives had changed substantially. They were now young men, accepted as clansmen, but more than this they were "Five Beast Slayers." A Farlain bard named Mesric had immortalized them in song and their deeds were the envy of the young boys of all clans.

The mystery of the Queen was much discussed, but upon that theme the druids remained silent. Taliesen had questioned the boys at length on their conversation with the woman, but he gave them no further hint as to her history. All five spent a great deal of time thinking back over the Hunt, and the changes it forced on them.

Layne, the deepest thinker, saw Gaelen with new eyes, seeking his company often and recognizing in the scarred youngster the signs of a natural leader.

Lennox drove himself hard once his broken arm had mended. He hauled logs, lifted rocks, spent all his spare time building up his strength. The huge frame gathered power and added muscle and still he drove himself on. His strength had been something he could rely on in a world where his wits were not as keen as his brother's. The beast had been stronger and Lennox was determined no enemy would best him again.

Gwalchmai no longer feared being unpopular, born as this had been from a sense of inferiority. He had always known Gaelen was a leader, and been happy to follow. But he watched Lennox pushing himself to greater limits and recognized in the young giant the kind of fear he once had himself.

For Gaelen the world had changed. He realized now that his life of loneliness in the city had been, by a freak of chance, the perfect apprenticeship. He had learned early that a man had to rely on himself. More than this—that such a man was stronger than his companions. And yet, having tasted the chilling emptiness of a life alone, he could value the clan as no other clansman ever would.

There was a natural arrogance now about the tall young man with the white blaze in his red hair. He ran like the wind, reveling in his speed. And though his bowmanship was merely average, he threw a spear with more accuracy than many tried warriors. He boxed well, emotions in check as Caswallon had taught him, and his sword work was dazzling. Yet the arrogance he showed in his skills was missing in his life, and this made him popular without effort on his part.

The wise men among the Farlain marked him well, watching his progress with increasing interest. All of which hurt Agwaine, who saw in Gaelen a rival for the ultimate prize.

The Hunt had changed Agwaine more than any of them. He had been schooled to believe he was more than special, a talented natural leader to follow his father. And nothing that had transpired in the mountains had changed that. All that had changed was that Agwaine feared Gaelen was the better man. Before the encounter with the beast he would have hated Gaelen for bringing home such a truth. Now he could not.

They took part in their first Games together in the five-mile run, Gaelen beating Agwaine by forty paces, the boys arriving home in ninth and tenth place.

Cambil had been furious. "He is faster, Father," said Agwaine, toweling the sweat from his face. "There is nothing more to it."

"You must work harder: drive yourself. You must not let him beat you ever again."

Agwaine was stricken, and for the first time he saw his father in a fresh light. "I will work harder," he said.

Layne and Gwalchmai delighted the younger clansmen by competing to the finals of their events, Layne in the spear tourney and Gwalchmai in the bow. Layne took third prize, beating the Loda champion into fourth place; Gwalchmai finished last of the eight finalists, but was satisfied, for by next year he would have added height and strength to his frame and believed he could win. For Lennox the Games were a sad affair, for his injured arm robbed him of the chance to lift the Whorl Stone.

Summer drifted into a mild autumn and on into a vicious winter.

Caswallon and Gaelen spent their time forking hay to the cattle and journeying high into the mountains to rescue sheep trapped in snowdrifts. It was a desperately hard time for all the clans, yet Gaelen absorbed the knowledge Caswallon imparted readily.

In winter, Caswallon told him as they sheltered from a fierce blizzard high on the eastern range, it is vital not to sweat. For sweat turns to ice beneath the clothing and a man can freeze to death in minutes. All movement should be slow and sure, and all camps prepared hours before dusk.

That afternoon, trapped by a fierce snow squall, Caswallon had led them to a wooded ridge. Here he had pulled four saplings together, tying them with thongs. Then he carefully threaded branches between them and built a fire in the center. As the snow continued it piled against the branches, creating a round shelter with thick white walls. The fire within heated the walls to solid ice and the two men were snug and safe.

"Make the storm work for you," said Caswallon, stripping off his sheepskin jerkin and allowing the fire's heat to reach his skin. "Take off your outer clothes, Gaelen."

"I'll freeze," answered the young man, rubbing his cold hands together.

"Clothes keep heat in, but similarly they can keep heat out. Remove your coat."

Gaelen did as he was told, grinning sheepishly as the heat in the shelter struck him.

Later Gaelen found himself staring into the glowing coals, his mind wandering. He rubbed his eyes and scratched at the jagged scar above.

"What are you thinking?" Caswallon asked.

"I was thinking of the Queen."

"What about her?"

"About her coming again."

"She is dead, Gaelen. Dead and buried."

"I know. But she seemed so sure. I wonder who she was."

"A queen—and I would guess a great one," said Caswallon. Silence settled around them, until Caswallon suddenly grinned. "What's this I hear about you and Deva?"

At the mention of Agwaine's sister Gaelen began to blush.

"Aha!" said Caswallon, sitting up. "There is more to this business than rumor."

"There's nothing," protested Gaelen. "Really, there's nothing. I've hardly even spoken to her. And when I do, my tongue gets caught in my teeth and I seem to have three feet."

"That bad?"

"It's not anything. I just . . ." Glancing up, he saw Caswallon raise his right eyebrow, his face mock-serious. Gaelen began to giggle. "You swine. You're mocking me."

"Not at all. I've never been one to mock young love," said Caswallon.

"I'm not in love. And if I was, there would be no point. Cambil cannot stand me."

"Do not let that worry you, Gaelen. Cambil is afraid of many things, but if young Deva wants you he will agree. But then it's a little early to think of marriage. Another year."

"I know that. And I was not talking about marriage . . . or love. A man can like a girl, you know."

"Very true," admitted Caswallon. "I liked Maeg the first moment I saw her."

"It is not the same thing at all."

"You'll make a fine couple."

"Will you stop this? I'm going to sleep," said Gaelen, curling his blanket around him. After a few moments he opened his eyes to see Caswallon was still sitting by the fire looking down at him.

Gaelen grinned. "She's very tall—for a girl, I mean."

"She certainly is," agreed Caswallon, "and pretty."

"Yes. Do you really think we'd make a good couple?"

"No doubt of it."

"Why is it that whenever I talk to her the words all tumble out as if they've been poured from a sack?"

"Witchcraft," said Caswallon.

"A pox on you," snorted Gaelen. "I'm definitely going to sleep."

The winter passed like a painful memory. Losses had been high among the sheep and calves, but spring was warm and dry, promising good harvests in summer.

Cambil accepted an invitation from Asbidag, leader of the Northern Aenir, to visit Ateris, now called Aesgard. Cambil took with him twenty clansmen. He was treated royally and responded by inviting Asbidag and twenty of his followers to the Summer Games.

Caswallon's fury stunned Maeg, who had never seem him lose control. His face had turned chalk-white, his hands sweeping across the pine tabletop and smashing pottery to shards.

"The fool!" he hissed. "How could he do such a thing?"

"You think the danger is that great from twenty men?" Maeg asked softly, ignoring the ruined jugs and goblets.

Caswallon said nothing. Taking his cloak and staff, he left the house and set off in a loping run toward the hills and the cave of Oracle.

Taliesen sealed shut the door to his private chambers and opened a small, hidden recess in the wall. Reaching in he touched a sensor and light bathed the small room, radiating from panels set in the four walls. With another touch he activated the viewer. The oak veneer of his crudely carved desktop slid back and revealed a dark screen, which rose into a vertical position. Taliesen moved to the rear wall. Scores of paper sheets were pinned to the paneling here, each covered in lines and scrawled with symbols. To the unskilled eye the drawings would appear to be of winter trees, with hundreds of tiny, leafless branches. Taliesen stared at them, remembering the perilous journeys through the Gateways that each represented. Here and there, on every sheet a branch would end with a single stroke drawn through it. By each was a hastily drawn star. Taliesen counted them. Forty-eight. On the desktop, beside the dark screen, was a newly drawn tree that showed no stars. Taliesen pinned it to the wall.

This was the tree of the Hawk Eternal.

The tree where Sigarni regained her sword that was stolen. Where she did not die in some last despairing battle, but survived to reach the Farlain and save the children. Taliesen gazed at the drawing. "Simple to see," he said, "but where are you? Which of the Time Lines will bring me to you?"

Seating himself before the screen, he opened the right-hand desk drawer and removed a round earring with a spring clip. It was in the shape of a star. Clipping it to his ear, he closed his eyes. The screen flickered, then brightened. Taliesen took a deep, calming breath and opened his eyes.

"Be careful," he warned himself. "Do not seek to see too much. Concentrate on the minutiae." The screen darkened, and with a soft curse Taliesen reached up and touched the star upon his ear, pressing it firmly. The screen leaped to life, and the old druid stared hard at the scene that appeared there.

For more than an hour he watched, occasionally scribbling short notes to aid his memory. Then he removed the earring, touched a button below the desktop, and stood. The screen folded down; the oak veneer covered it once more.

Taliesen studied the notes, adding a line here and there. Rising, he moved to the wall, pinning the notes alongside the tree of the Hawk Eternal. He shook his head. "Somewhere there is a rogue element," he said, "and it has not yet shown its face. What, where, and when?" A thought struck him and his mouth tightened. "Or perhaps I should be asking: Who?" he mused.

"Pah! Do not be so foolish," he told himself. "There is no one. You are the Master of the Gates, and the rogue element is a figment of your paranoia. If there was someone you would have found him by now. Or seen greater evidence to point toward him. You are an old fool! The secret lies with the Hawk Eternal—and you will teach him."

His eyes were drawn to the stars scrawled on the sheets. Focusing on each, he dragged the painful memories from the depths of his mind. The most galling of them was the last. Having defeated Earl Jastey, Sigarni contracted a fever and died in the night. By Heaven, that was hard to take. Taliesen had all but given up then.

For several months he had made no attempt to scan the Lines, in order to find a new Sigarni. The quest felt hopeless. Yet as he gazed down on the valleys of the Farlain, and at the butchery taking place in the Lowlands, he knew he had to struggle on.

Intending to make more notes now, Taliesen returned to his desk. Weariness swamped him as he sat, and he laid his head on his arms. Sleep took him instantly.

What had once been the gleaming marble hall of the Ateris Council was now strewn with straw and misty with the smoke from the blazing log fire set in a crudely built hearth by the western wall. A massive pine table was set across the hall, around which sat the new Aenir nobility. At their feet, rolling in the straw and scratching at fleas, were the war hounds of Asbidag—seven sleek, black, fierce-eyed dogs, trained in the hunt.

Asbidag himself sat at the center of the table facing the double doors of bronze-studded oak. Around him were his seven sons, their wives, and a score of war councillors. Beside the huge Aenir lord sat a woman dressed in black. Slim she was, and the gown of velvet seemed more of a pelt than a garment. Her jet-black hair hung to her pale shoulders and gleamed as if oiled; her eyes were slanted and, against the somber garb, seemed to glitter like blue jewels, bright and gold; her mouth was full-lipped and wide, and only the mocking half smile robbed it of beauty.

Asbidag casually laid his hand on her thigh, watching her closely, a gap-toothed grin showing above his bloodred beard.

"Are you anxious for the entertainment to begin?" he asked her.

"When it pleases you, my lord," she said, her voice husky and deep.

Asbidag heaved himself to his feet. "Bring in the prisoner," he bellowed.

"By Vatan, I've waited a long time for this," whispered Ongist, swinging around on his stool to face the door.

Drada said nothing. He had never cared much for torture, though it would have been sheer stupidity to mention it. The way of the Grey God was the way of the Aenir, and no one questioned either.

Drada's eyes flickered to his other brothers as they waited for the prisoner to be dragged forth. Tostig, large and cruel, a man well known for his bestial appetites. Ongist, the second youngest, a clever lad with the morals of a timber wolf. Aeslang, Barsa, and Jostig, sons of Asbidag's long-time mistress Swangild. They remained in favor despite Asbidag's murder of their mother—in fact they seemed unmoved by the tragedy—but then Swangild had been a ruthless woman as devoid of emotion as the black-garbed bitch who had replaced her. Lastly there was Orsa the Baresark, dim-witted and dull, but in battle a terrible opponent who screeched with laughter as he slew.

The sons of Asbidag . . .

The great doors swung open, admitting two warriors who half dragged, half carried a shambling ruin of a man. His clothes were in rags, his body covered in weeping sores and fresh switch scars that oozed blood. His hands were misshapen and swollen, the fingers broken and useless, but even so, his wrists were tied together. The guards released the man and he sank to the floor, groaning as his weight fell on his injured hands.

Drada stole a glance at his father's mistress. Morgase was watching the crippled man closely. Her eyes shone, her white cheeks were flushed, and her tongue darted out over her stained red lips. He shuddered and returned his gaze to the man who had commanded the Lowland army. He had met him once at court; a strong, proud warrior who had risen through the ranks to command the northern legions. Now he lay weeping like a babe at the feet of his conquerors.

"Now that is how an enemy should look," said Asbidag. Dutiful laughter rose around him as he left the table to stand over the prisoner. "I have good news for you, Martellus," he said, turning the man over with his foot. "I'm going to kill you at last."

The man's swollen eyes fought to focus and his mouth sagged open, showing the remains of his teeth, black and broken.

"Are you not going to thank me, man?"

Just for that one moment Drada saw a glint of anger in the man's eyes. For a fleeting second manhood returned to the ruined warrior. Then it passed and tears re-formed.

"How should we kill him, Morgase?" asked Asbidag, swinging his body to face the table.

"Let the dogs have him," she whispered.

"Poison my dogs? No. Another way."

"Hang him in a cage outside the city walls until he rots," shouted Tostig.

"Impale him," said Ongist.

Drada shifted in his seat, forcing his mind from the spectacle. For more than a year one task had filled his waking hours: planning the defeat of the clans.

The problems were many. The clans had the advantage of terrain, but on the other hand, they lacked any form of military discipline and their villages were widely spaced and built without walls. Each clan mistrusted the others and that was an advantage for the Aenir. They could pick them off one by one.

But it would be a massive operation, needing colossal planning.

Drada had worked for months to be allowed to enter the Farlain with a small company of men. Always his requests had been politely refused. Now, at last, Cambil had agreed they should be guests at the Games. It was a gift from the Grey God.

All the clans gathered in one place, a chance to meet every chieftain and Hunt Lord. An opportunity for the Aenir to scout valleys, passes, and future battlegrounds.

Drada was hauled back to the present, even as the hapless prisoner was dragged from the hall. Asbidag's shadow fell across him. "Well, Drada, what do you think?"

"Of what, Father?"

"Of my decision with Martellus?"

"Very fitting."

"How would you know that?" snapped Asbidag. "You were not listening."

"True, Father, but then you have planned his death for so long that I knew you would have something special for him."

"But it doesn't interest you?"

"It does, sire, but I was thinking about that problem you set me today, and I have a plan that may please you."

"We will talk later," said Asbidag, returning to his place beside Morgase.

"They're going to skin him," whispered Ongist to Drada.

"Thank you."

"Why must you take such risks?"

"I don't know. I was thinking about something else."

"It is good you are a thinker, brother. For you know Father cannot stand you."

"I know—but then I think he likes none of us."

Ongist laughed aloud. "You could be right," he whispered, "but he raised us to be like him, and we are. If I thought I'd get away with it I'd gut the bloated old toad. But you and my other dear brothers would turn on me. Wouldn't you?"

"Of course. We are a family built on hatred."

"And yet we thrive," said Ongist, pouring mead into his cup and raising it to toast his brother.

"Indeed, we do, brother."

"This plan of yours, it concerns the clans?"

"Yes."

"I hope you suggest invasion. Boredom sits ill with me."

"Wait and see, Ongist."

"We've waited a year already. How much longer?"

"Not long. Have patience."

The following afternoon Drada made his way to the ruins of the Garden of the Senses, a half acre of blooms, trees, and shrubs that had once been a place of meditation for the Ateris intellectuals. Many of the winding paths had disappeared now, along with a hundred or so delicate flowers choked by weeds and man's indifference.

And yet, so far, the roses thrived. Of all things Drada had yet encountered on this cruel world, the rose alone found a place in his feelings. He could sit and gaze at them for hours, their beauty calming his mind and allowing him to focus on his problems and plans.

As he had on so many such afternoons, Drada pushed his way through the trailing undergrowth to a rock-pool fringed with wooden benches. Unclipping the brooch that fastened his red cloak, he chose the west-facing bench and sat in the sunshine.

Unwilling to incur Asbidag's displeasure, he had spent the morning watching the flaying of Martellus. The scene had been an unpleasant distraction to the young Aenir warrior; he had seen men flayed before, indeed had witnessed more barbarous acts. And they bored him. But then most of what life had to offer ultimately left Drada bored. It seemed to the young warrior that the journey from birth screech to death rattle was no more than a meaningless series of transient pleasures and pain, culminating at last in the frustration of missed moments and lost opportunities.

He thought of his father and grinned wolfishly. Asbidag, the destroyer of nations, the bringer of blood. The most brutish warrior of a generation of warriors. He had nothing to offer the world, save ceaseless agony and destruction. He had no genuine thoughts of empire, for it was alien to him to consider building anything of worth. He lived to fight and kill, dreaming only of the day when at last he would be summoned to the hall of the Grey God to recite the litany of his conquests.

Drada shivered, though the sun was warm.

Asbidag had sired eleven sons. Three had died in other wars, one had been strangled by Asbidag soon after birth during a row with the mother. She had died less easily.

Now seven sons remained. And what a brood, cast as they were in the image of their father.

Of them all Drada hated Tostig the most. A vile man of immense power, Tostig possessed all the innate cruelty of the natural coward. A pederast who could only gratify himself by killing the victims of his lust. One day I will kill you, thought Drada. When Father is dead. I will kill you all. No, he thought. Not all. I will spare Orsa the Baresark, for he has no ambition, and despite his frenzy in battle, carries no hate.

Drada leaned his head back, closing his eyes against the bright sunlight.

"So this is where you plan your campaigns."

Drada opened his eyes. "Welcome, lady. Please join me." He didn't like to be disturbed here, but with Morgase he was careful to mask his feelings.

As always she was dressed in black, this time a shimmering gown of silk and satin. Her dark hair was braided, hanging over one marble-white shoulder. She sat beside him, draping her arm along the back of the bench, her fingers hovering near his neck. "Always so courteous, Drada. A rare thing among the Aenir."

"My father sent me away as a child to the court of Rhias. I was brought up there."

"You were a hostage?"

"More a viper in the bosom of a future enemy."

"I see." Her hand dropped to his shoulder, squeezing the firm flesh of his upper arm. "Why do you not like me?" she asked, her bright eyes mocking him.

"I do not dislike you," he countered, with an easy lie. "But let us assume that I made love to you here and now. By tonight my bloody corpse would be alongside the unfortunate Martellus."

"Perhaps," she said, interest fading from her eyes. She took her hand from his shoulder and glanced around the garden. "A pretty place."

"Yes."

"Are you planning a war against the clans?"

"They are not the enemy."

"Come now, Drada, do you think I never talk with your father? Do you see me merely as a mistress? Someone who shares only his bed?"

"No, lady."

"Then tell me."

"I am planning for our visit to the Farlain. We have been invited to view the Games."

"How dull."

"Indeed it is," he agreed.

"Tell me, then, if you *were* planning a war against the clans, how would you go about it?"

"This is a game?"

"Why not?"

"Very well. First tell me how *you* would plan it, lady, and then I shall add my own refinements."

"Are you always this cautious?"

"Always," he said, smiling.

She leaned back, closing her eyes as she relaxed in thought. She was beautiful but Drada instantly quelled the desire that surged within him. It confused him momentarily, for in the six months she had been with Asbidag, Drada had never been attracted to her. Her eyes flickered open and the answer came to him. There was something reptilian in those eyes. He shuddered.

"Extermination," she said triumphantly.

"Explain," he whispered.

"Conquering a city can be considered in a number of ways. You may desire to take over the existing enterprise of that city; therefore you would take it with a minimum loss of life and make the inhabitants your servants. In this way you would merely transfer ownership of the enterprise. But with the clans it is a different matter. The Aenir desire only the land, and obviously the livestock. But not the people. They are a wild race, they would not tolerate serfdom. Therefore an invasion against the Farlain would be a prelude to the extermination of the people."

"You would not advocate taking the women as slaves?" asked Drada.

"No. Use them by all means to satisfy the lusts of the warriors, but then kill them. Kill all the clans. Then the land is truly Aenir."

"That is fine as the object of the war. How would you go about invasion?"

"I don't know the terrain, and therefore could not supply answers to logistical problems," said Morgase.

"Neither do I."

"And that is why you plan so carefully for your visit to their Games?"

"You speak of logistical problems, Morgase. You have been involved in the planning of war?"

"Are you surprised?"

He considered the question for a moment. "No, I am not."

"Good. We should be friends, Drada, for we have much in common."

"It would appear so, lady."

"Tell me then, as a friend, what do you think of me?"

"I think you are intelligent and beautiful."

"Don't speak the obvious," she snapped. "Speak the truth."

"I do not know enough about you to form a stronger opinion. Before today I thought you were merely an attractive woman, bright enough, who had seduced my father. Now I must think again."

"Indeed you must. For I have plans of my own—great plans. And you can help me."

"How so?"

"First the Aenir must take the Farlain. Then we will talk."

"Why is that so important? You have no dealings with the clans; they can mean nothing to you."

"But then, my dear Drada, you do not know all that I know. There is a prize within the Farlain beyond the understanding of lesser mortals: the gateway to empires beyond counting."

"How do you know this?"

"It is enough that I know."

"What do you seek, Morgase?"

Her eyes glittered and she laughed, reaching out to stroke his bearded face. "I seek revenge, my handsome thinker. Simply that, for now."

"On whom?"

"On a woman who murdered my father and ordered my mother raped. A woman who stole an empire that ought to have been mine—that *would* have been mine." Her reptilian eyes glittered as she spoke, and her tongue darted over her lips. Drada hid his distaste. "Will you be my friend, Drada? Will you aid me in my quest?"

"I serve my father, lady. But I will be your friend."

"I admire caution, Drada," she said, rising. Her fingers stroked the skin of his throat and he was amazed to find arousal once more stirring his blood. "I admire it—as long as it is accompanied by ambition. Are you ambitious?"

"I am the son of Asbidag," he said softly.

As he watched her leave, the fear began. He had underestimated her. She was chilling, clever, and utterly ruthless. Yet another viper in our basket, he thought.

Caswallon was gone for three days, returning just after dawn as Maeg administered to the infant, Donal. He stood silently in the doorway, listening to the gentle words she crooned as she cleaned and oiled him. Caswallon closed his eyes for a moment, his emotions rising and threatening to unman him. He cleared his throat. She turned, her hair falling across her face, then she swept it back and smiled.

He knelt beside her. The child reached for him, giggling.

Caswallon lifted the boy and patted his back as his son's small chubby arms tried to encircle his neck.

Caswallon returned Donal to his mother, who dressed him in a woolen undershirt and a light tunic, and they moved downstairs to the kitchen where Kareen was preparing breakfast. Leaving Donal with the girl, Caswallon took Maeg by the hand and they left the house to watch the sunrise over Druin. Maeg said nothing as they walked, sensing the weight of sadness Caswallon carried.

They reached the crest of a hill and sat beneath a spreading oak. "I am so sorry, Maeg, my love," said Caswallon, taking her hand and kissing it.

"For what? A man will give way to anger now and again."

"I know. But you are the one person in the world I'd never seek to hurt."

"Foolish man, do you think you can hurt me with a little broken crockery?"

"Why did you marry me?" he asked suddenly.

"Why are men so foolish?" she countered.

"No, I mean it. Why?"

She looked at him closely and then, seeing the sorrow in his green eyes, sensed the burden he was bearing. Reaching up, she stroked his beard and then curled her arm about his neck and pulled him down to kiss her.

"No one can answer such a question. I didn't like you when you approached me at the Games; I saw you as an arrogant Farlain raider. But after Maggrig sent you away I found myself thinking about you often. Then, when I awoke that day and found you in my room, I hated you. I wanted you slain. But as the days passed thoughts of you grew in my mind. And when you walked into the Long Hall on that winter's night, your beard stiff with ice, I knew that I loved you. But now tell me why you risked your life to wed me."

Gently he eased her from him, cupping her face in his hands. "Because before I saw you I had no life to lose," he said simply.

For a long time they sat beneath the tree, saying nothing,

enjoying the warmth of the risen sun, until at last Maeg spoke. "Now tell me truly, Caswallon, what is troubling you?"

"I cannot. I have given a promise. But I can say this: The old days are finished, and what we have here is perhaps the last golden summer of the Farlain. I know this, and the knowledge destroys me."

"The Aenir?" she asked.

"And our own stupidity."

"No one lives forever, Caswallon. A man, or a woman, may die at any time. That is why today is so important."

"I know."

"Yes, you do. But you've not lived it. Suppose you are right, and the Aenir destroy us next month, or next year. Suppose, further, that they kill us both . . ."

"No! I'll not even think of that!"

"Think of it!" she commanded, pulling away from him. "What difference all this heartache? For the Aenir are not here today. On this morning we have each other. We have Donal and Gaelen. We have peace, we have love. How often have you said that tomorrow's problems can be dealt with tomorrow?"

"But I could have changed it."

"And that is the real reason for your sorrow. You refused to be considered for Hunt Lord, and denied yourself a place on the Council. Now you suffer for it. But one man will not thwart a race like the Aenir. They are killers all. What do they seek? War and death. Conquest and bloodshed. They will pass, for they build nothing."

"I have made you angry," he said.

"Yes, you have, for you have allowed fear to find a place in your heart. And there it has grown to fill you with defeat. And that is not what I expect from you, Caswallon of the Farlain."

"What do you expect?" he asked, smiling.

"I expect you to be a man always. You are angry because Cambil has allowed an Aenir company to attend the Games."

"Yes."

"Why?"

"Because they will scout our lands and learn that which should have cost them blood."

"Then see they are escorted here. Surround them with scouts."

"I cannot do that. The Council . . ."

"A pox on the Council! You are one of the richest men in the three valleys. As such, you are a man of influence. There are others who agree with you: Leofas, for example. Find a hundred men to do your bidding. And one more thing. Kareen was walking on the east hills yesterday and she saw men running around the walls of Ateris. Others were practicing with the bow and spear."

"So? The Aenir have Games of their own."

"We've not seen such a practice before."

"What are you suggesting?"

"The Aenir are bringing twenty men. I think they will ask to be allowed to take part in the Games."

"For what purpose?"

"To win."

"It would never be allowed."

"Cambil is Games Lord this year," she said.

"It is unthinkable," he whispered. "But there could be many advantages. If they could prove themselves superior it would boost the morale of their warriors and, equally, diminish our own. And they would earn the right to travel the mountains."

"That is better. That is the Caswallon I know."

"Indeed it is. I should have spoken to you before, Maeg."

Caswallon took Gaelen and Gwalchmai with him to observe the strange antics of the Aenir. It seemed that half of Asbidag's army at Aesgard was at play. The plain before the city was sectioned off by tents, stalls, and ropes, creating a running track, an archery field, a series of spear lanes, and a vast circle at the center of which men wrestled and boxed, or fought with sword and shield. Strength events were also under way.

"It is like the Games," said Gwalchmai. "How long have they been doing this?"

Caswallon shrugged. "Kareen saw them yesterday."

"They have some fine athletes," observed Gaelen. "Look at that white-haired runner leading the pack. He moves like the wind."

On the plain below Drada and Ongist were watching the foot races with interest. Ongist had wagered ten pieces of gold on Snorri Wolfson to beat Drada's favorite, the ash-blond Borak. Snorri was trailing by thirty paces when they reached the last lap.

"A curse on the man!" snarled Ongist.

"He is a sprinter," said Drada, grinning. "He's not built for distance."

"What about a wager against Orsa?"

Drada shook his head. "No one will beat him in the strength events." The brothers wandered across the running track to the twelve men contesting the weights. They were drawing lots to decide which man would first attempt the hurling and Drada and Ongist settled on the grass as the draw was decided.

One man approached a cart on which was set a block of marble. It was shaped as a ball and carefully inscribed with the names of Ateris's greatest poets. Before today it had rested on a velvet-covered stand in the city library.

It weighed over sixty pounds.

The man placed his hand on either side of the sphere, bent his knees, and lifted it to his chest. He approached the marker stake, hoisted the sphere above his head, and with a grunt of effort, threw it forward. With a dull thud it buried itself in the ground some five paces ahead. Three officials prized it loose with spears and rolled it back to the marker stake, lifting it for the next thrower.

Drada and Ongist watched with scant interest as the men took their turns until, at last, Orsa stripped himself of his shirt and stood grinning by the stake. He waved to his brothers.

Two officials lifted the sphere into his arms. Even before they were clear Orsa shifted the weight to his right hand, dipped his shoulder, and hurled the sphere into the air. It sailed over the other marks by some three paces; as it landed it shattered into a score of pieces.

"Must have hit a buried rock," muttered Ongist.

Orsa ambled across to them. "Easy," he said, pointing at the ruined marble.

Drada nodded. "You are still the strongest, brother."

"No need for proof," said Orsa. "Waste of time."

"True," Drada agreed.

"I'm hungry," said Orsa, wandering away without another word. Drada watched him go, marveling anew at the sheer size of the man. His upper arms were as large as most men's thighs.

"By Vatan, he's a monster," said Ongist.

Drada looked away. In a family of monsters it seemed ironic that Ongist should so describe the only one among them who hated no one.

High on the hillside the three clansmen stood to depart. They had seen enough. "I think Maeg is right," said Caswallon. "Tell me, Gaelen, do you think you could beat that white-haired runner?"

"I fear we will find out next month," said Gaelen. "I think I can. But he wasn't stretched today; he set his own pace. Still, if they do bring a team I hope that giant comes with them. I'd love to see him against Lennox."

Chapter Six

Deva awoke in the first moments of dawn, as the sun lanced its light through the slats of her window. She yawned and stretched, rolling to her side to watch the dust motes dance in the sunbeams. Kicking aside the down-filled quilt, she opened the shutters and leaned on the stone sill, breathing deeply.

The cool early-morning breeze held the promise of autumn, and already the leaves on the distant trees were dappled with rusty gold. Mountain ash and copper beech glistened and their leaves looked like coins, rich and freshly minted.

Deva was always first to rise. She could hear her brother Agwaine snoring in the next room. Stripping her woolen nightdress from her slender body, she poured water into a clay bowl and washed her face. She was a tall girl, willowy and narrow-hipped. Her features were clean-cut, not beautiful, but her large, grey eyes with traces of tawny gold gave her magnificence. Most of the young men of the Farlain had paid court to her and she rejected them all. The mother of kings! That's what the old tinker woman had predicted at her birth. And Deva was determined to fulfill her destiny. She would not do that by marrying a Highland boy! Over the door hung a silvered mirror. Wiping the water from her face and neck she walked over to it, looking deep into her own eyes. Grey they were, but not the color of arctic clouds, nor winter seas. They were the soft grey of a rabbit's pelt, and the glints of gold made them warm and welcoming. She smiled at herself, tilting her head.

She knew she was attractive. She combed her fingers through her corn-gold hair, shaking her head to untangle the knots. Then she remembered the visitors her father Cambil had welcomed the night before.

Asbidag, Lord of the Aenir! She shivered, crossing her arms. The Aenir was a large man with powerful shoulders and a spreading gut. His face was broad, his mouth cruel, and his eyes evil. Deva didn't like him.

No more did she like the woman he brought with him—Morgase, he called her. Her skin was white as any Ateris statue and she seemed just as cold.

Deva had heard much talk during the last few months about the dangers of the Aenir, and had dismissed it from her mind, believing as she did in the wisdom of her father. Last night she had thought afresh.

Asbidag brought two of his sons to the house. Both were handsome, and had they been Farlain Deva might have considered allowing them to join her at the Whorl Dance. The dark-haired Ongist had smiled at her, but his eyes betrayed his lust and she had lost interest in him. The other, Drada, had merely bowed and kissed her hand. Him she had seen before. His voice was deep, yet soft, and in his eyes she saw only a hint of mockery.

Now *he* was interesting . . .

Deva had been looking forward to the Games all summer. As the Games Maiden, elected by the Council, she would preside over the Whorl Dance and be the only woman to choose her dancing companions. No man could refuse the Games Maiden.

In her mind's eye she could see herself walking the lines of waiting men, stopping momentarily, lifting a hand. She would halt by Gaelen and smile. As he stepped forward, she would walk on and choose Layne.

She giggled. Perhaps she would choose Gaelen . . .

The thoughts were delicious.

She dressed quickly in a flowing skirt of leaf-green and a

russet shirt with billowing sleeves. Then she walked downstairs.

The woman Morgase was in the kitchen, talking to Drada. Their conversation ceased as she entered. "Good morning," she said as they turned.

They nodded at her and she felt uncomfortable, as if she had blundered in on a secret assignation. Moving past them, she opened the kitchen door and walked into the yard beyond.

The Games fields in the valley below were ablaze with color. Tents of every shade and hue had sprouted overnight like immense flowers. Ropes had been staked, creating tracks and lanes, and enormous trestle tables were ready for the barter of goods. Several cooking pits had been dug in preparation for the barbecue and the barrels of mead were set in the center of the field where the Whorl Stone had been placed on a bulging hill.

Already the clans were gathering. Her eyes scanned the surrounding hillsides. Everywhere was movement. They came from the Pallides, the Haesten, the Loda, the Irelas, the Dunilds, the Clouds—from every clan, large and small.

Today they would muster and pitch their tents. Tomorrow Cambil, the Games Lord, would announce the order of events. And then Deva would start the first race.

Movement to her left caught her eye. She turned and watched as the Druid Lord approached her. "Good morning, Taliesen," she said, smiling to hide her apprehension. She didn't like the old man; he made her skin crawl and she had often heard her father speak of his eldritch magic.

"Good morning, Deva. How is the Games Maiden?"

"I am well, my lord. And you?"

"I am as you see me."

"You never seem to change."

"All men change. You cannot fight the years. I wondered if you might do me a small service?"

"Of course."

"Thank you. Will you walk with me a way?"

"Where?" she asked, fear taking the place of apprehension.

"Do not worry. I shall not harm you. Come."

The old man moved away toward the western woods and Deva followed some paces behind. Once in the trees Taliesen stopped and retrieved a long bundle lying behind a fallen trunk. Unwrapping it, he removed the sword found by Agwaine.

"What are you doing?" asked Deva, stepping back.

"This must be returned to its owner," he told her.

"I thought the old woman was dead."

"She is—and she is not."

Deva felt the color ooze from her face. "You're not going to conjure her ghost?"

"No, not her ghost." He smiled gently. "Trust me, little one. Take the sword in your hands." He offered it to her, hilt forward. She took it; it was heavy but she was strong and held it firmly.

Taliesen closed his eyes and started to whisper sibilantly in a language Deva had never heard. The air about her began to crackle and a strange odor pervaded the wood. She wanted to run, but was frozen in fear.

The druid's eyes opened and he leaned toward Deva. Walk into the mist," he said. Deva blinked and stepping back she saw a thick grey mist seeping up from the ground, billowing like smoke some ten paces before her. "There is no danger, girl," snapped Taliesen.

Deva hesitated. "What is waiting there?"

"You will see. Trust me." Still she did not move and Taliesen's patience snapped. "By God, are you a Farlain woman or some Lowland wench afraid of her own shadow?"

Deva steeled herself and walked forward, holding the sword two-handed, the blade pointing the way. The mist closed around her. Ahead she saw flickering lights. Her feet were cold now. She glanced down and saw, to her amazement, that she was walking in water. No, not in. Upon! Momentarily she stopped as a large silver fish swam beneath her. "Go on!" came the voice of Taliesen in her mind.

To her right she heard the sound of a waterfall but it was strangely muted, muffled. Looking straight ahead she walked across the lake pool, and saw a crowd of armed men at the poolside carrying torches. At their center stood a young woman. She was beautiful, though her hair was bright silver, and she wore dark armor.

"Stop now!" came Taliesen's voice. Deva waited, the sword heavy in her hands. The warrior woman waded out into the pool. The water was thigh-deep as she approached where Deva stood.

"Who are you?" the armored woman asked.

"Say nothing!" ordered Taliesen. "Give her the sword."

Obediently Deva reversed the blade, offering it to the woman.

For a moment their eyes met, and Deva felt chilled by the power in the other's gaze. "Can you read the future, spirit?" asked the Queen. Taliesen whispered another order and Deva turned away, walking slowly back across the surface of the pool and reentering the mist.

The old druid waited for her in the sunshine. He was sitting on the grass, his cloak of feathers wrapped around his scrawny shoulders, his face grey with exhaustion.

Deva knelt beside him. "Who was she?" she asked.

"A queen in another time," he answered. "Tell no one of what passed here today."

The following day almost four thousand clansmen, women, and children thronged the fields, gathering around the Whorl Hill on which was set the legendary stone of Earis, by which he had pledged to lead the Farlain to safety beyond the Gate. The stone itself was black, but studded with clusters of pearl-white deposits that caught the sunlight and sparkled like tiny gems. Although a man could encompass it with his arms, it weighed more than two hundred pounds.

Around the stone stood the Hunt Lords of the clans, and in

their midst Asbidag of the Aenir. The clan lords were clearly uncomfortable.

Maggrig of the Pallides was furious. The Games were a clan affair, yet last night Cambil had sprung upon them his invitation for the Aenir to enter a team. The argument had raged for over an hour.

"Are you mad?" Maggrig had stormed. "Has the addled Farlain mind finally betrayed you?"

"I am the Games Lord this year. They are on Farlain land; it is my decision," Cambil answered, fighting to control his anger.

"Be that as it may, Cambil," put in the white-haired Laric, Hunt Lord of the Haesten, "but should any one man be allowed to set a precedent others will be forced to follow?" He was known to be a man rarely aroused to anger. Yet his thin face was flushed now, his fists clenched.

"It is my decision," Cambil repeated stonily.

Laric bit back his anger. "The Aenir have no friends— only vassals. They have tried to scout all our lands and been turned back. You realize that if they win outright we are obliged to allow them access? The Games Champions can travel and hunt where they will."

"They will not win," said Cambil. "They are not clansmen."

"Calling you a fool serves nothing," said Laric, "for you have proven that beyond my speculation. What breaks my heart is that one man's foolishness could bring about the ruin of the clans." There was a gasp from the assembled Hunt Lords and Cambil sat very still, his face ashen.

Maggrig rose. "I am tempted to take the Pallides home, away from this stupidity, yet I cannot," he said, "for without them the Aenir would have a greater chance of victory. I suspect it is the same for every lord here. But I tell you this, Cambil. Until now I have had scant respect for you. From today even that is a thing of the past. It matters not a whit to me if the Farlain are run by a fool; that hurts only the Farlain. But when you put the Pallides at risk I cannot forgive you."

Color drained from Cambil's face. "How dare you! You think I care what some potbellied out-clan thinks of me? Take your ragbag carles home. With or without the Aenir your Pallides would win nothing, only humiliation."

"Hark, the Aenir lapdog can still bark," snapped Maggrig.

"Enough of this!" stormed Laric, as Maggrig and Cambil moved toward each other. "Listen to me. I have no love for the Farlain, nor for the Pallides. But we are clansmen and no man will violate the spirit of the Games. There will be no violence among the Hunt Lords. The thing has been done and long will it be argued over. But it is *done*. Now let us consider the order of events, or we'll be here all night."

Later, as Maggrig and Laric walked back to their tents in the moonlight, the taller Haesten lord was deep in thought. Maggrig also kept silent. Laric—the oldest Hunt Lord in Druin, approaching sixty years of age—was also by far the wisest. Maggrig liked him, though he'd swallow live coals rather than tell him so.

They reached Laric's tent first and the older man turned to Maggrig, resting a hand on his shoulder. "Cambil is a fool. He cannot see that which should be clear to every clansman. The Aenir are tomorrow's enemy. My land borders yours, Maggrig, and we have had many disputes ere now, but if the Aenir cross Pallides land I shall bring my clansmen to your aid."

Maggrig smiled. It was a nice ploy, but the fact remained that for the Aenir to cross Pallides borders they must march through either Farlain land or Haesten—and the Haesten were less powerful than the Farlain. Laric was asking for an ally.

"Between us we have perhaps two thousand fighting men," said Maggrig. "Do you think they could stop an Aenir army?"

"Perhaps."

"Agreed, then. We will be allies. I would expect, of course, to be War Lord."

"Of course," said Laric. "Good night."

*   *   *

The following morning Maggrig stood alongside Asbidag, biting back his anger. The two men could have been brothers. Both had striking red beards flecked with silver, both were powerfully built. Deva watched them with anxiety. They were so similar—until you looked into their eyes. There was no evil in Maggrig. Deva looked away.

Cambil's opening speech of welcome was short, and he quickly outlined the order of the Games. The first event would be the mountain run, five miles on a twisting circuit through woods and valleys. Three hundred men were entered and the Hunt Lords had decided on six qualifying races. The first five in each race would contest two semifinals, and fifteen of the fastest, strongest clansmen would run the final on the last day.

Other qualifying events were outlined and then it was left to Deva, in a flowing dress of white linen garlanded with flowers, to signal the start of the first race. The named athletes, Gaelen and Agwaine among them, jostled for position as Deva's arm swept up, hovered momentarily, then flashed down and the race began.

Caswallon watched the start, saw Gaelen running smoothly in the center of the pack, and knowing the youth would qualify easily, he strolled to the market stalls on the edge of the field.

The stalls were doing brisk business in brooches, daggers, trinkets and tools, cloth, furs, blankets and shoes, meats, cheeses, fruit and vegetables. Caswallon eased through the massed crowds seeking a necklace for Maeg. Finding nothing to his taste, he bought a jug of mead and an oatmeal loaf. There were still one or two empty tables at the edge of the field and he chose a place away from the crowd where he would be alone with his thoughts. Since his talk with Maeg he had been less obsessed with the Aenir threat, but now, as was his way, he thought the problem through, examining every angle.

Morgase and Drada were sitting less than thirty paces away, but hidden by the crowd Caswallon did not see them. Morgase was bored, and her eyes flickered over the mass of people, seeking something of even passing interest. She saw the tall man walking to the empty table and her gaze lingered, her eyes widening in alarm. He wore a leaf-green cloak and a tunic of polished brown leather, while across his chest hung a baidric bearing two slim daggers. By his side was a long hunting knife. His trews were green laced with leather thongs. Morgase stared intently at the face. The short trident beard confused her, but the eyes were the same deep green she remembered so well.

And with such hatred . . .

She stood and walked over to where he sat. "Good morning," she said, her throat tight, her anger barely controlled.

Caswallon looked up. Before him was a woman dressed in black, a sleek-fitting gown that hid nothing of her slender figure. Her dark hair was braided and curled like a crown on her head and pinned with gold. He rose. "Good morning, lady." He gestured for her to be seated and asked if he could bring her refreshments. Then she saw Drada approaching, carrying two goblets of wine.

"How are you, Caswallon?" asked Drada.

"Well. Will you introduce me to the lady?"

"You do not know me then?" asked Morgase, surprised.

"I have been known to be forgetful, lady, but not insane. Such beauty as yours is unforgettable."

She seemed confused, uncertain. "You are very like someone I once knew. Uncannily like."

"I hope he was a friend," said Caswallon.

"He was not."

"Then allow me to make up for it," he said, smiling. Will you join me?"

"No, I must go. But please, since you two know each other, why don't you finish your drinks together?"

The men watched her walk away. "A strange woman," said Drada.

"Who is she?"

"Morgase, my father's consort. Beautiful but humorless."

"She thought she knew me."

"Yes. Are you taking part in the Games?"

"I am."

"In what event?" asked Drada.

"Short sword."

"I thought you were a runner?"

"I was. You are well informed. And you?"

"No, I'm afraid I excel at very little."

"You seem to excel in the field of selection," said Caswallon. "Rarely have I seen men train as hard."

Drada smiled. "The Aenir like to win."

"I wonder why?"

"What does that mean? No man likes to lose."

"True. But no clansman trains for the Games; they are an extension of his life and his natural skills. If he loses, he shrugs. It is not the end of the world for him."

"Perhaps that is why you are clansmen, living a quiet life in these beautiful mountains, while the Aenir conquer the continent."

"Yes, that is what I was thinking," said Caswallon.

"Was it your idea to have us escorted here?"

"I was afraid you might get lost."

"That was kind of you."

"I am a kind man," said Caswallon. "I shall also see that you are escorted back."

"Cambil assured us that would not be necessary. Or is he not the Hunt Lord?"

"Indeed he is, but we are a free people and the Hunt Lord is not omnipotent."

"You take a great deal on yourself, Caswallon. Why can we not be friends? As you have seen, the Aenir have respected your borders. We trade. We are neighbors."

"It is not necessary for you and me to play these games, Drada. I know what is in your heart. Like all killers, you fear that a greater killer will stalk you as you stalk others. You cannot exist with a free people on your borders. You must always be at war with someone. And one day, if you ever achieve your ambition, and the Aenir rule from sea to sea in every direction, even then it will not end. You will turn on yourselves like rabid wolves. Today you strike fear into men's hearts. But tomorrow? Then you will be thought of as a boil on the neck of history."

The words were spoken without heat. Drada sipped his wine, then he looked up to meet Caswallon's gaze. "I can see why you think as you do, but you are wrong. All new civilizations begin with bloodshed and horror, but as the years pass they settle down to prosper, to wax and to grow fat. Then, as they reach their splendid peak, a new enemy slips over the horizon and the bloodshed begins anew."

"The Farlain will be your undoing," said Caswallon. "You are like the man poised to stamp on the worm beneath his feet—too far above it to see it is a viper."

"Even so, when the man stamps the viper dies," said Drada.

"And the man with it."

Drada shrugged. "All men die at some time."

"Indeed they do, my bonny. But some die harder than others."

For ten days the Games progressed and the fear of the Hunt Lords grew. The Aenir competed ferociously, bringing new edge to the competitions. Gone was any semblance of friendly rivalry—the foreigners battled as if their lives depended on the result.

By the evening before the last day an overall Aenir victory had moved from possibility to probability. Only the athletes of the Farlain could overhaul them. The Aenir had won all but two of the short sprint finals, had defeated Gwalchmai in the archery tourney, but lost to Layne in the spear. Caswallon had beaten the Aenir challenger in the short sword, but lost the final to Intosh, the Pallides swordsman. Gaelen and Agwaine had fought their way to the final five-mile race planned for the morrow, though Agwaine had only reached it when a Haesten runner twisted his ankle hurdling a fallen tree. His disappointment in qualifying in such a manner was deepened by the fact that the Aenir athlete, the white-haired Borak, had beaten Gaelen into second place in their semifinal.

Lennox, in an awesome display of sheer power, had strolled comfortably to the final of the strength event, but here he was to face the fearsome might of the giant Orsa, himself unbeaten. The Aenir had won grudging respect from the clansmen, but all the same the Games had been spoiled.

Cambil remained withdrawn throughout the tournament, knowing in his heart the scale of his error. The unthinkable was on the verge of reality. The Aenir were two events from victory. He had summoned Gaelen and Agwaine to him and the trio sat before the broad empty hearth of Cambil's home.

"Are you confident of beating this Borak, Gaelen?" Cambil asked, knowing now that his own son could not compete at their level.

Gaelen rubbed his eye, choosing his answer carefully. "I saw no point in making a push yesterday; it would only show him the limit of my speed. But, on the other hand, he concealed from me his own reserves. No, I am not confident. But I think I can beat him."

"What do you think, Agwaine?"

"I can only agree with Gaelen, Father. They are superbly matched. I would not be surprised either way."

"You have both performed well and been a credit to the Farlain. Though you are adopted, Gaelen, you have the heart of a clansman. I wish you well."

"Thank you, Hunt Lord."

"Go home and rest. Do not eat too heavy a breakfast."

Gaelen left the house and wandered to the pine fence before the yard. Turning, he looked up at Deva's window hoping to see a light. There was none. Disappointed, he opened the gate and began the short walk through the woods to Caswallon's house in the valley.

The night was bright, the moon full, and a light breeze whispered in the branches overhead. He thought about the race and its implications. It was true that he was not confident of victory, but he would be surprised if the Aenir beat him. He thought he had detected an edge of fatigue in the blond runner as he came off the mountain on the last circuit of the field. Gaelen hadn't pressed then, but had watched his opponent carefully. The man's head had been bobbing during the last two hundred paces, and his arms pumped erratically.

Gaelen had finished all of thirty paces adrift and it would be closer tomorrow. Caswallon had pointed out one encouraging thought; no one had yet tested Borak. Did he have the heart to match his speed?

A dark shadow leaped at Gaelen from the left, another from the right. He ducked and twisted, using his forearm to block a blow from a wooden club. He hammered his fist into the belly of the nearest man, following it with a swift hook to the jaw. The attacker dropped as if poleaxed. As he hurled himself to the right, Gaelen's shoulder cannoned into the midriff of the second man. The grunting whoosh of his opponent's breath showed he was badly winded. Scrambling to his feet, Gaelen kicked the fallen man in the face. More men ran from the trees; in the darkness Gaelen could not recognize faces, but they were dressed like clansmen.

He caught an attacker with a right cross to the chin, but then a wooden club thudded against his temple. Gaelen reeled to the left, vainly holding up his arm to protect his head. The club hammered into his thigh and agony lanced him. Another blow to the calf and he collapsed to the ground, struggling to rise as a booted foot crashed into his face. Twice more he felt blows to his right leg, and he passed out.

It was dawn before he was found. Caswallon came across the unconscious body as he made his way to Cambil's home. The clansman had been worried about Gaelen staying out all night before the race, but had assumed he was sleeping at the house of the Hunt Lord. Carefully he turned Gaelen to his back, checking his heartbeat and breathing. He probed the dried blood on the youth's temple; the skull was not cracked. With a grunt of effort, he lifted Gaelen to his shoulder and stumbled on toward the house.

Deva was the first to be awakened by Caswallon kicking at the door. She ran downstairs, pulled back the bolts, and let him in. Walking past her, Caswallon eased Gaelen down into a leather chair. Deva brought some water from the kitchen and a towel to bathe Gaelen's head.

Cambil, bare chested and barely awake, joined them. "What has happened?" he asked, bending over the unconscious youth.

"From the tracks, I'd say five men set on him after he left here last night," Caswallon told him.

"Why?"

Caswallon glanced at him, green eyes blazing. "Why do you think? I was a fool not to consider it myself."

"You think the Aenir . . . ?"

"You want further proof?" Caswallon carefully unlaced the thongs of Gaelen's leggings, pulling them clear. His right leg was mottled blue, the knee swollen and pulpy. He groaned as Caswallon checked the bones for breaks. "Skillfully done, wouldn't you say?"

"I shall cancel the race," said Cambil.

"And what reason will you give?" snapped Caswallon. "And what purpose would it serve? We need to win both of today's events. Canceling one will only give the trophy to the Aenir."

Agwaine stood at the foot of the stairs watching the exchange. He said nothing, moving past his father and making his way to the yard. From there he gazed out over the Games field and the mountains beyond. Deva joined him, a woolen shawl across her shoulders, her white nightdress billowing in the morning breeze. Curling her arm about his waist, she rested her head on his shoulder.

"What are you thinking?" she asked.

"I was thinking of Father."

"In what way?"

"Oh, I don't know. Many ways. He's wrong, I know that now. The Games were ruined from the moment he allowed Drada to honey-talk him into allowing an Aenir team. But they flattered him so."

"You are disappointed?"

"Yes, I suppose I am. Do not misunderstand me, Deva. I love Father dearly, and I would give anything for him to be respected as he desires to be. But, like all men, he has limits, he makes mistakes."

"Gaelen's waking up."

"Yes, but he won't run today."

"No, but you will, brother."

"Yes," he answered, sighing. "Yes, I will."

The field was packed, the stalls deserted as three thousand clansmen thronged the start of the Mountain Race. The fifteen runners, dressed only in kilted loincloths and moccasins, were separated from the crowd by a lane of corded ropes staking the first two hundred paces, before the long climb into the timberline.

Agwaine eased his way through the athletes to stand beside the tall Borak. The man looked to neither right nor left, his eyes fixed ahead, ears tuned for the command to run.

As Games Lord it was Cambil's duty to start the race. Beside him stood Asbidag and Morgase, Maggrig, Laric, and the other Hunt Lords of minor clans.

Cambil lifted his arm. "Ready yourselves," he shouted. The crowd fell silent, the runners tensing for the race. "Race!" yelled Cambil and the athletes tore away, jostling for position in the narrow roped lane.

Agwaine settled in behind Borak, and was pulled to the front of the pack as the lean Aenir surged ahead. Gaelen, walking with the aid of a staff, watched, feeling sick with disappointment. Beside him, Lennox and Layne were cheering their cousin.

The runners neared the base of the mountain, Agwaine and the Aenir some twenty paces ahead of the pack. Borak shortened his step, leaning forward into the hill, his long legs pounding rhythmically against the packed clay. A thin film of sweat shone on his body and his white-gold hair glistened in the sunlight. Agwaine, his gaze pinned on his opponent's back, was breathing easily, knowing the testing time would come before the third mile. It was at this point that he had been broken in the semifinal, the Aenir increasing his pace and burning off his opponents. He had learned in that moment the strength-sapping power of despair.

The crowd below watched them climb and Asbidag leaned over to Cambil. "Your son runs well," he said.

"Thank you."

"But where is the boy with the white flash in his hair?"

Cambil met his gaze. "He was injured last night in a brawl."

"I'm sorry to hear that," said Asbidag smoothly. "Some trouble between the clans, perhaps?"

"Yes, perhaps," answered Cambil.

The runners reached the two-mile mark and swung along the top of the slope, past a towering cliff of chalk, and into the trees on the long curve toward home. Agwaine could no longer hear the following runners, only his heart hammering in his chest and the rasping of his breath. But still he kept within three paces of the man before him.

Just before the three-mile mark Borak increased the length of his stride, forging a ten-pace lead before Agwaine responded.

Caswallon had pulled the young Farlain aside earlier that day, after Gaelen's wounds had been tended. "I know we don't see eye-to-eye on many things, cousin," Caswallon had told him. "But force yourself to believe what I am going to tell you. You know that I won the Mountain Race three years ago. The way I did it was to destroy the field just after halfway—the same method the Aenir used in the semifinal. So I know how his mind works. He has no finish sprint, his one gamble is to kill off his opponents. When he breaks away, it will hurt him. His legs, just like yours, will burn and his lungs will be on fire. Keep that in mind. Each pain you feel, he feels. Stay with him."

Agwaine didn't know how the Aenir felt at this moment, but as he fought to haul back the distance between them the pain in his legs increased and his breathing grew hot and ragged. But step by step he gained, until at last he was nestled in behind the warrior.

Twice more Borak fought to dislodge the dogged clansman. Twice more Agwaine closed the gap.

Up ahead, hidden behind a screen of bushes, knelt an Aenir warrior. In his hand was a leather sling, in the pouch of which hung a round black stone. He glimpsed the runners and readied himself. He could see the shorter clansman was close to Borak, and he cursed. Difficult enough to fell a running man, without having the risk of striking his comrade. Still, Borak knew he was here. He would pull ahead.

The runners were nearer now and the Aenir lifted his sling . . .

"Are you lost, my bonny?"

The warrior swung around, dropping the sling hurriedly.

"No. I was watching the race."

"You picked a good position," said Caswallon, smiling.

"Yes."

"Shall we walk back together and observe the finish?"

"I'll walk alone," snapped the Aenir, glancing away down the trail in time to see the runners leave the woods on the last stretch of slope before the final circuit.

"As you please," said Caswallon.

Borak was worried now. He could hear the cursed clansman behind him and within moments he would be clear of the trees. What in Vatan's name was Snorri waiting for?

Just before they came in sight of the crowds below, Borak chopped his pace. As Agwaine drew abreast of him, Borak's elbow flashed back, the point smashing Agwaine's lips and snapping his head back. At that moment Borak sprinted away out of the trees, on to the gentle slope and down to the valley.

Agwaine stumbled, recovered his balance, and set off in pursuit. Anger flooded him, swamping the pain of his tired legs.

In the field below, three thousand voices rose in a howling cheer that echoed through the mountains. Cambil couldn't believe it. As Games Lord it behooved him to stay neutral, but it was impossible. Surging to his feet he leaped from the platform and joined the crowd, cheering at the top of his voice.

Borak hurtled headlong into the wall of sound, which panicked him for he could no longer hear the man behind him. He knew it was senseless to glance back, for it would cost him speed, but he couldn't help himself. His head turned and there, just behind him, was Agwaine, blood streaming from his injured mouth. Borak tried to increase his pace—the finishing line was only fifty paces away—but the distance stretched out before him like an eternity. Agwaine drew abreast of him once more—and then was past.

The crowd was delirious. The rope lanes were trampled down and Agwaine swallowed by the mass, only to be hoisted aloft on the shoulders of two Farlain men. Borak stumbled away, head bowed, then stopped and sought out his master.

Asbidag stood silently gazing down from the Hunt Lord's platform. Borak met his gaze and turned away.

"There is still Orsa," said Drada.

His father nodded, then watched the broken Borak walking away from the tents of the Aenir.

"I don't want to see his face again."

"I'll send him south," said Drada.

"I don't want *anyone* to see his face again."

Clan fervor, which had seemed to reach a peak following Agwaine's unexpected and courageous victory, hit new heights during the long afternoon. No one toured the stalls, nor sat in comfort at the tables sipping mead or wine. The entire crowd thronged the central field where Lennox and Orsa battled for the Whorl Trophy, awarded to the strongest man of the mountains.

That the two men were splendidly matched had been obvious from the culling events, when both had moved comfortably to the final. Both towered over six feet. In physique they were near identical, their huge frames swollen with thick, corded muscle. Deva thought them equally ugly, though the male watchers gazed in frank admiration.

The event had five sections. The first man to win three of them would be the Whorl Champion.

The first saw Orsa win easily. A sphere of lead weighing twenty pounds had to be hurled, one-handed. Orsa's first throw measured eighteen and a half paces. Lennox managed only thirteen. But the clansman drew level in the next event, straightening a horseshoe.

Watching the contest with Gaelen and Maeg, Caswallon was concerned. "The Aenir is more supple, and therefore his speed is greater. That's why he won the hurling so easily, and it must make him the favorite for the open wrestling."

The third event involved lifting the Whorl Stone and carrying it along a roped lane. Lennox was first to make the attempt.

The black boulder had been carried to a wooden platform at the head of the lane. Two hundred pounds of slippery stone. Lennox approached it, breathing deeply, and the crowd fell silent, allowing him to concentrate on the task ahead. The weight was not the problem. Set the boulder on a harness and Lennox could carry it across the Druin range. But held across the chest, every step loosened the grip. A strong man could carry it ten paces; a very strong man might make twenty; but only those with colossal power carried it beyond thirty. The man now known as Oracle had, in his youth, made forty-two paces. Men still spoke of it.

Lennox bent his knees and curled his mighty arms around the stone, tensing the muscles of his shoulders and back.

Straightening his legs with a grunt of effort, he slowly turned and began to walk the lane.

At fifteen paces the stone slipped, but he held it more firmly and walked on. At thirty paces the steps became smaller. Gone was the slow, measured stride. His head strained back, the muscles and tendons of his neck stood out like bars of iron.

At forty paces his face was crimson, the veins on his temples writhing, his eyes squeezed shut.

At forty-five paces Lennox stumbled, made one more step, then jumped back as he was forced to release the weight. Three men prized the stone clear, while a fourth marked the spot with a white stake.

Sucking in great gasps of air, Lennox sought out his opponent, reading his face for signs of concern. Orsa ran his hand through his thick yellow hair, sweeping it back from his eyes. He grinned at Lennox, a friendly, open smile. Lennox's heart sank.

To the stunned amazement of the crowd, Orsa carried the Whorl Stone easily past the stake, releasing it at fifty-seven paces. It was an incredible feat, and even the clansmen applauded it. Men's eyes switched to Lennox, knowing the blow to his morale would be great. He was sitting on the grass watching his opponent, his face set, features stern.

Cambil called for a halt to allow the contestants to recover their strength before the rope haul, and the crowd broke away to the mead tables and the barbecue pits.

Caswallon and Gaelen made their way to Lennox, along with Agwaine, Cambil, and Layne. "Can you beat him?" asked Cambil.

"Not now, cousin," snapped Caswallon. "Let him rest." Cambil's eyes flashed angrily and he turned away. Agwaine hesitated, then followed his father.

"How do you feel?" asked Caswallon, sitting down.

Lennox grinned and shrugged. "I feel broken. How could any man carry that stone for almost sixty paces? It's inhuman."

"I thought the same when you carried it for forty-six."

"I don't think I can beat him."

"You can."

"You've not been watching very closely, cousin."

"Ah, but I have, Lennox, and that's how I know. He took a lower grip, and kept his head down. Your head went back. That shortened your steps. You could have matched him; you still can."

"Don't misunderstand me, Caswallon. I shall do my best. But he is stronger, there's no doubt of that."

"I know."

"But he's not Farlain," said Gaelen. "You are."

Lennox grinned. "So speaks our limping cousin, who allowed a mere five Aenir to remove him from the race."

Gaelen chuckled. "I meant it, though. I don't think he can beat you, Lennox. I don't think there's a man alive to beat you. You'll see."

"That's a comforting thought, Gaelen. And I thank you for it." Lennox grunted as he stretched his back.

"Roll on your stomach," commanded Layne. "I'll knead that muscle for you."

Caswallon helped Gaelen to his feet, for his leg stiffened as he sat. "Let's get some food. How do you feel?"

"I ache. Damn, Caswallon, I wish I'd run in that race."

"Why?"

"I wanted to do something for the clan. Be someone."

"You *are* someone. And we all know you would have won. But it was better for Agwaine to do it."

"Why?"

"Because Agwaine needed to do it. Today he learned something about himself. In some ways he's like his father, full of doubts. Today he lost a lot of them."

"That may be good for Agwaine, but it doesn't help me."

"How true," said Caswallon, ruffling Gaelen's hair. "But there is always next year."

That afternoon began with the rope haul, a supreme test of a man's strength and stamina. The contestant looped a rope around his body and braced himself. On the other end three men sought to tug him from his feet. After ten heartbeats a fourth man could be added to the team, ten beats later another man, and so on.

This time Orsa went first. The men trying to dislodge him were Farlain clansmen. Bracing his foot against a deeply embedded rock, he held the first three men with ease, taunting them and exhorting them to pull harder. By the time six men were pulling against him he had run out of jeers, saving his breath for the task in hand. The seventh man proved too much for him and he fell forward, hitting the ground hard. He was up in an instant, grinning and complaining that the rock beneath his foot had slipped.

Lennox stepped up to the mark, a blanket rolled across his shoulders to prevent rope burn. Swiftly he coiled the rope, hooking it over his shoulder and back. Then he checked the stone; it was firm. He braced himself and three Aenir warriors took up the slack.

A fourth man was sent forward, then a fifth. Lennox wasted no energy taunting them; he closed his mind to his opponents. He was a rock set in the mountain, immovable. A tree, deeply rooted and strong. His eyes closed, his concentration intense, he felt the building of power against him and absorbed it.

At last the pressure grew too great and he gave way, opening his eyes to count his opponents.

Nine men!

Dropping the rope, he turned to Orsa. The Aenir warrior met his gaze and nodded slowly. He was not smiling now as he walked forward to stand before the dark-haired clansman. Blue eyes met grey. Orsa was in his late twenties, a seasoned warrior who had never been beaten and never would be. His confidence was born of knowledge, experience, and the pain borne by others. Lennox was nearing eighteen, untried in war and combat, but he had faced the beast and stood his ground.

Now he faced the Aenir and his gaze remained cool and steady. Orsa nodded once and turned away.

With two events each, the Whorl Championship would be decided in the open wrestling, a cultured euphemism for a fight where the only rule was that there were no rules. It was held in a rope circle six paces in diameter, and the first to be thrown from the ring was the loser. As they prepared, Caswallon approached Lennox and whispered in his ear. The huge clansman nodded, then stepped into the circle.

Orsa stepped in to join him and the two men shook hands, acknowledging the cheers of the crowd. Then they backed away and began to circle, hands extended.

Suddenly Lennox stepped inside and lightly slapped Orsa's face. Expecting a punch, the Aenir ducked and stepped back. Lennox flicked his hand out again, this time slapping Orsa's arm. Someone in the crowd began to laugh and others joined in. Lennox dummied a right, then slapped Orsa once more, this time with his left hand. The laughter swelled.

Orsa's blue eyes glittered strangely and he began to tremble. With a piercing scream he charged his tormentor. No more did he seek merely to throw him from the circle. Now only death would avenge the insult.

Orsa was once again a baresark!

Lennox met the charge head-on, swiveling to thunder a right hook to Orsa's bearded chin. The Aenir shrugged off the blow and charged again. This time Lennox hit him with both hands, but a wildly swinging punch from Orsa exploded against his ear. Lennox staggered. A left-hand punch broke Lennox's nose, blood spattering to his chin. Warding off the attack with a desperate push, the clansman moved back to the edge of the circle. Orsa charged once more, screaming an Aenir battle cry. At the last moment Lennox dropped to his knees, then surged upright as Orsa loomed over him. The speed of the rush carried Orsa on, flying headlong over his opponent to crash into the crowd beyond the circle.

The fight was over and Lennox had won. But Orsa in his berserk rage knew nothing of tournaments and petty victories. Hurling aside the men who helped him to his feet, he leaped back into the circle where Lennox was standing with arms raised in triumph.

"Look out!" shouted Gaelen and a score of others.

Lennox swung around. Orsa's massive hand encircled the clansman's throat. Instinctively Lennox tensed the muscles of his neck against the crushing strength of the man's fingers. His own hands clamped down on Orsa's throat, blocking his demonic snarling.

The crowd fell silent as the two men strained and swayed in the center of the circle.

Then the tall, red-caped figure of Drada appeared, pushing through the mass. In his right hand he carried a wooden club that he hammered to the back of his brother's skull. Orsa's eyes glazed and his grip loosened. Drada hit him once more and he fell. Lennox stepped back, rubbing his bruised throat.

Orsa staggered to his feet, turning to his brother. "Sorry," he said, and shrugged. He walked to Lennox, gripping his hand. "Good contest," he said. "You're strong."

"I don't think any man will ever carry the Whorl Stone as far as you did," Lennox told him.

"Maybe so. Why did you slap me?" The question was asked so simply and directly that Lennox laughed nervously, unable at first to marshal his thoughts. But Orsa waited patiently, no sign of emotion on his broad face.

"I did it to make you angry, so you would lose control."

"Thought so. Beat myself—that's not good." Still nodding, he walked away. Lennox watched him, puzzled, then the crowd swamped him, slapping his back and leading him onto the Hunt Lord's platform to receive the congratulations of the Games Lord.

As the crowd moved away, Drada approached Caswallon. "It was your advice, was it not, to make my brother baresark?"

"Yes."

"You are proving to be troublesome, Caswallon."

"I'm glad to hear it."

"No sensible man should be glad to make an enemy."

"I haven't made an enemy, Drada. I've recognized one.
There is a difference."

The Whorl Dance had begun around a dozen blazing fires,
and the eligible maidens of the Farlain chose dancing companions from the waiting ranks of clansmen. There was
music from the pipes, harsh and powerful; from the flute,
wistful and melodic; and from the harp, enchanting and fey.
It was mountain music, and stronger than wine upon the
senses of the men and women of the clans.

Deva danced with Layne, the Spear Champion, while
Gaelen sat alone, fighting a losing battle against self-pity.
His leg ached and he eased it forward under the table, rub-
bing at the swollen thigh.

Gwalchmai found him there just before midnight. The
young archer was dressed in his finest clothes, a cloak of soft
brown leather over a green embroidered tunic. "No one should
be alone on Whorl Night," said Gwal, easing in to sit opposite his comrade.

"I was just waiting for a girl with a swollen left leg, then
we could hobble away together," said Gaelen, pouring more
mead wine into his goblet.

"I have two legs, but have not found a partner," said Gwal,
helping himself to Gaelen's wine.

"Come now, Gwal, there must be five hundred maidens
here."

"They are not what I want," said Gwalchmai sadly. Gaelen
glanced at his friend. Gwal's hair was flame-red in the firelight, his face no longer boyish but lean and handsome.

"So what do you want . . . a princess?"

Gwalchmai shrugged. "That is hard to answer, Gaelen.
But I know I shall never wed."

Gaelen said nothing. He had known for some time, as had
Layne and Lennox, that Gwalchmai had no interest in the
young maidens of the Farlain. The boys did not understand it,
but only Gaelen suspected the truth. In Ateris he had seen

many who shared Gwalchmai's secret longings. "You know what I am, don't you?" said Gwalchmai, suddenly.

"I know," Gaelen told him. "You are Gwalchmai, one of the Beast Slayers. You are a clansman, and I am proud to have you for my friend."

"Then you don't think . . . ?"

"I have told you what I think, cousin," said Gaelen, reaching forward to grip Gwalchmai's shoulder.

"True enough. Thank you, my friend." Gwalchmai sighed—and changed the subject. "Where is Caswallon?"

"Escorting the Aenir back to Aesgard."

"I am not sorry to see them go," said Gwal.

"No. Did you hear about Borak?"

"The runner? What about him?"

"He was found this evening hanging from a tree on the west hill."

"He killed himself?"

"It seems so," said Gaelen.

"They're a strange people, these Aenir. I hope they don't come back next year."

"I think they will, but not for the Games," said Gaelen.

"You're not another of those war bores?"

"I'm afraid so."

"What could they gain? There are no riches in Druin."

"War is a prize in itself for the Aenir. They live for it."

Gwalchmai leaned forward on his elbows, shaking his head. "What a night! First I lose in the archery, then I get maudlin, and now I'm sitting with a man who prophesies war and death."

Gaelen chuckled. "You were unlucky in the tourney. The wind died as the Aenir took his mark, and it gave him an edge."

"A thousand blessings on you for noticing," said Gwal, grinning. "Have you ever been drunk?"

"No."

"Well, it seems the only enjoyment left to us."

"I agree. Fetch another jug."

Within an hour their raucous songs had attracted a small following. Lennox and Agwaine joined them, bringing fresh supplies, then Layne arrived with Deva.

The drink ran out just before dawn and the party moved to sit beside a dying fire. The songs faded away, the laughter eased, and the talk switched to the Games and the possible aftermath. Deva fell asleep against Layne; he settled her to the ground, covering her with his cloak.

Gaelen watched him gently tuck the garment around her and his heart ached. He looked away, trying to focus on the conversation once more. But he could not. His gaze swept up over the mountains, along the reddening skyline. Caswallon had told him his theory of the Aenir plan to demoralize the clans. The scale of their error was enormous. By the end they achieved only the opposite. Men of every clan had cheered Agwaine and Lennox against a common enemy; they had united the clans in a way no one had in a hundred years.

He heard someone mention his name and dragged his mind back to the present.

"I'm sorry you missed the race," said Agwaine.

"Don't be. You were magnificent."

"Caswallon advised me."

"It was obviously good advice."

"Yes. I'm sorry he and my father are not friends."

"And you?"

"What about me?"

"How do you feel now . . . about Caswallon, I mean?"

"I am grateful. But I am my father's son."

"I understand."

"I hope that you do, cousin." Their eyes met and Agwaine held out his hand. Gaelen took it.

"Now this is good to see," said Lennox, leaning forward to lay his hand upon theirs. Layne and Gwalchmai followed suit.

"We are all Farlain," said Layne solemnly. "Brothers of the spirit. Let it long remain so."

"The Five Beast Slayers," said Agwaine, grinning. "It is fitting we should be friends."

Deva opened her eyes and saw the five young men sitting silently together. The sun cleared the mountains, bathing them in golden light. She blinked and sat up. Just for a moment she seemed to see a sixth figure standing beyond them—tall, she was, and beautiful, silver-haired and strong. By her side hung a mighty sword and upon her head was a crown of gold. Deva shivered and blinked again. The Queen was gone.

Chapter Seven

Gaelen stood on the lip of a precipice looking down on Vallon from the north, listening to the faint sounds of the falls echoing up through the mountains. Spring had finally arrived after yet another bitter winter, and Gaelen had been anxious to leave the valley to stretch his legs and open his heart to the music of the mountains. He had grown during the winter, and constant work with axe and saw had added weight to his arms and shoulders. His hair was long, hanging to his shoulders, and held back from his eyes by a black leather circle around his brow. Kareen—before her marriage to the west valley crofter, Durk—had made it for him, as well as a tunic of softest leather, polished to a sheen, and calf-length moccasin boots from the same hide. His winter cape was a gift from Caswallon, a heavy sheepskin that doubled as a blanket. During the cold winter months he had allowed his beard to grow, shutting his ears to gibes about goose down from Maeg and Kareen. It had taken long enough but now, as he stood on the mountainside in the early morning sunshine, it gave him that which he desired above all else—the look of manhood.

Gone was the frightened, wounded boy brought home by Caswallon two years before. In his place stood a man, tall and strong, hardened by toil, strengthened by experience. The only reminders left of the hunted boy were the blood-filled left eye, and the white streak in his hair above the jagged scar on his forehead and cheek.

The black and grey war hound by his side growled and

rubbed against him. Gaelen dropped his hand to pat its massive head. "You don't like these high places, do you, boy?" said Gaelen, squatting beside the animal. It lifted its head, licking his face until he pushed it away laughing.

"We've changed, you and I," he said, holding the dog at bay. It had the wide jaws of its dam and the heavy shoulders of its breed, but added to this it also had the rangy power of the wolf that had sired it.

The wolf in it had caused problems with training, and both Caswallon and Gaelen had despaired at times. But slowly it had come around to their patient handling, until at last Gaelen had walked it unleashed among a flock of sheep. He told it to sit, and it obeyed him. But its eyes lingered over the fat, slow ewes and its jaws salivated. After a while it had hunkered down on its haunches and closed its eyes, unable to bear such mouth-watering sights any longer.

Under Caswallon's guidance, Gaelen taught the hound to obey increasingly complex instructions, beginning with simple commands such as "sit," "heel," and "stay." After that it was taught to wait in silence if Gaelen lifted his hand palm outward. Finally Caswallon built a dummy of wood and straw, dressed it in old clothes, and the hound was taught to attack it on Gaelen's command of "kill." This training was further refined with the call "hold," at which command the dog would lunge for the dummy's arm.

Painstakingly they honed the dog's skills. Once it attacked, only one call would stop it: *Home.* Any other call, even from Gaelen, would be ignored.

"This," said Caswallon, "is your safeguard. For a dog is a creature of instinct. You may order it to attack, but another voice may call it back. 'Home' should remain a secret command. Share it not even with your friends."

Gaelen called the beast Render. The hound's nature was good, especially with Caswallon's son Donal, now a blond toddler who followed Render—or Wenna, as he called it—about the house, pulling its ears and struggling to climb on its back. Attempts to stop him would be followed by floods of tears and the difficult-to-answer assertion, "Wenna like it!"

Maeg was hard to convince that Render was a worthy addition to the household, but one afternoon in late winter it won her over. Kareen had ventured into the yard to fetch wood for the fire, but had not secured the kitchen door on her return. Donal had sneaked out to play in the snow, an adventure of rare magic.

He was gone for more than half an hour before his absence was noted. Maeg was beside herself. Caswallon and Gaelen were at the Long Hall where Caswallon was being elected to the Council in place of an elderly clansman who had collapsed and died soon after the Games. Maeg wrapped a woolen shawl about her shoulders and stepped out into the storm. Within minutes it had grown dark and as she called Donal's name the wind whipped her words from her mouth. His track had been covered by fresh snow.

Kareen joined her. "He'll die in this," yelled Maeg.

Render padded from the house. Seeing the hound, Maeg ran to it and knelt by its side.

"Donal!" she shouted, pushing the dog and pointing out past the yard. Render tilted his head and licked her face. "Fetch!" she shouted. Render looked around. There was nothing to fetch. "Donal! Fetch Donal!" Render looked back toward the house and the open door that led to the warm hearth. The hound didn't know what the women were doing out in the cold. Then its ears came up as a wolf howled in the distance. Another sound came, thin and piping. Recognizing instantly the pup child of Caswallon, Render padded off into the snow.

Maeg's hands and feet were freezing, but she had no idea if the dog had understood her and she had not heard the faint cry, so she continued to search, terror growing within her and panic welling in her mind.

Render loped away into a small hollow hidden from the house. Here it found the toddler who had slipped and rolled down onto a patch of ice and was unable to get up. Beyond him sat two wolves, tongues lolling.

Render padded toward the boy, growling deep in his throat. The wolves stood, then backed away as the war hound advanced. Canny killers were the grey wolves, but they knew a better killer when they saw him.

"I cold, Wenna," said Donal, sniffing. "I cold."

Render stopped by the boy watching the wolves carefully. They backed away still farther, and satisfied, Render nuzzled Donal, but the boy could not stand on the ice. Render ducked his head, taking the boy's woolen tunic in his teeth. Donal was lifted clear of the ice and the huge dog bounded up the slope and back toward the house.

Maeg saw them and waded through the snow toward them, but Render loped past her and into the kitchen. He was cold and missed the fire. When Maeg and Kareen arrived Donal and Render were sitting before the hearth. Maeg swept Donal into her arms.

"Wolfs, Mama. Wenna scare 'em away."

Maeg shuddered. Wolves! And her child had been alone. She sat down hurriedly.

Neither of the women told Caswallon of the adventure, but he knew something was amiss when Maeg explained she had given his own cold meat supper to the hound.

Caswallon's activities during the summer and winter puzzled many of the clansmen. He drove no cattle to Aesgard, nor delivered grain and oats. The fruit of his orchards disappeared, and no man knew where, though the carts were driven into the mountains by trusted workers. There, it was said, they were delivered to the druids.

In the meantime, Caswallon gathered around him more than a hundred clansmen, and several of these he paid to scout around Aesgard and report on Aenir movement.

Cambil had been furious, accusing Caswallon of amassing a private army. "Can you not understand, Caswallon, that such deeds make war more likely?" said the Hunt Lord. "You think me foolish for trying to forge friendships among the

Aenir, I know that. As I know they are a warlike people, harsh and cruel. But as Hunt Lord I must consider the long-term well-being of my people. We could not win a war with the Aenir; they would swamp us. What I have tried—and will continue to try—to do is to make Asbidag aware of the futility of war in the Highlands. We have no gold, no iron. There are no riches here. This he understands. What is more important is that he must feel no threat from us. It is in the Aenir nature to see enemies all around. If we can make them our friends, there will be no war."

Caswallon listened in silence until Cambil had finished speaking. "Under different circumstances I would agree with every word, cousin," he said at last. "War is the last beast an intelligent man would let loose. Where I think you are wrong is in believing that the Aenir see war as a means to an end. For them it is the end in itself. They live to fight, they lust for slaughter and blood. Even their religion is based on the glory of combat. They believe that only if they die in battle will their souls be blessed with an eternity of pleasure. Now that their war with the Lowlanders is over where else can they turn for war, save with us? I respect you, cousin—and I mean that truly. You have acted with honor. Yet now is the time to open your eyes and see that your efforts have been in vain. The Aenir are massing troops on the southern borders."

Cambil shook his head. "Asbidag assures me that the troops are being gathered in order for the majority of them to be disbanded and offered land to farm, as a reward for loyal service. You are wrong, Caswallon. And the wisdom of my course will be appreciated in the years to come."

Despite Cambil's assurances Caswallon advised the Council to marshal a militia against a spring invasion. They refused, agreeing with the Hunt Lord that there were no indications the Aenir nursed any hostile intent toward the clan. The feeling was not unanimous. Badraig and Leofas supported Caswallon openly. Beric, a tall balding warrior from the northern valley, voted with them, but said nothing.

"You have a hundred men, Caswallon," said Leofas as the

four met after the spring banquet. "I can muster eighty crofters. Badraig and Beric the same between them. When the Aenir come it will be like a sudden storm. Three hundred men will not stop them."

"Let us be honest," said Badraig. "The Farlain united could not stop them. If every man took up his sword and bow we would have . . . what? . . . five thousand. Against a force five times as great." Badraig had changed since the beast killed his son. His hair was grey and he had lost weight, growing haggard and lean.

"That is true," agreed Caswallon, "but we can wear them down. We'll fight no pitched battles; we'll harry them, cutting and running. Soon they'll tire and return to Aesgard."

"That will depend on why they're here," said Beric. "If they take the valleys we'll have no way to support ourselves. We'll die in the mountains, come winter."

"Not necessarily," said Caswallon. "But that debate can wait for a better time. What worries me is not the long-drawn-out campaign, but the first strike. If they hit the valleys unawares, the slaughter will be horrific."

"There is not a day we do not have a scout watching them," said Leofas. "We should get at least an hour's warning."

Six hours' march to the east, the crofter Arcis breathed his last. His arms had been nailed to the broad trunk of an oak and his ribs had been opened, splaying out from his body like tiny tattered wings.

The blood-eagle had arrived in the Farlain.

One Aenir army burst upon the villages and crofts of the Haesten, bringing fire and death into the darkest part of the night. Homes blazed and swords ran with blood. The Aenir swept into the valley of Laric, hacking and slaying, burning and looting. The Haesten had not time to group a defense, and the survivors streamed into the mountains, broken and panic-stricken.

A Pallides hunter, camped on the hillside inside Haesten territory, watched stunned as the Aenir charged into the valley. As if in a dream he saw the warriors in the garish armor and winged helms race down to the homes of the Haesten, thrusting burning brands through open windows. And he viewed with growing horror the massacre of the clan. He saw women dragged forth, raped, and then murdered; he saw babies speared; he saw small pockets of Haesten resistance swallowed up in rings of steel.

Then he rose and began to run, stumbling over tree roots and rocks in the darkness.

He reached the grey house of Maggrig two hours before dawn. Within minutes the war horn of the Pallides sounded. Women and children hastily packed clothing and food and were led into the mountains. Thinking there was only one Aenir army, Maggrig miscalculated, and the evacuation was still under way as a second Aenir force, led by Ongist, fell upon them.

Maggrig had eight hundred warriors at his back, with messengers sent for perhaps five hundred more. As he stood on the hillside, watching the Aenir pour into the valley, he reckoned their numbers were in excess of five thousand. Beside him the grim-eyed swordsman Intosh, the Games Champion, cursed and spat. The two men exchanged glances. Whatever decision they made now would lead to tragedy.

The enemy were sweeping down toward the last file of women and children. If Maggrig did nothing they would die. If the Pallides countercharged they would be cut to pieces. In his heart Maggrig knew it was sensible to leave the stragglers and fight a defensive retreat, protecting the majority.

But he was Clan, and these stragglers were his people.

He lifted his sword, shifted his shield into place, and began to run down the hillside toward the Aenir. Eight hundred Pallides warriors followed him without hesitation. Seeing them come, the Aenir turned from the line of women and children. Their deaths would come later.

The two forces collided. Swords clashed against iron

shields, against close-set mail rings, against soft flesh and brittle bones. The clansmen wore little or no armor and yet the speed and ferocity of their assault made up for it. Intosh, fighting with two swords and no shield, cut a bloody swath through the Aenir, while Maggrig's power and cunning sword craft protected his right flank.

For some minutes the clan held, but then the weight of the Aenir pushed them back. Maggrig parried a wild cut from an axe-wielding warrior, countering with a swift thrust to the belly.

He glanced back at the mountainside. It was clear. With no way of estimating the losses among the warriors, Maggrig bellowed, "Pallides away!" The survivors turned instantly, sprinting for the mountainside. Screaming their triumph, the Aenir swept after them. Halfway to the trees, Maggrig glanced left and right. There were five hundred still with him.

"Cut! Cut! Cut!" he roared. At the sound of their battle cry the Pallides swung about and flung themselves on the pursuing warriors. In their eagerness to overhaul their enemy, the Aenir had lost the close-compacted formation of the battle in the valley. The swiftest of them had outdistanced their comrades and they paid with their lives.

"Pallides away!" shouted Maggrig once more, and the clansmen turned, racing for the relative haven of the trees.

The Aenir surged after them. A leading warrior screamed suddenly, his fingers scrabbling at a black-shafted arrow that hammered into his throat. Another died, and another. The Aenir fell back as death hissed at them from the darkness of the woods.

Within minutes, Maggrig sent his men forward to catch up with the clan, then beckoned Intosh to join him. Together they eased their way through to the women archers hidden by the timberline.

"Well done, Adugga," said Maggrig as a dark-haired woman rose up before him, bow in hand. "It was good thinking."

"It will not stop them for long. They'll outflank us."

"We'll be long gone by the time they do. They may be fine warriors, but they'll not catch us."

"That may be true, Hunt Lord. But where will we go?" asked Adugga.

"To the Farlain."

"You think we'll get a friendly welcome?" asked Intosh.

"Unless I am mistaken, the Aenir will be upon them before we arrive."

"Then why go there?"

"My son Caswallon has a plan. We've spoken of it often, and at this moment it seems to be the best hope we have. We are making for Attafoss."

Maggrig stepped forward, parted the bush screen, and gazed down upon the burning valley. The Aenir were sitting on the hillside just out of bowshot. "They're waiting for dawn," said Maggrig, "and that will not be long in coming. Let's away!"

In the first valley of the Farlain, Caswallon was awakened before dawn by a frenzied hammering at his door. He rolled from the bed and ran downstairs.

Outside was Taliesen. The old man, red-faced and wheezing, leaned on his oak staff. Catching his breath, he gripped Caswallon by the arm.

"The Aenir are upon us! We must move now."

Caswallon nodded and shouted for Maeg to dress Donal, then he helped the druid into the kitchen, seating him by the hearth. Leaving him there, Caswallon lifted his war horn from its place on the wall and stepped into the yard.

Three times its eerie notes echoed through the valley. Then it was answered from a score of homes and the clarion call was taken up, at last reaching the crofts of the outer valleys. Men and women streamed from their homes toward the Games field, the men carrying bows, their swords strapped to their sides, the women ready with provisions and blankets.

Caswallon opened the wooden chest that sat against the

far wall of the kitchen. From it he took a mail shirt and a short sword. Swiftly he pulled the mail shirt over his tunic and strapped the sword to his side. Taking the war horn, he tied its thong to his baldric and settled it in place.

"How long do we have, Taliesen?"

"Perhaps an hour. Perhaps less."

Caswallon nodded. Maeg came downstairs carrying Donal, and the four of them left the house. Caswallon ran on ahead to where hundreds of mystified clansmen were gathering.

Leofas saw him and waved as Caswallon made his way to him. "What is happening, Caswallon?"

"The Aenir are close. They've crossed the Farlain."

"How do you know this?"

"Taliesen. He's back there with Maeg."

Caswallon helped the druid push through the crowd to make his way to the top of the small hill at the meadow known as Center Field. The old man raised his arms for silence.

"The Aenir have tonight attacked the Haesten and the Pallides," he said. "Soon they will be here."

"How do you know this, old man?" asked Cambil, striding up the hillside, his face crimson with anger. "A dream perhaps? A druid's vision?"

"I know, Hunt Lord. That is enough."

"Enough? Enough that you can tell us that two days' march away a battle is taking place. Are you mad?"

"I don't care *how* he knows," said Caswallon. We have less than an hour to move our people into the mountains. Are we going to stand here talking all night?"

"It is sheer nonsense," shouted Cambil, turning to the crowd. "Why would the Aenir attack? Are we expected to believe this old man? Can any of us see here what is happening to the Pallides? And what if the Aenir have attacked them? That is Pallides business. I warned Maggrig not to be bullheaded in his dealings with Asbidag. Now enough of this foolishness, let's away to home and bed."

"Wait!" shouted Caswallon, as men began to stir and move. "If the druid is wrong, we will know by morning; all we will have lost is one night on a damp mountainside. If he is right, we cannot defend this valley. If Maggrig and Laric have been crushed as Taliesen says, then the Aenir *must* attack the Farlain."

"I'm with you, Caswallon," shouted Leofas.

"And I," called Badraig. Others took up the shout, but not all.

Debates sprung up, arguments followed. In despair Caswallon once more sounded his war horn. In the silence that followed he told them, "There is no more time to talk. I am leaving now for the mountains. Those who wish to follow me, let them do so. To those who do not, let me say only that I pray you are right."

Cambil had already begun the long walk back to his home and a score of others followed him. Caswallon led Maeg and Taliesen down from the hill and through the crowd. Behind him came Leofas, Layne, Lennox, Badraig, and many more.

"Ah, well, what's a night on the mountains?" he heard someone say, and the following crowd swelled. He did not look back, but his heart was heavy as he reached the trees. Of the three thousand people in the first valley more than two thousand had followed him. Many of the rest still stood arguing in Center Field; others were returning to their homes.

It was at that moment that a ring of blazing torches flared up on the eastern skyline.

Cambil, who was almost home, stopped and stared. The eastern mountainside was alive with armed men. His eyes scanned them. At the center on a black horse sat a man in heavy armor and horned helm. Cambil recognized the Aenir lord and cursed him.

"May the Gods preserve us," whispered Agwaine, who had run to join his father.

Cambil turned to him. "Get away from here. Now! Join Caswallon. Tell him I am sorry."

"Not without you, Father."

Cambil slapped his face viciously. "Am I not Hunt Lord? Obey me. Look after your sister."

On the hill above Asbidag raised his arm and the Aenir charged, filling the night air with strident screams that pushed their hatred before them like an invisible wall. It struck Cambil to the heart and he blanched. "Get away!" he yelled, pushing Agwaine from him.

Agwaine fell back a step. There were so many things he wanted to say. But his father had drawn his sword and was running into the valley toward the Aenir. Agwaine turned away and ran toward the west, tears filling his eyes.

In Center Field hundreds of stragglers drew swords ready to charge to the aid of their beleaguered kin, but Caswallon's war horn stopped them. "You can do nothing for them!" he yelled in desperation. "Join us!"

The valley beyond was filled with Aenir warriors. Fires sprang up in the nearby houses. The clansmen in the Center Field were torn between their desire to aid their comrades and their need to protect their wives and children beside them. The more immediate love tie took hold and the crowd surged up the hillside.

Cambil raced down the slope, sword in hand, blinking away the tears of shame filling his eyes. Memories forced their pictures to his mind—unkind, ugly pictures. Maggrig, calling him a fool at the Games. Taliesen's eyes radiating contempt. And, way back, the cruelest of all, his father, Padris, telling him he wasn't fit to clean Caswallon's cloak.

His feet pounded on the grass-covered slope. The Aenir force had swung ponderously around, like a giant horseshoe, to begin the encirclement of the defenders who waited, grim-faced, swords in hand.

Cambil increased his speed. Another hundred paces and he could die among the people he loved, the people he had betrayed with his stupidity. At least the enemy had not yet seen the exodus led by Caswallon.

Breathless and near to exhaustion, Cambil joined the circle, standing beside the councilor Tesk. "I am so . . . sorry," said the Hunt Lord.

Tesk shrugged. "We all make mistakes, Cambil, my lad. But be warned—I might not vote for you again." The older man gently pushed Cambil back into the circle. "Get your breath back and join me in a little while."

Grinning, Tesk shifted his shield into place, transferring his gaze to the screaming horde almost upon them. He could see their faces now, feel their bloodlust strike him like a malignant breeze.

"The stars are out, Farlain!" he yelled. "It's a fine night for dying."

The Aenir broke upon them like waves upon a rock, and the slaughter began. But at first it was the flashing blades of the Farlain that ripped and tore at the enemy, and many were the screams of the Aenir wounded and dying as they fell beneath the boots of their comrades.

Cambil forced himself alongside Tesk and all fear left the Hunt Lord. Doubts fled, shredding like summer clouds. He was calm at last and the noise of the battle receded from him. A strange sense of detachment came upon him and he seemed to be watching himself cutting and slaying, and he heard the laughter from his own lips as if from a stranger.

All his life he had known the inner pain of uncertainty. Inadequacy hugged him like a shadow. Now he was free. An axe clove his chest, but there was no pain. He killed the axeman, and two others, before his legs gave way and he fell. He rolled to his back, feeling the warmth of life draining from the wound.

He had finally succeeded, he knew that now. Without his sacrifice Caswallon would never have had the time to escape.

"I did something right, Father," he whispered.

"Bowmen to me!" shouted Caswallon. Beside him the silver-haired warrior, Leofas, stood with his sons Layne and Lennox. "Leofas, lead the clan toward Attafoss. Throw out a wide screen of scouts, for before long the Aenir will be hunting us. Go now!"

The clan began to move on into the trees, just as the sun cleared the eastern peaks. Many were the backward glances at the small knot of fighting men ringed by the enemy, and the eyes that saw them burned with guilt and shame.

Three hundred bowmen grouped themselves around Caswallon. Each bore two quivers containing forty shafts. They spread out along the timberline, screened by bushes, thick gorse, and heather.

As the light strengthened Caswallon watched the last gallant struggle of the encircled clansmen. He could see Cambil in with them, battling bravely, and some of the women had taken up swords and daggers. And then it was over. The sword ring fell apart and the Aenir swarmed over them, hacking and slashing, until at last there was no movement from the defenders.

Asbidag rode down the valley and removed his helm. He summoned his captains.

Caswallon could not hear the commands he issued, but he could guess, for the eyes of the Aenir turned west and the army took up its weapons and ran toward the mountainside.

"Do not shoot until I do," he called to the hidden archers. Caswallon notched a shaft to the string as the Aenir spread out along the foot of the slope. They advanced cautiously, many of them lifting the face guards of their helms the better to see the enemy. Caswallon grinned. He singled out a lean, wolfish warrior at the center of the advancing line. At fifty paces he stood, in plain sight of the Aenir, and drew back on the string. The shaft hissed through the air, hammering home in the forehead of the lead warrior.

The Aenir charged . . .

Into a black-shafted wall of death. Hundreds fell within a few paces, and the charge faltered and failed, the enemy warriors sprinting back out of bowshot.

Caswallon walked out into the open and sat down. Laying his bow beside him he opened his hip pouch, removing a hunk of dark bread. This he began to eat, staring down at the milling warriors.

Stung by the silent taunt of his presence, they charged once more. Calmly Caswallon replaced the bread in his pouch, notched an arrow to his bow, loosed the shaft, and grinned as it brought down a stocky warrior in full cry, the arrow jutting from his chest.

The Aenir raced headlong into a second storm of shafts that culled their ranks and halted them. Caswallon, still shooting carefully, eased his way back into the bushes, out of sight. The Aenir fled once more, leaving a mound of their dead behind them.

A young archer named Onic crept through the gorse to where Caswallon knelt. "We've all but exhausted our shafts," he whispered.

"Pass the word to fall back," said Caswallon.

In the valley Asbidag walked among the bodies, stopping to stare down at Cambil's mutilated corpse. "Remove the head and set it on a spear by his house," he told his son Tostig. The Aenir lord unbuckled his breastplate, handing it to a grim-faced warrior beside him. Then he looked around him, eyes raking the timber and the gaunt snow-covered peaks in the distance.

"I like this place," he said. "It has a good feeling to it."

"But most of the Farlain escaped, Father," said Tostig.

"Escaped? To where? All that's out there is wilderness. By tonight Drada will be here, having finished off the Haesten. Ongist will be harrying the Pallides, driving the survivors west into our arms. Once they are destroyed we will take our men into the wilderness and finish the task—that's if Barsa doesn't do it before we arrive."

"Barsa?"

"He is already in the west with two thousand forest-trained warriors from the south. They call themselves Timber Wolves, and by Vatan they're a match for any motley ragbag of stinking clansmen."

"We took no women," complained Tostig. "Most of the young ones killed themselves. Bitches!"

"Drada will bring women. Do not fret."

Asbidag began to move among the bodies once more, turning over the women and the young girls. Finally he stood up and walked toward the house of Cambil.

"Who are you seeking?" asked Tostig, walking beside him.

"Cambil's daughter. Hair like gold, and a spirited girl. Unspoiled. I didn't like the way she looked at me. And I told you to set Cambil's head on a spear!"

Tostig blanched and fell back. "At once, Father," he stammered, running back to the bodies and drawing his sword.

Durk of the Farlain was known as a morose, solitary man. He had no friends and had chosen to spend his life in the high country west of the valley, where he built a small house of timber and grey stone and settled down to a life of expected loneliness. Durk had always been a loner, and even as a child had kept himself apart from his fellows. It was not, he knew, that he disliked people, more that he was not good with words. He had never learned how to engage in light conversation. Crowds unnerved him, always had, and he avoided the dance and the feasts. Girls found him surly and uncommunicative, men thought him standoffish and aloof. Year by year the young clansman felt himself to be more and more remote from his fellows. Durk found this hurtful, but knew that the blame lay within his own shy heart.

But that first winter alone had almost starved him out until his neighbor Onic introduced him to Caswallon's night raids on bordering territories.

In the beginning Durk had disliked Caswallon. It was easy to see why: they were night and day, winter and summer. Where Caswallon smiled easily and joked often, Durk remained sullen with strangers and merely silent with companions.

Yet, for his part, Caswallon seemed to enjoy Durk's company

and little by little his easygoing, friendly nature wore away the crofter's tough shell.

Through Caswallon Durk met Kareen, the gentle child of the house and, in spite of himself, had fallen in love with her. In the most incredible slice of good fortune ever to befall the dark-bearded Highlander, Kareen had agreed to marry him.

She transformed his dingy house into a comfortable home and made his joy complete by falling pregnant in the first month of their marriage. With her Durk learned to laugh at his own failings, and his shyness retreated. At their marriage he even danced with several of Kareen's friends. Laughter and joy covered him, drawing him back into the bosom of the clan, filling the empty places in his heart.

Four days ago, in her eighth month, Kareen had returned to the valley to have the babe in the home of Larcia, wife of the councillor Tesk and midwife to the Farlain.

But last night Durk had heard the war horns blaring and he had set out for the valley, filled with apprehension. In the first light of dawn he had met the column of fleeing clansmen.

Tesk was not among them.

Caswallon had run forward to meet him, leading him away from the column. There Durk heard the news that clove his heart like an axe blade. Tesk had died with Cambil and almost eight hundred others. With them was Kareen. Caswallon had seen her in the circle at the last, a hunting knife in her hand, as the Aenir swept over them.

Durk did not ask why the rest of the clan had not raced back to die with them, although he dearly desired to.

"Come with us," said Caswallon.

"I don't think that I will, my friend," Durk replied.

Caswallon bowed his head, his green eyes sorrowful. "Do what you must, Durk. The Gods go with you."

"And with you, Caswallon. You are the leader at last."

"I didn't want it."

"No, but you are suited to it. You always were."

Now Durk stood at the timberline, gazing down into the

valley, past the gutted homes and the Aenir tents, and on to the mounds of bodies in the center of the field.

He left the trees and began the long walk to his wife.

Two Aenir warriors watched him come. They stood, discarding their food, and moved to intercept him. He was walking so casually, as if on a morning stroll. Could he be a messenger, seeking peace? Or one of Barsa's Timber Wolves, dressed like a clansman.

"You there!" called the first, holding up his hand. "Wait!"

The hand vanished in a crimson spray as Durk's sword flashed through the air. The return cut clove the man's neck. As he crumpled to the grass the second drew his sword and leaped forward. Durk ducked under a whistling sweep to gut the man.

He walked on. Kareen had been no beauty but her eyes were soft and gentle, and her mouth seemed always to be smiling, as if life held some secret enchantment and she alone knew the mystery of it.

In the valley Aenir warriors were moving about, eating, drinking, and swapping stories. The invasion had gone well and their losses had been few, save for the night before against the ferocious clan sword ring. Who would have believed that a few hundred men and women could have put up such a struggle?

Durk moved on.

No one stopped him or even seemed to notice him as he walked to the mound of bodies and began to search for Kareen. He found her at the center, lying beneath the headless corpse of Cambil. Gently he pulled her clear and tried to wipe the blood from her face, but it was dried hard and did not move.

By now his actions had aroused the interest of five warriors who wandered forward to watch him. Durk felt their eyes upon him and he laid Kareen to the ground. He stood and walked toward them, his face expressionless, his dark eyes scanning them.

They made no move toward their swords until he was almost upon them. It was as if his calm, casual movements cast an eldritch spell.

Durk's sword whispered from the scabbard . . .

The spell broke.

The Aenir scrabbled for their blades as Durk's sword licked into them. The first fell screaming; the second tumbled back, his throat spraying blood into the air. The third died as he knelt staring at the gushing stump of his sword arm. The fourth hammered his sword into Durk's side, then reeled away dying as the clansman shrugged off the mortal wound and backhanded a return cut to the man's throat. The fifth backed away, shouting for help.

Durk staggered and gazed down at the wound in his side. Blood flowed there, soaking his leggings and pooling at his feet. More Aenir warriors ran forward, stopping to stare at the dying clansman.

"Come on then, you woman killers! Face a man!" he snarled.

A warrior ran forward with sword raised. Durk contemptuously batted aside his wild slash and reversed his own blade into the man's belly.

The clansman began to laugh, then suddenly he choked and staggered. Blood welled in his throat and he spat it clear.

"You miserable whoresons," he said. "Warriors? You're like a flock of sheep with fangs."

Dropping his sword, he turned and staggered back to Kareen's body, slumping beside her. He lifted her head.

A spear smashed through his back and he arched upward violently.

His vision swam; his last sight was Kareen's face.

"I'm so sorry," he said. "I should have been here."

Orsa gazed down at the body, then tore the spear from the clansman's back.

"He was a madman," muttered a warrior behind him.

"He was a *man*," said Orsa, turning and pushing his way through the throng.

The Aenir milled around the corpses for a while, then drifted back to their forgotten meals.

"He was a fine swordsman," said a lean, wolfish warrior, dusting off the chicken leg he'd dropped in the dirt.

"It was stupid," offered a second man, gathering up a bulging wineskin.

"He was baresark," said the first.

"Nonsense. We all know what happens to a berserker—he goes mad and attacks in a blind frenzy."

"No, that's what we do. The clansmen are different. They go cold and deadly, where we are hot. But the effect is the same. They don't care."

"Taken to thinking now, Snorri?"

"This place makes you think," said Snorri. "Just look around you. Wouldn't you be willing to die for a land like this?"

"I don't want to die for any piece of land. A woman, maybe. Not dirt, though."

"Did you enjoy the clanswoman you took last night?"

"Shut your stinking mouth!"

"Killed herself, I hear."

"I said shut it!"

"Easy, Bemar! There's no need to lose your temper."

"It's this place, it gets under my skin. I knew it wouldn't be easy. I felt it in my bones. Did you see the look in that clansman's eyes? Like he thought we were nothing. A flock of sheep with fangs! You could laugh, but he had just slain seven men. Seven!"

"I know," said Snorri. "It was the same last night with their sword ring. It was like hurling yourself against a cliff face. There was no give in them at all; no fear. That scout Ongist caught and blood-eagled—he didn't make a sound, just glared at us as we opened his ribs. Maybe they're not people at all."

"What does that mean?" asked Bemar, dropping his voice to a whisper.

"The witch woman, Agnetha. She can turn men into animals. Maybe the clans are all animals turned into men."

"That's stupid."

"They don't act like men," argued Snorri. "Have you heard one clansman beg? Have you heard any tales of such a thing?"

"They die like men," said Bemar.

"I think they are more. You've heard Asbidag's order. Not one man, woman, or child to be left alive. No slaves. All dead. Doesn't it strike you as strange?"

"I don't want to think about it. And I don't want to talk about it," muttered Bemar, hurling aside the wineskin.

"Wolf men, that's what they are," whispered Snorri.

Caswallon watched helplessly as Durk walked back toward the valley. He knew the clansman was seeking death, and he could not blame him for it. Kareen had been his life, his joy. Even as Maeg meant everything to Caswallon.

The clan column moved on and Caswallon took his place at the head alongside Leofas. Crofters from outlying areas joined the exodus as the day wore on, and many were the questions leveled at the new lord.

Where were they going? What would they do? What had happened to one man's sister? Another's brother? Why did they not turn and fight? Why had the Aenir attacked? Where was Cambil? Who elected Caswallon?

The clansman lost his temper before dusk, storming away from the column and running quickly to the top of a nearby hill. Around him the dying sun lit the valleys of the Farlain, bathing them in blood. Caswallon sank to the ground, staring out over the distant peaks of High Druin.

"It's all a lie," he said softly. Then he began to chuckle. "You've lived a damn lie."

Poor Cambil. Poor, lonely Cambil.

"You should not have feared me, cousin," Caswallon told the gathering darkness. "Your father knew; he was wiser than you."

The night before the young Caswallon had left his foster father's house for the last time, Padris had taken him to the northern meadow and there presented him with a cloak, a dagger, and two gold pieces.

"I will not lie to you, Caswallon," Padris had told him, his keen eyes sorrowful. "You have been a disappointment to me. I have raised you like my own son and you have great talents. But you are not worthy. You have a sharp mind, a good brain, and a strong body. You will prosper. But you are not worthy. There is in you a fear that I cannot fathom. Outwardly you are brave enough, and you take your beatings like a man. But you are not clan. You don't care. What is it that you fear?"

"I fear nothing," Caswallon had told him.

"Wrong. Now I see two fears. The one that you hide, and now the fear of showing it. Go in peace, Caswallon of the Farlain."

"You were right, Padris," Caswallon whispered to the sky. "This is what I feared. Chains. Questions. Responsibilities."

Giving judgments over land disputes, settling rows over cattle or sheep, or thefts, or wayward wives and wandering husbands. Sentencing poachers, granting titles, deciding on the suitability of couples in love, and granting them the right to wed. Every petty problem a double-edged dagger.

And so he avoided the elections.

But what had it gained? The Farlain invaded and thousands dead throughout Druin. And what price the future?

He swore as he heard footsteps approaching. Leofas slumped down beside him, breathing hard. "No sign of pursuit," said the old warrior.

"Good."

"Talk, boy. Shed the burden."

"I would shed the burden if you agreed to lead."

"We've been over that before. I'm not the man for it."

"Neither am I."

"Whisht, lad! Don't talk nonsense. You're doing fine. So far we've saved the greater number of our cousins, and with luck there's another two thousand crofters who would have heard the horns and taken to the hills."

"Damn you, old man. I never gave you much of an argument before, and I should have. You've been on the Council since before I was born. You're respected, everyone would follow you. You're the natural choice. What right have you to shirk your responsibility?"

"None whatsoever, Caswallon. And I cannot be accused of it. A man needs to know his strengths if he is to prosper, and his weaknesses if he is to survive. I know what you are going through but, believe me, you are the best man we have. I'll grant that you would make a bad Hunt Lord; you don't have the application. But this is war. With luck it will be a short, sharp exercise, and you're the man to plan it. Think of it as a giant raid. Ye Gods, man, you were good enough at that."

"But it isn't a raid," snapped Caswallon. "One mistake and we lose everything."

"I didn't say it was easy."

"That's true enough."

"You have faith in Taliesen, do you not?"

"Yes."

"Well, he said you were the only man capable of pulling a victory from this catastrophic beginning. And I believe him."

"I wish I had your faith."

"It's because you don't that convinces me," said Leofas, slapping him on the shoulder. "I'm going to say this once, boy, for I'm not given to compliments. There's a nobility in you, and a strength you've not begun to touch. Rescuing Gaelen showed it to me. It was a fine, bonny thing. But more than that, I remember when we hunted the beast. You lifted Cambil that night when his fear for his son threatened to unman him, and among men who despised you it was you they followed when you walked to the north. When the Queen was dying and delirious you gave her words of comfort. You it was who planned the victory at the Games, and you again who brought us out of the valley.

"So don't sit here bemoaning your fate. You are where you should be: War Lord of Farlain. Do I make myself clear?"

"I should have spoken to you ten years ago," said Caswallon. "Maybe I would have been different."

"Ten years ago you wouldn't have listened. Whoring and stealing filled your mind."

"Good days, though," said Caswallon, grinning.

"Don't say it as though you're letting me into a secret. I was whoring and stealing before you were born. And probably making a better job of it!"

Gaelen awoke, rolling to his back and rubbing his eyes. The night was silent, save for the movement of bats in the trees above him and the skittering sound of badgers in the undergrowth off to the left. These were sounds he knew well. But something else had pierced his dreams, bringing him to wakefulness. His mind was hazy, confused. It had seemed as if horns were blowing far away, whispering in the night breeze.

But now there was silence as Gaelen sat up and looked around him. Render was gone, hunting his supper, and the fire had died down within its circle of rocks. Gaelen added fuel, more for light than heat. As the blaze flared he pushed back his blanket and stood up, stretching the muscles of his back. He was hungry. The sky was lightening and the dawn was not far off. Gathering his bow and quiver, he made his way to the edge of the woods, looking down onto a gently sloping field, silver in the waning moonlight. Upon it were scores of rabbits nibbling at grass and clover. Gaelen settled down on his knees and strung the bow; he then selected an arrow and notched it to the string. Spotting a buck some twenty paces distant, he drew and loosed the shaft. As the buck fell, the other rabbits disappeared at speed. Returning to the fire he skinned the beast, gutting and slicing it for the pot. Render loped through the bushes, jaws bloody, and squatted down beside him, waiting expectantly for the remains.

Gaelen threw the offal to the hound, who set to work on his second meal of the night. As dawn light seeped into the sky, Gaelen found himself thinking of the Queen Beyond. Often her face would come to him, sometimes in dreams but more often as he went about the chores of the day. She had died for him—for them—and Gaelen wished, with all his heart, that he could have repaid her. And what did she mean when she promised to come again?

By midmorning Gaelen and Render were picking their way down a wooded slope alongside a tumbling stream. Every forty or fifty paces the water hissed over rocky falls, gushing at ever-increasing speed toward the valley below. Birds sang in the trees, and crimson flowers bloomed by the water. Every now and then, as they came to a break in the trees, Gaelen stopped and gazed on the mountains, still snow-capped, like old men in a line. Gaelen knew he should be feeling guilty about his leisurely pace and the wide western swing he was making, for there was plenty of spring work back home. But after the winter cooped up in the valley, he needed the solitude.

A woman's scream pierced the glade. Render's head came up, a deep growl starting in his throat. Gaelen flashed his hand up, palm outward, and the dog fell silent. The scream came from the right, beyond a thicket of gorse. Gaelen eased his hunting knife into his hand, released his pack and bow from his shoulders, and moved forward silently. Render padded beside him.

Once in the thicket other noises came to them—the rending of cloth, and slapping sounds as if openhanded blows were being struck. Creeping forward, bent double, Gaelen came to the edge of the thicket. Three Aenir warriors had pinned a young girl to the ground. Two held her arms, the third crouched over her, slashing her clothes with a knife and ripping them from her.

Gaelen calmed the dog and waited. He couldn't see the girl's face, but from the clothes she was Farlain. The Aenir stripped her naked, then one forced her legs apart, dropping

his hand to loosen his breeches. As he did so Gaelen pointed
to the warrior holding the girl.

"Kill!" he hissed. Render leaped forward, covering the
ground in three bounds, snarling ferociously. The three
whirled at the sound, dragging their knives clear. Render's
great jaws closed upon the throat of his victim, the Aenir's
neck snapping with a hideous crack. Gaelen, long hunting
knife in hand, was just behind the dog. He hurdled the beast,
batting aside a wild slash from the second Aenir, then himself backhanded a cut across the man's face. The warrior's
cheek blossomed red and he fell back, dropping his knife.
Gaelen threw himself forward to plunge his own blade
through the man's leather jerkin, up under the ribs, seeking
the heart. The man's eyes opened in shock and pain. Gaelen
twisted the blade to free it from the suction of the man's body
and tore it loose, kicking him away. Spinning, he was just in
time to parry a thrust from the third warrior who aimed a vicious cut at his head. Gaelen ducked beneath it, stepping inside to hammer the knife into the man's groin. The Aenir
screamed and fell. Gaelen dragged the knife clear, punching
it to the man's throat and cutting off his screams. Render, still
growling, tore at his victim, though the man was long dead.

"Home!" hissed Gaelen. In the following silence he listened intently. Satisfied the Aenir were alone, he ran to the
girl.

It was Deva, her face bruised and swollen, her lips cut and
bleeding. She was unconscious. Gaelen gathered what remained of her clothes and lifted the girl to his shoulder. Then
he made his way back through the thicket to his pack and labored on up the slope, keeping to the rocky paths and firmer
areas that would leave less sign of his passing.

His breathing was ragged as he reached the highest point
of the slope, cutting into a sheltered glade where he lowered
Deva to the ground. She was breathing evenly. Her shirt was
in tatters and he threw it to one side. Her skirt had been
ripped in half. Removing it, he spread the cloth and sliced an
opening in the center. Sheathing his knife he lifted the girl to

a sitting position and put the skirt over her head, widening the slash until the garment settled over her shoulders like a cape that fell to her knees. He tore her shirt into strips and fashioned a belt that he tied around her waist, then he laid her back.

"Stay!" he ordered Render and the hound settled down beside the girl. Gaelen gathered up his bow and quiver and retraced his steps to the slope, crouching in the undergrowth, eyes searching the trail.

There were so many questions. Why were the Aenir so far into the Farlain? What was Deva doing alone in the wilderness? What manner of men were these warriors who dressed like foresters and carried hunting knives like the clans? Had the war begun, or were they merely scouts? How many more were searching these woods? He could answer none of the questions.

He had been lucky today, waiting until the men's lust was at its height before launching an attack. But once the enemy discovered the bodies they would be on his trail like wolves after a wounded deer. More than luck would be needed to survive from now on, he knew.

He was at least two days from the valley, but if the war had begun there was no point going east. If it had not, there was little point heading for Attafoss, a day or more to the northeast.

Down the slope he saw a flash of movement and drew back into the bushes. A man appeared, then another, then a file of warriors bearing bows. They did not seem to be hunting a trail, but if they kept moving along the track they would find the bodies. Gaelen waited until the file had passed, counting them, despair growing as the figure topped one hundred.

This was no scouting party.

Pulling back out of sight he ran to the glade, kneeling over Deva, lifting her head and lightly stroking her face. She came awake with a start, a scream beginning as his hand clamped over her mouth.

and rolling his blanket. Taking up his pack, he unstrapped his bow and strung it.

Glancing around, he saw that Render had gone hunting.

"We have a problem," he told the girl.

"They are ahead of us?"

He nodded. "Only two of them. Scouts. They passed in the night."

"Then give me a bow. My marksmanship is good, and you'll need your hands clear for knife work."

He handed her the weapon without hesitation. All clanswomen were practiced with the bow and Deva had the reputation of being better than most.

Slowly they made their way north and east, wary of open ground, until at last the trees thinned and a gorse-covered slope beckoned beyond. It stretched for some four hundred paces.

"You could hide an army down there," whispered Deva, crouching beside him in the last of the undergrowth before the slope.

"I know. But we have little choice. The main force is behind us. They have sent these scouts ahead to cut us off. If we remain here the main body will come upon us. We must go on."

"You go first. I'll wait here. If I spot movement I'll signal."

"Very well. But don't shoot until you are sure of a hit."

Biting back an angry retort, she nodded. What did he think she was going to do? Shoot at shadows? Gaelen left the cover of the trees and moved slowly down the slope, tense and expectant. Deva scanned the gorse, trying not to focus on any one point. Her father had taught her that movement was best seen peripherally.

A bush to the right moved, as if a man was easing through it. Then her attention was jerked away by a noise from behind and she turned. A hundred paces back along the trail, a man had fallen and his comrades were laughing at him. They were not yet in sight, but would be in a matter of moments. She was trapped! Fighting down panic, she notched an arrow to the bow. Gaelen reached the bottom of the slope and glanced back. Deva lifted both hands, pointing one index finger left, the other right. Then she jerked her thumb over her shoulder.

Gaelen cursed and moved. He broke into a lunging run for the gorse, angling to the right, his knife in his hand. Surprised by the sudden sprint, the hidden archer had to step into the open. His bow was already bent.

Deva drew back the bowstring to nestle against her cheek. Releasing her breath slowly, she calmed her mind and sighted on the motionless archer. Gaelen threw himself forward in a tumbler's roll as the man released his shaft. It whistled over his head. Deva let fly, the arrow flashing down to thud into the archer's chest. The man dropped his bow and fell to his knees, clutching at the shaft; then he toppled sideways to the earth.

Coming out of his roll, Gaelen saw the man fall. The second Aenir, a huge man with a braided yellow beard, hurled his bow aside and drew his own hunting knife. He leaped at the clansman, his knife plunging toward Gaelen's belly. Gaelen dived to the left—and the Aenir's blade raked his ribs. Rolling to his feet Gaelen launched himself at the warrior, his shoulder cannoning into the man's chest. Off balance, the Aenir fell, Gaelen on top of him. The blond warrior tried to rise but Gaelen slammed his forehead against the Aenir's nose, blinding him momentarily. As the man fell back Gaelen rolled onto the warrior's knife arm and sliced his own blade across the bearded throat. Blood bubbled and surged from the gaping wound, drenching the clansman. Pushing the body under thick gorse, Gaelen rolled to his feet and ran back to the first man. Deva was already there, struggling to pull the body out of sight into the bushes. Together they made it with scant moments to spare.

Huddled together over the corpse, Gaelen put his arm around Deva, drawing her close as the Aenir force breasted the slope. "If they find the other body we're finished," he said. His knife was in his hand and he knew with bleak certainty that he would cut her throat rather than let them take her.

The enemy moved down the slope. Grim men they were, and they moved cautiously, many notching arrows to bow-strings, their eyes flickering over the gorse. Gaelen took a deep breath, fighting to stay calm; his heart was thudding against his chest like a drum. He closed his eyes; Deva leaned against him and he could smell the perfume of her hair.

The Aenir entered the gorse, pushing on toward the east. Two men passed within ten paces of where they lay. They were talking and joking now, content that the open ground was behind them.

The last of the Aenir moved away out of earshot. Gaelen felt cramped, but still he did not move. It was hard to stay so still, for hiding was a passive, negative thing that leached a man's courage.

"You can let go of me now, clansman," whispered Deva.

He nodded, but did not move. Deva looked up into his face, seeing the tension and fear. Raising her hand, she stroked his cheek. "Help me get this swine's jerkin," she said.

Gaelen released her, smiling sheepishly. He pulled her arrow from the man's ribs and they worked the brown leather jerkin clear. Deva slipped it on over her tunic. It was too large by far and Gaelen trimmed the shoulders with his knife.

"How do I look?" she asked him.

"Beautiful," he said.

"If this is beautiful, you should have been struck dumb at the Whorl Dance."

"I was."

Deva giggled. She looped the man's knife belt around her waist. "You were so forlorn, Gaelen. I felt quite sorry for you, with your swollen leg."

"I felt quite sorry for myself."

"What are your plans now? Why are we heading north?"

"With luck the clan will be there."

"Why should they be?"

"I believe the war has begun. The Aenir will have raided the valleys. But Caswallon has a plan."

"Caswallon!" she snapped. "Caswallon is not Hunt Lord!"

"No, but he should be," hissed Gaelen. A sound in the bushes jolted them, but relief swept over Gaelen as Render's great black and grey head appeared. Kneeling, he patted the dog affectionately, using the time to let the angry moment pass.

"I'm sorry," he said at last. "I did not mean that."

"You meant it. Let's talk no more of it. We've a long way to go."

Chapter Eight

Drada arrived in Farlain valleys on the second day of the invasion, having completed his attack on the Haesten. Throughout the day his men had been scouring the mountains, hunting down clansmen and their families, killing the men and older women, taking the young girls alive. So far they had killed more than a thousand Highlanders.

Leaving a third of his force behind to harry the remnants of Laric's people, he moved on to join his father. There was no word from Ongist and his force, apart from the first message that told of Maggrig's flight into the mountains.

With twenty men Drada rode ahead of the marching army, reining his mount on the high slope above the first valley. Below him were a dozen or so gutted houses; the rest had been taken over by the Aenir, whose tents also dotted the field. Drada was discontented. The assault had not been a complete success. The Haesten were all but wiped out, but the Pallides and the Farlain were still at large.

Barsa's Timber Wolves would harry them in the northwest, but Drada did not share his father's scant regard for the clans' fighting abilities. And he had heard of Cambil's death with regret.

Not that he liked the man, more that he was easy to read, and if the Farlain had to escape Drada would have rested more easily knowing Cambil was Hunt Lord. He didn't need to be a prophet to predict the next leader:

Caswallon!

The viper beneath the Aenir heel.

Spurring his mount he rode down into the valley, past the field where cattle and sheep grazed contentedly. His brother Tostig saw him coming and walked out to meet him, standing before the cairn that housed the combined dead of the first assault.

"Greetings, brother," said Tostig as Drada dismounted, handing the reins to a following rider. "I told you the war would be short and sweet."

Drada stared into his brother's ugly face. "It is not over yet," he said evenly.

Tostig spat. "There's no real fight in these mountain dogs. They'll give us sport for a few weeks, that's all."

"We'll see," said Drada, pushing past him. He entered the house of Cambil, seeking his father. Asbidag sat in the wide leather chair before the hearth, drinking from a silver goblet. Beside him was a jug of mead and a half-eaten loaf. Drada pulled up a chair opposite and removed his cloak. Asbidag was drunk; ale dribbled to his red beard at every swallow, flowing over the crumbs of bread lodged there. His bloodshot eyes turned to Drada and he belched and leaned forward.

"Well?" he snarled.

"The Haesten are finished."

Asbidag began to laugh. He drained the last of the ale and then lifted the silver goblet, crushing it suddenly, the muscles of his forearm writhing as his powerful fingers pressed the metal out of shape.

"Finished? What about the Farlain? Your plan was a disaster." The words were slurred but the eyes gleamed with malevolent intelligence.

"We have the valleys and the Farlain have nowhere to go, and no food supply."

"So you say."

Morgase entered the room and Drada stood and bowed. Ignoring him, she moved to Asbidag and knelt by the chair, stroking the bread from his beard. Asbidag's eyes softened as he gazed on her cool beauty. He lumbered to his feet, pulling her up beside him, his huge hand sliding down her flank. He leered at her and left the room, stumbling on the stairs.

"Wait here," said Morgase. "I shall see you presently."

"I think not, lady. I fear you will be preoccupied for some little while."

"We shall see."

Drada moved from the hard seat to the wide leather chair his father had vacated, easing himself back and lifting his feet to a small table. He closed his eyes, enjoying the comfort. He was tired, he hadn't realized quite how tired. The light was fading. He cursed softly and pushed himself upright, gathering candles from the kitchen. Taking a steel tinderbox from his pouch he struck a flame and lit a candle, placing it in a brass holder on the wall above the hearth. Near the door was a crystal lantern that he also trimmed and lit. Returning to the chair, he tried once more to relax but he could not. He was overtired and filled with the tension only the planning of war could produce.

Morgase slipped silently into the room wearing only a dark silken robe. She knelt by him as she had knelt by his father. He looked down into her cold blue eyes; her cheeks were flushed, her lips swollen and red. By candlelight her face looked younger, softer.

"He is sleeping," she whispered.

"Good. I wish I was."

"Soon, Drada. Soon. Listen to me. I promised you the Gateway to empires. Do you still desire it?"

"Of course." Leaning forward, he rubbed his tired eyes.

"The druids guard the Gateway. They have a hiding place near the great falls called Attafoss. You must lead an army to the north."

"What is this Gateway?"

"I don't know what it is, only what it does. It is an entrance to my own world—a land full of riches and ripe for conquest."

"What do you mean? There is no world to the north, only mountains and sea."

"You are wrong. I was raised in a far land, not of this world. My father was an earl. He was killed in a rebellion when I was seven years old. The land is ruled now by a warrior queen but her armies have fought many battles and they are tired, weary to the bone."

"I have heard of no queen . . ." Drada began.

"Listen to me, you fool," she hissed, her eyes angry. "My brothers and I fought her for six long years, but our army was crushed. I fled north with two trusted servants; they brought me to a druid who lived in the eastern mountains and he told me of a Gate I could pass that would lead to safety. The entrance was marked by a carving at the mouth of the cave, where someone long ago had chipped out the shape of a goblet. He took me there and we entered the cave, which was shallow and dripping with water. He spoke some words by the far wall, and it shimmered and disappeared. Then he beckoned me to follow him and stepped through where the wall had been. I followed and found myself in the mountains near a great waterfall.

"It was like a dream. The old man stepped one pace back—and disappeared. I tried to follow him but there was no way back. I walked south for many days until I reached the city of Ateris in the distance. There I met your father."

Drada was awake now. "You say the Farlain druids control this Gateway?"

"Yes."

"And they can transport men *wherever* they wish to go?"

"Yes. Now do you see?"

"I do indeed."

"The druid who helped me told me that if ever I wished to return I should seek a man named Taliesen."

"I've met him," said Drada.

"He guards the Gate, and controls its power."

Drada leaned back in his chair, the tension easing from him, his weariness slipping away. "Such a Gateway allowed the Aenir to invade these lands," he said. "But once we were through it closed behind us, becoming solid rock. For years we sought sorcerers and witches to open them but none succeeded. What are these Gates? Who made them?"

"I don't know. The old druid told me they had existed for centuries. In my land we have legends of trolls and giants, beasts and dragons. The druid said these were all creatures which had passed through random Gates."

Drada sat back, saying nothing. This was a prize greater than any before. Dreams of empire grew in his mind. Suppose the Gates could send a man *wherever* he wished? Who could resist an army that appeared *within* a walled city? But was it possible? He looked down at Morgase, taking her chin in his hand. "Have you told my father?"

Her hand came down to rest on his thigh. "No, you are the man to lead the Aenir." At her touch he stiffened, his eyes flickering to the darkened doorway.

"Have no fear, Drada. I slipped him a sleeping potion. He will not wake for hours."

He lifted her to his lap and kissed her, his hand slipping beneath her robe.

"Are you worth dying for?" he asked, his voice husky, his face flushed.

"Find out," she told him.

Gaelen and Deva spent their second night in a shallow cave, the entrance hidden by a hastily erected screen of bushes. The day had been fraught, and their trail had been picked up by a second band of Aenir foresters. At one stage they had been sighted and chased for almost a mile before slipping their pursuers. Deva was exhausted, her feet grazed and blistered. Gaelen sliced strips of leather from her jerkin and she set to work shaping them into moccasins; but the leather was soft and they would not last long in the mountains.

They could light no fire and the night was cold. They spent it together, wrapped in Gaelen's blanket.

Gaelen was desperately worried now. The enemy were all around them and there was still open ground to cross. They would never make it. Deva slept on, her head resting on his shoulder. His back was cramped and sore, but he did not move. She was more tired than he, and needed the rest.

What would Caswallon do? he wondered. There must be a way to escape the Aenir net. Closing his eyes, he pictured the route to Attafoss. There were four sections of open ground, where the land dipped away into broad valleys with little or no cover. There was no way to avoid crossing at least one of them. Traveling by day would be suicidal. By night it would be almost as hazardous for, up to now, Gaelen had seen no sign of the Aenir campfires. They could blunder straight into an enemy camp.

In two days Gaelen had killed five enemy warriors. He had often dreamed of the day when he would pay them back for his terror and his wounds. But now be realized there was no joy or satisfaction to be found. He wished they had never come to the Farlain. Wished it with all his heart.

Render stirred beside him, his great head coming up with ears pricked. Gaelen gestured the hound to silence and woke Deva gently, his hand over her mouth.

"Someone's coming," he whispered. Carefully he crept to the mouth of the cave, easing aside the leaves and branches masking the entrance.

The Aenir had returned and were once more scouring the hillside for tracks.

With infinite care Gaelen withdrew his hand, allowing the branches to settle back. Then he drew his knife and waited. Render moved to him, laying his head on Gaelen's shoulder, nostrils quivering as he scented the Aenir. The cave was marginally below ground level, the entrance only three feet high, and Gaelen had uprooted two thick bushes, pulling them into the cave roots first. From outside they would appear to be growing at the base of the cliff.

For an hour or more the Aenir continued their search, then they moved farther down the mountainside out of sight. Gaelen relaxed and crept back to Deva, putting his mouth close to her ear.

"We must wait until nightfall," he whispered. She nodded.

Outside the sun shone brightly, but its warmth could not penetrate the chill of the cave and they sat wrapped in Gaelen's blanket throughout the long afternoon.

Just after dusk Gaelen pushed aside the bushes and climbed from the cave, eyes searching the mountainside. The Aenir had moved on. Deva passed out his pack and bow, then joined him in the open. Gaelen pushed the bush screen back in place.

"We may need to get back here," he said. "It leaves us one hiding place."

They set off in silence, threading a path through the trees toward the first valley. The night was brighter than Gaelen would have liked, a three-quarter moon shining in the clear sky. They stopped at the timberline, wary of leaving the sanctuary of the trees, and remembering the hidden Aenir scouts of the day before.

Stepping out into the open, Gaelen started the long walk to the shadow-shrouded valley. Deva, an arrow notched to the bow, walked just behind him, while Render loped out in a wide circle, content merely to be free of the narrow confines of the cave. The wind was in Gaelen's face and that pleased him, for Render would pick up any scent. Frequently Gaelen glanced at the hound, seeking signs of alarm. But there was none.

It took them an hour to cross the valley and climb the steep slope beyond. With one danger past, the next took its place.

They could not see anything within the trees; overhanging branches shut out the moonlight, creating a wall of darkness. Within the woods could be a hundred, a thousand, Aenir waiting for them.

They had no choice. Hand on knife, Gaelen walked into the darkness, leaning against a broad trunk and allowing his eyes to become accustomed to the stygian gloom. They moved on carefully. It was uncannily still among the trees, not a sound whispered in the night. The breeze had fallen away and above them the branches hung together forming an archway, the trees like colonnaded pillars. No bats skittered in the trees. No animals disturbed the undergrowth. It was like passing through a Hall of the Dead, murky and silent, pregnant with menace.

Render's head came up and he sniffed the air. He made no sound but looked away to the left. Gaelen patted him softly. About twenty paces away he could just make out the silhouette of a seated man. Gaelen stood statue-still. As he stared he could see more men lying on the ground, wrapped in blankets.

An Aenir camp!

Gesturing to Deva, he dropped to his hands and knees and began to crawl. The sentry coughed and spat. Gaelen froze. They eased their way past the group and into the forest beyond. They were climbing now and it became more difficult to move quietly. Sweat ran down Gaelen's face and his breathing grew ragged. He knew that stress was sapping his strength as much as the flight itself. Deva was bearing up well. He smiled grimly. But then she was Clan!

They climbed a steep slope and Gaelen peered over the rim, dropping back almost immediately. Beyond were another twenty Aenir asleep. A sentry was seated on a boulder on the far side. He had—thank God—been looking away when Gaelen appeared. Gaelen edged some thirty paces farther along the slope. Carefully he raised his head over the rim. There was a screen of trees now between them and the Aenir sentry. Swiftly he levered himself over the rim. Render scrambled up after him. Deva handed Gaelen the bow, then smoothly climbed to join them.

Once more in the trees, they breasted the rise and pushed on into the second valley. There was more gorse here and Gaelen felt his confidence rising. Then the breeze picked up once more—and saved their lives.

Render growled, hurtling forward into the gorse. A man's scream rent the night. Deva dropped to one knee, drawing the bowstring back to her cheek. Gaelen ran left, dropping his pack and drawing his knife. Three men ran from the bushes toward them. The first fell, Deva's arrow jutting from his right eye. Gaelen leaped feet first at the second, kicking him in the face; the man fell back. Gaelen hit the ground and rolled as the third Aenir raced past him toward Deva. The girl had no time to draw fully and let fly on half string. The arrow struck the man in the face, ripping open his cheek, but he tore it loose and kept coming. Deva hurled her bow aside as the man leaped upon her, bearing her to the ground.

"I have you now, you bitch!" he shouted, his knife poised above her throat. But a black shadow loomed, and Render's huge jaws clamped down on the man's face, fangs ripping away skin and flesh. Blood sprayed over Deva as the Aenir toppled from her. Weakly he tried to stab the hound, but then came the sound of crunching bones—and his skull shattered.

Gaelen rolled to his feet and hurled himself across the body of the second Aenir, who had been stunned by the kick and was struggling to rise when the young clansman dived upon him. Gaelen's knife plunged into his back. He screamed and thrashed his arms as Gaelen ripped the knife loose, whipping the blade across the man's throat.

Render padded toward him, jaws bloody. The silence that followed was broken by sounds of running men.

Grabbing his pack and bow Gaelen signaled to Deva and began to run, steering away from the pursuers and then cutting north. Beside him Deva ran easily, the bow looped over her left shoulder. Gaelen pushed the pace as hard as he dared, and Deva courageously matched him, though her lungs were burning and her legs aching.

They reached the trees ahead of their pursuers. What they needed now was somewhere to hide. The problem was that in the dark Gaelen had no way of knowing what sort of tracks they were leaving. He halted and grabbed Deva's arm. "Give them something to think about," he said. As the Aenir reached the bottom of the slope she sent a shaft into their ranks, catching a man high in the shoulder. The man cursed loudly, the rest diving to the ground. There were only ten men in the pursuing group, and none of them wanted to rush uphill toward a hidden archer.

"Now let's go," said Gaelen.

Deva shook her head, still fighting to catch her breath. "Need . . . a . . . moment," she said. Taking the bow, he crouched at the edge of the trees, trying to spot any attempt to outflank them.

After a few moments Deva tapped his shoulder. "I'm ready," she told him. He nodded and they slipped away into the trees.

As dawn lit the valleys Gaelen took a desperate gamble. Believing them clear of the Aenir he decided to push on through the day, reaching Attafoss before dark. He knew the risks were great, for there could well be enemy soldiers ahead. But, he thought, they would certainly catch up should he hide all day waiting for darkness. And he had no desire to repeat last night's adventures.

They crossed the open ground and found no sign of the enemy. Render loped out ahead of them, cutting off to chase a hare, but it ducked out of sight and the hound padded back to his master. High in the mountains now, the pursuit far behind them, Gaelen relaxed. Deva also felt tension easing from her.

"You don't say much, Gaelen," she said.

"No. I'm not very good with words."

"Is that true? Or are you just anxious around women?"

"That too."

"Do you like Layne?"

"Yes, he's a good friend."

"He wants to marry me."

Gaelen felt a knot of tension growing within him. Angry and uncertain, he said nothing.

"Well, speak, clansman."

"What is there to say? You did not ask a question. You know that I feel . . . that I would like . . . damn! As I said, I am not good with words. I lived alone for many years as a child. I talked to few people; I never learned the art of conversation. I am dull though I would prefer not to be. It would be nice to make people laugh with a witty jest, but it's not the way I am."

"You are fine the way you are," she said, feeling guilty and a little ashamed. "I'm sorry. I should not have teased you."

"You could have picked a better time," he said, smiling.

"Yes. Do you think the clan will be at Attafoss?"

"I hope so."

"You are a fine man, Gaelen. Truly fine."

"I am glad that you think so. Will you wed Layne?"

"No," she told him softly. "When I was born an old tinker woman made a prediction for me. She said I would be the mother of kings."

"What does that mean? There are no kings."

"Not here in the Highlands," she said, "but there are tales of faraway lands where kings and princes rule. One day a man will come—and I will wed him."

"I don't begin to understand," he said. "What is so important about wedding a king? Or being the mother of one, for that matter? What about love, Deva? Happiness?"

"How could you understand?" she said. "You were an orphan and a thief. It wasn't your fault. But I shall live in a palace, and my name will be known throughout the world. Perhaps forever."

He stood silently for a moment. "I would marry you," he said, "and spend my life making you happy. It is a dream I have had since first I saw you. But I cannot give you a palace, Deva."

She looked up at him and, for a single heartbeat, felt like taking him in her arms and turning her back on the dream she had nurtured. But the dream was too strong and Deva shook her head. "I know that I love you, Gaelen. Truly. But you must find another," she said softly, surprised that the words left her feeling empty and more than a little frightened.

Taking her hand he kissed it. "I'll not ask again," he told

her. "I wish you well in your quest, Deva. I hope your king comes for you."

Caswallon pushed his people hard throughout the days following the invasion. He sent a screen of warriors to the northeast and west, led by Badraig and Onic. Then he chose five hundred men and held them back to form a rear guard against any force the Aenir should send against them. He was desperate for news of Laric and Maggrig. Had the Pallides survived as a clan, or were they sundered throughout the mountains, leaderless? He needed to know. He called for volunteers from among the single men, skilled hunters and trackers, to journey back to the southeast and gather information. Among those who came forward were Layne, Gwalchmai, and Agwaine. Caswallon chose five men, Agwaine among them.

He took them aside, briefing each one, until at last only Agwaine was left. Caswallon placed both hands on the young man's shoulders. "I am truly sorry about what happened to your father," he said. "He was a fine man, a man of honor and great nobility."

"He was a fool, Caswallon. But I loved him well. Better than he knew."

"I doubt that. You meant everything to him. When we tracked you, as you fought the beast, he told me he would leave the Farlain if you did not survive. You were his joy. And as to his being a fool, I want you to think on this: He was made to look foolish by the brutal stupidity of the Aenir. Cambil was right in his philosophy, Agwaine. Sensible men will go to great lengths to avoid the vileness of war. Yet it is also a tragic truth that when war is inevitable, there is no place for sensible men. Intelligence can be a double-edged weapon. One of the blessings of a fine mind is that it allows a man to see both sides of a problem, therefore preventing him from acting in a blind or blinkered way. Your father was such a man. He believed that the Aenir would also see the wisdom of his view. That they did not is not a reflection on him, but a judgment upon them."

Agwaine shook his head. "I would like to believe all that. But you are an intelligent man—and the Aenir did not fool you, did they?"

"No," answered Caswallon slowly, "but then I did not have thousands of lives resting on my deeds, coloring my thoughts, feeding my hopes. Cambil knew that war would mean colossal loss of life. It does make a difference, Agwaine."

"Thank you, cousin, for your words. As you advise, I will think on them. Now what do you want me to do?"

"Find Maggrig and gather as many of the Pallides as you can. Then make for the eastern shore of the lake above Attafoss. There we will plan the destruction of the enemy."

"Do you believe we can win?"

"Be certain of it, Agwaine of the Farlain."

Agwaine grinned. "It would be nice to be certain."

Caswallon took the young man by the arm and led him away from the column. They sat down on the hillside, the stars gleaming above them like gems on a velvet cloak.

"Your father and I grew up together, you know that. You also know we were never friends," said Caswallon softly, meeting Agwaine's glance and noting, with sadness, the man's resemblance to Cambil. "He did not like me, but I don't blame him for that. I never did. He saw in me everything that could destroy the clan: selfishness; disregard for the customs that bound us together. I see that clearly now, and I wish he was here so that I could tell him. Instead, I tell his son.

"The clan thrives because we care for one another. Being Clan is as much a state of mind as a racial fact. Without it we are no different from the Aenir. Cambil understood this. Caring makes us strong, gives us courage."

"Why are you telling me this?" asked Agwaine.

"Have you noticed," countered Caswallon, "how nature gives and takes? The weakest dog in the litter is always the most cunning, the short man often more competitive, the ugly woman given the disposition of an angel. So it is with character. You saw it at the Games. Borak was faster than you, stronger. He even had an accomplice in the woods to ensure victory. And yet he lost, as his kind will always lose. For courage is born of caring. Evil has no depth of character to call on. You want certainty, Agwaine? I give it to you. They cannot conquer the clan."

Agwaine bowed his head. "At this moment," he said, "we are in flight. They outnumber us and they have killed thousands."

"Yes, and many more clansmen will die," said Caswallon, "but we shall not lose. Do not think of their numbers. It means nothing if the terrain is right. Think of your father, and his few hundred men. Aye, and women. Think of how the Aenir broke upon that sword ring. I would wager three Aenir died for every clansman. Think on it. For the Aenir will.

"Deep in their hearts they know the truth. Let you know it too. We are the Farlain, and though we may be ill-suited to it, we carry the torch of light in this war. And the Aenir darkness will not extinguish it."

Agwaine chuckled suddenly, leaning back to rest on his elbows. "Caswallon, you've only been with the Council for a few months and already you're spouting rhetoric."

"I know, and it surprises me. But what is more surprising, perhaps, is that I believe it. With all my soul."

"You believe the force of good will always defeat the force of evil?"

"I do—ultimately."

"Why?"

"I can't argue it, for it springs from the heart and not the mind. Why did the Queen come when you needed her?"

"Chance?"

"From where did you get the strength to beat the faster man?"

"I don't know. But why did the Lowlanders fall? They were not evil."

"I don't say that darkness does not have small triumphs. But we are not Lowlanders, we are the Farlain."

"Now *that* I will agree on," said Agwaine. "And now I'd better be heading for Maggrig."

"Are you more certain?"

"I don't know, but I feel the better for talking."

"Then that must be enough," said Caswallon, rising.

"Take care, Caswallon—and look out for Deva. She should be clear of them. She was visiting Lars with her friend Larain."

"I will send out scouts."

The clan had made camp on the northern slope of a group of hills, where their campfires could not be seen from the south. As night stole over the countryside Caswallon ordered the fires doused, lest the glow be seen against the sky. He sought out Taliesen and together they walked to the hilltop, the old druid leaning heavily on his oak staff. He wore his birds'-feather cloak over a white robe. Caswallon thought him dangerously tired.

"How are you faring?" he asked as they sat together under the bright stars.

Taliesen's eyes gleamed and he smiled. "I will not die on you, Caswallon."

"That does not answer my question."

"I am exhausted. But then I am old." He looked at the young warrior beside him, his eyes full of guile. "Do you know how old?"

"Seventy? Eighty?"

"If I told you my age, would you believe me?"

"Yes. Why would you lie?"

"I will not lie, Caswallon. I am over a thousand years old."

"I was wrong," said Caswallon, grinning. "I do not believe you."

"And yet I speak the truth. It was I who brought Earis here so many centuries ago. On this very hill, he and I looked down on the Farlain and knew joy."

"Stop this jest, Taliesen . . ."

"It is no jest, Caswallon, and I am not speaking to impress you. Of all the clansmen, you alone have the capacity to understand what I am going to tell you. You have an open, inquiring mind and a rare intelligence. You are not prey to superstitions. You make your own judgments. I am more than one thousand years old. I was born out there!" The old man's bony hand flashed out, pointing to the stars. "You've heard tales of the elder race, the vanished people. I am the last of those elders; the last true-blooded anyway. We made the Gates, Caswallon, and we journeyed across distances so great I could not impress on you the scale of it. Think of an ant crossing the Farlain and multiply it a thousand times, and you would have but the first step of my journeys.

"We came here, and from here we spread across the Universe. We were the Star Walkers. We birthed religions and created mythologies wherever man saw us. But then came catastrophe." The druid bowed his head, staring at his hands.

"What happened?" asked Caswallon.

"The Great Gates closed. Suddenly, without warning. Our links with home and distant empires were severed, gone without trace. All that remained were the Lesser Gates: playthings created for students like myself who wished to study the evolution of primitive societies in a controlled environment."

"I do not understand any of this," said Caswallon. "But I read men well, and I believe what you say. Why are you telling me now?"

"Because I need you. Because you are the catalyst. Because the future of the Farlain—my chosen people—rests with you. And because you will see great wonders in the days to come and your mind must be prepared. I cannot explain to you the nature of the skills that created the Gates. So think of it as magic, impossibility made reality. You know that I have a hiding place for the clan. I am going to tell you now where that hiding place is: Golfallin, the first valley of the Farlain."

"What nonsense is this? You will take us back where we have come from?"

"Yes. But there will be no Aenir, no crofts and homes, only virgin land."

"How so?"

"As I did with Earis," said the old man. "The Gates do not merely link different lands, Caswallon. I shall take you all through time itself. We are going back ten thousand years, to a time before the clan, before the Aenir."

"That would be magic indeed."

"You, however, will not be going back. There is a task you must perform."

"Name it."

"You must find the Queen who died and bring her to the Farlain with her army. Only then can you hope to crush the Aenir."

"You want me to find a dead woman?"

"Time, Caswallon. Where I will send you she is still young."

"Why should she aid us?"

The old druid shrugged. "There are some questions I will not answer. But let me say this: The chaos we are enduring was caused—in part—by one selfish man. I am doing all in my power to reverse it."

"Oracle?"

"Yes."

"He told me of his journey," said Caswallon, "and that is why I believe you. He said he took his men through the Gate and came to a realm torn by war. He chose to serve the Queen and gained prominence. He told me he fought many battles until at last he crossed the Gateway once more and became a king in a far land, with an army of thousands at his back. But then he suffered betrayal and fled back to the Gate."

"He did not tell you all, Caswallon. Men rarely do when speaking of their mistakes. He became a king, even as he said, but to do so he made alliances with evil men. One such was Agrist, a rare brute. In return for Agrist's services Ora-

cle gave him the secret of the Gate, and Agrist led his people
through in search of riches and plunder. They thrived in their
new world and grew strong. They became the Aenir, who now
pillage the Farlain. For the Gate Oracle gave them brought
them to the recent past of our world."

"He did tell me," said Caswallon.

The druid gave a thin smile. "Did he also tell you of the
night after Sigarni's great battle when he found the enemy
general's widow and her daughter hiding in a cave? Did he
describe how he raped the mother in front of the daughter,
and of how the noble lady slew herself?"

"No," replied the clansman.

"No," echoed Taliesen. "Nor did he say how he stole the
legendary Sword of Ironhand from the Queen, and used its
power to build his own kingdom from the blood of innocents. As I said men rarely tell the whole truth of their iniq-
uities. I have spent years, Caswallon, trying to repair the
damage his pride and ambition caused."

Caswallon turned away to gaze out over the silhouetted
mountains, black against a grey sky. "I feel like a child taught
to scrawl his name, who is given a book and told to read it. I
can make out some of the letters, but the words are lost to
me. Gateways, journeys through time." He glanced at the old
man, holding his gaze. "If we can make such journeys, why
can we not merely go back a few days and save all the people? We could hit the Aenir *before* they invade."

Taliesen nodded. "What if I told you that we did? And that
it failed and the Farlain were destroyed?"

"Now you have lost me utterly."

"That is what makes the chaos so terrible," said Taliesen.
"There are so many alternative realities. If I told you now
how many times I have tried to prevent an Aenir victory you
would think me mad. The complexities and paradoxes created are legion. Armies out of their time, dead men who were
destined to live and achieve greatness, women who should
have borne proud sons murdered in their childhood. Destiny
thwarted, changed—the Gateways themselves trembling

under the weight of the chaos." Taliesen sighed. "Do you know how many times you and I have had this conversation? Of course you don't, but it runs into scores, Caswallon. And how many times have I seen the clans destroyed, the Aenir triumphant? Hundreds. Now I grow older and more frail, and the task is as great as ever it was."

Caswallon smiled grimly. "I doubt that I can learn what you have to teach, old man. You are taking the clan back to before they were born, and then I shall seek help from a queen already dead. Do you hold more surprises for me, Taliesen?"

The Druid Lord did not answer. He leaned back, gazing at the stars, naming them in his mind until he fastened on the farthest, its light flickering like a guttering candle.

Taliesen pushed himself to his feet, his heart heavy, his mind tired. "Aye, I have more surprises, War Lord," he said. "If we are to win, Caswallon, which is not likely, then you will change and suffer as no Farlain has before you." Taliesen sighed. "I do not yet know how all this will come to pass, but I know that it will, for I have seen the Hawk Eternal."

Caswallon was about to speak, but Taliesen raised his hand for silence. "No more words tonight, War Lord. For I am weary unto death."

Oracle watched the Aenir in the valley below. They had slaughtered three prime steers and were preparing a feast. Since the invasion three days before not one enemy warrior had approached the cave. Heavy of heart, Oracle walked back to the entrance and on into the small room at the rear of the cave. He had seen the death of Durk, and now from beneath his narrow cot bed he pulled an oak chest, brass-edged and finely worked. From it he took a rusting mail shirt and helm and an old broadsword wrapped in oiled cloth. He donned the mail shirt noting, with a wry grin, that it no longer hung well on his bony frame. Man aged less well than iron. Pushing back his white hair, he placed the helm firmly on his head. Looping sword and scabbard about his waist, he moved back into the sunlight and began the long walk into the valley.

Many were the thoughts as he strode down toward the feast. He remembered his childhood, and the first Hunt, his glory at the Games when he carried the Whorl Stone farther than any man before him. He remembered his love, Astel, a spirited lass from among the Haesten, and how she had sickened and died during their first winter together. The sense of loss crippled him still, though she remained young in his memory while he withered in reality.

The trees thinned out and he walked on.

Then had come the day when he approached the Council following his success in the war against the Lowland raiders. Great days, when his name was sung throughout the Farlain. He believed they would make him king. Instead they had rejected him, and in his fury he had sworn never to return to the clan.

With a few valiant followers he had risked everything sailing to Vallon. There he overpowered the druids who manned the Gate, and journeyed to the world beyond. For two years he fought alongside the Battle Queen, Sigarni. Regret touched him as the long suppressed memory of his shame rose to his mind. Sigarni had dismissed him, stripping him of rank. Oracle and his followers had then crossed the Gate once more to a distant land.

And what a land it was, green and fertile, with rolling hills and verdant valleys, broad plains and tall cities of glowing marble. It was a country riven by civil war, petty chieftains and robber princes vying with one another for control. Oracle had arrived in a world made for his talents. Within two years he was a general. Within five he led an army of three thousand men against Vashinu, the Prince of Foxes, and smashed him in a battle near Duncarnin. Five years later he crowned himself king and was acclaimed from northern mountains to southern seas as the undisputed Lord of the Isles, High King.

Had he been possessed of compassion, or even foresight,

he might have changed that troubled land, bringing peace and prosperity to his subjects. But he had been a man of war, and had learned nothing of diplomacy, nor forgiveness. He persecuted his enemies, creating greater hatreds and thus more enemies. Two rebellions he crushed, but the third saw his army broken.

Wounded and alone, his few close friends dead or captured, he fled north and there vainly attempted to gather a force. For three years he fought minor campaigns, but always the great victories slipped away until at last he was betrayed by his lieutenants and turned over to his enemies. Sentenced to death, he had broken from his prison, killing two guards, stolen a horse, and made his way southeast to the Gateway once more. Twice they almost caught him, an arrow piercing his back. But he had been strong then, and he carried the wound to the druid's cave—the cave he had stumbled from so many years before, when first he laid eyes on the Land of Isles.

There had been a druid there, who had gazed upon him, shocked and bewildered. He had been one of the men Oracle had overpowered long before on Vallon. Oracle, weak from loss of blood, asked the man to send him back home. He had done so without argument.

Now the old man gazed down on the fruits of his ambition, and bitter was the taste. The valley was scarred by the invasion, burnt-out homes black against the greenery, enemy soldiers trampling the wheat in the fields. By the long hall were the guards, and within were the captured women of three clans, kept in chains to endure the lusts of the conquerors.

Men looked up from their work as the old man came in sight, then began to gather and point at him. Laughter began and sped as warriors came running to watch him. The laughter touched Oracle's mind like acid. In his day men had quailed to see him thus attired. Now he was a figure of fun. He drew his sword, and the laughter subsided.

Then someone called, "Run, lads. It's the entire clan army!"

And they mocked him, spreading out in a circle about him.

"Where is your leader?" he asked.

"Hark, it speaks! You can talk to me, old man. Tell *me* your business."

"I seek the dog, not its droppings," said Oracle.

The man's face reddened as he heard the laughter and felt the acid. He drew his sword and leaped forward. Oracle parried his thrust, reversing a cut that half severed the man's neck.

The laughter died, replaced by the sharp, sliding hiss of swords being drawn.

"Leave him. He interests me," said Asbidag, striding through the crowd—Drada to his right side, Tostig at his left. He halted some five paces from Oracle, grinning as he noticed the rusted mail shirt.

"I am the leader. Say what you must."

"I have nothing to say, spawn of Agrist. I came here to die. Will you join me?"

"You want to fight me, old man?"

"Have you the stomach for it?"

"Yes. But first tell me where your clan has gone. Where are they hiding, and what do they plan?"

Oracle grinned. "They are hiding all around you, and they plan your destruction."

"I think you can tell me more than that. Take him!"

The men surged forward. Oracle's sword flashed twice and men fell screaming. The old man reversed his blade, driving it deep into the belly of the nearest warrior. In his pain and rage the Aenir lashed back with his own sword, cleaving Oracle's ribs and piercing his lungs. He doubled over and fell, blood gushing from the wound.

"Get back, you fools!" shouted Asbidag, punching men aside. Oracle struggled to rise, but the Aenir War Lord pushed him back to the earth, kneeling beside him.

"You got your wish, old man. But you'll be blind in Valhalla, for I'll cut out your eyes unless you tell me what I wish to know."

Oracle heard his voice as from a great distance, and then another sound burst upon his mind: a woman's voice, screaming in hatred. He thought he recognized it, but his vision swam and he did not feel the knife blade that pierced his throat.

Asbidag turned as Morgase plunged the knife again and again into the old man's neck. Tears were falling from her eyes and her sobbing screams unsettled the warriors around her. Asbidag hauled her to her feet, slapping her face; she calmed down then, her eyes misting over as she exerted her will, blanketing down the hatred that had overwhelmed her.

"You knew this man?" asked Asbidag softly.

"Yes. He was a general in the army that saw my father slain. He raped my mother and after that she killed herself. He was Caracis, Sigarni's general."

"I don't know these names," said Asbidag. "You told me your land was ten thousand leagues from here. You must be mistaken. This old man was a clansman."

"Do you think I would forget such a man?"

"No, I do not. But there is something you have left out, my little dark lady. How is he here?"

"I thought he was dead. He . . . vanished twenty-five years ago." Asbidag grunted, then kicked the corpse. "Well, whatever he was, he's dead now," said Asbidag, but his gaze rested on Morgase as she walked back to the house.

Drada wandered to his father's side. "Do you really think she would remember? She must have been a small child twenty-five years ago."

"It worries me," answered Asbidag, still watching the woman. "I've never heard of her realm. I think she's bewitched."

"What will you do?"

"What I choose. I think she's lying about something, but it can wait. She's far too good a bed partner to spoil now."

"And the Farlain, Father?"

"We'll set after them tomorrow. Ongist has driven the Pallides west and outflanked them, driving them back toward the east, and Barsa's Timber Wolves. Tomorrow we march, and if Vatan favors us we'll arrive while there is still a little sport."

The journey deep into the mountains was difficult, for many of the clan folk were old, while others struggled to carry babies and infants. Even among the young and strong, the defeat and the flight that followed it brought a strength-sapping sense of despair. Rain made the slopes slippery and treacherous, but the straggling column moved on, ever closer to Attafoss. Maeg passed the sleeping Donal to a clansman, who grinned as he settled the boy's head on his shoulder. Then she walked away from the column to where Caswallon was issuing orders to a group of warriors. He saw her coming and waved the men away. Maeg thought he looked tired; there was little spring in his step and his eyes were dull. He smiled and took her hand.

"You're not resting enough," she said.

"Soon, Maeg."

Together they watched the clan make their way toward the last slope of the mountains before Attafoss. Already in the distance they could hear the roaring of the great falls. Day by day more stragglers joined the exodus and now almost six thousand people followed Caswallon. The long column of men, women, and children was moving slowly, suffering from the frenzied pace of three days' marching. The old and the very young were placed at the center of the column. Behind these came the rear guard, while young women strode at the head armed with bows and knives. There was little conversation. The young men were desperate to leave their families in safety on Vallon, so that they could turn back and rend the enemy. The old men were lost in thoughts of youth, regretting their inability to wreak vengeance on the Aenir and ashamed of their faltering pace. The women, young and old, thought of homes lost behind them and the danger their men would face in the days ahead.

Warriors took it in turns to carry the younger children.

These tasks were done in good heart, for they were all clan. All one in the spirit of the Farlain.

"You saved the clan, Caswallon," said Maeg, slipping her arm around her husband's waist and smiling up at him, noting the lines of tension on his face, the dark circles beneath his green eyes.

He kissed her hair. "I don't need lifting, lovely lady, but thank you for saying it. I seem to be clinging by my fingertips to an icy cliff. There are so many problems. A messenger from Badraig says there is a force in the east. We know the Aenir are also following in the south. I am frightened by all of it. There is no room for a wrong decision now."

"You will do what is best," she said. "I have faith in you."

"Oh, I have faith in myself, Maeg. But all men make mistakes."

"Maggrig always said you were as cunning as a fox, and trying to out-think you was like catching wood smoke with your fingers."

He grinned and the tension fell from him, though the fatigue remained.

"I will feel better when the clanswomen and children are safe and my thoughts can turn once more to simple tasks—like killing the Aenir."

"You think that will be more simple?"

"Indeed it will. They think they have won, they see us running and believe us broken. But we will turn and they will find themselves staring into the tawny eye of the killing wolf."

She turned to him, staring up into his angry eyes. "You will not let hate enter your soul?"

"No. Do not fear for me in that way. I do not hate the Aenir; they are what they are. No more do I hate the mountain lion who hunts my cattle. And yet I will fight and kill the lion."

"Good. Hate would not sit well with you, Caswallon of the Farlain."

"How could I hold you in my heart and find room for

hate?" he said, kissing her lips. "Now you must go, for I have much to do."

Hitching up her skirt she ran along the column, found the warrior holding Donal, and thanked him for his help. The child was still sleeping and she took him back in her arms and walked on.

Caswallon wandered to the rear of the column where Leofas walked with the rear guard. Surrounded by younger men the burly warrior seemed grizzled and ancient, but his eyes shone as Caswallon approached.

"Well, we made it without incident," he said.

"It looks that way," Caswallon agreed.

Leofas scratched his beard. There was more grey than red in the hair, and Caswallon thought it had the look of rust on iron. Leofas was old, but he was tough and canny, and the day had not dawned when an enemy could take him lightly. He wore a glistening mail shirt of iron rings sewn to a leather base with silver thread. By his side were two short swords and in his hand an iron-capped quarterstaff.

"Did you mean what you said, Caswallon? About sending out people through the Druid's Gate?"

"Yes."

"Will they be safe?"

"Safer than here, my friend, believe me. A hundred of the older men will go with them, to help with the hunting and building."

"And then what?"

"Then you and I will hunt a different game."

The older man's eyes gleamed and he grinned wolfishly. "It's about time. I do not feel right heading away from the devils. My legs keep turning me about. I never thought the day would come when I'd care about what happened to the Pallides," Leofas went on, "but I hope that old wolf Maggrig is safe."

"He's not a man to be surprised by a sudden attack. He would have had scouts out."

"Yes, but so did we, Caswallon."

*   *   *

Forty miles to the south and east Maggrig's anger was mounting. He was tired of being herded toward the west, tired of skulking away from the enemy, and filled with a sense of dread. The Aenir had caught up with them on the afternoon of the day following the attack, but Pallides scouts had hit them with a storm of arrows and slowed their pursuit. Since then they had outflanked the clan to the east and the two groups were seemingly engaged in a deadly race, the Aenir endeavoring to outrun them and prevent the northward exodus. Rare cunning and an intimate knowledge of the land enabled Maggrig to stay ahead, but always the angle of the march was being shifted and the wily Pallides Hunt Lord had begun to suspect they were being herded west for a reason other than the obvious. It had seemed at first that the Aenir commander wanted to force a direct battle by cutting off their flight, but he had spurned two opportunities to do so. Once could have been put down to ignorance or lack of thought.

Twice was a different tale.

As the swordsman Intosh had pointed out, it could still be stupidity. Maggrig had grunted, dismissing the idea. "Any general who needs to rely on his opponent being an idiot is in sore trouble. No, I don't think he wants a confrontation yet. I think there's another Aenir force to the west of us. We are between a hammer and a hard rock."

"We have limited choices," said Intosh, squatting to the earth and sketching a rough map of the terrain ahead. "All we can do is react. We are hampered by the presence of our women and children."

"According to our scouts," said Maggrig, "the enemy has two thousand men. We have eight hundred who can fight, and seven hundred women. With older children who can handle a bow, we could muster sixteen hundred fighters."

"To what purpose?" said Intosh. "We cannot take them on."

"We must," said Maggrig sadly. "Yes, we can continue to

run, but each mile brings us closer to disaster. We must take the initiative."

"We cannot win."

"Then we'll die, my friend, and we'll take as many of the swine along the path as we can."

Intosh's eyes focused on Maggrig. The swordsman was also tired of running. "It is your decision and I will stand by you. But where do we make this stand?"

Maggrig knelt beside him and together they selected the battle site, tracing the lines of the land in the soft earth.

Dawn found the Aenir under Ongist marching through a wide valley. Ahead was a range of hills, thickly wooded with ancient oaks on the left slope, and to the east a higher hill clear of trees. Upon that hill was the shield ring of the Pallides, the rising sun glistening on the swords, spears, and helms of the clan, and shining into the eyes of the Aenir.

Ongist called his scouts to him. "How long before Barsa reaches us?"

"Another day," said a lean, rangy forester. "Do we wait?"

Ongist considered it. To wait would mean sharing the glory—and the women. Shading his eyes he scanned the hill, making a rapid count. "How many would you think?"

The forester shrugged his shoulders. "Fifteen hundred, maybe two thousand. But half of them must be women. Vatan's balls, Ongist, we outnumber them by three to one!"

Drada had been insistent that no major battle should be joined until Barsa's troops had linked with his, but what would Father say if Aenir warriors merely waited, apparently fearful of attacking a hill defended by women, old men, children, and a handful of warriors?

Calling his captains forward, Ongist ordered the advance.

The Aenir swept forward, screaming their battle cries and racing toward the hill. The slope was steep and arrows and spears hurtled among them, but the charge continued.

On the hilltop Maggrig drew his sword, settling his shield firmly in place on his left arm. The Aenir were halfway up the hill, the last of their warriors on the lower slopes, when Maggrig gave the signal to the warrior beside him. The man lifted his horn to his lips and let sound the war call of the Pallides.

In the woods behind the Aenir, eight hundred women dropped from the trees, notching arrows to the bowstrings. Silently they ran from cover, kneeling at the foot of the slope and bending their bows. The Aenir warriors running with their shields before them were struck down in their scores as black-shafted death hissed from behind. Ongist, at the center of the mass, turned as the screams began.

Hundreds of his men were down. Others had turned to protect themselves from this new assault. These only succeeded in showing their backs to the archers above.

Ongist cursed and ducked as an arrow flew by him to bury itself in the neck of his nearest companion. The charge had faltered. He had but one chance of victory, and that lay in charging the women archers below. He bellowed for his men to follow him and he began to run.

But at that moment Maggrig sounded the horn once more and the shield ring split as he led his fighters in a reckless attack on the enemy rear. Intosh beside him, the burly Hunt Lord cut and thrust his way into the Aenir pack. A sword nicked his cheek before the wielder fell with his throat opened, to be trampled by the milling mass.

Shaft upon shaft hammered into the Aenir ranks. Death was ahead of them—and behind they could hear the shrill battle cry of the Pallides: "Cut! Cut! Cut!" Faced with a hail of missiles many of the Aenir broke to the left, streaming away toward the safety of the trees, desperate to be clear of the rain of death. Ongist was furious. With a hard core of his personal carles he stood his ground, but the battle was lost. Arrows tore into his men, opening a gap in the shield wall, exposing Ongist to the enemy. Two shafts pierced the air, ripping into Ongist's chest. With a grunt of pain he broke off the jutting shafts. Turning, Ongist saw Maggrig before him, his beard dark with blood, his eyes gleaming and his lips drawn back from his teeth in a feral snarl.

Ongist lashed out weakly. Maggrig parried the blow with ease, lifting his hand for the archers to cease shooting. Ongist, the last Aenir alive, staggered, then gazed on the enemy with new eyes. His legs buckled and he fell to the ground, pushing himself to his knees with great effort.

"Bring him," muttered Maggrig, walking past the dying Aenir general and on toward the trees.

Within the hour the Pallides were once more marching north and west. Behind them the crows settled on the Aenir dead—more than eleven hundred bodies stripped of armor and weapons littered the hillside. And nailed to a tree hung the body of Ongist, his ribs splayed grotesquely, his innards held in place with strips of wood. His eyes had been put out and his tongue torn from his mouth.

Maggrig also knew of the Aenir dream of Valhalla.

Ongist's shade would neither speak nor see as it was led to the Grey God's hall.

Gaelen and Deva scrambled over the last skyline before Attafoss, staring out at the great falls and the spreading forests, the wide valleys and the narrow rocky passes beyond.

In the distance he could just make out the moving column, like ants crawling across a green blanket. He sank to the ground beside Deva. He was tired now but she was exhausted, her moccasins cut to rags by the flinty rock and the scree slopes. Her feet were bleeding and her face was grey with fatigue; her golden hair, once so beautiful, hung in greasy rats' tails to her grimy neck.

She laid her head against his neck. "I did not think we would get here safely," she said.

He stroked her hair, saying nothing. Beside them Render spread himself out, resting his head on his paws. He had not eaten for two days, and gone was the sleek shine of his fur. Three times they had dodged their pursuers, hiding in caves and beneath thick bushes, and once sheltering in the branches of a broad oak as the Aenir searched beneath.

Twice they had stumbled on the tortured bodies of clansmen nailed to trees and splayed in the horrifying blood-eagle. Deva had wanted the bodies cut down, but Gaelen refused, pointing out that such an action would only alert the trackers.

Now they were clear, with only an hour's gentle downhill stroll to meet with the clan. Gaelen rubbed his sweat-streaked face, scratching idly at the jagged white scar above the blood-filled left eye. He scanned the falls and the rushing white water, then transferred his gaze to the column as it moved with painful lack of speed toward the woods. Suddenly Gaelen jerked as if stung. From his vantage point he could see into the trees, and just for a moment, he caught a glimpse of a warrior, running bent over. The man had been wearing the horned helm of the Aenir.

"Oh, no!" he whispered. "Oh, Gods, no!"

"What is it?" asked Deva, swinging her head to glance back down the trail, expecting to see their pursuers close by.

"The Aenir are in the woods," he said. "They're waiting to hit the clan and I can't warn them."

Deva shaded her eyes, searching the timberline.

"I see nothing."

"It was only one man. But I know there were more."

Despair washed over the young man. "Let's move," he said, and they began to run down the grassy slopes, angling away from the woods.

Far below them Caswallon halted the column. Ahead was the forest of Atta, the dark and holy place of the druids. Beyond that, according to Taliesen, was the invisible bridge to Vallon. Caswallon called Leofas to him—and Badraig, who had returned from the west with news that the Aenir had split into several forces, the majority racing east at speed, the others vanishing into the mountains in small groups.

The scouting party had cornered twenty Aenir warriors and destroyed them, taking one alive whom they questioned at length. He would tell them little, save that they had been pursuing a man and a girl. Badraig killed the man swiftly and led his party back to Caswallon.

"What do you think?" asked Badraig. "Gaelen?"

"It could be. The girl might be Deva. Dirak's scouts found the mutilated body of a clan girl they thought was Larain, and Agwaine said the two girls were together."

"Why should the Aenir split their forces?" Leofas asked.

"I would bet it is Maggrig. The wily old fox is probably leading them a merry dance."

Taliesen joined them, leaning on his oak staff, his long white hair billowing in the morning breeze. "Can we move on, War Lord? I am anxious to be on safe ground."

"Not yet," said Caswallon. "I am concerned about the second force you mentioned, Badraig. Why did they split up, do you think?"

"To re-form elsewhere. Why else?"

"Then where are they? We've searched the west."

"They could have returned to the south."

"Or come north," said Leofas.

"My thoughts exactly," said Caswallon, switching his gaze to the dark trees of Atta.

"How many would you say were in this second force?" Leofas asked.

Badraig shrugged. "It could be anything from two hundred to a thousand. Not more, though."

"Then for once we are not outnumbered," said Caswallon. "I think we'll camp here, and tonight we'll set fires. We know no force from the south can be on us before tomorrow past the noon."

Badraig and Leofas spread the word and the women of the column cast around for firewood, though none approached the trees.

Within the forest Barsa waited patiently with his seven hundred and fifty archers, watching the Farlain make camp.

Unlike his half brother Ongist, Barsa was not a reckless man. Though neither was he intuitive, as his half brother

Drada. Barsa was simply a trained killer of men who relied on his experience more than his intellect. Experience told him the Farlain did not know of his presence; he had avoided their scouts and taken only the best of his men, breaking into small parties and heading north, re-forming at the falls. He had been guessing as to the line of the clan march and was secretly pleased at the accuracy of his guess. He had no idea where they were ultimately heading, for the north was a mystery to the Aenir save that men said the sea was not far off. And when he had received the message from Ongist saying the Pallides were also racing north he had acted at once, dispatching three thousand to join his brother and taking eight hundred with him to this place.

It would please his father, and Barsa looked forward to basking in his praise. He could decimate the Farlain with his first volley. They would break and run and his men would have their pick of the clan maidens. Sadly they would then have to kill them. It was the one order that made no sense to Barsa; always the Aenir had taken captured women as house slaves and concubines—even wives. But in the mountains Asbidag's orders had been specific.

Kill all the clansmen, women, and children.

An Aenir forester crept to Barsa's side. "They are making camp. Should we attack tonight?"

It was a thought, but Barsa was loath to commit his men in the open for the clans outnumbered him. "No. We'll wait for morning, as they enter." The man nodded and moved silently back into the deeper darkness.

Beyond the line of campfires flickering on the open ground, Caswallon silently led a thousand warriors south and then east, circling toward the blackness of Atta forest. Once in the east the Farlain split into three forces, one led by Caswallon, the others led by Leofas and Badraig. Armed only with short swords and hunting knives the men entered the trees, moving silently forward. It was slow progress.

The moon was bright above the mountains, but its light was diffused by the overhanging branches of the ancient oaks that made up the bulk of the forest. Every three or four steps Caswallon closed his eyes, focusing on the sounds around him, listening for movement in the bushes ahead. The hoarse rasp of cloth on wood came to him and Caswallon raised a hand. The men behind him stopped. He pointed to the bushes; a clansman crept forward with knife in hand.

In the bushes the Aenir archer dozed—and died without waking as the razor-sharp hunting knife slid across his throat. Beyond him slept scores of warriors. With bright knives the clansmen moved in among them, killing them as they slept.

The night hunters moved on. Leofas and his group crept deep into the forest to the north, continuing their silent slaughter before working their way down the western side while Badraig, reaching the northernmost point, turned south.

An hour before dawn a cry split the night silence as a clansman's blade slit open an Aenir throat. The man awoke as the knife cut into him, screaming a warning before dying as six inches of iron slashed through his neck.

Barsa leaped to his feet, knowing instantly that he had been tricked. He bellowed a warning to those nearest and drew his sword. Aenir foresters ran to him and then he saw the clansmen bearing down in the gloom. He glanced right and left. He had fewer than a hundred men with him. But if the men of the clan had entered the forest, that left the women alone on open ground. Barsa turned and sprinted south. If they could only hack their way past the women and old men they would be clear.

The Aenir ran from the trees and Barsa's heart sank. A line of women kneeling in the grass, bows bent. He threw himself to the ground as the shafts whistled home.

A second volley hammered into their ranks and then the clansmen were upon them. Barsa leaped to his feet and parried a thrust from a short sword, sweeping a double-handed blow to the clansman's unprotected head and caving in the skull. A second man fell to his sword, and a third, as he roared his defiance at them. Then the clansmen fell back, and a warrior strode through their ranks. The man was tall, his long black hair tied at the nape of the neck, a trident beard giving him a sardonic appearance. His eyes were green and in his hand he carried a short sword. Beside Barsa the last of the Aenir foresters died with an arrow in his ribs. Barsa was not afraid of death. He had earned his place in the Grey God's hall.

Leaning on his sword, he grinned at the blood-drenched clansman.

"Come on then, mountain dung. I'll see your corpse before you see mine."

The clansman stepped forward as Barsa's sword flashed in the air. He parried it, ducking beneath the swing to thrust at the Aenir's groin. Barsa leaped back, his blade plunging downward. The clansman blocked the blow, iron clashing on iron as the men circled. The Aenir had the advantage of the long sword, but the clansman moved swiftly, his green eyes probing for weaknesses in the Aenir's defense.

"Frightened, clansman?" sneered Barsa. The man did not reply, but leaped forward with a sword raised. Barsa slashed wildly. The man parried, then spun on his heel to hammer his elbow into Barsa's face. The Aenir staggered back, then felt the searing agony of a sword blade buried deep in his belly. An awful cry tore from his throat and he pitched to the ground, writhing and straining to free the blade. Then the pain faded, washed from his body by the rushing blood. He rolled to his back, looking up at the sky above him, waiting to see the Valkyrie ride down for his soul.

He wondered if Asbidag would mourn for him. "I'll cut out his eyes," he heard someone say. Barsa knew panic; he did not want to be blind in the Hall of Heroes.

"Leave him be," said the clansman who had cut him.

Relief and release came together, and the light faded.

Chapter Nine

In the early-morning sunlight the clanswomen stripped the Aenir dead of all weapons and dispatched those warriors still clinging to life. Caswallon walked into the forest with many others of the attacking party, stopping at a fast-moving stream and removing his blood-covered clothes.

The night's work had appalled the new War Lord. More than six hundred Aenir warriors had been butchered in their sleep; it was no way for a man to die.

Caswallon stepped into the stream, shivering as the icy mountain water touched his skin. Swiftly he washed, then returned to the bank, sprawling out alongside Leofas and the young raven-haired warrior Onic, the finest quarterstaff fighter in the mountains.

"A fine night," said Leofas, grinning. Stripped of his clothing, the old warrior looked even more powerful. His barrel chest and muscular shoulders gave evidence of his great strength, yet his belly was flat and taut, the muscles of the solar plexus sharp and clean.

"It was a victory, anyway," said Caswallon wearily.

"You're a strange man, Caswallon," said Leofas, sitting up and slapping the younger man between the shoulder blades. "These swine have come upon us with murder and rape and now, I sense, you regret last night's slaughter."

"I do regret it. I regret it was necessary."

"Well, I enjoyed it. Especially watching you gut that tall son of a whore."

A group of clanswomen, led by Maeg, came to the stream

carrying clean clothes for the men. Caswallon dressed, and spotted Taliesen sitting on a fallen tree; the War Lord joined him in the sunshine.

"There is the smell of death in this forest," said Taliesen. "It reeks of it." The druid looked impossibly old, his face ashen, the skin dry. His cloak of feathers hung limply on his skeletal shoulders, the colors faded and dust-covered. "But still, you did well, War Lord."

Caswallon sat beside the old man. "Who are you, druid? What are you?"

"I am a man, Caswallon. No more, no less. I was a student centuries ago and I joined the trek from the stars to see more of life. I wanted to learn the origins of man. The Gates were a means to an end."

"And what are the origins of man?"

Taliesen chuckled, his tired eyes showing a glint of humor. "I don't know. I never will. My teacher was a great man. He knew the secrets of the stars, the mysteries of the planets, and the structure of the Gates. And yet, he never learned the origins. Together we journeyed and studied, and ever the great mystery eluded us. I sometimes fear the cosmic force I cannot see, and he laughs at me in my vanity.

"My teacher, Astole, became a mystic in a far land. It happened soon after the Prime Gate failed. You see, we could never travel back far enough, anywhere, to find the first man. The Gates would always be pushed back. Wherever we went, there was a man, developed to some degree. Several hundred years ago I developed a theory of my own, and I left Astole in the deserts of his world and journeyed to a northern land, a Highland kingdom. The people there were under threat, even as you are, and I led them to the Farlain to watch them grow and to see how they would develop. I thought the development would assist my studies."

"And did it?" asked Caswallon.

"No. Man is a singularly irritating creature. All that happened was that I grew to love the people of the Farlain. My studies were ruined anyway two hundred years ago, when the last of my people wed into the race. We had no women, you see, and every man needs companionship. I recruited many of their children, and so the order survives, but many of those now practicing the skill do not appreciate any longer the . . . arts behind the machines.

"You, Caswallon, are of my race. You are the great-grandson of the daughter of Nerist. A bright man was Nerist. He alone of all my pupils said we would never reopen the Great Gates. You cannot understand the awful sense of separation and loss we experienced when those gates closed. You see, what happened was an impossibility."

"Why should it be impossible?" asked Caswallon. "All things have a beginning and an ending."

"Indeed they do. But when you play with time, Caswallon, you create circles. Think of this: Today you will see the last of the Middle Gates. Today. *Now.* You will gaze upon it, and your people—our people—will pass through it. But tomorrow, let us say, the Gate disappears. We are worried at first, but then we think: It was there yesterday. Therefore we step through a Lesser Gate into yesterday. What should we find?"

"The other Gate should once again be there," said Caswallon.

"Aye, it should—for we saw it yesterday . . . passed through it. But that is the mystery, my boy. For when the Great Gates disappeared, they vanished *throughout* time. Impossible, for it does not correspond with reality."

"You told me," said Caswallon, "that magic was impossibility made reality. If that is true, there should be no problem accepting the reverse. What happened to your Gates was simply reality made impossibility."

"But who made it happen?"

"Perhaps someone is studying you, even as you study us," said Caswallon, smiling.

Taliesen's eyes gleamed. "Astole believed just such a thing. I do not."

At that moment Gaelen entered the clearing, calling Caswallon's name. The War Lord leaped to his feet, opening his arms as the young man ran to him. They stood there for several moments, hugging each other. Then Caswallon took hold of Gaelen's shoulders and gently pushed him away.

"Now, you're a sight to ease my mind," said Caswallon.

"And you. Deva and I thought to find you cut to pieces by the Aenir. We saw you from the peaks yonder."

"Just for once we out-thought them. You look tired, and there is dried blood on your tunic."

We've been chased over the mountains for three days."

"But you came through."

"You taught me well."

Caswallon grinned. "Where is Deva?"

"Upstream, washing the grime from herself."

"Then you do the same. Much as I am glad to see you, you smell like a dead fish. Away with you!"

Caswallon watched the young man walk to the stream and his eyes glowed with pride. Taliesen stood beside him. "He is a fine young man. A credit to you."

"A credit to himself. You know, Taliesen, as I carried him on my back from the destruction of Ateris I wondered if I was being foolish. His wounds were grievous—and he was all skin and bone anyway. My legs ached, and my back burned through every step. But I'm glad I didn't leave him."

"He is tough," agreed the druid. "Oracle did well to heal him."

"Yes. I hope the old man survived the assault."

"He did not," said Taliesen.

"How do you know?"

"Let us leave it that I know. He was a strong man, but vain."

"That is not much of an epitaph," said Caswallon.

"It is the best I can offer. Now get the clan ready. We must cross the bridge before dusk."

Almost six thousand people thronged the shoreline as the sun cleared noon. Silence fell upon them as a druid appeared on the island's shore, some forty yards across the foaming water. He tied a slender line to a sturdy pine, then looped the long coil over his shoulder and stepped out on the water. A gasp rose from the watchers, for the man was walking several feet above the torrent. After some twenty paces he stopped, reaching down, and stroked the air in a vertical line by his feet. Then he looped the twine around the invisible post and walked on. This he did every twenty paces, and amazingly the twine hung in the air behind him. Slowly the man made his way to the waiting clan, stopping to tie the end of the twine to a small tree. Then he approached Taliesen and bowed.

"Welcome, lord, it is good to see you again. How many of the clan survived?"

"Just under six thousand. But there could be more hidden in the mountains."

"And the Pallides?"

"No one knows. But the Haesten were crushed, and I don't doubt many lesser clans were annihilated."

"Sad news, lord."

The druid, who seemed almost as ancient as Taliesen, turned to Caswallon. "You will instruct your people to hold on to the twine and follow it. There is no danger, and the path is wide enough to make a line of five men. Let them approach slowly. All children to be carried. If anyone falls they are dead. They will be carried over Attafoss within seconds. Instruct your people."

Caswallon was the first to cross, the clan filing slowly behind him. It was an uncanny sensation, placing weight upon solid air. He soon found it inadvisable to look down, for his sense of balance threatened to betray him.

Behind him the clan followed in silence and there were no mishaps.

Once on the island the clan spread out and pitched their camps. They found dried meat and fruit waiting for them, sacks of grain and oats, bags of salt, and huge tubs of honey, warm blankets and soft hides: all the product of Caswallon's land that had so mysteriously disappeared the previous autumn.

Caswallon himself called a War Council and they met in a cavern beneath Vallon's highest hill.

At the center of the cavern was a long table of pine, around which were fifty chairs. These were soon filled. Caswallon took his place at the head of the table, flanked by Leofas and his sons Lennox and Layne; beside them sat Gwalchmai and Gaelen, and beyond them Onic and the pick of the Farlain warriors.

"Before we begin," Caswallon told them, "there is a matter to settle. It is our custom to elect our leaders. Most of the Council were slain with Cambil in the valley. We here now constitute a new Council. I offer myself as War Lord, but if there is any here with a hankering to lead, let him speak."

No one stirred.

"It is accepted then that I lead the Farlain until this war is concluded?"

"Of course it is, Caswallon. Do you think us fools?" said Leofas.

"Very well. Then let us begin the real business of the day. How best can we hurt the enemy?"

Asbidag gazed at the ruin that had been his son. Maggots writhed in the dead flesh, and the sharp beaks of crows had torn at the body, but still it was recognizable as Ongist. In full armor, his helm held in his hands, Asbidag stood before the tree soaking in the sight, feeding his fury and his hatred. Behind him stood Drada and Tostig and beyond them twenty-five thousand Aenir warriors.

Asbidag felt no remorse, no sadness at the death of his child. He had not liked Ongist; he liked none of his offspring. But the boy had been his: blood of his blood. He could hear him praying for vengeance at the door of the Grey God's hall.

Through his anger he felt frustration. How could he wreak vengeance upon the clans? Already his armies had slain four thousand. Many were the blood-eagles decorating the countryside. But he wanted—needed—more.

The clans feared him now, but terror was his desire.

He turned to Tostig.

"Fetch Agnetha from Aesgard. Do it now."

The color drained from the warrior's face and he thought of asking his father to send another. But Asbidag's eyes were cold and distant and Tostig knew from experience that he was on the edge of a killing frenzy. He nodded and backed away to his horse.

Drada stood silently as his brother departed. He had scouted the hill where Maggrig made his stand, and had received reports from the foresters as to the ploy the Pallides used. It was a clever plan, but it would have failed against any captain less impetuous than Ongist. Maggrig had gambled the lives of his people on one perilous venture, and he had succeeded. But it proved the measure of the man, and Drada knew he could best him when next they met.

Two serious errors had been made by Maggrig. On the night of the first attack he had led his warriors on a suicidal charge to protect a few women and children, and now he had staked everything on one battle. He was obviously a man ruled by his heart.

Drada hoped his success would make him bold.

Asbidag stalked from the tree, and several warriors moved forward to cut down the body, preparing it for the funeral pyre on the hillside.

Drada joined his father in the black tent at the base of the hill. Asbidag was drinking heavily, and Morgase sat in the background saying nothing. "We will not catch the Pallides before they link with the Farlain," said Drada.

"Good," said Asbidag. "I want them all together."

"Do you want to press on today?"

"No, we will wait for Agnetha."

Drada left his father and wandered through the camp to where his own tent had been pitched. Once inside, he stripped off his armor and spread his blankets upon the ground. It was early yet, but weariness was upon him and he slept through the afternoon. He awoke to the smell of cooking meat. One of his carles brought him a platter of beef and some bread and he joined the men outside.

For the first time in many years these fierce warriors were fighting not for gold, nor women, nor glory but for land. And he sensed the difference in them.

"It will not be easy," said his carle captain Briga, a swarthy black-haired veteran who had been Drada's first Aenir tutor.

"Nothing worth having comes easy," Drada told him.

The man grinned. "They fight well, these clansmen."

"Did you expect less?" Drada asked him.

"Not after the Games."

"No." Drada finished his meal and returned to his tent. Briga watched him go. He had been Drada's carle captain for five years, and before that his sword master. He liked the boy; he was unlike his brothers, but then he had been brought up as a hostage in a foreign city and upon his return was less Aenir than foreigner. He was soft, and his learning sat heavily upon him. Asbidag had made him Briga's charge.

In the years that followed Drada had learned of battle and death, horror and hate. But blood had run true and he had become, outwardly at least, as much an Aenir as his brothers. Only Briga knew of the lack.

Drada did not love war. He loved the *planning* of war.

Briga did not care. He sensed that Drada would one day rule the Aenir, and he waited patiently for the day to come.

The Aenir warriors were anxious to push on, but Asbidag gave no orders to move. For ten days they remained in camp until, on the morning of the eleventh day, Tostig rode in alone, reining his lathered mount outside his father's tent. Asbidag hauled him from the saddle, eyes blazing.

"Where is the witch woman?" he stormed. "If you have failed me I'll kill you! Your body will hang on the same tree as your brother."

"She is coming, Father, I swear it. She refused to ride, said she would come in her own way."

Asbidag hauled him to his feet. "She had better," he hissed.

At midnight, as the fires burned low, a bitter wind blew up, flashing sparks from the coals. Men shivered as dark clouds obscured the stars and Asbidag, sitting alone before his tent, drew his red cloak around him. A shadow fell across him, and glancing up, he saw the old woman standing before him leaning on a staff. She was as grotesque as ever—almost bald, the remaining greasy white patches of hair hanging like serpents to her emaciated shoulders. Her teeth were broken and black, and her face adorned with wrinkled, leathery skin, as if her skull had shrunk to half its size, leaving the flesh around it to sag monstrously. She wore a matted cloak of human scalps and her tattered gown was said to have been made from the skins of flayed maidens. Asbidag believed it to be true.

"What do you want of me?" she asked, her voice a sibilant hiss.

"Terror among the clans."

"You have brought terror to the clans. What do you want of me?"

"I want your sorcery."

"And what will you offer the Grey God?"

"Whatever he asks."

Her eyes gleamed. "Whatever?"

"Is your hearing going, woman? Whatever!"

"A hundred virgins slain by midsummer."

"You shall have it."

"And seven of your strongest men slain tonight."

"My men?"

"Yours. And I'll need your war dogs. Bring them to the woods in an hour."

Asbidag's carles roamed the camp until the seven men had been chosen, bound, and gagged. Together with the Aenir Lord's Hunt Master Donic, and his seven hounds, they were taken to a circular clearing within the woods. Asbidag was waiting there with Drada, Morgase, and Tostig; the woman, Agnetha, sat close by on a round boulder.

The bound men were forced to kneel before the woman

and she waved away Asbidag's carles who returned, relieved, to the camp. Agnetha called Donic forward, ordering him to set each dog before a bound man. He did so, then ran back to his blankets and the guttering fire behind Asbidag's tent.

In the clearing the kneeling men were sweating freely as they stared into the eyes of Asbidag's hounds. Agnetha glanced at the Aenir lord and nodded.

"Kill!" he shouted.

The hounds lunged forward, ripping at the exposed throats before them.

Agnetha ran along the line of dying men, hurling a grey misty powder over them and chanting. One by one the dogs sank to the earth, their teeth embedded in the flesh of the slain men. The witch woman lifted her arms to the night sky, screaming the name of the Grey God over and over again.

"Vatan! Vatan! Vatan!"

By her feet the hounds began to writhe and swell, while the Aenir corpses twisted and shriveled. Morgase turned away. Drada swallowed hard, flicking a glance at his father. Asbidag was grinning. Tostig squeezed shut his eyes.

Within seconds the dead warriors were bone-filled husks, while the hounds had grown to triple their size. Their front paws had stretched into taloned fingers, and their dark fur-covered forms parodied men—long muscular legs, deep powerful chests, and round heads ending in elongated maws and sharp fangs.

Agnetha danced around them, bidding them rise. Releasing the empty husks, the beasts pushed themselves to their feet, red eyes scanning the clearing. Their gaze fell upon Asbidag and their howling rent the night. Tostig stepped backward in terror and fell. Morgase gripped Drada's arm.

"Is this what you wanted, Asbidag?" said Agnetha.

"Yes."

"Once unleashed they can never be brought back. They will follow no one. They are created out of hate and they will kill any man they find, be he Aenir or clan. Is this what you want?"

"Yes, curse you! Just send them north."

"They will go where they will. But I will send them north. Have you done with me now?"

"I have."

"Remember your promise, Asbidag. One hundred maidens by midsummer. Or the werehounds will hunt *you*."

"Don't threaten me, hag," thundered Asbidag.

The woman cackled and turned to the silent beasts. Lifting her arm, she pointed north and the ghastly pack loped away into the darkness.

Asbidag walked forward, pushing his boot against a shriveled corpse. A dried bone split the skin and fell to the grass. He shook his head and began to laugh.

Agnetha stopped him, placing her bony hand upon his arm. "What is so amusing?"

"This," he answered, pushing the corpse once more. "This was Anias, son of my brother Casta. Only yesterday I told him he was empty-headed. Now his body matches his head."

Drada approached Agnetha. "How can those things live?"

"In the same way as you, Lord Drada. They breathe and they eat. It is an old spell, and a fine one, taught to me by a Nadir shaman in another age."

"But what are they now, hounds or men?"

"They are both—and neither."

"Do they have souls?"

"Do you?"

"Not anymore," said Drada, gazing down at the corpses.

The pack made their first kill that night, drifting silently through the pine forests in the northwest. The leader's head came up, nostrils flaring in the breeze. His red eyes turned to the northeast and he led the group deeper into the trees.

A young Haesten clansman and his two daughters were hidden in a cave. Having escaped the assault on their valley, they had met a Farlain scout who told them to head for Vallon. The clansman traveled by night carrying his youngest child, a girl of six years. His other daughter was eleven and she walked beside them. On this night, exhausted and hungry, they had made an early camp in the pine woods after spotting the Aenir army to the south.

The man had fallen into a light sleep when the werebeasts struck and he died without a struggle, his eyes flaring open to see wide jaws lined with fangs flashing toward his face. He had no time to scream.

His elder daughter, Jarka, took hold of her little sister and sped from the cave—only for talons to lance into her back, dragging her to a stop. In the last moment of her young life, Jarka hurled her sister into the undergrowth. The child screamed as she crashed through the bushes; then she was up and running, the awful sound of howling echoing behind her.

For an hour or more the beasts fed, then they slept by the remains of their kill. At dawn they left the cave, their hunger not totally appeased.

The leader dropped to all fours, sniffing at the earth around the cave. His head came up as the breeze shifted. And they set off in pursuit of the child.

Maggrig was angry. An hour before he had been furious. Caswallon had calmly told him that the clans would fight as one, and the one would be led by Caswallon. Maggrig could not believe his ears. The two men had been alone in a tiny cell, the bedchamber of a druid. Caswallon sat beside Maggrig on the narrow cot outlining his plans.

"I have plans of my own," said the Pallides' chieftain. Caswallon had been dreading this moment and took a deep breath.

"I know it is hard for you, but think about it deeply. The death toll among the clans has been enormous. I have perhaps four thousand fighting men, you have eight hundred. Even together we are no match for one fighting wing of the Aenir army."

"I accept that, Caswallon. But why should you lead? What experience do you offer? Great Gods, man, you've turned down responsibility all your life! Granted you've led us here, and our women and children are safe. But to lead in war calls for more than that."

"It calls for a cool head," said Caswallon.

Maggrig grunted. "You'll not lead the Pallides."

"Let me make this clear to you. You are on Farlain land, under the protection of the Farlain clan. If you do not accept me, then I will require you, and all your people, to leave tomorrow."

"And where would we go?"

"Wherever you choose. Those that remain will follow me without question."

"You would really do this thing? Turn out women and children to be slaughtered by the Aenir?"

"I would."

"What have you become, Caswallon? I mean, I've always liked you, boy. You were different, yes; but you were a clansman. Now you sit here and calmly say you would sacrifice my people for your ambition?"

"No, that is what *you* are saying," Caswallon told him. "During the Games you made an agreement with Laric that you would support him in any war—as long as you became War Lord. You reached that decision on the grounds that your men outnumbered the Haesten. That argument should surely still apply, can you not see it? If I were to agree that you lead, then most of the Farlain men would quit and go; they would not follow you."

"You think the Pallides would follow *you*?"

"Yes."

"Why? What makes you so different?"

"I am your son by law, for I wed your daughter. That gives me the rights of a Pallides warrior. They cannot argue."

"All right," said Maggrig at last, "I will follow you. But only as long as I think you are right."

"No," said Caswallon. "You will take my hand and swear allegiance to me as War Lord. You will offer me your life, as your carles have done for you."

"Never!"

"Then prepare your people to move."

Maggrig had stormed from the room seeking Intosh and together they walked among the trees of Vallon, avoiding the dark entrance to the Druids' Hall. Maggrig emptied himself of fury, his words tumbling over one another as he poured scorn on his son-in-law, the Farlain, the Druids, and the One Angry God for bringing him to this pass.

Intosh remained silent, merely walking beside his lord and absorbing his words. Finally exhausted, Maggrig stopped and sat by the water's edge, staring into the torrent. "Well, what do you think?" he asked.

"Of what?" answered the swordsman.

"Where can we go?"

"There is nowhere."

"We could go north," said Maggrig.

"And fight the Dunilds, the Loda, and the Sea Clans?"

"Then what do you suggest?"

"Agree to serve Caswallon."

"Are you serious?"

"He has done well."

"I know that—and all credit to him. But to serve my own son-in-law . . ."

"He has the power," said Intosh, shrugging. "It makes sense."

"He demanded I swear the vassal oath."

"You would have done the same."

"That's not the point," snapped Maggrig.

"No, Hunt Lord?"

An hour later Maggrig swore the vassal oath and was amazed his tongue did not fall out.

That same afternoon Caswallon and Maggrig led the women and children of the Pallides into the Druids' Hall entrance and down into the broad underground chamber housing the Middle Gate.

Maggrig blinked. At the end of the hall was a black marble archway. Yesterday a solid wall of stone had stretched between the pillars. Now that wall was gone and the Pallides

Hunt Lord gazed down on the first valley of the Farlain, where already men and women were pitching tents and felling trees for shelter. The archway was twice the height of a man and ten paces across. The two men stood in the Gateway looking down on the valley. Within paces of them a tall pine was waving in the breeze, but no breath of wind touched their faces.

"Where are the Aenir?" asked Maggrig as his people bunched behind him, looking down in wonder.

"That is the Farlain ten thousand years ago," said Caswallon.

Maggrig's eyes widened. "This is sorcery, then?"

"It most certainly is," Caswallon told him.

Maggrig stepped through the Gateway, flinching as rushing colors blinded him momentarily. Caswallon walked through behind him, waving the women to follow.

On the other side the breeze was cool, the sunlight warm and welcoming.

"It is not possible," whispered Maggrig, watching his people materialize from the air. From this side there was no sign of the Gate, only the rolling green countryside.

Caswallon led the Pallides down into the meadow where Leofas was supervising the building work. "I'm glad to see he survived," said Maggrig. "He always was the best of the Farlain." The old warrior grinned as he saw Maggrig, stepping forward to grip the Hunt Lord by the hand.

"So you got here, you dog," said Leofas.

"Did you expect a few Lowlanders to stop me?"

"Certainly not. I expected you to chase the swine from our lands, leaving nothing for the Farlain to do."

"I was tempted," said Maggrig with a broad grin.

Caswallon left the men talking and sought out Gaelen; he found him chatting to Deva by the river's edge. Apologizing for disturbing them, Caswallon led Gaelen up into the timberline and they sat beneath the pines.

"I want you to do something for me," said Caswallon, "but it is hazardous."

"Name it," said Gaelen.

"Don't make hasty judgments. I want you to take some men and head back into the Haesten, gathering as many warriors as you can. I want you to bring them to Axta Glen in three weeks."

"Why the glen?"

"It is there we will tackle the Aenir."

"But that is open ground."

"I know. Have faith in me. I am hoping there will be upward of a thousand clansmen still in hiding. I have sent messages to the Dunilds, the Loda, and many other smaller clans, but I don't know if they will come to our aid. But we must get more men; you must find them."

"I'll do the best I can."

"I know that, Gaelen."

"Why me?"

"Because you are known as an outsider. You are accepted within the Farlain, there is no doubt about that. But similarly you are not Farlain; the Haesten may follow you."

"Even if I did add a thousand to our army, we would still be outnumbered five to one. And on open ground . . ."

"I am also going on a journey," said Caswallon. "If it is successful, we will have another ally."

"Where will you go?"

"Through the Gate. I am seeking help from the Queen Beyond."

Gaelen shivered. "You mean the daughter of the woman who saved us from the beast?"

"No, the woman herself."

"She is dead."

"As we sit here in this valley, Gaelen, neither of us is born. Our birth cries are ten thousand years in the future. Is it so strange then to think of seeking a dead queen?"

"Why would she come?"

"I don't know. I only pray that she does—and that her strength will be sufficient."

"What if she does not?"

"Then the clans will face a difficult day in Axta Glen."

"What are our chances?"

"Taliesen says they are minimal."

"What do *you* say?"

"I'd say Taliesen was being wildly optimistic."

Gaelen returned to Deva at the stream and told her of his mission. She listened quietly, her grey eyes grave. "It will be dangerous for you. Take care," she said.

"I would be the more careful," he said tenderly, "if I knew you would be waiting for me when I returned." She looked away then, but he took her hand. "I have loved you for such a long time," he told her.

Gently she pulled her hand clear of his. "I love you too, Gaelen. Not just because you saved my life. But I can't promise to wait for you, nor for any Farlain warrior. I know you think me foolish to believe in the prophecy—but Taliesen confirmed it; it is my destiny."

Gaelen said nothing more. Rising, he moved away and Deva returned to the waterside. Her thoughts were confused as she sat, trailing her hand in the stream. It was senseless to refuse love when all she had was a distant promise, Deva knew that. Worse, her feelings for Gaelen had grown stronger during the time they spent together, being hunted by the Aenir. All her doubts surfaced anew, and she remembered confiding in Agwaine. He had not scoffed, but he had been brutally realistic.

"Suppose this father of kings never comes? Or worse. Suppose he does, and he does not desire you? Will you spend your life as a spinster?"

"No, I am not a fool, brother. I will wait one more year, then I will choose either Layne or Gaelen."

"I am sure they will be glad to hear it," he said.

"Don't be cruel."

"It is not I who am being cruel, Deva. Suppose they don't wait? There are other maidens."

"Then I will marry someone else."

"I hope your dream comes true, but I fear it will not. You sadden me, Deva, and I want to see you happy."

"A year is not such a long time," she had said. But that had been before the Aenir invasions, and already it seemed an eternity had passed. Her father was dead, the clan in hiding, the future dark and gloom-laden.

Gaelen chose six companions for the journey south— Agwaine, Lennox, Layne, Gwalchmai, plus Onic and Ridan. Onic was a quiet clansman, with deep-set eyes and a quick smile. Almost ten years older than Gaelen, he was known as a fine fighting man with quarterstaff or knife. He wore his black hair close-cropped in the style of the Lowland clans, and around his brow sported a black leather circlet set with a pale grey moonstone. His half brother, Ridan, was shorter and stockier; he said little, but he had also fought well in the retreat from the valley. Both men had been chosen for their knowledge of the Haesten, gained from the fact that their mother had come from that clan.

Taking only light provisions and armed with bows, short swords, and hunting knives, the seven left Vallon before dawn. A druid guided them over the invisible bridge, for the twine had been removed lest the Aenir march to the island.

Gaelen had mixed feelings about the trip. The responsibility placed upon him weighed heavily. He loved Caswallon, and trusted him implicitly, but to battle the Aenir on the gentle slopes of Axta Glen? Surely that was madness. During the last two years Gaelen had enjoyed many conversations with Oracle about battles and tactics, and he had learned of the importance of terrain. A large, well-armed force could not be met head-on by a smaller group. The object should be a score of skirmishes to whittle down the enemy, disrupting his supply lines and weakening his morale. Oracle had likened such war to disease invading the body.

Agwaine was content. For him the mission provided an outlet for his grief over the death of his father and a chance to achieve victory for the Farlain. He didn't know if a Haesten force survived. But if it did, he would find it.

The group moved through Atta forest, past the swelling Aenir corpses and on into the first valley. They moved warily, knowing the Aenir could be close. Only in the high passes, where the woods were thick and welcoming and they trusted their skills above those of the enemy, did they relax.

Toward dusk Lennox scouted out a hollow where they made camp. It was set within a pine woods and circled by boulders and thick bushes. There was a stream nearby and Gaelen lit a small fire. It was a good campsite and the fire could not be seen outside the ring of trees. Lennox, as always, was hungry, having devoured his three-day rations by noon. The others mocked him as he sat brooding by the fire watching them eat.

Lennox had grown even larger in the last year, his shoulders and arms heavy with muscle, and he now sported a dark beard close-cropped to his chin. Coupled with the brown goatskin jerkin, it created the appearance of a large, amiable bear.

"We are comrades," he pleaded. "We should share a little."

"I saw some berries on a bush back there," said Gwalchmai. "I am sure they will prove very tasty." He bit into a chunk of oatcake, and swung to Agwaine. "I think the honey in these cakes is better this year, don't you, Agwaine? Thicker. It makes the cakes so succulent."

"Decidedly so. It gives them extra flavor."

"You're a bunch of swine," said Lennox, pushing himself to his feet.

Laughter followed him as he walked into the darkness in search of berries. The woods were quiet, moon shadows dappling the silver grass. Lennox found the bush and plucked a handful of berries. They served only to heighten his hunger, and he toyed once more with the idea of appealing to his comrades. His stomach rumbled and he cursed softly.

A movement to his right made him turn, dropping into a

half crouch with arms spread. He saw a flash of white cloth disappear beneath a bush, and a tiny leg hastily withdrawn.

Lennox ate some more berries and then ambled toward the bush, as if to walk past. As he came abreast of it he lunged down, pulling the child clear. Her mouth opened and her face showed her terror, but no sound came out. Lennox took her in his arms, whispering gentle words and stroking her hair. She clung to the goatskin tunic with her tiny hands clenched tight, the knuckles white as polished ivory.

"There, there, little dove. You're safe. I didn't mean to frighten you. There, there. Don't worry about Lennox. He's big, but he's not bad. He won't hurt you, little dove. You're safe." All the while he stroked her head. She burrowed her face into his jerkin, saying nothing.

Lennox made his way back to the camp. Instantly his companions gathered around, plying him with questions. He shushed them to silence. "She's terrified," he said, keeping his voice low and gentle. "She must have lost her parents in the woods." Looking at his comrades, he silently mouthed the words "Probably killed by the Aenir."

Gwalchmai, always a favorite with children, tried to get the girl to speak, but she pushed her face deeper into Lennox's jerkin.

"I have never seen a child so frightened," said Agwaine.

"Where are you from?" whispered Lennox, kissing her head. "Tell your uncle Lennox." But the child remained silent.

"I don't recognize the girl," he said. "Do you, Gwal?"

"No. She could be Pallides, or Haesten, or even Farlain. Or even a crofter's daughter from the Outlands."

"Well, we can't take her with us," said Ridan. "One of us must take her back to Vallon."

"I'll do it in the morning," Lennox agreed.

The fire burned low and the companions took to their blankets, ready for an early rise. Lennox sat with his back to a boulder, cuddling the child who had fallen into a deep sleep. He felt good sitting there. Children had never been easy around him—Layne said his great size frightened them—but whatever the reason, it had always hurt Lennox, who loved the young.

In sleep the child's face relaxed, but her left hand still clutched his tunic. He pushed her yellow hair back from her eyes, gazing down into her face. She was a pretty little thing, like a doll stuffed with straw. As the night grew chill Lennox wrapped his blanket around her.

A strange thought struck him.

This was probably the most important moment of his life.

He was not normally a man given to abstract thoughts, but he couldn't help thinking about the child. Here she was, tiny and helpless and full of fear. She had been suffering the worst days of her young life. And now she slept safe in the arms of a powerful man, content that he would look after her. With no more action than a gentle embrace Lennox had ended her terror. What in life, he wondered, could be more important to her?

If her parents were still alive and making for Vallon they must be sick with worry, he thought. But what if—as was likely—they were dead?

Lennox chewed the problem over for a while. He would take her to Maerie; she was a fine lass with only one child, who would take the girl in and love her into the bargain.

The girl's eyes opened, she blinked and yawned. Lennox felt her move and glanced down, stroking her hair. Her eyes were brown and he smiled at her.

"Are you feeling better?" he asked.

"You're not my papa."

"No, little dove. I'm your uncle Lennox."

"My papa's gone. Wolfs et him up," she said, tears glistening. She blinked. "Et up Jarka too."

"Wolves?" asked Lennox.

"Big wolfs. Big as you. Et him up."

"You've been dreaming, little one. There's no wolves, and certainly none as big as me."

"Lots of wolfs," she persisted. "They chased me, to eat me up."

"Uncle Lennox won't let them. You're safe now. Go back to sleep, we'll talk in the morning."

"Did you know my papa?"

"No. Was he nice?"

"He played games."

"He sounds like a good man. Where is your mama?"

"Men with swords took her away. She was all bleeding."

"Well, it's over now. You're with your uncle Lennox, and he's the strongest man in all the world. Nothing will harm you."

"Are you stronger than the wolfs?" she asked.

"Aye, lass. And I swear upon my soul no harm will come to you while you're with me. You believe me?" She smiled, closed her eyes, and put her thumb in her mouth.

In the bushes beyond the firelight, bloodred eyes watched for the flames to die down.

Taliesen took Caswallon deep underground to a small chamber set with walls of shining silver and gold. Soft light filled the room, but Caswallon could not see the source. The druid beckoned him to a tall chair of white leather, then sat upon an oak-topped table.

"This is my inner sanctum," he told the warrior. "Here I observe the Farlain and I keep my notes—notes no one will read in my lifetime." He gestured to the shelves, but there were no books there, only small silver cylinders neatly stacked from floor to ceiling. The far wall was covered with sheets of paper, upon which were curious drawings and symbols.

Caswallon studied them. "What do these represent?" he asked. Taliesen joined him. "They are Time Lines, and chart my attempts to aid Sigarni."

Caswallon ran his eyes over the symbols. "And the stars?"

"Each time Sigarni dies I mark the spot and pursue a new Time Line—a different reality. It is very complex, Caswallon. Do not seek to stretch your mind around it."

"When must I seek the Queen?"

"As soon as you are ready."

"I'm ready now."

"Then observe," said the druid. Turning, he walked to the wall by the door and opened a hidden panel. The desktop slid back and a screen rose silently from it. Lights blazed from the screen, forming the image of a walled city.

"That is Citadel town, where the Queen currently resides—currently being a relative term," added the druid with a dry chuckle.

"How is this done?" whispered Caswallon.

"It is merely an image. It is summer and Sigarni has won a great battle. She has returned to the north to celebrate with her captains. The enemy has been pushed back . . . for now. But the Outland King is gathering a huge force against her. Now, before I send you through, you must understand this, Caswallon: We will meet again on the other side of the Gate. Ask me nothing of the events that are transpiring now. Do not speak of the Aenir invasion."

"I don't understand."

Taliesen sighed. "Trust me, Caswallon. In other . . . realities . . . our meeting beyond the Gate has already taken place. Many times. And I have found it disadvantageous to view the possible futures. It all becomes too confusing."

Caswallon stood silently for a moment, then his green gaze fastened on the druid's dark eyes. "And I have died in these other realities?" he asked.

"Yes," admitted Taliesen. "Do you still wish to go?"

"Can we win if I do not?"

"No."

"Then let us go."

Taliesen pressed a button on the screen and the image of the city disappeared. He stood and led Caswallon back to the Druids' Hall and the black-arched Gate.

Maeg was waiting there. She stood as he approached, opening her arms, and Caswallon walked into her embrace.

She kissed him, her eyes wet with tears. "The world has changed, as you said it would," she told him.

"We'll change it back."

"I don't think so," she said sadly. "Even if you beat the Aenir, nothing will ever be quite the way it was."

He did not argue. Instead he kissed her. "There is one constant fact, Maeg. I love you. I always have. I always will."

"I have something for you," she said, pulling away from him. Turning, she lifted a buckskin shirt from the back of a chair. The skin was soft and beige while on the chest, in crimson-stained leather, was a cunningly crafted hawk with wings spreading to each shoulder. "If you are to meet a queen, it is fitting you look your best," she said.

Caswallon slipped out of his woolen shirt, donning the buckskin. The fit was perfect.

Leofas stepped from the shadows with Maggrig.

"Are you sure about this plan, Caswallon?" he asked.

"No," admitted the War Lord. "But Taliesen is, and I can think of no other."

"Then may the Gods guide you." The two men shook hands.

Taliesen walked to the archway, lifted his hands, and began to chant. The view of the Farlain vanished, to be replaced instantly by a sloping plain and a distant city.

Maggrig curled his arm around Maeg's shoulder. "He will come back," he said.

Caswallon stepped into the archway—and vanished.

Suddenly the view from the Gate disappeared, a blank grey wall replacing it. Maeg moved forward and touched the cold stone.

Caswallon found himself in a forest glade in the last hour before dusk. Shafts of sunlight lanced the branches of mighty oaks and birds sang in every tree.

But there was no city in sight. Perplexed, he stepped back to where the Gate had been.

It was gone . . .

Cursing, he drew his short sword and started prodding the air, seeking the entrance. After a few minutes he gave up and sat back on a jutting tree root. He was loath to leave the spot, and had no idea what plan to pursue.

His thoughts were broken by the sounds of shouting. Looking around him, he marked the spot in his mind and set off toward the sound. Perhaps the Gate had merely sent him too far, and he had come out on the other side of the city. He seemed to recall seeing a woods there.

The shouts became triumphant, and Caswallon guessed the men to be hunters who had cornered their prey. Then a voice cried out. "Lord of Heaven, aid your servant!"

Caswallon broke into a run. Ahead of him three men had surrounded a bald, elderly man in robes of grey who was holding a tightly wrapped bundle in his arms.

"Surrender it, priest," ordered a tall man in a red cape.

"You cannot do this," said the old man. "It is against the laws of man and God."

The red-caped warrior stepped forward, a bright sword in his hand. The sword flashed forward. The old man twisted the bundle away from the blade, which lanced into his belly. He screamed and fell.

Caswallon hurdled a fallen tree, his own short sword glinting in the dying light. "What vileness do we have here, my bonnies?"

The three spun around and the leader walked forward, his sword dripping blood to the grass.

"It is none of your concern, stranger. Begone."

"Frightened as I am to face three heroes who can so valiantly tackle old men, I feel I must debate the point," said Caswallon.

"Then die," shouted the man, leaping forward. Caswallon parried the lunging blade, his own sword flashing through the man's neck. The remaining warriors ran forward. Caswallon blocked the first thrust, hammering a punch to an unprotected chin, and the attacker staggered.

Pushing past him Caswallon engaged the third, slipping his

hunting knife into his left hand. He ducked beneath a vicious swipe, sticking his sword behind the man's knee; with a scream he fell. Caswallon whirled as the second man was almost upon him, sword plunging for his chest, but Caswallon parried the blow, punching his hunting knife through the man's tunic. The blade slid between the man's ribs, cleaving the heart. Dragging the knife free, he saw the third man crawling toward the bushes, leaving a trail of blood behind him. Ignoring him, Caswallon ran to the old man, gently turning him.

"Thank the Source," said the priest. "For He has sent you in my hour of need." Blood was seeping fast, drenching the old man's clothes.

"Why did they attack you?"

"It wasn't me, my son; they wanted the babe." The old man pointed to the bundle by his side. Caswallon lifted the blanket and there lay a sleeping infant no more than a week old. She was tiny and naked, her downy hair pure white.

"Lie still," urged Caswallon, ripping open the priest's robes, seeking to stem the outflow of blood from the wound. The assassin's sword had ripped down through the man's lower belly, opening the artery in his groin. There was no hope for him, and his face was already losing color.

"Where are you from?" whispered the dying man.

"Another world," said Caswallon. "And I am lost."

The old man's eyes gleamed. "You passed through a Gate?"

"Yes."

"Was it Mordic sent you?"

"No."

"Cateris, Blean, Taliesen . . ."

"Yes, Taliesen."

"Take the babe back through the Chalice Gate."

"I do not know where it is."

"Close by. North. I opened it myself. Look for a cave on the hillside; it has a goblet fashioned in the rock of the entrance. But . . . beware . . . Jakuta Khan will follow."

"Who are you?"

"Astole. I was Taliesen's teacher." Horns sounded in the

forest to the south. "They are coming for the child. Take her and run. Go now! I beg you." The old man slumped back.

Sheathing his sword and knife, Caswallon scooped the bundle into his arms and began to run. Behind him he could hear the barking of dogs and the shrill call of hunting horns. He was angry now. Thwarted from his quest, he was being hunted by an enemy he did not know, in a forest that was strange to him.

Dropping his pace to a gentle jog, eyes scanning the undergrowth, he searched for a way to lose his pursuer. He could hear running water away to the left and he cut toward it. A small stream gurgled over rocks. Splashing into it, Caswallon followed it upstream for about thirty paces and then left it on the same side, walking through soft mud to stop before a massive oak.

Without turning he looked down and walked backward, placing his feet in his own prints. Slowly he backtracked to the stream, then carried on walking through the water. It was an old trick, which in daylight would fool no skilled tracker, but with dusk approaching fast it could hold up the pursuit.

The child opened her eyes, pushing her tiny fist into her mouth. Caswallon cursed. She was hungry and that meant there were scant moments left before she began to cry for food.

Turning again toward the north, he scanned the hillside for the cave the old man had spoken of. The babe in his arms gave out a thin piercing wail and Caswallon cursed again. The sun was slowly sinking behind the western peaks. As it fell below the clouds a shaft of bright light lit the hillside, and Caswallon saw the dark shadow of the cave entrance, some thirty paces above him and to the right.

The barking of hounds was closer. Twisting, he saw four sleek black shapes emerge from the tree line below, no more than fifty paces behind him. Holding firm to the child, Caswallon sprinted up the slope and into the cave. It was like a short tunnel. Behind him the dying sun was bright against the rocks, yet ahead was a forest bathed in moonlight.

Caswallon spun, for the first of the hounds had reached the cave. As it leaped his sword slashed down across its neck, smashing through flesh and bone. Turning again, he saw the moonlit forest begin to fade. Taking two running steps he hurled himself through the Gateway. He fell heavily, bracing his arm and shoulder so that the babe would be protected.

Rolling to his feet he swung to face his enemies—and found himself staring at a solid wall of grey stone. The sound of a waterfall came to him and he sheathed his sword and walked toward it. I know this place, he thought. But the trees are different. This was Ironhand's Pool, and if he climbed above the falls he would see High Druin in the distance. The wind shifted, bringing the smell of wood smoke to his nostrils. Moving to his left into the wind, the smell grew stronger. Ahead was a cottage of stone, with a thatched roof, and a cleared yard containing a small flower garden and a coop for chickens. Caswallon ran to the cottage, tapping softly at the door. It was opened by a young woman with long fair hair. "What do you want?" she asked, her eyes wide with fear.

"Food for a babe," he answered, handing her the child. Her eyes changed as she gazed at the small face.

"Come inside."

Caswallon followed her. At a pine table sat a large man with a heavy beard of red-gold.

"Welcome," said the man. Caswallon noticed that one of his hands was below the table, and guessed a blade was hidden there.

"I found the babe in the forest," he said lamely.

The man and woman exchanged glances. "Do you know whose child it is?" the man asked.

"I know nothing of her," said Caswallon.

"We lost our own daughter three days ago," said the man. "That is her crib there, in the corner. You can leave the child with us, if you will. My wife is still milk-swelled—as you can see." The woman had opened her shirt and was feeding the babe.

Caswallon pulled up a chair and seated himself opposite

the man, looking deep into his clear grey eyes. "If I leave her with you, will you care for her as you would your own?"

"Aye," said the man. "Walk with me awhile." He rose, sheathing the hunting knife he had held below the table. He was taller than Caswallon, and broader in the shoulder. Stepping out into the night he walked to the far side of the cabin, seating himself on a bench crafted from pine. Caswallon sat beside him. "Who are you?" he asked. "Your clothes are clan, but you are not Loda."

"I am Caswallon of the Farlain."

"I have dealings with the Farlain. How is it I have never heard of you?"

Caswallon let out a sigh and leaned back against the bench. "Is there a town near here, on the edge of the Lowlands, called Ateris?"

The man shook his head. "There is Citadel town. The Outlanders control it now. And I ask you again—who are you?"

"I am a clansman, as I have said." He laughed suddenly. "Were our positions reversed, my friend, and you were to tell me the story of how you found the babe, I would think you mad."

"I am not you," said the man. "So speak."

Quietly Caswallon told him of the Aenir invasion and of his journey through the Gateway, of the dying priest, and the men and hounds who had sought the death of the child. The man did not interrupt, but listened intently. As he finished Caswallon stood and looked down into the man's deep-set grey eyes, awaiting a response.

At that moment the ground trembled. Thrown off balance, Caswallon lurched to the right. The moonlight brightened and gazing up, both men saw two moons shining in the sky. For moments only the land was bathed in silver brilliance, then the second moon faded.

As it did so the figure of Taliesen appeared beside them. The old man stumbled and fell to his knees as the crofter leaped to his feet, his knife snaking into his hand. "No!" shouted Caswallon. "He is the druid I told you of."

Taliesen tried to stand, failed, and sat glumly on the ground. "I think the journey almost killed me," he grumbled. As Caswallon helped him to his feet, the little sorcerer sighed. "You have no idea of the energy I have expended to arrive here. Who is this?"

"I am Cei," said the crofter.

"I must see the child," said Taliesen, shaking himself free of Caswallon's support and moving off to the cabin.

Cei approached Caswallon. "You were wrong. I did not think you mad. Yesterday an old man came to us as we were mourning the death of our babe. He told us he would come, and that he would bring us joy—and sorrow."

"This man, was he bald and wearing grey robes?"

Cei nodded.

Both men returned to the cabin, to find Taliesen kneeling beside the crib where the baby was sleeping. When Caswallon and Cei looked closely they saw that the child's silver hair was now corn-gold.

Taliesen stood and turned toward the crofter. "Enemies will come after this babe," he said. "Be warned. I have changed the color of her hair. As I have told your wife, you must raise her as your own; no one must know how she came here. Your wife says the death of your child is not known among your friends in the clan. Keep it that way."

"Who is she?" asked Cei. "Why is she in danger?"

"She is your daughter. You need know no more than that— save that she is of the blood royal," said Taliesen. "Now we must go."

Lennox added fuel to the fire and the flames leaped and twisted. He wasn't cold, he merely wanted to see the child's face in sleep. Her thumb had slipped from her open mouth and she was breathing evenly. Lennox carefully hitched her into the crook of his right arm, stretching his back.

Gaelen yawned and stretched, sitting up and rubbing his eyes. Seeing Lennox still awake, he moved around the fire to join him. "How is she?"

"She is all right now. She says her father was eaten by wolves . . . and her sister."

"It's unlikely," said Gaelen. "She would not have escaped a pack. A dream, do you think?"

"I don't know. She said the wolves were as big as me."

"Wolves attack at night and they move fast. A child that small might think them overlarge."

"I agree, Gaelen, but she's clan; her father was clan. How could he be surprised by wolves? It makes no sense. I can't remember a clansman ever being killed by a pack. Wolves don't attack men. I've never heard of such a thing."

"Perhaps he had no fire, or had been forced to flee without weapons. Perhaps the wolves were starving."

The two men sat in silence for a while, then Gaelen spoke. "More likely it was the Aenir and the child was confused. Many of them wear wolfskin cloaks. And at the Games I saw a man with a wolf's head for a helm. An attack at night?"

"She says her mother was killed by men with swords. I don't think she's that confused. I think you should walk warily tomorrow," said Lennox.

"We'll miss you on the trip," said Gaelen, gripping Lennox's shoulder.

"Yes, but you don't need me. She does. I'll get her to the island and then join my father. We'll see you in Axta Glen."

"I hope so. I pray there is an army of Highlanders ready to be gathered. But if not I shall still see you there, Lennox. Even if I am alone. I promise you."

"I know you will, cousin. I'll look forward to it."

Soon after dawn the companions bade farewell to Lennox and the child and set off to the south. Lennox hoisted the girl to his shoulder and headed north.

As they walked he discovered that her name was Plessie and her clan Haesten; she was the niece of Laric, the Hunt Lord. He was tempted to run back and find the others, for Laric would be well disposed toward a group that had rescued his niece. But Plessie's fearful glances behind them forced him to dismiss the idea.

Whatever had happened to her had left a terrible scar.

Throughout the morning he climbed through the timber-line, and they stopped to eat at a rock pool below a small falls. The companions had given Lennox some oatcakes and these he shared with Plessie. The child sat upon a rock dangling her feet in the water, giggling at its icy touch. Lennox smiled—and froze. He slowly climbed to his feet, aware suddenly that he was being watched. Fear grew in his heart—not fear for himself, but for the child. He had promised she would be safe and a promise was a sacred thing among the clans.

Casually he glanced around at the thick undergrowth. He spotted a patch of darkness beyond a blossoming heather, but allowed his eyes to skip over the bush. He had the feeling the dark patch was fur, and if that was so the thing was either a bear or a wolf.

Plessie was sitting in the shade of a tall pine, and a long branch extended above the water. Lennox scooped her into his arms and lifted her high onto the branch.

"Sit there for a moment, little dove," he said.

"Don't want to," she wailed.

"Do it for your uncle Lennox. And be careful now."

Even as he spoke a werebeast charged from the undergrowth, jaws wide, taloned fingers reaching for the clansman. As it leaped it gave a terrifying howl. Beasts of the wild always roar or screech on attacking their prey. The sound freezes the victim.

But Lennox was not a hunted animal. Nor even an ordinary man.

He was the most powerful warrior in the long history of the Farlain.

As the beast broke cover Lennox whirled, bellowing his own scream of fury. He charged it, smashing a right cross to its open jaws. Fangs snapped, the jawbone disintegrating under the impact. The beast screamed and fell, rolling to all fours and howling in pain. A second creature leaped forward, and twisting to meet it, Lennox charged again. Talons lashed across his shoulder, scoring deep through the flesh. The jaws lunged for his face, and throwing up his hand, he fastened his fingers to the furry throat. The downward lunge was halted, the fangs inches from his face. Lennox could feel hot, rancid breath on his skin. The power of the beast was immense. He threw a left-hand blow that thundered against the werebeast's ear; the creature fell back, then leaped again. This time Lennox stood his ground until the beast was almost upon him. As it rushed forward he caught it by the throat and groin, and hurled it with all his strength against the trunk of a pine. It hit with a sickening thud—spine exploding into shards, ribs splitting and piercing the great lungs beneath. Blood flowing from his wounds, Lennox drew his sword. The first beast attacked again, its jaw hanging slack. As its talons lashed out, Lennox ducked beneath the swinging arm and hammered his sword into its unprotected belly.

The creature writhed in agony, then crumpled to the earth, thrashing in its death throes. Lennox dragged his sword loose and drew his hunting knife, eyes scanning the bushes. There was no movement there. But he had to be sure.

"Stay in the tree, Plessie. Uncle Lennox won't be a moment."

"No," she wailed. "Don't leave me. Wolfs eat me up!" Her tears cut through him, but he moved on, searching the tracks within the undergrowth. Satisfied there were only two of the creatures he returned to the weeping child, lifting her down and cuddling her.

"There, there! You see, I was only a moment or two."

"Don't leave me again, Uncle Lennox."

"I won't. Now, you are going to have to be a brave girl and help me to stop this bleeding. Can you do that?" With a grunt of pain Lennox removed his ripped shirt. There were four deep slashes across his right shoulder blade, but he could reach none of them.

"There's lots of blood, Uncle Lennox."

"The bleeding will clean the wounds," he said, moving to his pack. "Can you sew?"

"Mother taught me," said Plessie.

"That's good, little one." Rummaging into his pack, he found needle and thread. "I want you to close these little scratches for me. Then we'll move on. Will you do that for me?"

"I don't know how."

Lennox could see the fear returning to her. "It's easy," he told her, forcing a smile. "Trust me. I'll show you. First thread the needle. My hands are too big and clumsy for it." Plessie took the thread, licked the end, and carefully inserted it into the eye of the needle. She looked up expectantly at Lennox. Twisting his head, he could see the ragged red line of the first cut on the top of his shoulder. Taking the needle, he pricked it through the skin. "You do it like this," he told her, as a wave of nausea hit him. "Just like this."

Plessie began to cry. "You're not going to die, are you, Uncle Lennox?"

"From little scratches like this? No. Now come around to my back and show me your sewing."

Taliesen led Caswallon away from the cabin, and on into the trees. It was not cold, but the breeze brought a promise of autumn in the air. "The child will be the future queen—if she lives," said the druid.

Caswallon stopped. "What do you mean, if she lives? We know she lives. I watched her die after killing the beast."

Taliesen gave a dry laugh. "My boy, you saw *one* Sigarni. But it would take too long to explain the infinite possibilities when one deals in time, the paradoxes created. Merely hold to the concept of impossibility made reality. This child is in great danger. First and foremost is the sorcerer Jakuta Khan. He was hired to bring about the fall of the King, Sigarni's real father, and in exchange he was offered wealth—and the life of the King's daughter. He is a gifted magicker, Caswallon. He will track her down; the crofter cannot stand against him."

Caswallon sat down on a fallen tree. "The thought fills me with sorrow, Taliesen, but what can we do? My people need me. I cannot stay here and protect the babe. Nor can you. We do not have the time."

"That word again—time," responded Taliesen, sitting beside the taller man. "It matters not how long we wait here, for when you return no *time* will have passed in the world you know. There is a small settlement close by; we will rest there, and be offered food. Then we will journey back to the falls and make camp by the rock face where the Gateway opened. There you will see in one day what few mortals will ever see."

The following evening Caswallon built a small fire by the rock face, and the two men sat eating a meal of honey biscuits and watching the fragmented moon dance upon the rippling water of the falls pools.

"How long do we wait?" asked Caswallon.

"Until I feel the magic of Jakuta Khan," said Taliesen. "But now there is someone I must summon." Rising, the little sorcerer moved to the poolside. As Caswallon watched, Taliesen began to chant in a low voice. The wind died down and a mist formed above two boulders close to the pool's edge. Caswallon's eyes widened as the mist rose into an arch some ten paces in front of the sorcerer. Tiny lights, like fireflies, glittered in the archway, and then a man appeared, tall, impossibly broad-shouldered, wearing a silver breastplate and a shining mail shirt of silver steel. His hair was moonwhite, his beard braided.

"Who calls Ironhand?" he asked, his voice low and deep like distant thunder. Caswallon rose and walked to stand beside Taliesen.

"I call upon you, High King," said the sorcerer. "I, Taliesen, the Druid Lord. Your daughter lives, but she is in peril."

"They killed me here," said the ghostly warrior. "My body

lies beneath those boulders. They killed my wife, and I cannot find her spirit."

"But your daughter lives: The babe sleeps in a cabin close by. And the hunters will come for her, the demons will stalk her."

"What can I do, Taliesen? I am a spirit now."

"You can do nothing against men of flesh, Ironhand. But I have planted a seed in the child's mind. When the demons materialize she will flee here. The creatures, though flesh, are also summoned through spirit spells. You can fight them."

"When you need me, call upon me," said the Ghost King. The archway shimmered and vanished, and Caswallon once more felt the night breeze upon his skin.

"She is Ironhand's daughter? Sweet Heaven!"

"Aye," whispered Taliesen, "she is of the blood most royal. Now let us return to the fire. There is a spell I must cast before I leave you." The druid banked up the fire, and once more began to chant. Caswallon sat silently until he had finished, then Taliesen took a deep breath. "There is a man I must see. He is a dreamer and a drunkard, but we will need him before long. Stay here, and do not for any reason venture from the fire." He smiled. "I think what you are about to see will keep you well entertained until I return."

Rising, he ambled away along the line of the pool. Caswallon leaned back against the rock face. Suddenly the moon sped across the sky, the sun flashing up to bathe the pool in brilliant light. Then as suddenly as it had come the sun fell away, and the moon reappeared. Astonished, Caswallon gazed around the pool. There was no sound now, but night and day appeared and disappeared in seconds. Beyond the firelight the grass grew long, withered and dried, died and was replaced. Trees sprouted branches before his eyes. Leaves opened, glistened, withered, and fell. Within the space of a moment snow appeared beyond the fire, thick and deep. Then it was gone, instantly replaced by the flowers of spring.

He watched the seasons pass by in heartbeats, in blazes of color and streams of light.

When the snow had appeared for the sixth time, the rushing of time began to slow. The moon reared up and stopped in mid-heaven.

The cold of winter now whispered past Taliesen's spell and Caswallon shivered. Movement to his right caught his eye and he saw Taliesen trudging through the snow toward him. The old man was carrying a short hunting bow and a quiver of arrows. "How did you make the seasons move so fast?" asked Caswallon.

"Not even I can do that," answered Taliesen wearily. "You are sitting beside a Gateway. I merely activated it. It flickered *you* through the years."

"It is a memory I shall long treasure," said the clansman.

"Sadly, we have no time to dwell upon it," Taliesen told him, "for the evil is almost upon us." He squatted down by the fire, holding out his long, thin fingers to the flames. "I am so cold," he said, "and tired." He handed Caswallon the bow and arrows.

"What are we facing?" asked the clansman, stringing the bow and testing the pull. It was a sturdy weapon.

"Men would call them demons, and so they are, but they are also flesh and blood from another dimension . . . another land, if you will. They are huge beasts, Caswallon, some reaching eight feet tall. In build they are much like great bears, but they move with greater speed, and are upright, like men. Their fingers are taloned, each talon the length of your hunting knife. They have fangs also, and short, curved tusks. They do not use the tusks in combat; these are for ripping flesh from the leather-skinned beasts they have hunted in their own world."

"Should we not make our way to Cei's cabin? He cannot face them alone."

Taliesen shook his head. "Cei's life is over, boy. It was over the moment he agreed to take the babe. The beasts will materialize there."

"What?"

"They will be conjured there," snapped Taliesen. "Jakuta

Khan is a spellmaster; he has located Sigarni and will cause the beasts to appear inside the cabin. I have observed him, Caswallon. He has used these beasts before; he makes them invisible to the human eye. The first moment the victim knows of their existence is when the talons rip out his heart. Trust me, we do not want to be inside the cabin when that happens."

"How then do we save the babe?"

"She is no longer a babe. You have seen the seasons fly by and she is six now. And she will make her way here. I planted a seed in her mind, and that of her mother. As soon as the terror manifests itself, both will act instinctively. The child will run here."

Caswallon rose and tied the quiver to his belt. "And how am I to fight these invisible beasts?" he asked softly.

"As best you can, clansman. Come, kneel by me, and I will give you all that I can."

Dropping to one knee, Caswallon looked into the old man's eyes. The druid was more than tired. His eyes were dull and purple-ringed, his skin dry. Lifting his hand, Taliesen covered Caswallon's eyes and began to chant. Heat emanated from his fingers, lancing into Caswallon's brain like an arrow of fire. The clansman groaned but Taliesen's voice whispered to him: "Hold on, boy, it will not last much longer."

The hand fell away and Caswallon opened his eyes. "What have you done?" he whispered. The trees by the pool had changed now, becoming sharp and unreal, like a charcoal sketch upon virgin paper. Taliesen's features could no longer be seen; he was merely a glowing form of many colors, red in the belly and eyes, purple over the heart, the rest a shifting mix of orange, yellow, and white.

"Now you will see them, Caswallon," said the shimmering druid. "They will come from the south, hard on the heels of the child. Best you find a place to smite them."

"How many will come?"

"I would guess at two. It needs a mighty spell to summon just one. Jakuta Khan will expect little resistance from a crofter. But there might be more; he is young and arrogant in his strength."

Caswallon moved out onto the frozen pool and headed south, moving high into the tree line. An old oak stood beside the trail, its two main branches—some ten feet high— spreading out like the arms of a supplicant. Caswallon climbed to the right-hand branch and sat with his back to the tree bole.

His thoughts were many as he waited for the beasts. He had never lacked physical courage—in fact, he had often courted danger merely for the thrill of it. But now? The Farlain were under threat, and his wife and child were in peril in another world. No longer able to afford the luxury of danger, he felt fear rise within him. What if he died here? What would become of the Farlain, or Maeg, and Donal? His mouth was dry. His thoughts swung to the child, Sigarni: an innocent hunted by demons. Yet what was her life when set against his entire clan?

"I will fight, but I cannot die for you," he said softly. "I cannot risk that.

His decision made, he relaxed. Looking down at the glimmering colors that were his hands, he realized that the fingers had become difficult to see, and they were cold. He rubbed his palms together and looked again. For a few heartbeats they shone with a dull red light, then faded once more. Tugging his fleece-lined gloves from his belt, he pulled them on. Ice formed in his beard as he waited in the tree. Glancing back, he saw the shimmering colors he recognized as Taliesen moving across the ice. The old man must be frozen, he thought. The cloak of feathers would do little to keep out the bitter cold.

A bestial scream tore through the silence of the night. Caswallon removed his gloves and notched an arrow to the bowstring. For some moments there was no movement, then a small figure ran into sight, the colors glowing around her bright and rich. The figure stumbled and rolled in the snow.

Pulling his gaze from her, Caswallon looked back up the trail. Something huge loomed over the hillside, then another.

To his left was a third, moving through the trees. Caswallon cursed, gauging the beasts to be around eight feet tall. The first of the creatures lumbered down the slope. Its colors were strong, mostly purple, orange, and red; the purple area spread from the neck to the belly in two vertical circles joined by a red ridge. Caswallon drew back on the bowstring until it touched his right cheek, then he let fly. The arrow hammered home in the upper circle of purple and instantly the color changed, flowing from the wound as golden light. Caswallon loosed a second shaft that punched through the lower circle. The creature gave a terrifying shriek, tottered to the left, and fell heavily.

Twisting around, Caswallon saw that the child had reached the poolside. Two beasts were converging on her. Of Taliesen there was no sign. Dropping from the tree, Caswallon notched an arrow and raced down the icy slope. His foot struck a tree root hidden by snow and he was pitched forward. Releasing the bow, he tried to roll over and stop his slide, his hands scrabbling at the snow. Another tree root saved him, his fingers curling around it. Scrambling to his feet he saw the first of the beasts almost upon the helpless child. His bow was some twenty paces up the slope. Drawing his short sword and hunting knife Caswallon ran forward. As the beast reared up, he ducked under a sweeping slash from a taloned paw and stabbed his knife hilt deep into the creature's belly. A backhanded blow took him high on the shoulder, lifting him from his feet and hurling him through the air. Falling hard, he struck his left shoulder against a tree trunk, paralyzing his arm. The mortally wounded beast staggered and fell, but the third demon reared up and advanced on the clansman.

With an angry curse Caswallon rose, eyes glittering.

"Run, you fool!" shouted Taliesen as the beast loomed before the clansman. Deep in his heart Caswallon knew that he should take that advice. There was so much to live for, so much still to be achieved.

The beast turned away from him—toward the child at the

water's edge. In that moment Caswallon felt relief flood over him. He was safe! I live and she dies, he thought suddenly.

Without further thought he took three running steps and hurled himself at the beast, plunging his sword into its broad back. The creature screamed and spun. The sword was ripped from the clansman's hand, but remained jutting from the beast's rainbow flesh. Talons ripped into Caswallon's shoulder, pain searing through him as he was thrown to the ground.

In that moment a bright light blazed and Caswallon saw the massive, shimmering figure of Ironhand standing over the child, sword held two-handed and raised high. The beast gave a low growl and sprang at the ghost. The dead King stepped forward to meet it, his silver sword slashing through the air in a glittering arc; it passed through the creature seemingly without leaving a wound.

But the demon froze, tottered, and toppled backward to the snow.

Taliesen emerged from his hiding place in the undergrowth and ran to the child. Caswallon's vision blurred, the spell placed over his eyes fading. He blinked and saw the druid kneeling beside Sigarni. The girl was sitting silently, her eyes wide open and unblinking. Taliesen placed his hands on the child's head. "Is she hurt?" asked the Ghost King.

Taliesen shook his head. "Her body is safe, her spirit scarred," he said.

With a groan Caswallon pushed himself to his feet. Blood was flowing freely from the gash to his shoulder. "What will happen to her now?"

"There is one coming who will look after her. His name is Gwalch; he is a mystic," Taliesen told him.

"I hope this is an end to her adventures with demons," said Caswallon.

"It is not," whispered Taliesen. "But the next time she must fight them alone."

"Not alone," said the King. "For I shall be here."

*   *   *

With time against him, Gaelen led the companions over the most hazardous terrain, skirting the Aenir army on the third day of travel. From their hiding place on a wooded hillside, the companions gazed down on the horde moving through the valley.

The size of the enemy force dismayed the clansmen. It seemed to stretch and swell across the valley, filling it. There were few horsemen, the mass of fighting men striding together, bearing round shields painted black and red, and carrying long swords or vicious double-headed axes.

Gaelen was worried. For the last day he had been convinced that the companions were being followed. Agwaine shared his view, though when Gwalchmai and Layne scouted the surrounding woods they found only animal tracks. Onic and Ridan, anxious to push on, accused Gaelen of needless caution.

That night they made late camp on open ground and lit a fire. The moon was hidden by a dark screen of storm cloud and the night covered them like a black fog. Gaelen was glad of the darkness and curled into his blanket. Onic had suggested they head for Carduil, a jagged, unwelcoming series of peaks to the east, and Gaelen had agreed. The companions had moved south at first, hugging the timberline, gradually veering toward the distant mountains. Tomorrow they would head into the rising sun over the most dangerous stretch, wide valleys with little cover. Making a cold camp in a hidden hollow, Gaelen took the first watch. After an hour Layne moved through the darkness to sit beside him.

"Can't you sleep?" asked Gaelen.

"No, cousin. I wish you had brought Render with you. I feel uneasy."

"He's well trained," said Gaelen, "but he's still a hound, and his hunting might have alerted the Aenir."

"It is not the Aenir that concern me," whispered Layne.

"You are still thinking about the wolves?"

"Aye—and the beast which killed the Queen." The moon

cleared the clouds and Gaelen looked at his friend. Layne's hair glinted silver in the moonlight.

Gaelen shivered. "You think they might be demons?"

"I hope not," said Layne. "But if they are—and they continued to follow the child—I fear for Lennox."

Gaelen put his arm around his friend's shoulder. "If any man can survive against such beasts, Lennox will. I have no fears for him."

Layne smiled. "He is uncommonly strong." For a time they sat together in silence, then Layne spoke again. "Did you propose to Deva?"

"Yes. She spurned me."

"Me too. Some nonsense about birthing kings. I think she'll grow out of it. Will you continue to court her?"

"No, Layne."

"I shall. Once we have crushed the Aenir, I shall pursue her with such ardor that she will melt into my arms." He grinned, looking suddenly boyish again.

Gaelen smiled. "I wish you good fortune, my friend."

"I think I'll get some sleep now," said Layne.

"Layne!" whispered Gaelen as his friend rose.

"What?"

"I never really thanked you for standing up for me on that first day, when Agwaine drew his knife. You made me feel welcome among the Farlain and I'll not forget it. And if ever you need me, I will be there for you."

Layne said nothing, but he smiled and then moved back to his blanket. Gaelen kept watch for another two hours, then he woke Ridan.

"You've ruined a fine dream," muttered the clansman, sitting up and yawning.

Gaelen crossed the clearing and lay down. Sleep came instantly, but a faint rustling brought him awake. Was one of the others moving around? He took a deep breath, releasing it slowly, and listened again.

Silence.

No! There was the sound again, away to the right.

An animal? A bird?

Gaelen curled his hand around the short sword lying next to him, gently easing it from the leather scabbard. He felt foolish, thinking back to the first night he had spent in the open with Caswallon, when the fox had terrified him.

A crunching noise, followed by a bubbling gurgle, brought him to his feet and the clouds above moved away from the moon. A scene of horror met his eyes. Five huge beasts were crouching in the camp. Ridan lay dead, his throat ripped apart, while another body was being dragged toward a screen of bushes.

Gaelen froze.

One beast, red eyes glinting, reared up on its hind legs and ran silently toward him. Gaelen shouted a warning and Onic rolled to his feet, his arm flashing back and then forward. His hunting knife shot across the camp to plunge deep into the beast's back; it howled then, rending the night silence. Gaelen leaped forward, ramming his sword into the beast's chest. Talons lashed at him and he jumped back, releasing the blade. Then Gwalchmai ran forward and hurled his knife, which thudded into the creature's neck.

And the clouds closed, darkness blinding them all.

Gaelen dived for his pack, scrabbling at the canvas lip. Delving inside, he produced his tinderbox. There were only a few shredded leaves inside, but he was desperate for light. Twice the sparks jumped and then a tiny flame licked out. Holding up the box like a flickering candle, Gaelen turned. He could see Agwaine, Onic, and Gwalchmai standing together with swords in hand. On the ground nearby lay the hideous corpse of the dead beast. Elsewhere there was no sign of the pack.

The others joined him, gathering twigs and branches, and they built a fire, heedless of any danger from the Aenir. Agwaine took a burning branch and moved to the spot where Layne had slept. The ground was wet with blood, and his body was lying some twenty feet away. Ridan's corpse was nowhere in sight.

Gaelen moved to where Layne lay and with trembling

hands turned over the corpse. Layne's throat had been ripped away, but his face was untouched and his grey eyes were open, staring at nothing. Gaelen sank back. Gwalchmai knelt by the body and reached out, his fingers tenderly brushing the skin of Layne's face. "Oh, God," said Gwalchmai. Gaelen lifted Layne's hand, picturing him as he had been only a few hours before—tall, handsome, and in love.

"I promised to be there for you, and I wasn't," he said. "I am so sorry, Layne."

"We must bury him—deep," said Agwaine.

"We can't," said Gaelen. "The fire will have alerted the Aenir, and the beasts could return at any time. We must push on."

"I'll not have him devoured by those creatures!" stormed Agwaine.

Gaelen rose, tears shining in his eyes. "You think I do not feel exactly the same, Agwaine? But Layne is gone. His spirit has fled; all that is left is dead flesh which, even if we bury it, will be devoured by maggots. The Farlain need us, Layne does not. Now let us move."

"But we don't know where those creatures are," objected Gwalchmai. "We could run right into them."

"And if we don't," snapped Gaelen, "then by morning we'll all be blood-eagled to the trees."

"Gaelen is right. It's time to move," said Agwaine. "Kill the fire."

Donning their packs they set off toward the east, where the dark line of the Carduil range could be seen against the sky. They walked with swords in hand, saying little, and the journey was fraught with fear. The storm clouds passed over them, lightning flashing to the south, and the moon shone bright.

"By the Gods, look!" exclaimed Gwalchmai.

On either side of them, some twenty paces distant, dark shadows could be seen moving from bush to bush.

"How many?" hissed Agwaine.

"Four," answered Onic.

Swiftly they doffed their packs, stringing the short hunting bows.

"Wait!" said Gaelen. "Let us each pick a target, for once they learn the power of the bow they will be more wary."

Gwalchmai eased back on the string. "All right. I'll take the one on the left at the rear."

Choosing their targets they waited patiently, Gwalchmai and Onic kneeling, Agwaine and Gaelen facing right with bows half drawn.

The werebeasts crouched in the bushes, confused and uncertain. They could not see the shining talons that had cut down their comrade, only long sticks of wood. But they were wary. The leader edged forward, raising his head. The scent of warm flesh caused his stomach to tighten and saliva dripped from his maw. He moved into the open on all fours, edging still closer. A second followed him. On the other side a third beast was in view.

More clouds bunched above them, the sky darkening.

Gaelen cursed. "Let fly . . . NOW!"

Shafts hissed through the night air. The leader howled as the missile sliced into his chest, spearing his lungs. Blood filled his throat and the howling ceased. Behind him the second thrashed about in the bushes, an arrow through his eye.

To the left Gwalchmai's target had dropped without a sound, shot through the heart. Only Onic had not let fly. His target had remained in the bushes. Alone and frightened, it sprinted away to the west.

Chapter Ten

Taliesen led Caswallon to a long room beneath the Vallon caves. The walls were lined with shelves of old oak, some of them twisted and cracked with age. Upon some of them were parchment scrolls, leather-bound books, and sheafs of paper bound with twine. Others were stacked with metal cylinders or small glass bottles sealed with wax. On the far side of the hall two druids were sitting at one of the many tables, poring over scrolls and scribbling notes with quill pens.

Maggrig, Leofas, and Maeg were waiting there when the druid and the clansman arrived. While Maeg examined the shallow wound in her husband's shoulder, Maggrig pressed Caswallon about his journey through the Gateway. He told them of the baby, and the old man who had been carrying her.

As she spoke the old man's name Taliesen sank to a chair, eyes wide, mouth agape. It was the first time Caswallon had seen him so surprised. "You did not tell me it was Astole," he whispered. "Still alive!"

"He's not alive now," said Caswallon. "He died there in that forest."

Taliesen shook his head. "Unlikely. He had remarkable powers of recuperation," said the druid. "He is twice as old as I am. And I once saw a spear pierce his chest, the point emerging alongside his spine. He made me draw it from him; I did, and watched the wound heal within seconds."

"Alive or dead, he cannot help us now," said Caswallon. "So what do we do?"

"We try again—if you feel strong enough. Do you?"

"Is there a choice, druid?"

Taliesen shook his head. Maggrig loomed over the druid. "Except that after the last mistake," he said, "you might now waft him away to the center of the Aenir camp, and he can demand their surrender."

"It was not a mistake," snapped the druid. "It was destiny."

"Well, if there is a moment of *destiny,*" promised Maggrig, "I'll pierce your scrawny ears with your teeth!"

"That will be hard to do—after I've turned you to a toad!" Taliesen countered.

"Enough!" said Maeg sharply. "Go back to the Gate—all of you. I need to speak to my husband." Maggrig swallowed his anger and followed Taliesen and the old warrior Leofas from the room.

When they had gone, Maeg took Caswallon's hand and looked deep into his sea-green eyes. "I love you, husband," she said, "more than life. I want so much to ask you—to beg you—to refuse Taliesen. Yet I will not . . . even though my heart is filled with fears for you."

He nodded, then lifted her hand to his lips. "You are mine, and I am yours," he said. "You are the finest of women, and I have not the words to tell you what you mean to me." He fell silent as a single tear rolled to Maeg's cheek. "I love you, Maeg. But I must do what I can to save my people."

The clansman stood, and hand in hand he and Maeg walked to the Gate. It stood open, the bright sunshine of another world blazing down upon hills and mountains. Taliesen stood waiting on the other side. Maeg kissed Caswallon and he felt the wetness of her tears on his cheek. Maggrig gripped his hand. "Take care, boy," he said gruffly.

Recovering his sword, Caswallon stepped through the archway onto the hillside above Citadel town.

"Remember, Caswallon," said Taliesen, "the Queen must have her army assembled within ten days. Take her to the falls where we fought the demons. Tell her Taliesen needs her help."

"You think she will remember you after all these years?"

"She saw me only yesterday," said Taliesen. "Well . . . yesterday to her. And now it is time to go. Come back here at dawn in four days and report on your progress."

Leaving the druid behind him, Caswallon set off down the slope toward the city. There were sentries at the gates, but many people were passing through and the clansman was not challenged. As he walked Caswallon gazed at the buildings; they were not like the houses of Ateris, being higher and more closely packed, built of red brick and stone, the windows small.

There were narrow, open sewage channels on both sides of the street, and the stench from them filled the nostrils. Crowds of revelers were gathering on every side, drunken clansmen and mercenaries, many singing, others dancing to the tune of the pipes. Caswallon threaded his way through them, heading for the Citadel above the town.

At the gates he was stopped by two guards wearing bronze breastplates and leather kilts. Both carried lances. "What is your business here?" asked the shorter of the two.

"I seek the Queen," replied Caswallon.

"Many men seek the Queen. Not all are allowed to find her."

"It is a matter of importance," said Caswallon.

"Do I know you?" asked the guard. "You seem familiar."

"My business is urgent," said Caswallon. The man nodded once more, then called a young soldier from the ramparts. "Take this man to the city hall. Ask for Obrin."

The soldier saluted and walked away. Caswallon followed. The man stopped before a wide flight of marble steps, at the top of which were double doors of bronze-studded oak. Before the doors were four more guards in bronze breastplates; each of these wore crimson cloaks and leather breeches cut short at the calf. The soldier led the way up the stairs and whispered to one of the sentries; the man tapped at the door and passed a message inside. After a wait of several more minutes the door opened once more and an officer came out.

He was tall and of middle years, his beard iron-grey, his eyes a frosty blue. He looked at Caswallon and smiled. Taking the clansman by the arm, he led him inside the hall. "The Queen is holding a victory banquet," he said, "but you will not find her in a good mood."

The hall was vast, with ten high-arched windows. A huge curved table was set at the center, around which sat more than two hundred men and women feasting on roast pig, swan, goose, chicken, and sundry other meats and pastries. The noise was incredible and Caswallon found himself longing for the open mountains. Swallowing down his distaste, he followed the officer forward.

At the far end of the hall, where the table curved like an upturned horseshoe, sat the Queen. She was a tall woman, silver-haired and yet young, and she wore a plain dress of white wool. Caswallon had seen this woman die in the Farlain three years before. Then she had been handsome but old; now she was a beauty, proud and strong, her clear grey eyes sparkling with life and energy. The eyes turned on Caswallon and Sigarni rose from her seat, a delighted smile on her face.

She hesitated, as if not believing what she saw. Then she was running to meet Caswallon. "Redhawk!" she shouted joyously. "You've returned!"

Caswallon returned the Queen's embrace, his mind racing as Sigarni gripped his shoulders.

"Let me look at you, Redhawk. By Heaven, how is it you have become young again? Have you dyed that beard? It was almost pure silver the last time we met."

"I hear you have done well," countered Caswallon, his mind racing.

"Well? Now, that is an understatement. The Outland King is slain, his army in ruins. The war may not be won, but we have gained valuable time. Time! Morgase is defeated—but she has vanished. Not one word of her in six months. But enough of that. Where have you been these last two years? I needed you."

"I have been in my own land, among my own people."

"You are ill at ease, my friend. What ails you?"

"I am merely tired, my lady."

She smiled. "Join us at table. We'll eat and hear a few songs," said Sigarni, leading him forward. "Later we'll talk."

The feast seemed to last an eternity, and great was his relief when eventually it ended. A servant led him to an upper bedchamber. It was small, with a single window and a long pallet bed. A fire was burning in the hearth. Moving to the window, Caswallon pushed it open and gazed out over the mountains. Confused, he remembered again the Queen's death near Attafoss, and her last words.

"Now the circle is complete," the Queen had said. "For you told me you would be with me at my death." And then at the last she had asked, Was I truly the Queen you desired me to be?" The cold winds of approaching winter made him shiver. Closing the window, he crossed the room to sit on the rug before the fire. He thought he had been prepared for anything, but the sight of the Queen had shaken him. She was stunningly beautiful, and despite his love for Maeg, he found in himself a yearning for Sigarni that he would not have believed possible.

For some time he sat there, then felt the draft on his back as the door opened.

Sigarni entered. She was dressed now in a simple woolen shirt of white that showed the curve of her breasts, and dark brown leggings that highlighted her long, slim legs. She sat down on the bed. No more the Queen, she looked now like a clanswoman—tall and strong, fearless and free. Her mouth was astonishingly inviting, and Caswallon found his heart beating wildly.

"What are you thinking, my wizard?" she asked, her voice more husky than he recalled from her greeting in the hall.

"You are very beautiful, lady."

"And you are changed," she said softly, her grey eyes holding to his gaze.

"In what way?" he countered.

Sigarni slid off the bed to sit next to him by the fire.

"When I greeted you I saw the surprise in your eyes. And now I am here beside you—and yet you do not seek to hold me. What has happened to you, Redhawk? Have you forsaken me for another? I will understand if that is true. By Heaven, I have said my share of farewells to lovers. I would hope to have the strength to accept similar treatment. Is that what is happening here?"

"No," he said, his mind reeling. Moving back from her, he stood and returned to the window. The moon was high over the mountains and he stared up at the sky, fighting to make sense of her words. They were lovers! How could this be? For Caswallon loyalty was not like a cloak, to be worn or discarded, but an iron code to live by. And yet . . .

"Talk to me, Redhawk," said Sigarni.

He swung to face her. Once more her beauty struck him like an arrow. "Taliesen told me that you understood the Gateways. You know, therefore, that they allow us to move through time as well as to other lands?"

"Of course," she told him. "What has that to do with you and me?"

He took a deep breath. "In all my life I have seen you only four times. Once as a babe in the forest, the second time by Ironhand's Falls, the third"—he hesitated and looked away—"in my own realm . . . and the fourth tonight in the great hall. Everything you say to me—about us—is . . . new and strange. If we are to be lovers, it is not now but in a time—for me—that is yet to be. As I stand here I have a wife, Meg, whom I adore, and a small child, Donal." He saw she was about to speak and raised his hand. "Please say nothing, for I know I would never betray Maeg while she lived. And I do not want to know what the future holds for her."

Sigarni rose, her face thoughtful. "You are a good man, Redhawk, and I love you. I will say nothing of Maeg . . ." She smiled. "Just as you hesitated about our meeting in your own realm. I will leave you now. We will talk in the morning."

"Wait!" he called out as she opened the door. "There is something I must ask of you."

"The debt," she said. Then, noting his incomprehension, she smiled softly. "You always said there would come a time when you would ask me a great favor. Whatever it is, I will grant it. Good night, Redhawk."

"You are a rare woman, Sigarni."

Turning back, she nodded. "You will one day say that to me with even more feeling," she promised.

Taliesen sat alone in the semidarkness of his viewing chamber. It was cold, and idly he touched a switch to his right. Warm air flowed through hidden steel vents in the floor and he removed his cloak. Leaning back against the headrest of the padded leather chair, he stared at the paneled ceiling, his mind tired, his thoughts fragmented.

He transferred his gaze to the gleaming files. Eight hundred years of notes, discoveries, failures, and triumphs.

Useless.

All of it . . .

How could the Great Gates have closed?

And why were the Middle Gates shrinking year by year?

The Infinity Code had been broken a century before his birth by the scientist Astole. The first Gate—a window really—had been set up the following year. It had seemed then that the Universe itself had shrunk to the size of a small room.

By the time Taliesen was a student his people had seen every star, every minor planet. Gates had been erected on thousands of sites from Sirius to Saptatua. Linear time had snapped back into a Gordian knot of interwoven strands. It was a time of soaring arrogance and interstellar jests. Taliesen himself had walked upon many planets as a god, enjoying immensely the worship of the planet-bound humanoids. But as he grew older such cheap entertainment palled and he became fascinated by the development of Man.

Astole, his revered teacher, had fallen from grace, becoming convinced of some mystic force outside human reality. Mocked and derided, he had left the order and vanished from the outer world. Yet it was *he* who had first saved the baby, Sigarni. Taliesen felt a sense of relief. For years he had feared a rogue element amid the complexities of his plans. Now that fear vanished.

He understood now the riddle of the Hawk Eternal.

"You and I will teach him, Astole," he said, "and we will save my people." A nagging pain flared in his left arm, and rubbing his biceps, he rose from the chair. "Now I must find you, old friend," he said. "I shall begin by revisiting the last place Caswallon saw you." His fingers spasmed as a new pain lanced into his chest. Taliesen staggered to his chair, fear welling within him. He scrabbled for a box on the desk-top, spilling its contents. Tiny capsules rolled to the floor . . . With trembling fingers he reached for them. There was a time when he would have needed no crudely manufactured remedies, no digitalis derived from foxglove. In the days of the Great Gates he could have traveled to places where his weakened heart would have been regenerated within an hour. Youth within a day! But not now. His vision swam. The fear became a tidal wave of panic that circled his chest with a band of fire. Oh, please, he begged. Not now!

The floor rose to strike his head, pain swamping him.

"Just one more . . . day," he groaned.

His fingers clenched into a fist as a fresh spasm of agony ripped into him.

And as he died the Gates vanished.

During the week that followed Caswallon's departure Maggrig led his Pallides warriors on a series of killing raids, hitting the Aenir at night, peppering them with arrows from woods and forests. Leofas, with four hundred Farlain clansmen, circled the Aenir force and attacked from the south.

Whenever the Aenir mustered for a counterattack the clans melted away, splitting their groups to re-form at agreed meeting places.

The raids were no more than a growing irritation to Asbidag, despite the disruption of his supply lines and the loss of some three hundred warriors. The main battle was what counted, and the clans could not run forever.

But where was Barsa? Nothing had been heard of his son and the Timber Wolves he led.

Drada trapped a raiding party of twenty Pallides warriors in a woods twelve miles from Attafoss, and these—bar one— were summarily butchered. The prisoner was tortured for seven hours, but revealed nothing. He had been blood-eagled on a wide tree. But the main force, led by Maggrig, escaped to the north, cutting through the ring of steel Drada had thrown around the woods. Still, twenty of the enemy had been slain, and Drada was not displeased.

In the southeast Gaelen and his companions had found more than eighty Pallides warriors in the caves of Pataron, a day's march from Carduil. These he had persuaded to march with him on his return. It was a start.

On the fifth day of travel Gaelen and his group entered the thick pines below Carduil, and as they climbed they felt the chill of the wind blowing down from the snowcapped peaks. As they neared the opening to a narrow pass, a tall woman in leather breeches and a hooded sheepskin jerkin stepped out from the trees, a bow half drawn in her hands.

"Halt where you stand," she commanded.

"We are seeking Laric," Gaelen told the clanswoman.

"Who are you?"

"Gaelen of the Farlain. I come with a message from the War Lord Caswallon and his friend Maggrig of the Pallides."

The warrior woman eased down the bowstring, returned the shaft to the quiver, and moved forward. "I am Lara," she said, holding out her hand. "Laric's daughter. My father is dead. He led the men on a raid to Aesgard; they were taken and slain to the last man."

"All dead?" asked Agwaine, pushing forward.

"Yes. The Haesten are finished."

"I am sorry," said Gaelen, his heart sinking.

"No more than we are," said Lara. "We are camped within Carduil. Join us."

The companions followed her into the pass, and up to the winding trail below the caves. Once within the twisted caverns Lara pushed back her hood, shaking loose her dark hair. Leaving the companions at a fire where food was being prepared, she took Gaelen to a small rough-cut chamber in which lay a bed and a table of pine.

"There used to be a group of druids here," she said, stripping off her jerkin. Tossing it to the bed, she pulled a chair from beneath the table and sat.

Gaelen sat on the bed, his misery evident. "You thought you'd find an army?" she asked softly.

"Yes."

"How many Farlain warriors escaped?"

"Close to four thousand."

"And Pallides?"

"Less than a thousand."

"They'll fight well," said the girl. "Would you like something to drink?" Gaelen nodded. She stood and crossed the chamber, bending to lift a jug and two goblets from behind a wooden chest. The soft leather of her breeches stretched across her hips. Gaelen blinked and looked away, suddenly uncomfortable.

She passed him a goblet of honeyed wine. "Are you warm?" she asked.

"A little."

"Your face is flushed. Take your jerkin off."

She really was quite striking, he realized as he removed the garment. Her eyes were the blue of an evening sky, her mouth wide and full-lipped.

"Why are you staring?"

"I'm sorry," he stammered.

"I saw you run in the Games," she said. "You were unlucky to miss the final."

"Luck had little to do with it," he said, happier to be on firmer ground.

"I heard—you were attacked. Still, the clans won."

"Yes."

"They will win again."

"At this moment I don't see how," said Gaelen. "Nothing has gone right for us. We have lost thousands and the Aenir are hardly touched."

"I have eight hundred warriors at my command," she said.

"What? Where are you hiding them?"

"They are not hidden. They are here, with me."

"You mean the women?"

"If that patronizing look does not fade soon, you Farlain pig swill, then you'll be leaving here faster than you came."

"I . . . apologize," he said.

"Well, stop apologizing!" she snapped. "It seems you've done nothing else since you arrived. You're the Lowlander Caswallon brought home, are you not?"

"I am."

"Then, this once, I will forgive you for not thinking like a clansman. All our women are skilled with the bow. We can also use knives, though swords are a little unwieldy. Our men are dead and our clan finished. None of us have any reason to go on living like beasts in the mountains. Even if we survive and smash the Aenir, there will be no Haesten. Our day is gone. The best we can hope for is to find husbands from other clans. Believe me, Gaelen, that is not a happy thought."

"Let us start again, Lara," he said. "I did not wish to insult you. And though I was once a Lowlander, I am well aware of the skill of clanswomen. I will accept your offer, if you still hold to it. You must forgive me. It has been a long spring and much has happened; I have been hunted, attacked, and have seen my closest friend slain. The enemy that destroyed your people did this to me when I was a child in Ateris," he told her, pointing to the blood-red eye and the jagged white scar above. "I had few friends in that city, but those were brutally murdered. Youngsters I grew to like among the Farlain are now rotting corpses. I was sent here to gather an army that could descend upon the enemy and, perhaps, turn the tide of battle. I do not patronize you, I admire you. But still I am disappointed."

"That I can understand," she said, her voice softening. "You were one of the Beast Slayers, were you not?"

"That seems so long ago now. There were five of us—and one of those lies dead back in the forest . . . or at least he would, had he not been devoured by another demon beast."

"Who died?" she asked.

"Layne."

"The handsome brother of the mighty Lennox," she said. "That is indeed a loss. You say there are more of these creatures still roaming the mountains?"

"One only. We slew the others."

"Good," she said with a smile. "You know you are now part of clan myths."

He nodded. "A small part."

"The Lowlander and the Ghost Queen."

"Is that what they call her?"

"Yes. The story is that she was the daughter of Earis returned from the grave."

"I don't know about that," he told her. "Her name was Sigarni, and she was a mighty warrior queen—the sort of woman you would follow into the caverns of the damned."

"I like the sound of her. I'll get us something to eat," she said, rising and taking his empty goblet.

"Tell me," he asked suddenly, "was your man killed?"

"I had no man."

"Why?"

"What business is it of yours?"

"I . . ."

"And don't apologize!"

He watched her leave the chamber, too aware for comfort of her sensual grace and the sleek lines of her body.

Maggrig was horrified when the young druid, Metas, brought him the news of Taliesen's death. The Pallides leader was still reeling from the trap that had been sprung on him that morning when the Aenir encircled his force. He had escaped, but only by good fortune.

Now he was thunderstruck. He sent a message to Leofas and retired with Intosh to the forest caves to await him. It was late afternoon when Leofas was led to him; with the old warrior was his giant son, Lennox.

"You have heard?" asked Maggrig, rising and gripping the old man's hand.

"Yes." Leofas was grey with fatigue and he slumped to the ground beside the crackling fire. "How could it happen?" he asked.

"Damned if I know. Druid magic. Taliesen was found dead in his chambers; they'd run to him to report the disappearance of the Gates. Metas tells me they've tried all the words of power, but none work anymore."

"All our women and children gone. Caswallon trapped in another land. Gods, it's hopeless," said Leofas.

"The druids are searching through Taliesen's records. So far they've achieved nothing."

Leofas rubbed his face, scratching at his iron-streaked beard. "It seems as if the Gods are riding with the Aenir."

"Let them," said Maggrig. "I've never had a lot of time for them. A man stands alone in his life; if he stops to rely on some invisible spirit, then he'll fail."

"Luck has a way of changing," said Intosh. "I don't believe we should do anything rash. We must proceed with the original plan."

"And commit suicide?" asked Maggrig. "The whole point of the Axta strategy was so that Caswallon could bring the Queen's army down on the enemy. Without that we will be wiped out within the morning."

"They could still reopen the Gates," said Lennox.

"I wouldn't trust those druids to open a pouch," snapped Maggrig. "It's hard to have faith in a group so prone to panic. Metas doesn't know his buttocks from a lump of cheese. And as for the rest, they're running around like headless chickens, so I'm told. If they reopen them in time, we'll stay with Caswallon's plan. If not—we must think again."

"There's worse news," said Lennox. The three men turned to him. "We caught an Aenir scout last night. He told us that Laric and his Haesten launched an attack on Aesgard. They were repulsed and trapped in Southwood by Orsa and two thousand Aenir, and were all slain. Laric's head was left on a spear. There will be no help from the south."

"Well, that's about it," said Maggrig. "All we need is a plague in our ranks and the day will be complete."

The four sat in silence around the fire, the burden of despair weighing them down.

A young Pallides warrior entered the cave. "The Loda Hunt Lord has arrived," he said.

"Bring him to me."

"I need no *bringing*!" said Dunild, pushing past the young warrior. The newcomer was short, but powerfully built. He had no beard, and his yellow hair hung to his shoulders beneath a woolen bonnet edged with leather and decorated with an eagle's feather.

Maggrig stood and forced a smile. "Well met, you poaching rascal!"

Dunild laid his round shield on the ground and gripped Maggrig's wrist. "You look fat and old, Maggrig," said the Loda Hunt Lord.

"That's because I *am* old and fat. But still a match for most men—including you. How many follow you?"

"Three hundred."

"Good news."

"I hear you've been suffering."

"I've had better days," admitted Maggrig. "What of Grigor?"

"I know nothing of the thieving louse," hissed Dunild.

"Now, that is not the whole truth, my friend," said Maggrig, "for you'd not have brought your clan and left your own valley unprotected."

Dunild grinned. "He says he will come and fight alongside *you*—as long as he doesn't have to fight alongside *me*!"

"How many will he bring?"

"He'll match me man for man, so I told him five hundred."

"I trust neither of you will leave any behind to raid each other's lands?"

"On the contrary. We've both done just that."

"I think you might be right, Intosh," said Maggrig. "Perhaps our luck is changing." The swordsman grinned and the newcomer joined them around the fire.

The discussion carried on into the night, and the men were joined by Patris Grigor, a skeletally lean, balding warrior and Hunt Lord to the Grigor clan. There were few better sword killers in the mountains than this taciturn clansman. He sat as far from Dunild as he could, and the two men exchanged not a word during the discussion, all comments directed at Leofas or Maggrig. The atmosphere was tense.

At dawn they received a report from the druid Metas. There had been no success with the Gates, and Taliesen's files had offered no solution. The Gates, he said, were closed forever.

For a time none of the leaders spoke. Their families gone, their hopes dashed, they sat in the silence of despair. Finally Leofas said, "All we have left now is to die—and take as many of the enemy with us as we can. Now is the time for a decision, Maggrig. Axta Glen is out of the question. So where do we make a stand?"

His words hung in the air. Maggrig, forcing his mind from thoughts of Maeg and his grandson, lost in time, glanced at Dunild and Grigor. The men had brought their warriors to fight alongside the other clans—not to throw their lives away. Maggrig saw the concern on their faces, and he knew what other thoughts would be stirring in their cunning minds. The Farlain and the Pallides had lost all their women and children. If, by some chance, they were able to destroy the Aenir they would then be forced to raid for women from other clans.

"We will find a way to open the Gates," he said, surprised at the confidence in his voice. "And more than that. I don't intend to merely lash out like a dying bear. I want to win. By the Gods, we're all clansmen here. Brothers and cousins. Together we will destroy Asbidag and his ragtag band of killers."

"A pretty speech, Maggrig," said Dunild softly. "But how—and where—will this be achieved?"

"That is for us to decide at this meeting," answered Maggrig. "Who will begin?"

An hour of discussion followed as the clan leaders suggested various possible battle sites, mostly occupying high ground. None of the sites offered even the possibility of a victory. Then Intosh suggested a mountain pass some twenty miles east. It was known as Icairn's Folly, following a battle there hundreds of years ago when a young chieftain had followed his enemy into the pass and been destroyed.

"We could man the pass walls with archers and lure the Aenir in upon us," said Intosh. "The mountain walls narrow to two hundred fifty paces apart at the center, and a small force could hold a larger one there."

"And what when we are pushed back? The pass is blocked and we would be like cattle in a slaughter pen," said Maggrig.

"Let's *not* be pushed back," said Intosh.

"But can we win there?" asked Grigor. "I don't like the idea of hurling my clan to doom on one battle."

"Can we win anywhere?" asked Leofas.

"The Folly does have one advantage," offered Maggrig. "Our archers will wreak a terrible slaughter among the enemy. The Aenir could break and run. They've done it before—when the Pallides crushed them."

"Even so, is it wise," asked Dunild, "to choose a battle site with no avenue of retreat?"

"All other areas are ruled out," said Intosh. "Although we cannot retreat, they cannot encircle us."

"We could continue to hit and run," suggested Lennox, who had remained silent for much of the planning.

"But we can't win that way," said his father. "I hate to admit it, but it seems we have run out of choices. I vote for Icairn's Folly."

The other leaders nodded, then Grigor spoke. "This is your war, Maggrig, not mine. I have come because we are all clan. But I'll not watch my men cut to pieces. My archers will man the left-hand slope of the pass. If you are crushed, we can still escape."

"What more could be expected from the Grigors?" snapped Dunild.

Patris Grigor started to rise, reaching for his sword, but Maggrig stopped him with a raised hand.

"Enough!" he said. "Patris is entirely correct. Dunild, you and your Loda warriors will hold the right-hand slopes, Patris the left. The Pallides and the Farlain will stand together at the center. If we are pushed back or scattered, the rest of you must get away with as many men as you can. Take to your own lands. But for the sake of all clansmen, do not go back to war with one another. For your lands will be next, I think."

"We are decided then?" asked Leofas.

"It seems so," said Maggrig.

Caswallon's first realization that anything was wrong came early on the fourth morning of his stay in Citadel. Borrowing a horse, he rode into the hills seeking Taliesen and the Gate. He was anxious to hear of the Aenir advance.

When he arrived at the slope he found no entrance. At first he was unconcerned and returned to the city, spending the day with Sigarni, listening as she talked warmly of her youth and the early days of her rule—days of bloody war and treachery, and close encounters with disaster. Through the conversations Caswallon's appreciation of the Queen grew. She was a natural tactician but, more than this, knew men, their strengths and weaknesses, and what drove them.

She had a close-knit band of followers, fanatically loyal, led by the powerful Obrin, the Queen's captain, a man of iron strength and innate cunning. Sigarni talked of a black general called Asmidir, who had died holding the rear guard against the Earl of Jastey and his army, and of a dwarf named Ballistar who had journeyed through a Gateway in the company of Ironhand's ghost. But of the Redhawk she had known she said little, save that he had appeared following the death of Asmidir and had helped her to train her men, leading the left wing against Jastey and his thousands.

"Do I have friends here?" he asked.

"Apart from me?" she countered with a quick smile. "Who would need more? But yes, there is Obrin. You and he became sword brothers. I think he is a little hurt that you have spent so little time with him."

The Queen had agreed to lead her warriors into the Farlain, but said she could gather only four thousand. The call went out, and the muster began.

At dawn Caswallon tried again to find the Gate. This time an edge of anger pricked him.

What was Taliesen doing, closing the Gate at such a time?

Taking supplies for three days, he rode north to the great falls of Attafoss. Leaving the horse tethered on a grassy meadow he swam across to the isle of Vallon and entered the deep honeycomb of caves beneath the hill. Near the entrance he was met by an elderly druid he had seen with Taliesen.

"Why has the Gate been closed?" asked Caswallon. The man wrung his hands. His face was pinched and tight as if he had not slept for days.

"I don't know," he wailed. "Nothing works anymore. Not one word of power."

"What does this mean?"

"The Middle and Lesser Gates have vanished—just like the Great Gates of yesteryear. We are trapped here. Forever."

"I will not accept that!" said Caswallon, fighting down the panic threatening to overwhelm him. "Now be calm and tell me about the words of power."

The man nodded and sank back on his narrow cot bed, staring at his hands. Caswallon's enforced calm soothed his own panic and he took a deep breath.

"The words themselves are meaningless, it is the *sound* of the words. The sounds activate devices set within the hillside here. It is not dissimilar to whistling for a hunting dog, which responds to sounds and reacts as it has been trained to do. Only here we are dealing with something vastly more complex, and infinitely beyond our comprehension."

"Something is . . . broken," said Caswallon, lamely.

"Indeed it is. But we are talking about a device created aeons ago by a superior race, whose skills we can scarce guess at. I myself have seen devices no bigger than the palm of my hand, inside which are a thousand separate working parts. We do not even have the tools to work upon these devices, and if we did we would not know where to start."

"So we cannot contact Taliesen?" asked Caswallon.

"No. I just pray he is working toward a solution on the other side."

"Are you one of the original druids?"

The man laughed. "No, my grandfather was. I am Sestra of the Haesten."

"Are there any of the elder race on this side of the Gate?"

"None that I know of."

Caswallon thanked him and returned to the mare. Two days later, weary to the inner depths of his soul, he rode back into Citadel town. Not to see Maeg again, and feel the touch of her lips on his. Not to see Donal grow into a fine man. Never to know the fate of his people. Doomed to walk the rest of his life in a foreign land under strange stars.

He sought the Queen, finding her in her private rooms at the east wing of the hall. He told her nothing of the disappearance of the Gates, but questioned her about the priest who had first brought her to the forest as a babe.

"What of him?" asked Sigarni.

"Did he survive?"

"You know that he did."

"I am tired, my lady, and my brain is weary. Forgive me. Does he still live, is what I meant."

"Only just, my love. He is the abbot of the Dark Woods, a day's journey to the east. But the last I heard he was blind and losing his wits."

"Can you spare a man to take me to him?"

"Of course. Is it important?"

"More important than I want to think about," said Caswallon.

With two horses each, Caswallon and a rider named Bedwyr rode through the day, reaching the Dark Woods an hour after dark. Both men reeled from their saddles and Bedwyr hammered at the door of the monastery. It was opened by a sleepy monk, whose eyes filled with fear as he saw the armor worn by the riders.

"Be at peace, man," said Bedwyr. "We're not raiders, we ride for the Queen. Does the abbot live?"

The man nodded and led them through narrow corridors of cold stone to a small cell facing west. He did not tap upon the door but opened it quietly, leading them inside. A lantern flickered upon the far wall, throwing shadows to a wide bed in which lay a man of great age, his eyes open, seeming to stare at the rough-cut ceiling.

"Leave us," ordered Caswallon. Bedwyr escorted the monk from the room and Caswallon heard the rider asking for food, and the monk's promise that he would find bread and honey. Caswallon walked forward and sat beside the abbot. He had changed much since Caswallon first saw him; his face was webbed with age and his sightless eyes seemed preternaturally bright.

"Can you hear me, Astole?" asked Caswallon.

The man stirred. "I hear you, Redhawk, my friend. There is fear in your voice."

"Yes. Great fear. I need your help now, as once you needed mine in the forest."

The man chuckled weakly. "There is no magic left, Redhawk. With all the wonders my mind encompassed I can now no longer lift this pitiful frame from the bed, nor see the brightest sunset. By tomorrow I shall have joined my Lord."

"The Gates have closed."

"That is ancient history."

"The Middle Gates."

"Again? That is not possible."

"Believe me, Astole, they have closed. How may I reopen them?"

"Wait a moment," said the old man. "When last did you see me?"

"You were in the forest with the infant Queen."

"Ah, I understand," said Astole. "It is so long since I played with time, and my mind is growing addled." His head sank back on the pillow and he closed his sightless eyes. "Yes, it is becoming clear. The Farlain is still under threat, the Queen has not yet passed the Gate, and you have yet to learn the mysteries. I have it now."

"Then help me," urged Caswallon. "Tell me how to reopen the Gate. I must lead the Queen through, or my people will perish."

"I cannot tell you, my boy. I can only show you, teach you. It will take many years—eleven, if I remember correctly."

"I don't have years," said Caswallon, hope draining from him. The old man was senile and making no sense. As if reading his mind Astole reached out a hand and gripped Caswallon's arm, and when he spoke his voice was strong with authority.

"Do not despair, my friend. There is much that you cannot understand. I made the Gates in my youth and arrogance. I discovered the lines of power that link the myriad pasts, the parallel worlds, and I made the machines to track them and ride them. It was I who allowed the Great Gates to close. My race was using the universe as an enormous whorehouse. I rerouted the prime power source to feed the Lesser and Middle Gates. But all power sources are finite—even those that flow from collapsed stars and make up the Sipstrassi. It is—in the *Now* that you inhabit—running to its finish. There are other sources, and I will teach you to find and realign them, and then the Gates will return. The man you see now is but the last fading spark of a bright fire. He will die tonight, and yet he will not be dead. We will meet again and he shall teach you.

"There is a cave behind this abbey; a chalice is carved upon the entrance. Let the muster of the Queen's men continue, and on the appointed day walk into the Chalice Cave and approach the far wall. It will appear as solid rock, but you will pass through it, for this Gate has not vanished but only shifted. On the other side, I shall be waiting."

"But you are dying!"

"We are speaking of events which have already happened, my boy. I was working upon a complex formula in my study when the Gateway flickered and you appeared. You told me that I had sent you, and you told me why. More I cannot say." The old man sighed, then gave a weak smile. "We are to be great friends, you and I. Closer than father and son. And yet I must say farewell to a stranger who is yet to be my friend. Ah, the tricks time plays . . ."

The old man fell silent and his eyes closed. Caswallon sat beside him, his mind tired, his burdens heavy. Was the abbot to be trusted? How could he tell? The future of his people rested with the promise of a dying monk. He sat with Astole until dawn's first light seeped through the wooden shutters of the window, then he lifted the abbot's hand from his arm.

Caswallon stood and gazed down at the old man. He was dead. The clansman lifted the blanket and pulled it over the abbot's face, pausing to study the man's expression. A faint smile was on the lips and a great feeling of peace swept over Caswallon.

He walked to the window, pulling open the shutters. The woods beyond shone in the early morning light. Behind him the door opened and the lancer Bedwyr stepped into the room.

"Did you find what you hoped for, Redhawk?"

"Time will tell."

"The old man died then," said the lancer, glancing at the bed.

"Yes. Peacefully."

"They say he knew great magic. Does that mean his spirit will return to haunt us?"

"I certainly hope so," said Caswallon.

Unaware of the growing drama, Gaelen led the Haesten women northwest, stopping only to meet the Pallides warriors. The eighty-man force had now swelled to one hundred ten, as other warriors crept in from the mountains and woods where they had hidden their families in derelict crofts or well-disguised caves. Ten men were to be left behind, to hunt and gather food for the hidden children, but the others were set to follow Gaelen.

The young clansman was truly concerned now, for he had never led such a force and was worried about the route. He conferred with Agwaine, Onic, and Gwalchmai. It was one thing for a small party to thread its way through the Aenir lines, quite another for an army numbering almost a thousand.

"We know," said Onic, "that the main army is before us, pushing north. We should have no real trouble for at least two days."

"You are forgetting Orsa," said Gaelen. "His force destroyed Laric in the south. We don't know if he will head north now and join his father. If he does, we will be trapped between them."

"Ifs and buts, cousin," said Agwaine. "We will solve nothing by such discussion. We are expected at Axta Glen and one way or another we must move on. We cannot eliminate all risks."

"True," admitted Gaelen, "but it is as well to examine them. So be it, we will head due north, and then cut west to Atta, and then on to the glen. That way we should avoid Orsa. But we'll push out a screen of scouts west and east, and you,

Gwal, shall go ahead of us in the north with five men to scout."

The self-appointed leader of the Pallides, a burly clansman named Telor, caused Gaelen's first problem. "Why should you lead, and make such decisions?" he asked when Gaelen told him of the plan.

"I lead because I was appointed to lead."

"I follow Maggrig."

"Maggrig follows Caswallon."

"So you say, Blood-eye."

Gaelen breathed deeply, pushing aside his anger. He rubbed his scarred eye, aware that Lara and the others were watching this encounter with detached fascination. Such was the way of warriors among the clans. Telor had now implied that Gaelen was a liar, and the two men were hovering on the verge of combat.

"Your land," said Gaelen at last, "has been overrun by an enemy. Your people are sundered and preparing to fight alongside the Farlain in a last desperate battle for survival. If they lose, we lose. Everything. And yet here you are debating a point of no importance. Now I will say this only once: I lead because I was chosen to lead. There is no more to discuss. Either draw your sword or obey me."

"Very well," said Telor. "I will follow you north, but once the battle is sighted I will lead the Pallides."

"No," said Gaelen.

The man's sword hissed from his scabbard. "Then fight me, Farlain."

The onlookers backed away, forming a circle around the two men.

"I do not desire to kill you," said Gaelen hopelessly.

"Then I lead."

"No," said Gaelen softly, drawing his sword. "You die."

"Wait!" shouted Lara, stepping forward with hands on hips. "It is well known that the Farlain are arrogant numbskulls, and that the Pallides have too long interbred with their cattle, but this is sheer stupidity. If you must fight, then fight, but let it be clear that if Gaelen conquers, then he leads ALL."

"What if Telor wins?" asked a young Pallides warrior.

"Then he leads the Pallides alone," said Lara. "I'll not follow a man with the brain of a turnip."

"You miserable Haesten bitch," snapped Telor. "You seek to rob the contest of any merit."

"It has no merit," said Gaelen. "Thousands of clansmen and their wives lie butchered by invaders, and you seek to add more clan blood to the soil."

Telor gave a harsh laugh. "Frightened, are you, Farlain?"

Gaelen shook his head. "Terrified," he said, dropping his sword and stepping forward, his forehead thundering against Telor's nose. The Pallides warrior staggered back, blood drenching his yellow beard, as Gaelen moved in with a left cross exploding against Telor's unprotected chin. The Pallides warrior pitched to his left, hitting the ground hard. Gaelen rolled the man to his back and drew his hunting knife, touching the point to Telor's throat. "Make a choice, live or die," he said coldly.

Telor lay very still. "Live," he whispered.

"The first wise choice you've made," said Gaelen. Rising, he gripped the man's right arm, hauling him to his feet. Telor staggered, but remained upright, blood dripping from his ruined nose. "Now, pick twenty Pallides to follow Agwaine and Onic. I want scouts east and west of us. Then you go, with three of your choosing, to the north to make sure our route is clear. Is that understood?"

Telor nodded.

Turning on his heel Gaelen set off, and the small army followed him. Lara moved up alongside him, grinning. "That was close," she said.

"Yes. Thank you for your help; it took away his concentration."

"It was nothing. I didn't want Telor to cut your ears off; he's second only to Intosh with a blade."

"Then I thank you again—with even more feeling."

"Are you a good swordsman?"

"I've recently learned to tell the point from the hilt."

"No, truly?"

"I am as good as most men."

"Have you killed any Aenir?"

"Yes."

"How many?"

"Gods, woman! What does it matter?"

"I like to know who I am following."

"I've killed five and wounded another."

"Five? That's not bad. Hand to hand, or with the bow?"

"Hand to hand. The wounded man I hit with an arrow."

"Marksmanship's not your strong point, then?"

"No. And you?"

"What about me?"

"Well, we seem to be talking about numbers killed, so I am asking you the same question."

"I see. Why?"

"Because I like to know the caliber of my followers," said Gaelen, grinning.

"I haven't killed any. But I will."

"I don't doubt it."

"Do you have a woman?" she asked suddenly.

"No."

"Why?"

"She refused me."

"I see," said Lara.

"What do you see?"

"I see why you are so nervous around women."

"I am not nervous around women, I am nervous with you," he said.

"Why is that?"

Gaelen was growing hot and beginning to feel like a hunted rabbit.

"Well?" she pressed.

"I have no idea, and I don't wish to discuss it," he said

primly. She laughed then, the sound deep and throaty, which only added to his discomfort.

On the first night of camp Gaelen avoided her, talking long into the night with Gwalchmai, who had returned from his scouting trip with Telor. Telor and his companions had remained in the north, and Gwal was due to rejoin them at first light.

"It was an uncomfortable day," said Gwalchmai. "I think we only exchanged three words."

"I'm sorry, Gwal. How does it look?"

"So far the route is clear. That Telor gives me cold chills, though."

"Yes. Let's hope he saves his anger for the Aenir."

"Let's hope they cut his damned heart out," muttered Agwaine, joining them.

Gaelen shook his head. "No wonder the clans are always at war," he said.

"How are you getting on with Lara?" asked Agwaine, his mouth spreading in a lecherous grin.

"What does that mean?" snapped Gaelen.

"She likes you, man. It's obvious."

"I don't want to talk about it."

"She's gorgeous, isn't she? Not beautiful exactly, but gorgeous. And those breeches . . ."

"Will you stop this?"

"I wish she liked me."

"I cannot believe this conversation is taking place. We are marching toward a battle, I'm trying to think about tactics, and all you can think about is . . . is . . . breeches."

"What about breeches?" asked Lara, moving up to sit with them.

"Yes, Gaelen, tell her about the breeches tactic," said Gwalchmai.

Gaelen closed his eyes.

"Well?" she said.

"You're the authority, Gwal. You explain it."

Gwalchmai chuckled. "No. If I'm to be with Telor by dawn, I'd best tuck up in my blankets. Excuse me."

Gwal moved off to fashion a bed below an overhanging pine. Agwaine grinned and also moved away—despite Gaelen's imploring gaze. "So?" said Lara. "What about breeches?"

"It was a jest. The clouds are bunching—there could be rain tomorrow."

"Come with me," she said, taking his hand. He followed her into the trees and they stopped some forty paces away in a circular clearing, screened by dense bushes. She led him to where she had placed her blankets and pulled him down beside her. The clansman was supremely ill at ease.

"What did you want to talk about?" he asked huskily.

"I don't want to talk, Gaelen." Leaning forward, she curled an arm around his neck and kissed him.

Thoughts of Deva vanished like ice on fire.

Leofas and Maggrig walked the length of the Folly as darkness gathered around them. The slopes on either side were steep and pitted with rocks and boulders, while the pass itself showed a steady incline toward the narrow center. The Aenir would be charging uphill and that would slow them. But not by much.

The two men were joined by Patris Grigor and a dozen of his archers. "It's a magnificent killing ground," said Grigor. "They'll lose hundreds before they reach you—if they come in, that is. What if they bottle up the mouth of the pass?"

"We attack them," declared Maggrig.

"That's not much of a plan," said Grigor, grinning.

"I'm not much of a planner," admitted Maggrig, "but I think they'll come at us. They've yet to learn fear."

"When your arrows are exhausted, we leave. If we can," said Grigor.

"Understood," said Maggrig, walking back toward the campfires in the wide pass beyond.

The walls of the box canyon rose sheer, reflecting the red light from hundreds of small fires. Leofas, who had remained silent on the long walk, sat back on a boulder, staring out over the clan army as they rested. Some men were already sleeping, others were sharpening sword blades. Many were laughing and talking.

"What's wrong, my friend?" Maggrig asked.

Leofas glanced up. In the flickering firelight Maggrig's beard shone like flames, his blue eyes glittering, his face a mask of bronze.

"I'm tired," said Leofas, resting his chin in his hands and staring out over the campfires.

"Nonsense! You'll be leading the victory dance tomorrow like a first-year huntsman."

The Farlain warrior looked up, eyes blazing. "Will you stop for a moment? I'm not a first-year huntsman, and I don't need you trying to lift me. I'm old. Experienced. I've seen war and death. Anyone who can tell a sword point from a hole in the ground knows we have little chance tomorrow."

"Then leave!" snapped Maggrig.

"And where would I go, Maggrig? No, I don't mind dying alongside you. In fact, I don't mind dying. My hope is that we cull their ranks enough for the other clans to have a chance of defeating them."

"You think I've been foolish?" asked Maggrig, slumping beside him.

"No. We ran out of choices, that's all."

For a time they sat in silence, then Maggrig turned to his companion. "Do you mind if I ask you a personal question?"

"I don't mind if you ask," said Leofas. "I may not answer."

"Why did you never remarry? You were only a young man when Maerie died."

Leofas switched his gaze to the stars and the years slipped away like falling dreams. He shook his head. Finally he spoke, his voice soft, his eyes distant.

"I miss her most at sunset, when we'd go to the ridge behind the house. There was an old elm there. I built a seat around the base and we'd sit there and watch the sun die. I'd wrap us both in my cloak and she'd rest her head on my shoulder. It was so peaceful, you could believe there was not another living being in the world. I felt alive then. I never have since."

"So why not remarry?"

"I didn't want anyone else. And you?"

"No one else would have me," said Maggrig.

"That's not true."

"No, it's not," admitted Maggrig. "But then Rhianna and I didn't watch many sunsets. In truth we spent most of our life together squabbling and rowing. But she was a good lass for all that. Maeg was four when Rhianna died, she wouldn't have taken to another mother."

"We're a pair of fools," said Leofas again. "Do you regret not having sons?"

"No," lied Maggrig. "And we're getting maudlin."

"Old men are allowed to get maudlin. It's a rule of life."

"We're not that old. I'm as strong as ever."

"I'm ten years older than you, Maggrig, and according to tradition, that makes me wise. Between us we muster a century or more. That's old."

"I never used to be old," said Maggrig, grinning. "Strange how it creeps up on a man."

They let the silence grow, each drifting on a river of memories. It was, they believed, their last night alive under the stars and neither wanted to talk about tomorrow.

Drada was angry, more angry than he could ever recall. The clans had mounted a series of raids, retreating always to the east. He sensed a plan behind the attacks and now it had become clear.

That morning Aenir scouts had reported a movement of the clans toward a pass six miles east. Drada, who had scouted the land personally some days before, knew that the pass was blocked and impassable to the north. Surely the clans would not consider a battle there? But they had, and now the Aenir force was waiting in the mouth of Icairn's Folly—and Drada was crimson with rage.

"But why attack, Father? It is unnecessary. There is no way out for them; if we wait they must attack us."

"I command here!" thundered Asbidag. "Why do you plead caution when we have them where we want them?"

"Listen to me, Father. The slopes within could hold a thousand archers. They will take a huge toll. The main army will be near the center of the pass, where the mountain walls narrow, which means our weight of numbers will be lessened. We will be fighting one to one. Of course we'll win—but we could lose thousands in there."

"They brought me Barsa's rotting corpse this morning," said Asbidag. "Now I have two sons calling for vengeance. And you want me to sit and wait."

"The clans have made a terrible mistake," said Drada. "They are hoping we will do exactly what you are planning. It is their *only* hope."

"What are you, a prophet now? How do you know what they are planning? I believe we have surprised them in their lair. Get the men ready to charge."

Drada swallowed his anger, and it tasted of bile. He turned away from his father then, so that he would not see the burning hatred in his eyes.

You are dead, Asbidag, Drada decided. After the battle, I will kill you.

The Aenir line assembled in the mouth of the pass, shield straps being tightened, sword hands rubbed in dust for better grip. Twenty-five thousand men peered at the rock-strewn slopes and the towering mountain walls beyond. There was no enemy in sight.

The war horns of the Aenir sounded and the armor-clad mass began to move slowly forward, Drada and Tostig together at the center, Asbidag's other sons to the left and right of them. Asbidag himself stayed at the mouth of the pass surrounded by his forty huscarles. Morgase stood beside him, her eyes bright, her heart hammering as she waited for the killing to begin.

The Aenir army moved on warily, with shields held high,

scanning the slopes. Ahead of them the pass narrowed and still there was no sign of the enemy . . .

Suddenly the Folly was alive with noise as the Farlain and the Pallides moved into sight to man the narrow center. A great roar went up from the Aenir as they surged forward, beating shields with their sword blades. On either side of them rose archers from the Dunilds and the Loda. Goose-feathered shafts filled the air. The screams of wounded men rose above the war cries and now the clans roared out their own battle cry that echoed in the mountains, booming and growing.

Dark clouds of hissing death flashed into the Aenir horde in a series of withering volleys. Some warriors broke from the ranks to charge the archers, but these were cut down by scores of shafts. The charge slowed, but did not stop.

At the front of the Aenir line the giant Orsa felt the bare-sark rage upon him. Hurling aside his shield, he raced ahead of his men bellowing his anger and swinging his broad-sword above his head. An arrow sliced into his thigh but he ignored it.

Lennox leaped from the line to meet him, holding a long-handled mace of lead and iron. He too threw aside his shield as Orsa ran forward slashing his blade toward the clansman's head. Lennox made no move to avoid the blow but lashed the mace into the blade, smashing it to shards. Orsa crashed into him and both men fell to the ground, Orsa's hands closing about Lennox's throat. Releasing the mace, Lennox reached up to cup his hand under Orsa's chin; then punching his arm forward, he snapped the Aenir's head back, tearing the man's grip from his neck. Rolling, Lennox came up with the mace and delivered a terrible blow to Orsa's skull, crushing the bones to shards and powder.

With scant seconds to spare Lennox rejoined the line, standing beside his father, Leofas, and the Pallides War Lord Maggrig. The front line of the Aenir bore down on the waiting clans. Maggrig lifted his sword, grinned at Intosh, then screamed the battle cry of the Pallides.

"Cut! Cut! Cut!"

The chant was taken up and the clans surged into the charging Aenir. After four years of war in the Lowlands the Aenir believed they were the finest fighters under the sky, but never had they met the fierce-eyed, blood-hungry wolves of the mountains. Now they learned the terrible truth, and as the blades of the clans slashed and cut their first line to shreds, the charge faltered.

Maggrig powered his way into the Aenir ranks, cleaving and killing, an awful fury upon him. Many were the Pallides dead whose faces he would never forget, whose souls hungered for vengeance. The War Lord forgot the plan to hold the center and forged ever deeper into the enemy. Intosh and the Pallides had no choice but to follow him.

Leofas gutted one warrior and parried a blow from a second, backhanding his shield into the man's face. Lennox aided him, braining the man with his mace.

"Sound the horn!" yelled Leofas. "Maggrig's gone mad!"

Lennox stepped back from the fray, allowing Farlain warriors to shield him from the enemy. Lifting his war horn to his lips, he blew three sharp blasts. The sound filtered through Maggrig's rage and he slowed in his attack, allowing the Pallides to form around him. The weight of the Aenir numbers was beginning to tell and the clans were pushed back, inch by murderous inch.

The deadly storm of arrows had slowed now, for the archers on the slopes were running short of shafts.

Dunild hurled aside his bow, lifting his shield and drawing his sword. His men followed suit. Now was the time to withdraw, for the battle could not be won; the Aenir had not broken.

Three hundred clansmen joined him, swords in hand. Looking across the slopes to where his enemy Patris Grigor had also drawn his sword, Dunild felt a strange calm settle on him. He lifted his sword in silent farewell to his enemy. There would never be peace while they both lived, for their hatred was stronger than any desire to beat a common foe.

"Cut! Cut! Cut!" yelled Dunild as he led his three hundred down the slope to reinforce the Farlain.

Patris Grigor could not believe his eyes. His enemy of twenty years had just surrendered his lands. Patris was now the undisputed lord of the northwest.

"What does he think he's doing?" yelled a man on his left. Grigor shrugged. Twenty years of hatred, and now Dunild was hurling his life away on a futile charge in a doomed battle. Grigor shook his head and dropped his bow.

"Do we leave now?" asked a clansman.

Grigor laughed. "You know what's happening down there?"

"The Aenir are about to win through. It's all over."

"That's right. And that brainless idiot Dunild has gone down there to die."

"Then we are leaving?"

"What do *you* think?"

The man grinned. "If we charge now we might just be able to hack our way through to Dunild and then, while no one's looking, I'll cut his throat."

Grigor chuckled and hitched his shield to his arm. "Yes, by damn. Let's do something noble for a change!" Raising his sword, he began to run down the slope. Five hundred Grigor warriors took up their swords and followed him.

The front line of the Aenir slipped and slithered over blood-covered rocks and sprawled bodies, only to be cut down by the slashing iron blades of the clansmen. Leofas, his cold blue eyes glinting with battle fever, stood at the center of the defenders, Maggrig and Lennox on either side. Again and again the Aenir swarmed forward, only to be turned back by the sharp blades and steadfast courage of the defenders.

Drada alone among the Aenir was not surprised by the resolute defense, but he had been a part of many battles and knew what must happen now. The clans would fall back, there was no choice. Their strength was failing fast and their losses were enormous. The two at the center were both old men and their stamina suspect. Once they had fallen, the line would break.

Beside him Briga was poised for the final rush. He had been a warrior for more than twenty years and always, he knew, there came a point where the fight could be read like a game, where the ebb and flow could be charted like a steady current. They had reached that point now.

And the clans were ready to break . . .

The feeling swept among the Aenir and the battle cries began again. Once more the forces clashed. The clansmen fought silently now, leaden-legged and heavy of arm, and inch by inexorable inch they were forced back toward the open pass beyond.

Briga felt joy surge in his veins. No army in the world could hold now. It was over. The clans were finished!

Maggrig felt it too, and he cursed aloud as he clove his sword through an Aenir neck and ducked under a slashing blade. Well, if he had to die he was damned if it would be in the open ground he had fought so hard to defend. Dropping to his haunches he hurled himself forward into the Aenir, cutting and stabbing. Caught up in the frenzy of the moment, Leofas joined him, with Lennox and Intosh.

And the clans rallied, surging forward to join their leaders. The ferocity of the assault stunned the leading Aenir warriors and they fought to pull back. Briga, just behind the front line, turned to Drada. "It's impossible!" he shouted. Drada shrugged.

As the Aenir front line backed away from him, Maggrig raised his sword defiantly. "Come on, you Outland scum. We're still standing!"

A huge warrior in a wolf's-head helm leaped from the Aenir ranks, sword raised. Maggrig parried the blow and reversed a cut to the warrior's neck. The blade hammered into the mail shirt and snapped. Dropping the useless hilt, Maggrig grabbed the man by his mail shirt and hauled him forward, butting him savagely and crashing his fist into the man's belly. The warrior doubled over, his head snapping back as Maggrig's knee came up to explode against his face.

Intosh threw Maggrig a sword, Maggrig caught it by the hilt and sliced the blade through the back of the wolf's-head helm. The Aenir died without a sound.

"You lice-ridden sons of bitches," shouted Maggrig. "Is that the best you can do?"

A roar rose from the Aenir and the line lunged forward.

The battle raged once more and now there were no blood-curdling battle cries—only the screams of the dying and the grim determination of the living to survive. The clansmen had been forced back, but their enemies had to climb a wall of their own dead to force a path to the dwindling band of defenders.

Asbidag had climbed into the saddle, the better to see the battle. His trained eye knew it had reached its final stage. A carle beside him screamed suddenly, pitching forward to the ground with a black-feathered shaft in his back. Arrows hissed through the air around him. Asbidag swung in the saddle, tearing his shield from the saddle horn.

At the mouth of the pass Gaelen lifted his war horn and blew three blasts. Eight hundred bows were bent and a dark cloud of shafts ripped into the horde.

Maggrig crashed his shield into the face of an attacker, hurling him from his feet, lancing his blade into a second man and dragging it clear.

"It's Gaelen!" shouted Lennox. "He must have a thousand men with him."

Maggrig staggered as an axe blade shattered his shield. He hammered his fist into the axe-man's face, feeling the man's teeth break under the impact. A lean Aenir swordsman pushed himself past Maggrig. Leofas blocked his blow, but lost his grip on the sword. Grabbing the man by the neck and groin, he hoisted him into the air and hurled him back among his comrades. The man vanished into the mass. Leofas recovered his blade, wincing as a sword cut into his shoulder.

Lennox leaped to the rescue, his blood-covered club smashing the swordsman's spine.

At the mouth of the pass Gaelen signaled for the women to scale the slopes on either side of the fighting men. Lara set off to the right with four hundred Haesten women behind her. As she climbed, Gaelen turned to Telor.

"Now let's see what you can do with that blade," he said.

Hitching his shield into place Gaelen ran at Asbidag's carles, a hundred Pallides warriors yelling their war cry behind him.

His horse rearing and kicking, Asbidag saw death running at him. An arrow knocked his helm from his head, another thudded into his shield. Panic overwhelmed him. Kicking his heels to his horse's side he rode through his own men, smashing their line, then veered away from the advancing clansmen. Arrows hissed around him and he ducked low over the horse's neck.

Lara saw his flight and notched an arrow to the string, drawing smoothly and sighting on Asbidag's broad back. The shaft sang through the air, punching through the Aenir's mail shirt at the shoulder. Then he was through and clear and riding south. His horse carried him for a mile before collapsing and pitching him to the earth. He rolled to his feet. Three arrows had pierced the beast's chest and belly; leaving it to die, Asbidag began the long walk south.

In the Folly, Asbidag's panicked flight had opened the way for Gaelen and his warriors to smash the shield wall and engage the carles. Gaelen ducked under a two-handed cut and drove his sword home into the man's chest. Beside him Telor leaped and twisted, his sword flashing in the sunlight, cleaving and killing. Two men ran at Gaelen. He blocked a blow from the first, gutting the man with a reverse stroke; his sword stuck in his opponent's belly, he saw the second warrior's sword arcing toward his head. Telor parried the blow, chopping his blade through the man's neck.

The burly Pallides grinned. "Be more careful, Farlain. I can't be watching out for both of us."

In the valley all was chaos as Drada fought to hold the Aenir steady. Arrows rained upon them from both sides of the pass and the clans were fighting like men possessed. But it was a losing battle. Drada could feel that success was but a matter of moments ahead. Once they pushed the enemy back into the wider pass beyond, nothing could prevent an Aenir victory.

Glancing about him, the young Aenir warrior was horrified at the losses his force had suffered. Considerably more than half his warriors were down: twelve thousand men sacrificed to Asbidag's stupidity!

But against this Drada had seen his father's flight and it filled him with joy. No need to kill him now, and risk death from his carles. No Aenir would follow him ever again. He would be a wolf's-head, disowned and disregarded.

Now Drada would have it all: the army, the land, and the magic Gates. He would build the greatest empire the world had ever seen.

"On! On!" he yelled. "The last yard!"

And it was true. The Aenir pushed forward once more.

Maggrig fell, slashed across the thigh. From the ground he stabbed upward, gutting his attacker. A blow sliced toward his head but Intosh blocked it—and died, an axe cleaving his skull.

Maggrig staggered to his feet, plunging his blade through the axe-man's chest. A sword lanced his side and he stepped back, lashing out weakly. Lennox bludgeoned a path to stand alongside him, mace dripping blood.

Above the noise of battle came the sound of distant horns. Then they felt the ground beneath their feet tremble, and the rolling thunder of galloping hooves echoed in the mountains. For a moment all battle ceased as men craned to see the mouth of the pass. A huge dust cloud swirled there, and out of it rode four thousand fighting men with lances leveled.

At the center was a warrior in silver armor. In her hand was a mighty sword of shimmering steel.

"The Queen comes!" yelled Leofas.

*   *   *

Maggrig could not believe his eyes. Blood streamed from the wound in his side and his injured leg, and he stepped back from the fray, allowing two Pallides warriors to join shields before him. Slowly he climbed to the top of a pitted boulder, narrowing his eyes to see the horsemen.

The Aenir moved back from the clan line, straining to identify the new foe. Drada was stunned. What he was seeing was an impossibility; there were no cavalry forces on this part of the continent. But it was no illusion. The thunder of hooves grew and the Aenir warriors facing the charge scrambled toward the rocky slopes on either side of the pass. Their comrades behind them threw aside their weapons and tried to run.

Other more stout-hearted fighters gripped their swords more tightly and raised their shields. It mattered not whether they ran or stood. The terrible lances bore down upon them, splintering shields and lifting men from their feet, dashing them bloody and broken to the dusty ground. Horses reared, iron-shod hooves thrashing down, crushing skulls and trampling the wounded.

The Aenir broke, streaming up onto the slopes into the flashing shafts of the Haesten women.

Leofas urged the Farlain forward, shearing his sword into the confused mass before him. The battle became a rout. Aenir warriors threw down their weapons, begging for mercy, but there was none. With swords in their hand or without, the Aenir were cut to pieces.

Dunild and Grigor fought side by side now—the remnants of their clans, blood-covered and battle-crazed, hacking and slashing their way forward.

The Aenir struggled to re-form. Drada sounded the war horn and the shield ring grew around him. An arrow punched through Tostig's helm to skewer his skull. With a bellow of rage and pain he slumped to the ground beside his brother. Drada raised his shield.

Sigarni, her silver-steel blade dripping crimson, wheeled

her grey stallion and led her men back down the pass. The Aenir watched them go, sick with horror. At the mouth of the Folly the Queen turned again, and the thunder of charging hooves drowned the despairing cries of the enemy.

Thrice more she charged and the shield ring shattered.

A lean Aenir warrior ran forward, ducking under Sigarni's plunging sword, stabbing his own blade into the horse's belly. It screamed and fell, rolling across the man who had ended its life, killing him as it died. Sigarni was thrown to the ground in the midst of the Aenir. She came up swinging the double-handed sword, beheading the first warrior to leap to the attack.

The Aenir closed around her. Gaelen and Telor, fighting side by side, saw the Queen go down.

"No!" screamed Gaelen. He cut his opponent from him and raced into the mass. Telor followed him, with Agwaine and Onic and a dozen Pallides.

"Hold on, my lady!" yelled Gaelen. Sigarni flashed a glance toward him, momentarily puzzled, then blocked a slashing attack from a long sword. Twisting her wrists and returning the blow, she clove the man from collarbone to belly. But the Aenir were all around her now. She swung and twisted and, too late, saw a blade slashing toward her neck. Gaelen's sword flashed up, parrying the death blow. "I am here, my lady!" he shouted above the clash of iron on iron.

Sigarni grinned and returned to the business of death.

Drada, with all hope of victory gone, tried to forge a path to the mouth of the pass. Beside him his carle captain Briga fought on, though a score of minor cuts poured blood from his arms and thighs. "I think we are done, Drada," shouted Briga. "But by Vatan there's been some blood spilled today."

Drada did not answer. Ahead of them a woman had climbed to a tall boulder and drawn back her bow. The arrow hissed through the air, thudding into Drada's throat, and with a look of surprise the Aenir leader fell sideways. Briga tried to catch him, but a sword slid between his ribs and he jerked upright.

He did not know it, nor would he have cared, but he was one of the last Aenir still alive in the Folly. His breath rasped in his throat and he dropped his sword as a great rushing noise filled his ears. Around him the pass was choked with bodies of the fallen, and Briga thought he could see the Valkyrie descending from the sky—the winged horses and the chariots of black. What tales he would tell in the Hall of the Dead . . .

He toppled from his feet, eyes still fixed on the black mass of crows and buzzards circling in the sky overhead.

Far to the south Asbidag, unaware of the clan victory, entered a thickly wooded section of hills. He was breathing heavily and tired to the bone. Stopping by a stream, he tore the arrow from his shoulder and stripped his mail shirt from him. He leaned over the water to drink. Looking down, he saw his reflection and just above it a face out of a nightmare.

Asbidag rolled to his back, scrabbling for his knife, but the werehound's talons snaked down, ripping his throat to shreds. Blood bubbled from the ruined jugular and the creature's jaws opened. Asbidag's eyes widened as the fangs flashed down. The creature backed away from the body and squatted on its haunches, staring down at the ruined face. In its mind vague memories stirred, and a low whine came from its throat.

Pictures danced and flickered. Racing ahead of the pack and the horsemen, leaping at the stag as it turned to face them. Curling up in the day by the stables, warm and comfortable. But other, stranger images confused it. A young woman with fair hair, smiling, her head resting on a cotton pillow. A child running, laughing, hands stretched toward . . . toward . . . it?

Lifting its head, the beast howled its despair at the night sky. Then moving back to the corpse the creature stretched out its taloned claw, pulling the dagger loose from the sheath. Turning the point to its breast, it plunged the blade home.

Pain, terrible pain . . .

Then peace.

*   *   *

Obrin found her hiding behind a boulder. He was tempted to slit her throat and be done with it . . . sorely tempted. He knew what she was, had always known.

The tall rider dragged her out by her hair. She was strangely quiescent, and her eyes were hooded and distant. "I'd like to kill you," he hissed.

Holding her hair, he led her past the bodies and out to the plain.

Sigarni was seated on a high-backed saddle placed before a small fire. She was drinking wine from a copper goblet and chatting to three of her lancers. She glanced up as Obrin hurled the woman to the ground at her feet.

"A surprise, my lady," said Obrin. "She was with the Aenir, I'm told."

Sigarni stood and pulled her gently to her feet. "How are you, Morgase?" she asked.

The raven-haired woman shrugged. "As you see me. Alone."

"I know how that feels," said Sigarni. "Accept that the war is over, and you may return with us. I shall restore you to your father's lands."

"In return for what? My promise of allegiance? My mother's soul would scream out against it. You saw my father slain, my mother raped. Kill me, Sigarni—or I will haunt you to your grave!"

Obrin's sword hissed from its scabbard. "This once I'll agree with the bitch!" he said. "Give the word, my lady."

Sigarni shook her head. "Fetch her a horse. Let her ride where she will."

Two soldiers took hold of Morgase and led her away. Twisting in their grip, she shouted out, "I will find a way back, Sigarni. And then you will pay!"

"Your decision burdens my spirit," said Obrin. "She is evil, Sigarni. There is no good in her."

"There is little good in any of us. We live and we die by the grace of God. A great wrong was done to her. It twisted her mind—as once such a deed twisted mine."

By dusk the druids had come out from hiding in the woods around the Folly and had begun to administer to the wounded clansmen. Maggrig, ten stitches in his side and twelve more in his thigh, sat on a boulder staring at the fluttering crows who were leaping and squawking over the stripped bodies of the slain.

The clan dead had been carried out of the Folly and laid together on the plain. A cairn would be built tomorrow. So many dead. Of the eight hundred Pallides only two hundred survived, many of these with grievous wounds. More than a thousand Farlain warriors had died, and another four hundred from the Loda and Dunilds. By a twist of fate both leaders had survived, fighting at the last back-to-back.

Maggrig sighed. The place looked like a charnel house.

Leofas, his wounds stitched and bandaged, joined him at the boulder. "Well, we won," he said.

"Yes. And we old ones survive. So many young men gone to dust, and we old bulls sit here and breathe free air."

Leofas shrugged. "Aye, but we are a canny pair."

Maggrig grinned. "Have you seen Caswallon?"

"No. Come on, let's seek out the Queen. The least we can do is thank her."

Leofas helped Maggrig to his feet and the two made their way through the bodies. The crows, bellies full and heavy with meat, hopped out of their way, too laden to fly.

At the mouth of the pass, beyond the tethered mounts, were the campfires of Sigarni's lancers, set in a circle at the center of which sat the Queen and her captains.

Sigarni rose as the clansmen approached. "Pour wine for them, Obrin," she told her captain.

Maggrig thrust out his hand. "Thank you, my lady. You have saved my people."

"I am glad we were here in time. I owe much to Redhawk, and it was a relief to part-settle the score."

"Where is Caswallon?" asked Maggrig.

"I know not," said the Queen. "He asked us to meet him at the island of Vallon."

Two riders brought high-backed saddles that they placed on the ground for the clansmen. "Be seated," said Sigarni. I wish to meet one of your clansmen; he saved my life today."

"I think it will be hard to find one clansman," said Leofas.

"Not this one. He has a blaze of white hair above his left eye and the eye itself is full of blood."

"I know him," said Leofas. "If he lives I will send him to you."

Obrin brought mulled wine and they drank in silence for a while.

The following morning, as work began on the cairn, most of the lancers had returned home through the Gate that had appeared in a blaze of light on the plain the night before. Sigarni remained behind with twenty men, including Obrin.

Leofas had found Gaelen sitting hand in hand with the Haesten girl in the woods skirting the mountains. "Well met, young Gaelen," he said.

Gaelen rose, introducing Lara to the older man.

Leofas bowed. "I have seen you before, girl, but never prettier than now."

"Thank you. I am glad you survived," said Lara.

"We might not have done, had you not appeared with your archers."

"A freak of chance," Lara told him. "We struck north to avoid the Aenir, and that meant we had to pass the Folly. How is it that the Queen arrived? Gaelen told me she was due at Axta Glen, and that's a day's ride from here."

Leofas shrugged. "I don't know, neither does the Queen. Caswallon's the man to answer the riddle. Now get a move on, boy, the Queen wishes to see you. But tell me, where is Layne?"

Gaelen looked into the old man's eyes, but could find no words. The smile faded from Leofas's face, and he looked suddenly so very old.

The white-bearded warrior sighed. "So many dead," he whispered. "Tell me how it happened." Gaelen did so, and could find no way to disguise the horror of Layne's passing. Leofas listened in silence, then turned away and walked off alone toward the trees.

Gaelen watched him, and felt the comforting touch of Lara's hand. "Come," she said, "the Queen wishes to see you."

He nodded and together they approached the Queen's camp. Sigarni strode out to meet him, hand outstretched. "Good to see you alive, my lad! There are a few questions I have for you."

Gaelen bowed, introducing Lara. The Queen smiled warmly at the clanswoman. "Now, what were you doing risking yourself to save me?" she asked, turning on Gaelen, her grey eyes glinting with humor. "I expect that from my lancers, but not from strangers."

"I owe you my life," said Gaelen simply.

"For coming here with my lancers, you mean?"

"No, lady. But I cannot speak of it. Forgive me."

"More secrets of the enchanted realm? You sound like Redhawk. All right, Gaelen, I shall not press you. How can I reward you for your action?"

Gaelen stared at her, remembering the day she had saved them from the beast. In that instant he knew where his road must lead. Dropping to one knee before the warrior Queen, he said, "Let me serve you, my lady. Now and forever."

If Sigarni was surprised she did not show it. "You will have to leave this realm," said the Queen, "and fight beside me in a war that is not of your making. Do you desire this?"

"I do, my Queen. More than anything. I love this land, but I have seen my friends slaughtered, their homes burnt, and their children massacred."

"Then rise, for my friends do not kneel before me; they walk beside me. Will your lady come too?" she asked, turning to Lara.

Gaelen rose and took her hand. "Will you?"

"Where else would I go?" she answered.

"I love you," he whispered, pulling her to him.

The Queen moved away from them then, joining Obrin at the fire.

With a high cairn now covering the clan dead, Leofas led the survivors back to Attafoss. Despite the victory the men were heavy of heart. Their loved ones were lost in the past, their friends dead in the present. Maggrig rode beside Sigarni, while Gaelen and Lara joined Lennox, Onic, Agwaine, and Gwalchmai at the head of the column.

Gaelen was the only one of the surviving Beast Slayers to have emerged unscathed from the battle. Lennox carried a score of stitches, while Gwalchmai had taken a spear in the shoulder. Agwaine had been stabbed in the leg and he walked with a painful limp.

"Are you really going to go with the Queen?" asked Agwaine. "And leave the mountains?"

"Yes," answered Gaelen. "I promised her years ago that I would follow her."

"Will she take me too, do you think?" Gwalchmai asked.

"I believe so."

"I shall not go," said Agwaine. "There is much to do here."

"Without Layne there is little to hold me here," said Lennox sadly. "I'll come with you, Gaelen."

An hour before dusk the column arrived at the invisible bridge to Vallon, and spread out along the banks.

A man appeared on the far shore, a tall man with greying hair, wearing a velvet robe the color of dark wine. He lifted his hand. Glittering lights rose from the water to hover in the air around the invisible bridge, which darkened, gleaming like silver in the fading light. Stronger and stronger grew the bridge as the light coalesced, shimmering and sparkling, until at last it seemed built of silver and gems. The man lifted his hand once more and stepped out upon the silver walkway. From behind him came the men and women of the Farlain and the Pallides.

A great silence settled on the clansmen as hope flared again in their hearts.

The man approached, his grey-streaked hair billowing in the breeze. He was full-bearded and his eyes were the green of a distant sea. "Caswallon!" shouted Gaelen, running forward to meet him.

Caswallon opened his arms, tears sparkling in his eyes. The two men hugged each other warmly, then Gaelen pulled back to look at his foster father. Caswallon seemed to have aged ten years since last they met.

"What has happened to you?" whispered Gaelen.

"We will talk later. First let us enjoy the reunion."

Wives and children ran to husbands and fathers, sons and brothers, and laughter swelled through the trees of Atta forest. "A long time since that sound was heard," said Caswallon.

Maeg was one of the last across the bridge. Silently she approached her husband, little Donal beside her riding on the back of the great hound, Render.

"Leave us for a while, Gaelen. I will see you later," said Caswallon. He took Maeg's hand, kissing her palm. Her eyes were full of tears and she leaned into him.

"What have they done to you?" she asked, holding back the sorrow and stroking his greying hair.

"They? There is no 'they,' Maeg. Time has done this. But it was necessary, for otherwise I would never have found you. It took me eleven years to learn all that I needed to fetch you home. But every day of that time I thought of you and I loved you."

Donal slipped from Render's back and tugged at the hem of Caswallon's velvet robe. He was crying. Caswallon lifted him to his chest and hugged him tightly.

"We won, Caswallon," said Maeg. "But the price was terrible."

He nodded. "It always is. But we are together now, and we shall rebuild."

Maeg caught sight of a silver-armored woman staring at them. "Who is that?" she asked Caswallon. He turned and saw Sigarni swing away and walk alone toward the trees.

"That is the Queen, Maeg," he said, taking her into his arms. "She saved us all."

"She looked so sad," said Maeg, then turned back to her husband. "Welcome home, my love," she whispered, kissing him.

He couldn't reply. Tears ran from his eyes and she led him away into the trees.

Chapter Eleven

Three days after the battle, Gaelen was summoned by an elderly druid and led to Taliesen's chambers below the hall of the Gate where Caswallon awaited him. In the harsh light of the chamber Caswallon seemed even older; his hair was thinning and had turned white near the temples.

"Welcome," he said, gesturing the clansman to be seated. He poured clear white wine into silver goblets, handed one to Gaelen, and then sat down in a wide leather chair.

"What happened to you, Caswallon?"

The older man chuckled. "Do I look so bad?"

"No," lied Gaelen, "just older."

"I *am* older. It is eleven years since I asked you to find Laric and bring his warriors to Axta Glen. Eleven long years . . . lonely years."

"The Queen told me you led her to the Chalice Gate and then you stepped through. Within seconds you returned, only you were older and dressed, as now, in robes of velvet."

"It is not easy for me to explain it to you, Gaelen. When I reached the Chalice Gate I was filled with fear. A dying monk told me the Gate was not closed, yet I could see for myself that it was. The cave was shallow and water dripped from the walls. I walked forward, sick with dread, and reached out. My hand passed through the stone as though through smoke. I walked on, and found myself on a plain overlooking a city of golden turrets and tall towers of polished marble.

"A man was waiting for me. His name was Astole and he greeted me like a brother, for I had saved his life in another place. He took me to his home—a palace with many servants—and there he began to instruct me in the Gates and the words of power to manipulate them. I was filled with terrible impatience, but he promised he could return me to within seconds of my departure. And I had to trust him.

"The years passed slowly. Sometimes I would be filled with joy at my newfound knowledge and dream of exacting a terrible revenge on the Aenir. At other times I felt an awful dread, wondering if I had been tricked. But always I learned. Impossibility made reality. You have seen the stone that attracts iron?"

"Yes. Onic has one."

"The force that pulls the metal cannot be seen, but its effects can be observed. It is the same with the power behind the Gates. Let me show you something." Caswallon lifted a small box set with colored stones. He pressed the ruby at the center and the far wall darkened, then became a window overlooking the Farlain.

"As you can see, that is the mountain of Carduil on the borders of Haesten territory. That is *now*. We can see that image as the light is reflected to our eyes. Had we been here yesterday, we would have seen rain over Carduil. But we were not. Yet the image was still transmitted. Astole discovered that light images linger, leaving traces that can last ten thousand years. Hence, with the turn of a dial, we can see . . ." The screen shimmered and the mountain appeared once more, cloud-covered and dull, sheeting rain pounding the slopes. Caswallon pressed a stone and the image disappeared.

"Astole made machines that could trace the Lines of Time, allowing man to view his own past. But then the greatest excitement of all. Within the traces Astole discovered particles of matter that did not deteriorate. Unchanging, they existed from day to day, from century to century. They were unaffected by the passing of time. Indeed, they seemed to exist outside time's laws.

"During his experiments Astole trapped several particles within a field of force—similar to that which works the stone that attracts iron. The field and the particles disappeared without trace. Astole constructed another and suddenly the first field reappeared, but the second vanished. The following day he constructed a third field, and the same thing happened. Excited beyond his experience, Astole made plans for two large fields, preparing his assistants beforehand. He placed himself at the center of the first field and activated it. He vanished instantly. His assistants, following his instructions, activated the second field and he reappeared. The particles had drawn him into a distant past. How, he did not know, but he had stumbled on the greatest discovery of them all, the Gates."

"I don't understand any of this, Caswallon," said Gaelen.

"I'm sorry, my boy. How can I tell you in minutes that which has taken a decade of my life? Anyway, I stayed with Astole, and I absorbed his knowledge. Together we journeyed to fabulous cities and kingdoms lost to the memory of man. We walked the Time Lines, seeing the births of civilizations and the deaths of empires. Finally he judged me ready and we journeyed to a desert, and there I met the man to answer all questions. As he spoke I felt my heart emptied and refilled. All dreams of vengeance died. Violence was washed from me."

"Who was he?" asked the clansman.

Caswallon smiled and laid his hand on Gaelen's shoulder. "If you thought the Gates were hard to comprehend, then do not ask about the man. He sent me home and I appeared in the Chalice Gate, even as you see me now. With my new words of power I activated the machines and scanned Axta Glen. You were not there. I searched the Farlain, coming at last to Icairn's Folly. Then I opened the Gate and the Queen led her lancers through."

"But you did not ride with them," said Gaelen.

"No. I am the Hawk Eternal, Gaelen, and I'll never wield a sword against any man again."

"You have changed, Father."

"All life is change. But I am the same man who carried

you from Ateris, the same man who loves his people. Only now I love them more. It is strange. I could have destroyed the Aenir single-handed; but with the gift of that power, I lost the desire to use it thus."

"How did Maeg take all this?" asked Gaelen.

"Hard. But love conquers all. And I love her—more than life."

"Will you remain as Hunt Lord?"

"Do I look like a Farlain Hunt Lord?" he asked, smiling.

"No."

"And I shall not be the Hunt Lord. I will remain here, at Vallon, and tend the Gates. There are many tasks before me, Gaelen, but first I must spend some time with Maeg and Donal. Then I will meet Astole again."

"I am returning with the Queen," said Gaelen. "Lennox, Onic, and Gwalchmai are coming with me."

"I know. We will meet again."

"Tell me, Caswallon, are you truly content?"

"More content than any mortal man has any right to be."

"Then I am glad for you."

"And I for you. You have a fine woman in Lara, and I know she will give you beautiful children. I wish for you a life enriched with love, for you deserve it."

"I shall miss the Farlain. Will I be able to return someday?"

"Ask me when next you see me."

"I must go. The Queen is waiting," said Gaelen.

Caswallon rose and walked around the table. "Walk always in the Light," he told Gaelen.

Caswallon watched the clansman leave and his heart ached. He had seen pity in Gaelen's eyes and knew the bond between them would never be the same. For to Gaelen, Caswallon was no longer a clansman. He had put aside his sword.

What could he have told Gaelen to make him realize? Should he have explained about the man in the desert?

Caswallon grinned wryly and filled his goblet. Tell him about a man who allowed himself to be dragged through a

city and murdered by the people he loved? Oh, yes, that
would have impressed him. He finished his wine and turned
to the black screen before him. Lifting the control box he
tuned the image, watching Sigarni, Gaelen, and his friends
crossing the Gates of Time.

He felt a cold breeze on his back and turned to see Maeg
standing in the doorway hugging a woolen shawl about her
shoulders. She seemed so distant, so withdrawn. Caswallon
swallowed hard, a sense of despair gripping him.

"You must be getting old, Caswallon," she said, "allowing
yourself to be surprised by a woman."

"Surprise, is it? When I heard the footsteps I felt it had to
be a mountain troll come to life."

She grinned at him then. "My feet are not so large. But
even if they were I think I'd sooner have that than vast areas
of my head losing hair."

"Did no one ever teach you to respect your elders,
woman?"

"Is it respect you want?" she asked, moving closer.

He opened his arms and held her close. "Do you still love
me, Maeg?"

"I love you, clansman. Above all things. And you're a fool
to believe otherwise. Now tell me what happened to you."

For an hour or more they sat together until he had emptied
himself of words. At last she led him from the chamber to
walk under the stars above Vallon.

Epilogue

Agwaine ruled the Farlain for twenty-seven years, having first led his warriors in the sack of Aesgard. The city was razed to the ground and all its inhabitants put to the sword. Thereafter peace came to the mountains.

Deva lived in Agwaine's house for seven years, refusing all offers of marriage, her eyes constantly on the horizon—waiting for the man who would be king. One bright day in summer she was brushing her hair when she saw, in the mirror, the first grey hairs appearing at her temple. No suitor had approached her for two years now. Fear touched her and she went in search of Caswallon. She found him sitting in the sunlight in the garden behind his house, tending his roses.

Caswallon welcomed her, offering her a cup of honey mead, and she sat beside him on a long, carved bench. "What is troubling you, Deva?" he asked.

"The prophecy hasn't come true, and if I wait much longer I shall be unable to bear children. Why hasn't he come, Caswallon?"

"Wait? Not so fast. What prophecy?"

"When I was born, a tinker woman told me I would be the mother of kings. Taliesen told me it was true. But where is this prince who will ask to wed me?"

"Wait here," he said, and walked slowly into the house. Deva sat in the sunshine for almost an hour, and was still there when the young Donal came walking in from the hills with the faithful hound Render beside him. Caswallon returned as the sun was setting. "I am sorry to have kept you so long, my dear," he said. "Come, I have something to show you."

Leading her into the house, he took a silvered mirror and placed it in her lap. "Look closely at the glass and you will see the prophecy." Holding it up to her face she looked into her own reflection, seeing the fine lines that were appearing around her eyes. The image faded, and she found herself looking down upon the scene in the front room of the old house. Cambil was holding a babe in his arms. An old woman was sitting on the rug before the young Hunt Lord.

The woman's voice came whispering into Deva's mind. "She will see the great and the strong, Hunt Lord. And a future ruler will ask for her hand. If she weds him, she will be the mother of kings."

The image faded. "I don't understand," said Deva. "That was my prophecy. So where is this king I have waited for so long?"

Caswallon took the mirror from her hands, then he sat beside her. "He asked for your hand, Deva, and you refused him."

"No!" she stormed. "There has been no prince!"

"The Queen who saved us named him as her heir and he will become king. He is a warrior and a great leader—and he loved you once."

"Gaelen," she whispered. "He is to be king?"

"Yes. I am only sorry you did not come to me before this."

Deva stood on trembling legs, then ran from the house. A year later she married a widower and raised three sons and a daughter.

Lennox returned twice to the Highlands, once for the funeral of his father Leofas, who died twelve years after Icairn's Folly, and once to bring Gwalchmai home after an Outland spear cut him down at the siege of Culceister. Gwalchmai had asked to be buried above Attafoss.

Gaelen never returned. On the death of Obrin he took over as captain of the Lancers and became known as the Queen's

Champion. He and Lara lived contentedly, raising two sons and three daughters.

The clansmen served the Queen for thirty years. In the fortieth year of her reign Sigarni was called to battle by Morgase and the last great Outland army. The battle was fierce and close-run, but as always, Sigarni won the victory, leading a last charge against the shield wall. Morgase took poison rather than be captured.

The Queen's wounds were grievous. Gaelen helped her from the field and in the last fading light of the dying sun carried her up the slopes beyond Citadel to the Chalice Cave—and beyond! There a young druid took charge of the Queen and Gaelen watched him half carry her toward a mountain cave.

Returning through the Great Gate, the aging warrior removed his helm and scratched at his thinning grey hair. Idly he rubbed the ancient scar above his eye.

Beyond the Gate four boys were preparing for their first Hunt. The sun was a globe of gold and the future full of promise. At that moment there was no beast, no danger, and the Aenir were a distant threat.

Gaelen turned back to stare down into the valley where the campfires blazed and the cairn was nearing completion. Below lay the bodies of the fallen, Highlander and Outlander together in death. Among them were Onic and Lennox. The giant had died swinging his massive club of iron and lead as the enemy swarmed forward. Onic had fallen beside him.

Now only Gaelen was left. "Farewell, my Queen," he whispered.

A shadow moved to his right. He turned and there was Caswallon, leaning on his staff of oak, his robes of velvet shimmering in the moonlight.

"And so it ends," said Caswallon, his wispy white beard swirling in the breeze like wood smoke.

"No, it begins," said Gaelen, pointing at the cave.

Caswallon nodded. "And now you will be king, Gaelen. How does that sit with you?"

Gaelen pushed his iron-grey hair back from his eyes. "I'd give it all up to be young again."

Caswallon turned and gestured to the Gate. "But you are young, Gaelen. Through that Gateway is a youth, who with his friends is walking the mountains. Even now the wind is in his hair, and the future is before him, bright and golden. Just a few steps away. Would you like to see him?"

Gaelen smiled. "Let us leave him to his life," he said, taking Caswallon by the arm and leading him down the mountainside.

And now a sneak preview from the launch of David Gemmell's ambitious new trilogy, set in the time of Troy. This is a tale of kings and queens, of legendary heroes and epic combat. The action begins with Book One,

LORD OF THE SILVER BOW

Coming in October 2005 from Del Rey Books

The Golden Ship

The storms of the past two days had faded into the west, and the sky was clear and blue, the sea calm, as Spyros rowed his passenger toward the great ship. After a morning of ferrying crewmen out to the *Xanthos,* Spyros was tired. He liked to tell people that at eighty years of age he was as strong as ever, but it wasn't true. His arms and shoulders were aching, his heart thumping as he leaned back into the oars.

A man was not old until he could no longer work. This simple philosophy kept Spyros active, and every morning, as he woke, he would greet the new day with a smile. He would walk out and draw up water from the well, gaze at his reflection in the surface, and say: "Good to see you, Spyros."

He looked at the young man sitting quietly at the stern. His hair was long and dark, held back from his face by a strip of leather. Bare chested, he was wearing a simple kilt and sandals. His body was lean and hard muscled, his eyes the brilliant blue of a summer sky. Spyros had not seen the man before and guessed him to be a foreigner, probably a rogue islander or a Kretans.

"New oarsman, are you?" Spyros asked him. The passenger did not answer, but he smiled. "Been ferrying men like you in all week. Locals won't sail on the Death Ship. That's what we call the *Xanthos*," he added. "Only idiots and foreigners. No offense meant."

The passenger's voice was deep, his accent proving Spyros's theory. "She is beautiful," he said amiably. "And the shipwright says she is sound."

"Aye, I'll grant she's good to look upon," said Spyros. "Mighty pleasing to the eye." Then he chuckled. "However I wouldn't trust the word of the Madman from Miletos. My nephew worked on the ship, you know. He said Khalkeus wandered about talking to himself. Sometimes he'd even slap himself in the head."

"I have seen him do that," agreed the man.

Spyros fell silent, a feeling of mild irritation flowering. The man was young and obviously did not appreciate that the gods of the sea hated large ships. Twenty years ago he had watched just such a ship sail from the bay. It had made two voyages without incident, then had vanished in a storm. One man had survived. He had been washed ashore on the eastern mainland. His story was told by mariners for some years. The keel had snapped, the ship breaking up in a matter of a few heartbeats. Spyros considered telling this story to the young oarsman. He decided against it. What would be the point? The man had to earn his twenty copper rings, and he wasn't going to turn back now.

Spyros rowed on, the burning in his lower back increasing. This was his twentieth trip out to the *Xanthos* since dawn.

There were small boats all around the galley, stacked with cargo. Men were shouting and vying for position. Boats thumped into one another, causing curses and threats to be bellowed out. Ropes were lowered and items slowly hauled aboard. Tempers were short both among the crew on the deck and the men waiting to unload their cargo boats. It was a scene of milling chaos.

"Been like this all morning," said Spyros, easing back on the oars. "Don't think they'll sail today. It's one of the problems with a ship that size, getting cargo up on that high deck. Didn't think of that, did he—the Madman, I mean?"

"The owner is to blame," said the passenger. "He wanted the largest ship ever built. He concentrated on its seaworthiness and the quality of its construction. He didn't give enough thought to loading or unloading it."

Spyros shipped his oars. "Listen, lad, you obviously don't know who you are sailing with. Best not say anything like that close to the Golden One. Helikaon may be young, but he is a killer, you know. He cut off Alektruon's head and ripped out his eyes. It's said he ate them. Not someone you want to offend, if you take my meaning?"

"Ate his eyes? I have not heard *that* story."

"Oh, there're plenty of stories about him." Spyros stared at the bustle around the galley. "No point trying to push my way through to the stern. We'll need to wait awhile until some of those cargo boats have moved off."

A huge, bald man, his black beard greased and twisted into two braids, appeared on the port deck, his voice booming out, ordering some of the cargo boats to stand clear and allow those closest to clear their cargo.

"The bald man there is Zidantas," said Spyros. "They call him Ox. I had another nephew sail with him once. Ox is a Hittite. Good man, though. My nephew broke his arm on the *Ithaka* a few years back and couldn't work the whole voyage. Still got his twenty copper rings, though. Zidantas saw to that." He turned his face toward the south. "Breeze is starting to shift. Going to be a southerly. Unusual for this time of the year. That'll help you make the crossing, I suppose. If it does get under way today."

"She'll sail," said the man.

"You are probably right, young fellow. The Golden One is

blessed by luck. Not one of his ships has sunk, did you know that? Pirates avoid him—well, they would, wouldn't they? You don't cross a man who eats your eyes." Reaching down he lifted a waterskin from below his seat. He drank deeply, then offered it to his passenger, who accepted gratefully.

A glint of bronze showed from the deck, and two warriors came into sight, both wearing breastplates and carrying helms crested with white horsehair plumes. "I offered to ferry them out earlier," muttered Spyros. "They didn't like my boat. Too small for them, I don't doubt. Ah well, a pox on all Mykene anyway. Heard them talking, though. They're not friends of the Golden One, that's for sure."

"What did they say?"

"Well, it was more the older one. He said it turned his stomach to be sailing on the same ship as Helikaon. Can't blame him, I suppose. That Alektruon—the one who lost his eyes—was a Mykene, too. Helikaon has killed a lot of Mykene."

"As you say, not a man to offend."

"I wonder why he does it."

"What? Kill Mykene?"

"No, sail his ships all over the Great Green. They say he has a palace in Troy and land in Dardania and somewhere else way north. Don't remember where. Anyhow, he is already rich and powerful. So why risk himself on the sea, fighting pirates and the like?"

The young man shrugged. "All is never as it seems. Who knows? Maybe he is a man with a dream. I heard that he wants to sail one day beyond the Great Green, to the distant seas."

"That's what I mean," said Spyros. "The edge of the world is there, with a waterfall that goes down forever into darkness. What kind of an idiot would want to sail off into the black abyss of the world?"

"That is a good question, boatman. A man who is not content, perhaps. A man looking for something he cannot find on the Great Green."

"There you go! There's nothing of worth that a man cannot find in his own village, let alone on the great sea. That's the problem with these rich princes and kings. They don't understand what real treasure is. They see it in gold and copper and tin. They see it in herds of horses and cattle. They gather treasures to themselves, building great storehouses, which they guard ferociously. Then they die. What good is it then?"

"And you know what real treasure is?" asked the young man.

"Of course. Most ordinary men do. I've been up in the hills these last few days. A young woman almost died. Babe breeched in the womb. I got there in time, though. Poor girl. Ripped bad, she was. She'll be fine, and the boy is healthy and strong. I watched that woman hold the babe in her arms and gaze down on it. The mother was so weak she might have died at any moment. But in her eyes you could see she knew what she was holding. It was something worth more than gold. And the father was more proud and happy than any conquering king with a vault of treasure."

"The child is lucky to have such loving parents. Not all children do."

"And those that don't get heart scarred. You don't see the wounds, but they never heal."

"What is your name, boatman?"

"Spyros."

"How is it you are a rower and a midwife, Spyros? It is an unusual pairing of talents."

The old man chuckled. "Brought a few children into the world during my eighty years. Developed a knack for delivering healthy babies. It began more than fifty years ago. A young shepherd's wife had a difficult birth, and the babe was born dead. I was there and picked up the poor little mite, to carry it away. As I lifted him he suddenly spewed blood, then started to cry. That began it, you know, the story of my skill with babies. My wife . . . sweet girl . . . had six children. So I knew more than a little about the difficulties of childbirth.

Over the years I was asked to attend other births. You know how it is. Word gets around. Any girl within fifty miles gets pregnant, and they'll send for old Spyros come the time. It is strange, you know. The older I grow the more pleasure I get bringing new life into the world."

"You are a good man," said the passenger, "and I am glad to have met you. Now take up your oars and force your way through. It is time for me to board."

The old man dipped his oars and rowed in between two long boats. Two sailors above saw the boat and lowered a rope between the bank of oars. Then the passenger stood and, from a pouch at his side, pulled out a thick ring and handed it to Spyros.

It glinted in his palm. "Wait!" shouted Spyros. "This ring is gold!"

"I liked your stories," said the man with a smile, "so I will not eat your eyes."